TEACH ME

Steamy Secrets, Book Two

DIANE DEMETRE

LUMINOSITY PUBLISHING LLP

TEACH ME
Steamy Secrets, Book Two
Copyright © November 2019 Diane Demetre

Paperback ISBN: 978-1-9993066-5-6

Cover Art by Poppy Designs

DEDICATION

For Tash
My Tiny Dancer
May we all dance forever, together

QUOTE

If I could tell you what it meant, there
would be no point in dancing it.
— Isadora Duncan

CHAPTER ONE

SAM'S SHOULDER SCREAMED IN protest as she lugged her suitcase up the narrow, creaking staircase. Uncertain if she was going to make it to the reception counter before she collapsed, she gave one final tug, hauling behind her stubborn suitcase, dance bag and hand luggage. Dumping the bags on the floor, her shoulder sagged in relief as she shoved the suitcase under the counter and tapped the desk bell.

With a skinny, roll-your-own cigarette balancing between yellowing teeth, an old man raised his head from behind the counter, like a tortoise peering out from its shell.

"Monsieur Boucher?" Sam's bright tone was in direct contrast to the landlord's unwelcoming frown. He nodded. "I have a reservation. My name is Samantha O'Brien. From Australia." Handing him the folded email with her reservation's details, Sam allowed herself to relax for the first time since she'd arrived in Paris only a few hours earlier. Monsieur Boucher stared at the email. He continued to scratch his chin and chew his wet cigarette.

"You see. Here." She reached toward the email pointing out the confirmation details between herself and Regina's Montmartre, the small hotel in which she'd planned to live. "You confirmed here and here. I have a reservation beginning today for the next six months." The triumph in her voice as to the veracity of the booking did little to convince Monsieur Boucher. Tilting his head to one side, his grapefruit-sour face squeezed tighter, and he shrugged. Pulling his tattered black beret a little further down his forehead, he nodded and lowered himself down to whatever was more interesting below the desk.

"Monsieur Boucher, I have a reservation. Here at this hotel, Regina's Montmartre," Sam's voice rose. "I've just flown all the way from Australia and would like to go to my room, *se il vous plait*." Sam knew her French was limited but she threw in the 'please' hoping it might sweeten the landlord's mood.

"Mademoiselle." The grapefruit face opened for a slow, deep voice to dribble out, but since Sam had no idea what he was saying, she became mesmerized by the cigarette that threatened to fall from his lips. With another shrug of his drooping shoulders, he returned to his disappearing act behind the counter.

Sam's fatigue from the recent travelling bubbled to the surface. "Now listen here to me, Monsieur Boucher. I have a reservation. There it is." Sam jabbed her finger so hard on the desk she thought she heard it crack. "I want to go to my room this very minute."

Monsieur Boucher reached below the counter and produced a reservations diary which looked as old as he. He flicked the pages, ran his nicotine-stained finger down the listings, found O'Brien and turned the diary to face Samantha.

"Good," she said, "About time." In a grand voice, she read the entry aloud. "The twenty-sixth of September 2016. What? My reservation wasn't for next year, it's for this year, 2015!" Sam's finger worked overtime stabbing her email while Monsieur Boucher's finger tapped at his entry.

Angry tears bit at her eyes while Sam tried to explain once more. Complicated by the language divide, the landlord's constant shrugging and apparent lack of any sympathy for her plight, made the situation excruciating. With her stomach twisting in knots and on the edge of screaming, she looked around and saw there wasn't even a couch on which to sit in defiant protest of such incompetence. Wedged at the counter, she could either remain trapped upright arguing with a man who showed no compassion or responsibility for ruining her life or trundle down the stairs to the unknown. Which version of hell to choose?

With a final nonchalant shrug, Monsieur Boucher made the decision for her. Unable to tolerate the scene any longer, Sam threw her bags back on her shoulder and stormed down the stairs, unconcerned about scraping the old timber from the steps with every thud of her trailing suitcase. At least, the landlord's angry yelling gave her some satisfaction. On reaching the bottom, she turned to see him standing at the top of the staircase, shaking his fists, his reddening face ready to implode on the quivering cigarette. Sam promptly responded by poking her tongue out. With a toss of her ponytail, she turned on her heel and strode away.

"Stupid old bastard," she spat as she battled with her luggage along the uneven pavement. Musing over the childishness of her tongue-poke made her smile, and as her temper subsided, so did the pace at which she marched down the Rue des Abbesses.

"Oh, God," she cursed under her breath. "What am I going to do now?" Dodging other pedestrians and with her resistant luggage in tow, she headed for the nearest café. Propped at a tiny red table under a pretty red awning, she sat in the red-light district of Paris awaiting *un café* as she scrolled to the number on her phone.

"*Bonjour. C'est* Moulin Rouge," came the friendly female voice on the other end.

"*Bonjour.* Do you speak English?" Sam asked sipping the worst coffee she'd ever tasted.

"*Oui.* How may I help you?"

"My name is Samantha O'Brien, from Australia and I'm one of the new dancers in the *Partie Paradise* show. I was booked to stay at Regina's Montmartre, but I've just arrived to be told they don't have my booking. I've got nowhere to live, and I'm stuck somewhere in Montmartre. I need to find somewhere else to stay. Can you help me please?" The longer she spoke, the more she struggled to swallow the emotion clawing at her throat.

"*Oui,* Samantha. You are not far away from the Moulin Rouge. If you hail a taxi, it will bring you here. Come to the box office and ask for Yvette. That is me. *Oui?*"

"Oh, thank you, Yvette. Yes. *Oui.* I'll be there soon. Thank you." Samantha gladly left her lukewarm, bitter coffee to hail a cab. Yvette was right. The Moulin Rouge was close by, giving Sam just enough time to compose herself in the back of the cab.

On paying the fare and with her suitcase and bags stacked beside her, Sam stood on the pavement in front of her new career. At twenty-four years of age and being blessed with a 1.85-metre-tall, long-limbed body, she'd made her dream come true. Her mother and Aunty Michele had both danced at the Rouge when they were about her age. Soon, the name Samantha O'Brien would become part of the legend, as one of the Dorris Dancers for the next Moulin Rouge production. Regardless of Monsieur Boucher's ineptitude, nothing could dampen the thrill of starting her new life in Paris. Looking up at the iconic red windmill, she took a deep breath, picked up her bags and headed to the box office. Through the entrance corridor she strolled, taking her time to study the current show's glass-encased posters which lined the walls. Stopping now and again to soak up the atmosphere and history, Sam reflected on the venue's fame that dated back to 1889. Daydreaming of the wonderful time she was about to have being part of one of the Rouge's famous cabaret productions, she relaxed and, for the first time since arriving in Paris, her luggage behaved.

When she stepped into the foyer, flaming shades of red leapt to engulf her. The carpet, the walls, the furnishings and the drapes; everything blazed such an exotic vermilion she could almost smell the cinnabar. Like a seductive lover, the pigment's brilliance beckoned her down the many stairs and toward the box office.

"*Bonjour.* I'm Samantha O'Brien."

"*Bonjour,* Samantha, I'm Yvette." A tiny redheaded young woman perched on a stool at the ticketing window. "I'm so sorry about your trouble, but Josette Deschamps was supposed to meet you at the airport. Did you not see her?"

"I know, but she wasn't there. At least, I couldn't find her."

"I will call her now. Just a moment." Yvette dialled and chatted in rapid French to the person on the other of the phone. "Josette says she was there but must have missed you.

I am so sorry, Samantha. One of our dancers is supposed to meet all new dancers at the airport and make sure everything is all right. Josette is on her way here now. Miss Faraday will be most displeased Josette missed you." It was common knowledge that the ballet mistress, Miss Faraday ruled the dancers with a fair, but iron will. Sam was relieved it'd be Josette and not her, who would attract Miss Faraday's scrutiny on this occasion.

"In the meantime, I've found somewhere for you to stay," Yvette said.

"You have? That's marvellous."

"Madame Lucette owns Hotel Hollandaise. She has one room left to let. It's a small hotel or how you say, a boarding guest house. Not far from here. You can walk from the Rouge to the hotel."

"Really? Oh, thank you so much, Yvette. I could kiss you."

"No, no. Not necessary." Yvette's petite hands waved Sam's gratitude away and at the same time, a leggy blonde leapt down the stairs two at a time, making a beeline to the box office window.

Her long eyelashes fluttered over sparkling sapphire eyes and her blonde ponytail kept two-four time, swinging like a metronome behind her head. She threw her arms around Samantha's neck. "I am so sorry. I don't know how I missed you at the airport. I even paged you, but you must have gone. Are you all right?"

Assuming this was Josette, Sam unclenched herself from her chaperone's fierce hug. "It's okay, Josette. I'm okay. Yvette has sorted everything out for me."

Again, Josette threw her arms around Samantha's neck. "Oh, that is wonderful news." Then on releasing Sam, she turned to Yvette and blew her lots of air-kisses smattered with innumerable *merci beaucoups.*

Josette spoke good English, less broken than Yvette's, so Sam gave an abridged version of her reservation fiasco and the new accommodation Yvette had secured at Madame Lucette's for her.

"Hotel Hollandaise," Josette shrieked in approval. "It is so cute. You'll love it. Come on. Let's go." She hauled Sam's bags onto each shoulder, leaving Sam to handle the suitcase and say a hurried farewell to Yvette, who returned to her normal ticketing duties.

~ ♥ ~

SOON THE PAIR STRODE down the Boulevard de Clichy. Zigzagging through the passing traffic, Josette was undeterred by the wrath of angry drivers, while Sam trailed behind, smiling and apologizing for their impertinence. Taking a left into Rue Puget, Josette finally slowed her marathon pace.

Josette turned to Sam with a dazzling showgirl smile. "So, are you excited?"

"Yes, very much," Sam said, mirroring Josette's smile.

Chatting idly, neither girl took much notice of the stares their presence produced. The local Parisians were used to seeing showgirls on the street, their long legs tucked into tight jeans and killer high heels. But it was the tourists, unaccustomed to seeing such poise and beauty close up, who turned as they passed by. Nearly a full head taller than mere mortals, Josette and Sam were a carbon copy of each other, except that Josette's flaxen hair was in direct contrast to Sam's thick, liquorice-coloured locks; remnants of her Irish ancestry, as were her emerald eyes.

Josette veered right into a small public courtyard and for the first time, Samantha took the chance to appreciate the prettiness of the 18th arrondissement of Paris. Two rows of sprawling linden trees with their canopies of rich, dark leaves stretched overhead like giant awnings. The diffused shade protected the graceful bodies of men and women as they relaxed on the park benches, enjoying their autumn lunch and talk of love. Manicured grass, plush as velvet crept to meet the cobbled pathway that threaded through the courtyard, caressing it with a lover's touch as if to match the furtive glances of a local's lunchtime tryst.

"This is *petite fontaine bleue*, small blue fountain," Josette said when they stopped at the cobalt-blue marble fountain in the middle of the courtyard. Held aloft by four nymphs, its cup of water trickled down into the cobblestone trough at its base, with only the slightest murmur.

"It's beautiful." Sam circled the fountain, pointing to the scattered coins in its base. "Is it a fountain of love?"

"*Oui*, all is love in Paris."

At the rear of the courtyard, and camouflaged by golden, honey locust trees, hid Hotel Hollandaise. A narrow, early twentieth century, three-story white-washed stone block structure, it stood wedged between larger period buildings like a little sister squashed between much larger brothers. With a tight central doorway splitting its façade and tiny balconies protruding from the rooms above, Hotel Hollandaise welcomed Samantha with its slender curtained windows and French doors winking in the sunlight.

"This looks perfect," she said, appreciating her new home away from home.

"Yes, it's so quaint. I know you'll love it here. It's where I lived when I first arrived from Monte Carlo a few years ago. And Madame Lucette is wonderful. She's a fortune-teller, you know. But you'll find that out for yourself."

Before Josette could continue, out from the front door launched a dynamic woman wearing a floating multi-coloured caftan and a black fringed shawl which failed to disguise her bony shoulders. Grey hair swirled atop her head in a loose bun skewered by two Chinese chopsticks. By the glint and jangle of bracelets, earrings and necklaces, she was a costume jewellery retailer's dream customer.

"*Bonjour. Bonjour.* You must be Samantha. Ah, Josette, it is good to see you."

Like a giraffe stretching down to drink, Josette exchanged double cheek kisses with her diminutive, ex-landlady whose face wore the friendliest of smiles.

"*Bonjour*, Madame Lucette. It's so good of you to take me in like this." Unexpected emotion welled in Sam's eyes and Madame Lucette rushed forwards, embracing her new tenant, reaching up with a kiss to her cheeks.

"There, there, *chère fille*. It is all right. I will look after you. Hotel Hollandaise is not the most beautiful hotel in Montmartre, but it is the most charming." With a flourish of her hand, Madame Lucette signalled the way into the hotel.

Crammed into a small corner in the foyer was the reception desk, behind which the wall was amateurishly painted in a scene depicting the nearby Sacré-Coeur, the famous white-domed Catholic church of Montmartre. The hotel tried to smell its age, but Madame Lucette's scented candles and incense burnt away its attempts. Although the walls needed fresh licks of paint, Sam noticed the foyer was clean and organized. Decorated with clusters of knick-knacks, fortune-telling cards and baubles, the atmosphere reminded her of a gypsy's caravan, warm and mysterious. Breaking the spell, a computer glowed in the corner. Madame Lucette squeezed behind the counter and arranged all the details of Samantha's reservation with efficiency and friendliness as her oversized, crystal droplet earrings jingled in time with her movements.

Large brass key in hand, Madame Lucette led the dancers up the stairs to the first floor. "I call this my *salle do soleil*, my sunshine room, Samantha. Every morning the sun shines in and fills it with light. I know you dancers like to sleep late, but it is so important to let light into your life." She turned back to Sam and winked for emphasis before continuing her climb. Josette nodded at Sam with a 'told-you-so' expression.

Turning the brass key in the lock, Madame Lucette opened the creaky door with pride. A double bed all but filled the room, its sagging mattress covered with clean sheets, mismatched blankets and a hand-made fringed quilt. Not more than four steps from the end of the bed, a small ornate fireplace lay claim to the wall. To one side of the bed crammed a nightstand, while on the other squeezed an old teak armoire, barely big enough to store the clothes Samantha had in her suitcase. Next to this squatted a bar fridge, which sat as sentinel to the door leading into the even tinier bathroom.

Not wanting to sound ungrateful, Sam said, "It's wonderful. Thank you. This will suit me perfectly."

"I know it is small, *chère fille*, but it is the room for you. The cards told me so." Madame Lucette placed the large key in Samantha's hands, kissed her cheeks once more and made a sweeping exit, all but catching her shawl in the closing door.

Sam pushed her suitcase into a corner and nodded at Josette to discard the other bags likewise. When they flopped onto the bed, it sank beneath their strictly controlled weight, making them laugh out loud.

"Well it's not what I expected but I have a roof over my head, a fireplace and a bathroom. I consider myself lucky. It's very expensive, though. I'll have to get mum and dad to send over some extra money to help out I think."

"Everything in Paris is expensive. Although, it would be better to have a stronger bed for when you make love to your new French boyfriend" Josette bounced up and down as proof of the poor performing mattress.

"I didn't come here to find a boyfriend. I came here to dance. I'm only interested in my career. I don't have time for boyfriends."

"*Idiote*," Josette scolded. "You are in Paris, the city of love. Of course, you will find love. It is all around you."

"No, Josette. I don't want love. I want a career. Love can wait." Samantha had worked long and hard for this opportunity and she wasn't going to lose her heart to some man and ruin her future.

"Poor Samantha," Josette said with sarcastic pity. "It doesn't matter what you want. You are in Paris and Paris is love." With a grand kick of her legs, she was off the bed and at the door. "I'll be back around seven o'clock tonight. We will go out and find you some love." As Sam repeated her rebuttal, Josette closed the door and was gone.

Pushing open the stiff French doors on the other side of the bed, Sam wiggled out onto her narrow balcony to watch her new friend prance away. Josette turned, did a perfect bump-and-grind and blew Sam a kiss. When nearby men whistled her impromptu performance, Josette took a bow and left the courtyard a quieter place.

Looking out at the wise, old trees and the lovers on the park benches below her, Sam smiled in contentment. This quaint, old-world hotel had become her new home and she wondered what the city of love had in store for her.

CHAPTER TWO

"I STILL CAN'T BELIEVE you rang me, Aunty Michele. It's two o'clock in the morning over there."

"That's okay, my Tiny Dancer. I promised your mum I'd call you in Paris since she's still on the flight home from London." Having been showgirls together years before at the Moulin Rouge and lifelong friends, Michele was calling Sam for SallyAnn, who'd be worried sick about her daughter's arrival in Paris.

"You know, Aunty Michele, I'm not that tiny anymore."

"I know, honey. But you'll always be my Tiny Dancer because that's what I called you when you started ballet. I'm so proud of you, you know that, don't you?"

"Yes, I do. Thanks for everything, Aunty Michele. Please make sure mum doesn't worry too much. But they'll need to organize some more money for me though so I can pay the rent here. Paris is so expensive. I doubt I'll be able to afford to eat anything other than coffee and salads."

"I'll let your dad know about the money in the morning. He'll sort it out. They'll just be happy that you found somewhere to live after all the mix-up. Now, remember, not only is Paris expensive, it's also very romantic. There's always lots of love on offer. Your mother had a wonderful affair when we danced there—"

"Okay. Too much information. I have to go, Aunty Michele. Josette is taking me out tonight. Love you."

"Love you too, Tiny Dancer."

Samantha had one hour to finish unpacking and get ready before Josette turned up. She recalled what Aunty Michele used to say, 'time to put your skates on' so Sam did just that and was ready and waiting downstairs just before seven.

~ ♥ ~

"I SEE YOU ARE going out, Samantha," Madame Lucette crooned from behind a large potted philodendron she was tending.

"Yes. Josette is going to show me around a little."

"It's a full moon tonight, Samantha." Madame Lucette glanced outside and then to Sam as if telepathically sharing the significance of the moon's cycle.

Sam smiled awkwardly and returned to curling up the cuffs of her white blouse, which she tucked once more into her low-slung blue jeans. With her long black tresses hanging loosely over her shoulders and her makeup artfully applied, she was a striking contradiction of youthful innocence and exotic sexuality.

"You are a very beautiful girl, Samantha, and Paris is a very beautiful city. But sometimes beauty is not always a blessing." Madame Lucette's gaze remained fixed on the leaves she lovingly polished.

"Oh, Madame Lucette, there are many more beautiful girls than me in Paris. Josette is far more beautiful than me." She shifted her weight uneasily from foot to foot.

"No, I do not think that is true, *chère fille.*" Madame Lucette looked up and met Samantha's green eyes. "I talk about inside beauty and you are filled with it." She paused and watched Samantha continue fidgeting. "But with beauty can also come demons. And the cards tell me you have both inside you . . ."

"*Bonsoir,* Sam. Are you ready for love?" Josette called in a bright voice as she strode to the front door where Samantha stood waiting to be saved.

"No. But I'm ready for a glass of wine." Samantha cast a farewell smile and a quick wave to Madame Lucette before making a hasty exit.

"Is something the matter?" Josette asked as they headed through the courtyard, their high heels navigating the cobblestone pathway.

"It's Madame Lucette. I thought you were joking when you said she was a fortune teller. I thought she was just eccentric, but she said something just now—"

"What?"

"Oh, it doesn't matter. I just need a drink." Sam dismissed her apprehensions and the odd conversation with the landlady with an elegant wave of her hand.

"That I can do." Josette linked her arm through Sam's and guided her to her first party night in Montmartre.

MADAME LUCETTE WAS RIGHT. Samantha's room was *salle do soleil*. Having forgotten to wear her eye mask, Sam was rudely awoken at seven o'clock by blistering sunlight. As she struggled against the light's insistence, her head joined the morning wake-up party with a staggering thud.

God, what was that drink? The green fairy? Absinthe? The night came crashing back. Just making it to the porcelain, Sam threw up what was left in her stomach, unsure whether it was the last of the lethal green drink or bile. Convinced she must have also heaved up an internal organ or two, Sam scanned the toilet bowl. Not noticing anything untoward as compared to the usual, she flushed the toilet and shuffled back to bed for more of the light show. After a few seconds of her hand rattling around in the nightstand drawer, she found her eye mask, strapped it to her face and fell unconscious.

~ ♥ ~

IT WAS DUSK BY the time Sam awoke for the second time on her second day in Paris. Praying her bathroom included steaming hot water she turned on the antique taps and waved her hand under the feeble spray. Although her hangover remedy never quite made it to the temperature or force she needed, she found the shower adequate. In fifteen minutes, she was towelled, dressed and with her wet hair twirled in a tight bun she padded down the stairs to the guest dining room.

Empty except for its six shabby-chic tables and a dozen matching chairs, the room opened onto a charming private courtyard through four French doors. Wandering outside, Sam admired the tiny quadrangle's unruly beauty of geraniums, nasturtiums, roses and dahlias squabbling for more space in the traditional border garden. Each autumn flower seemed compelled to be the finest flame of colour before winter arrived to strip away its glory.

"Being in nature is a wonderful gift to give oneself, Samantha."

Startled, Sam turned to see Madame Lucette resting on a wrought iron garden seat, in a halo of cigarette smoke. "Come sit beside me for a while." The landlady tapped the cold, hard metal and Sam accepted her offer, although the cigarette smoke made her wince.

"So how was your night out with Josette?"

"I drank too much absinthe and now I'm paying the price," Samantha said sheepishly.

"I see." Madame Lucette stubbed out her cigarette in an ashtray and pocketed her *Gitanes* under her shawl. "You would like some soup?

"Oh no, Madame Lucette. No food. Maybe tomorrow."

"But you must have a little something. Come. I will make you a special tonic my mama used to make for me when I was a reckless, young girl like you." Not waiting for consent, she clasped Sam's hand and led her back through the dining room, into the kitchen.

"Sit, sit." Madame Lucette pointed to one of two timeworn chairs nestled at the round table in the corner.

Samantha sat in silence and watched the landlady thrust her hands into the pantry retrieving an armful of ingredients which she whisked into a foamy, green mixture. Pouring a glass of the elixir, she slid it across the table to her guest. "Drink, Samantha. Drink."

Tentative as to whether her stomach could tolerate anything green-coloured again, she sipped. "Actually, this tastes good." Surprised that the tonic tasted far better than it looked, Sam drank it in a couple of swallows.

"*Bon.*" Collecting the empty glass Madame Lucette rinsed it and placed it in the wire dish rack. "Now, let us talk a little. Come to my room."

Leading the way through the door on the other side of the kitchen, Madame Lucette beckoned Sam to follow. Like the typical fortune-telling parlours in old Hollywood movies, Madame Lucette's room was filled with pink-glowing lamps draped with Tiffany shades, delicate shawls and scarves. Fragrant incense filled the room, its smoke flirting with the warm currents of air from the wall heater. The temperature in the room brought little beads of perspiration to Sam's face, and she tugged to loosen the collar of her dress. Like Sam's room, Madame Lucette's small bed-sit was engulfed by her double bed adorned with a mountain of colourful pillows, leaving little room for the fortune-teller's table tucked under a standard lamp in the corner. Madame Lucette glided to the table, pulled out a chair and nodded to Sam to be seated. Not one to disobey her elders, Sam lowered herself onto the cushioned chair and waited.

"First, let us see what the cards have to say." Madame Lucette lit the melted candle next to her and waited for the flame to steady. She reached for the deck of tarot cards in the middle of the table and began to shuffle and concentrate.

After a few silent moments, she placed the deck in front of Sam. "Now shuffle the cards and ask them a question in your mind, Samantha. Cut the deck and you will have your answer."

"But I don't have a question, Madame Lucette." Sam's stomach began to churn.

"But you do, Samantha. Everyone has a question. You must ask it."

Trying to think of the question she supposedly wanted to ask, Sam forced herself to ignore her uneasiness and focus on shuffling the deck. The tattered edges of the cards slipped through her fingers as the artwork on the back of each drifted past. Depicting a dark, tranquil night sky resplendent with a full moon peeping out from behind some stormy clouds, the cards worried in her hands as if eager to be freed. Wondering how, within forty-eight hours, she'd come to be in a French fortune-teller's parlour, recovering from the hangover from hell, sitting opposite an eccentric landlady and shuffling tarot cards, Sam cut the deck. She peered at the card, uncomfortable at the sight of the wizened old hag, ashen-faced, unkempt and with arthritic fingers, pointing into the black distance.

Madame Lucette studied the card. "Samantha this is the crone goddess. She tells of the end, of decay, of winter that is to come. The crone goddess is a dark lady who holds the souls of the dead in her embrace."

"But I'm not dying. I'm beginning a new life. Here in Paris." Sam's voice began to make its escape without her.

"The cards never lie, Samantha. Something is coming to an end in your life. There is natural termination. This may not be what you want or what you planned or expected. But there is an end."

"I don't understand." Sam fidgeted in her chair, desperate to leave.

"To resist this end will only cause more pain, Samantha. Something must end so another may begin. You must accept this inevitable change." With her shadowy eyes burning into Sam's, Madame Lucette leaned further forwards as if being closer would reinforce her message.

"I really must go, Madame Lucette. I need some sleep before tomorrow." Not waiting for a response Sam sprang up, her panic bumping the table. A bony hand ensnared her wrist. Sam imagined it felt like the old crone's hand from the tarot card, and for a moment, Madame Lucette's face seemed to wither and whiten, making the image complete.

With a softer tone in her voice, Madame Lucette said, "Samantha, do not be afraid. This is a card of great liberation. There is something you will soon be free of. This is good news, *chère fille*. Go now. Sleep well and dream of liberation." Madame Lucette released her grip and Sam forced a smile then dashed from the room. Through the kitchen, out the dining room and up the stairs she fled, until safe behind her locked door, she took a deep breath.

This is crazy, she thought as she tried to slow her heart rate and breathing. On the bed, her phone flashed a message. It was Josette checking that Sam would be ready by eight the next morning. Sam messaged back she would. The simple act of texting brought normality back to the evening, enough for Sam to ready herself for sleep.

Jet lag still plagued her body and last night's drinking had been foolish. As she crawled into bed, Sam left her eye mask off on purpose, knowing the sun would be her natural alarm clock. Finding comfort in the old mattress and soft pillows, she drifted into a deep sleep with thoughts of the French revolution and the music from *Les Misérables* swirling in her mind.

CHAPTER THREE

"*Bonjour,* Sam." Josette kissed Sam on both cheeks. "Ready for rehearsals?"

Unlike Josette who wore a face full of makeup, Sam's scrubbed face had only a lick of cherry lip gloss and a lashing of mascara. Both wore sweatpants and loose jumpers. Josette's rehearsal clothes screamed designer while Sam wore a Targét special, under which her dance gear of mesh tights and hi-cut leotards were concealed. Both had tied their hair back in tight buns, guaranteeing there'd be no distraction from wayward tendrils.

"As ready as I'll ever be. I'm terribly nervous, though. I could barely eat any breakfast, just a hard-boiled egg and a cup of tea. And that feels like it's about to perform an encore any minute." Sam rubbed her flat tummy trying to quell the nerves.

"You will be fantastic. Tony is a good guy. He will love you. Come let's go."

With their dance totes hitched over their shoulders, the pair retraced their steps back to the Moulin Rouge under the blue skies of a crisp autumn day. Though the birds chirped good morning in the courtyard and lovers kissed goodbye on their way to work, Sam noticed none of the nuances of the city of love.

~ ♥ ~

After the formalities of checking in as a new dancer, Sam followed Josette backstage. Narrow corridors wound like rabbit warrens branching left and right to unmarked doors, staircases and dark corners. The smell of over one hundred years of stage makeup, sweaty costumes and French artistry permeated the theatre's backstage area sending a thrill of excitement through Sam's body and a sharp jab of doubt into her mind. Josette called, waved and kissed, at least twenty other perfectly proportioned dancers, introducing Sam to each one. With no idea what they were saying Sam nodded, smiled and said *bonjour* to all. Most didn't respond with more than a nod and an ice princess appraisal before prancing off to join a group of friends.

"Oh, Josette, I am out of my depth here. These girls are so stunning," Sam whispered as they dropped their bags, stripped off their sweats and began to limber up.

"No, Sam. Once we begin, you will be fine." Josette used the handrail at the bottom of a staircase on which to stretch her legs. Shuffling over, she offered a spot for Sam, who threw her leg up and contorted with a professional dancer's flexibility. Face to foot Sam continued limbering up as she sneaked peeks at the other sixty or more dancers who, like her, formed the chorus of the *Partie Paradise* show. Every one of them, a towering vision of human genetic engineering, combined talent, beauty, confidence and poise with the discipline of a finely tuned machine. The male dancers were even taller and stronger, with faces chiselled as if from precious marble. For Sam, having been chosen to join such an illustrious company, was both inspiring and terrifying.

When the ballet mistress clapped her hands calling everyone to begin rehearsals, Sam raced onstage and froze with a gasp. She stood amongst the dancers, looking out into the auditorium where hundreds of patrons would dine and watch her perform two shows every night, six nights a week. She considered pinching herself to check she wasn't dreaming, but she knew it was real She was finally here. Although the Moulin Rouge auditorium was lit only with bright worker lights, not the subtle, sensual lighting that glowed during the performance, it still resonated with a class and ambience befitting its world-renown reputation.

Miss Faraday, the ballet mistress, welcomed the cast with a short speech and then introduced the assistant choreographer, Penny Capstan, the stunning, ex-Rouge principal who'd been with the company for years. Sam suspected that Penny's fresh-faced smile belied the ferociousness with which she was about to manage their first rehearsal.

With a lyrical flourish of her arm, Miss Faraday said, "And our choreographer and stage director, Tony Di Falco joins us once again for this show."

Sam studied her new boss, whose presence filled the cavernous venue when he stood at their applause. With thick, dark hair pulled back in a loose ponytail, a scruffy light beard, dark smouldering eyes and burnished skin, Tony Di Falco could not be mistaken for anything but Sicilian. Rumours preceded him of the death-stare he'd inflicted last year on a poor, stupid male dancer who asked him where in Italy he'd been born. To a Sicilian, the insult of being called an Italian was unforgivable. As expected, Tony hadn't invited that male dancer to return for this show. Everyone secretly referred to Tony as Ursu, meaning the 'bear' in Sicilian, and it wasn't because he was cute and cuddly.

With only a twitch of a smile, he greeted his new charges. "*Merci*, Miss Faraday. It is once again a pleasure to be here at the famous Moulin Rouge. We will work hard, we will have fun and we will be the best show in the world." Ever the consummate performer he paused for his cast's murmur of agreement then continued in a warm modulated voice cloaked in a sexy European accent. "Now let us begin. Penny, the can-can please." Sinking his tall, muscular frame back into the front row seat, Tony steepled his fingers together, tapping them to his lips. Eyes like a hawk he surveyed his prey on stage while his assistant sorted the cast into the various groupings for the show's most famous routine. A form of a quadrille with extravagant leaping, kicking, acrobatics and non-stop footwork, the Moulin Rouge's can-can was known as one of the most strenuous in the business.

Within a few hours and under Penny's relentless instruction, some of the new dancers were crippled over in the wings gasping for breath, clutching their stomachs, trying not to throw up before their next entrance.

"You are doing good, Sam." Josette jigged on the spot in the wings beside her.

"I feel much better now we've started." Sam pulled deep breaths into her lungs, her confidence growing. Following Josette's lead of a piercing scream, Sam ran onto the stage shrieking the call of the can-can.

A baritone voice boomed over the music. "What is your name?" Tony's stare singled Sam out and sent an icy chill through the rehearsals. All movement and music stopped.

"Samantha O'Brien." Arms hanging lank by her sides, she felt her insides crumble.

"Well, Samantha O'Brien we do not need your shrill screams until you have been taught how to make the right sound. So please just concentrate on the steps for now."

"Yes, Tony. I'm sorry. I was just trying to—"

"Here at the Moulin Rouge, we do not try. We do as instructed." His dismissal of her was absolute. Turning his attention to Penny, he waved his hand. "Continue."

Holding back tears, Sam looked at Josette, who shook her head in a 'not-to-worry' fashion. Sucking up her emotions with a dancer's discipline, Sam launched back into the routine, punishing herself with the steps while keeping one eye glued on her new boss, trying her utmost to please him for the rest of the rehearsal.

~ ❤ ~

EXHAUSTED SIX HOURS LATER, Josette and Sam found a table at the local *crêperie, Toutes les crêpes de jour,* a favourite haunt of the dancers. Most of the tables were already occupied by the cast as they chatted, smoked, drank coffee and waited for their crepes. With the evening beginning its slow descent, the electric blue of the night sky formed a fitting backdrop to the red awnings of the shops scattered along the narrow, cobbled street. Languishing at the tables, the experienced dancers looked relaxed and well pleased with themselves, while the newbies fidgeted trying to get comfortable while lactic acid charged through their muscles.

"That was awful," Sam said, reliving the humiliation she suffered on stage. "I was so looking forward to making a good impression on Tony. Now he just hates me. I'm so embarrassed."

"No, no. It does not matter. He does not hate you. He sometimes does that with dancers he really likes. Wait and see. Here are our crepes. Eat. You will feel better."

Fork in hand and with little appetite, Sam approached her meal when a voice behind interrupted. "Samantha O'Brien." Frozen, she had no intention of turning around. Once today she'd heard her name spoken by this voice and it hadn't ended well.

"Tony," Josette welcomed. "Join us."

"Thank you." The chair between the dancers skittered across the cobblestones as Tony steadied it to sit. Stony-faced he looked at Sam. "You did very well today, Samantha." He was so close to her, she could smell his power. She prayed he couldn't smell her fear.

"I did?" She glanced up, meeting his fathomless eyes.

"Yes. Aside from your over-enthusiastic screaming, you danced well." He offered both girls a cigarette and, on their refusal, lit one for himself. When he inhaled, he closed his eyes and Sam noticed how the features of his face were sculptured; strong cut jaw and defined chin, high sweeping cheekbones with a straight elegant nose set in perfect symmetry in the middle of his face. With his hair now released and falling in subtle curls on the collar of his leather jacket, his face softened as he exhaled through slightly parted lips. He opened his eyes to find Sam staring at him. Caught off guard again, she returned to her crepes, digging at them as if searching for buried treasure.

"Tony, do you want something to eat? I will call the waiter," Josette said.

"No. I don't eat very much during rehearsals, Josette. Too much going on in my head. But you two must eat. *Bonsoir*, ladies. I will see you tomorrow." He turned and fixed Sam in his steely stare. "Sleep well, Samantha, and dance good for me again tomorrow."

Rising to his full 1.9-metre height, he towered over the table, and when Sam lifted her eyes to meet his gaze, he half-smiled and sauntered away, leaving her skin on fire. In his faded black jeans, moulded to his neat dancer's arse and white converse sneakers, Tony Di Falco oozed restrained sex appeal. On his way, he stopped and chatted briefly to the other dancers then wished them goodnight.

Sam's fork clattered into her bowl and her head sunk into her hands. "How else can I embarrass myself with this man?"

"There are many ways you can do that."

Samantha raised her face to catch Josette wrapping her lips seductively around her spoon.

"I'm not that stupid, Josette."

"No? But I think Tony likes you. I think he likes you a lot."

"You're being silly. Why on earth would you think that?

"Because you are young, you are new, you are strong, and Tony Di Falco is a collector of young, new things with strong hearts."

"Well, this is one heart he won't be collecting." Appetite restored, Sam finished her crepes, but her eyes followed the faint glow from Tony's cigarette as he rounded the corner out of sight.

Rehearsals for tony were always gruelling. His mind never stopped. Reinventing the choreography, checking the design team was building the sets to his specifications, reviewing the costume designs as well as lighting design and other countless tasks, he loved it all, but nevertheless, the month or so of intensive work took its toll. Then there was the bevy of new dancers. The Australian girl, Samantha O'Brien was star material. A strong dancer, with a stunning face and body of death, she was destined to be a soloist. A bit unsure of herself, though. He needed to keep an eye on her, make certain she settled in okay. These foreign girls often got themselves involved in some foolish, passionate love affair which ultimately broke their hearts and careers.

Tony tapped out the last cigarette in his packet and lit it. He dragged back on it hard then exhaled the stale smoke through his nose. God, he wished he could give these awful things up. He'd tried a few times, but he was addicted. Much like the way he was addicted to beautiful women and cocaine. But as they say, bad things come in threes.

~ ♥ ~

Trudging up the stairs at Hotel Hollandaise, Sam was startled to find Madame Lucette leaving her room.

"Ah, Samantha, *bonsoir*. How was your first day at rehearsals?"

"Oh, it was good, thank you, Madame?" Sam stared from the landlady to her door asking the question.

"I have just placed some flowers in your room. I find my dancers are often tired after their first day and the autumn flowers from my garden add a little love and beauty when they get home." Madame Lucette's sweet smile left little room for Sam to be aggrieved at her privacy being invaded.

"Oh, ah. *Merci*. That was kind of you. I think I will go to bed now. Goodnight." Samantha squeezed past the old woman, and keeping her eyes downcast, hoped her retreat would be successful.

"And were you liberated today?"

"I beg your pardon?" Sam stopped on the steps, her mind trying to find a footfall.

"The crone goddess card foretold of you being liberated. Was it today?" Madame Lucette's eyes gleamed.

"No. Not today, Madame. Not today. *Bonsoir*." Sam turned her key in the lock and bustled into her sanctuary.

Perched in an antique crystal vase, Madame Lucette's garden flowers did add a touch of welcome to Samantha's small room. On the mantle of her fireplace, they seemed to greet her with a natural fondness. Sam undressed and relived her first day of rehearsals at the Moulin Rouge; the exhilaration, the physical pain, the sheer pleasure of it all. It had been everything she'd hoped for and more. Yet, like an errant child, her mind wandered back to the enigmatic Tony Di Falco.

Under the hot water in the shower, she remembered the impassive expression on his face tonight when he complimented her dancing. Although his words commended her, his body remained taut, restraining his intense power and gruff demeanour. Ursu, the bear, seemed to be an apt nickname for her new boss.

Rubbing the soap in her hand and up her arms, she felt the abrasiveness of his voice polishing her skin. Particularly when he chastised her on stage, he was purposeful, forceful and in command. At least then he'd expressed some emotion, even if it was dissatisfaction with her impromptu vocal performance when she screamed the wrong can-can squeal.

As Sam scrubbed the tension from her body, she imagined his hands; strong, lean, unforgiving, circling her legs, kneading the day's dance from them. Moving higher up her thighs, she closed her eyes, retreating to her fantasy. Sliding her soapy hands between her legs, she imagined Tony's voice telling her what to do, what he wanted.

Slipping her finger into her sudsy slit, she toyed with herself. Knowing how best to self-gratify, she slid down into the old claw-foot bathtub, splaying her legs over the sides and allowed the sharp pricks of hot water to bite at her open cleft. Visualizing Tony nibbling at her clit, punishing it with his mouth, she circled her throbbing bud as she raised her hips up toward his imaginary face. She moaned and tried to stave off her climax by rubbing at her clit, changing the rhythm to intensify the final release. All the while, Tony Di Falco growled in her ear, berating her for not dancing well enough, for not doing what she was told. Harder and harder he scolded her, harder and harder she damaged her sweetness until jamming her fingers deep inside, she launched upright pumping herself to orgasm.

Collapsing back in the tub, Sam's face transformed with an inscrutable smile, her unrepentant fingers still slithering in her engorged folds. Perhaps this was the liberation Madame Lucette read in the cards? But as Sam began another delectable assault on her sex, she suspected she'd cracked open a door that only Tony Di Falco could shut.

~ ♥ ~

By Saturday, one of the new dancers had resigned to return home to her boyfriend in Sweden, another had pulled a tendon and had to work overtime to catch up on the routines she'd missed, while Sam had managed to make it through the first week without severe injury to either her body or her psyche. In six days, they'd all suffered and agonized over five new routines and were now rehearsing the grand finale.

"And one more time please, *beddi*." Tony commanded Penny to put his 'lovelies' through their paces again while he prowled left to right across the front of the stage, calling corrections to individual dancers.

"This way. Look this way for God's sake." His growl rose above the sound of the pianist thumping the keyboard.

The male dancers' heads snapped to stage left.

"No, the Vegas Step needs a full half-turn. Get it right please," Tony hollered at a section of the female chorus as they scurried upstage in record time. "Now. Cue now!" he yelled louder still at another group of dancers entering a beat too late from the wings. His hands rapped out the beat, while Penny shouted more orders from stage left. On and on everyone danced, until with a final triumphant chord the routine ended with each dancer striking their pose. Dazzling smiles remained frozen, lungs struggled for air and muscles screamed. Although it was only a rehearsal, no one dared to break formation. Hold, hold, hold.

"All right, *beddi*. Come sit on the stage." Tony clapped once and waved his cast forward, while Penny flapped like a mother hen pushing her chicks to the front of the stage.

"Good work this week everyone. Well done. Relax tomorrow. I'll give notes on Monday before we start. See you then." For the first time, he allowed his cast to see his admiration and affection for them. A visible sigh could be felt as everyone applauded him for his creative vision. Elated and exhausted, everyone left the stage chatting about what they planned to do on their day off.

"I'm stuffed. This was sheer torture. I've never worked so hard in rehearsals, ever. I don't think I'll be able to move tomorrow." Sam threw her sweaty towel around her shoulders and dragged herself off stage.

"Tomorrow, you walk. Go see Montmartre, the Sacré-Coeur. I must visit with my mother, but you must walk, or you will not be able to dance on Monday." Josette's advice left no room for debate, and on consideration, Sam knew she was right. She needed to walk out her muscles or they'd seize up.

Bending over to cram her towel and water bottle into her dance bag, Sam's skin prickled at the brooding presence behind her.

"Samantha, you have danced well this week," Tony said.

Sam's sexual fantasy of Tony Di Falco had haunted her all week and now here he was, breathing fire down her spine.

"Thank you, Tony." Convinced a bright, breezy manner would be the best approach, Sam straightened to her full height, only slightly shorter than him. She threw her tote over her shoulder in readiness to leave, and with both hands clinging to the straps, hoped to protect herself from his intense scrutiny.

Dressed in his dance gear of tight black pants, white converse sneakers, white singlet and white long sleeve shirt knotted at the waist, he leaned back against the staircase railing. With one hand on his hip and the other relaxed by his side, he said, "Are you enjoying the rehearsals?" He cocked one foot up on the wall behind, drawing her attention downward with his movement. Her eyes glimpsed his crotch, and she wondered how any man had the right to look so goddamned beautiful and dangerous at the same time. "I'm loving the rehearsals, Tony. Very strenuous and exhausting. But that's okay by me. I like hard work."

"I'm sure you do." His dark eyes flashed. "Have a relaxing Sunday, Samantha. I'll see you next week." In an unexpected move, he reached out to wipe away a stray trickle of perspiration from her temple, then with predatory grace, he strolled back onto the stage.

Sam shuffled into the backstage darkness and watched him discussing lighting intricacies with his lighting director.

"*Oui*, Paris is love," Josette whispered in Sam's ear, making her flinch and nearly drop her bag.

"I am not in love. I admire Tony. He's a great director," Sam said with as much conviction as she could muster in a whisper.

"Great directors make great lovers. Come. Time to eat." Josette pulled Sam away from the object of her growing fascination.

Even as Tony strode off to find his lighting director, his thoughts remained on Samantha, with her flushed cheeks and sweaty brow. Two characteristics he found extremely appealing. She seemed a sweet girl, but nervy. Over the years, he'd initiated many sweet girls, enjoying them immensely. When he was just a young dancer in Rome, he'd had his choice of the chorus girls and a couple of the principals as well. In those days, his desire for fame was matched by his lust for female flesh. During that time, he'd learnt that discretion was the better part of valour — and of sex. After nearly being expelled from a company for his sexual exploits in a wild orgy with a few of the girls from the show, who later told too many people of their fuck-fest, Tony had decided he needed to rein himself in, both physically and metaphorically. Now older and wiser, he chose his casual sex partners not only on their beauty and willingness to oblige but also on their ability to be discreet. Even as recently as a couple of years ago, during his first show as stage director at the Rouge, he'd endangered his career with a showgirl who became fixated on him. Because they'd also enjoyed the odd line of coke, she threatened to expose his untamed predilections. What she didn't know was she was playing a dangerous game; one she couldn't win against a man who grew up as a bullied and battered kid in the south of Sicily.

The long-legged beauty was no match for Tony Di Falco and within weeks, she was offered a role she couldn't refuse in the Lido. Connections in this game were everything. But this Samantha stirred something else within him. She wasn't wild and untamed. She wasn't his usual type, and she was way too young. God, he needed a cigarette.

CHAPTER FOUR

HAVING WOKEN FEELING LESS stiff and sore than she expected, Sam accepted Madame Lucette's offer of a hot, English breakfast, complete with toast, marmalade and a steaming pot of *Twining's English Breakfast Tea*. Calculating the kilojoules she'd burned in rehearsals this week couldn't be replaced by one large meal, she allowed herself the rare privilege of enjoying her breakfast, guilt-free. With a street map in front of her, she studied how to get to the tourist sights on foot.

With hands wiping on her apron, Madame Lucette strolled out of the kitchen toward her new tenant. "Where are you off to today, Samantha? Sacré-Coeur? Place du Terte?"

"Yes. I want to get my bearings, so I'll spend the day just walking around."

"There is much history here, *chère fille*. Just keep going up the hill to the big white church." The unlit *Gitane* in Madame Lucette's hand waved in the air, indicating the way upward as she continued into the garden to light her cigarette.

MAP IN HAND, SAM threw her bag over her shoulder and set off to explore what the locals call the village of Paris. Deciding to follow her landlady's advice, Sam resisted the herd mentality, choosing not to follow the tourists up the hill, but to veer off onto the weaving cobblestone backstreets. Tucked away from the crowds, little shops, patisseries and delicatessens with bells on their doors and windows full of local fare, catered to the needs of the Parisians. French voices lilted from open doorways and from friends as they welcomed each other on their way to or from their day's activities. Like other cities across the world, Sunday was family day in Montmartre with children and parents spending time together, as evidenced by the laughter and shouting resounding down the laneways. Losing herself in the autumn sun's warmth, Sam soon relaxed and stopped checking her map, instead using the Basilica as her beacon. Its grand, white dome contrasted against the vivid blue of the sky, calling her upward.

Eventually, she stood at the bottom of the three hundred steps of Montmartre. Steep and lined with lampposts and deciduous trees now bare of their summer foliage, the steps seemed to slice a perfect pathway to heaven. Opting for the physical exercise, Sam allowed the tourists to clamber on board the funicular while she climbed up toward Sacré-Coeur.

She arrived at the top with plenty of breath and muscles grateful for the small workout. Not keen on joining the tourist hordes snapping souvenir pictures of the basilica, she decided to make another date with the church that was not a Sunday. She wandered the streets until she came upon the Place du Terte, a quaint square surrounded by cafés, restaurants and souvenir shops. Filled with African migrants, the Place du Terte buzzed with activity, as they peddled their cheap souvenirs. Ever vigilant, they remained on the look-out for police who systematically chased them away, only for them to return like ants to a picnic.

"Mademoiselle, mademoiselle." The hawkers pounced, thrusting cheap merchandise under her nose, pushing her to buy. Fending off their vehement sales pitch, Samantha smiled and shook her head, turning her attention to the portrait artists crammed in the centre quadrant of the square. Impressed by their skill, she watched one man pencil-sketch a remarkable likeness of a young girl in less than thirty minutes. Her American parents effused with delight as they parted with their cash in exchange for a wonderful memory of their trip to Paris.

Nearly eighty artists sat with their easels and pencils waiting for another subject to render on paper for a small sum. In berets and sipping mugs of rich smelling coffee, they smoked and chatted with each other while the rest of the world strayed past, deliberating who they would select to immortalize them.

"*Mademoiselle?*" The voice intoned recognition, but as Sam sought its owner, her eyes fell upon a stranger. Leaning against his easel, his legs casually crossed at the ankles, he seemed incongruent with the group of aging artists. Tall, lean, young and clean-shaven, he looked ethereal, as if he'd just flown down from the basilica on angel wings. His androgynous face, with its fine aquiline nose, translucent blue eyes framed by thick eyelashes and fine honey-coloured hair that danced defiantly over his forehead, glowed with vitality.

"*Mademoiselle?*" He nodded to her and beckoned her closer. Drawn by his beauty, Sam drifted over.

"Do I know you?" she asked in a shy voice.

"No. We have not met before, mademoiselle, but now we do. My name is Philippe Lacroix, and I am an artist." His sculptured hand reached out and on cue, Sam lifted hers. Dropping his lips to her skin, he kissed her hand.

"I'm Samantha O'Brien from Australia."

"Well Samantha O'Brien from Australia, would you like a portrait?" He still had hold of her hand, romancing her to be his subject.

A sales pitch, she thought. "No. I don't think I need a portrait at the moment."

"That is a pity, Samantha. I am a very good artist, and you are a very pretty young woman." He stepped down from beside his easel, meeting her face-to-face. "Perhaps instead, you would like a coffee or a sandwich?"

"I suppose that might be nice."

"Then I will take you to the best patisserie here in Place du Terte." He turned back to his colleagues advising them he was taking a break and escorted Sam through the milling crowds.

Shaking free of the spell he seemed to cast over her, Samantha reclaimed her hand and they walked the short distance to Le Pain de Pascal. Setting a steady pace and with Sam in tow, he maneuvered through the throng with ease, his lithe frame side-stepping the slower pedestrians. On entering the café, he brandished his hand at the establishment's sign, indicating their successful arrival. With the angelic smile never leaving his face, Philippe squeezed between the dozen or so terrace tables until he found one of his liking. He pulled the chair out and with an artistic flourish of his hand, beckoned Sam to sit. "They do the best baguettes in all of Paris and the best pastries," Philippe said with such pride, Sam wondered if he perhaps was a stakeholder in the thriving business.

"I'll just have tea please."

"What nothing to eat? I will order something for you." He called a waiter who scribbled down the order, nodded curtly and disappeared.

Before long, a magnificent baguette brimming with salad and chicken arrived, accompanied by a steaming pot of tea and a plate of delicious petit fours. While Philippe devoured his lunch, Samantha picked some salad from the baguette and drank her tea.

"You must be a dancer. No?"

"Yes. I am dancing at the Moulin Rouge. We just started rehearsals last week." Delight rang in Sam's voice.

"I thought so. Dancers never eat." He nodded to her fussing over the food.

"Well, we have to be very careful with our weight otherwise we might lose our job."

"Samantha, you are too beautiful to lose your job." He reached over, cut a slab of baguette and foisted it firmly onto her plate. "Eat."

She wrapped her fingers around his command, lifted the baguette to her mouth and bit down hard. The flavours and the soft, chewy texture of the French bread settled onto her tongue, and she chewed deliberately, delaying its departure while an appreciative smile stretched across her face.

"Better," he said, captivating her with a smile of straight, white teeth framed by the perfectly bowed lips of a renaissance artwork. "You cannot live in Paris and not eat a baguette."

The delight with which he dug deep into his baguette enchanted Sam. She'd never seen anyone eat with such passion. Aside from his art, she wondered what else he did with such passion.

"Philippe, Philippe." The loud cry came from the older man running toward them, waving his arms wildly. Sam had no idea what he said, but its impact on her new friend was immediate.

"Samantha, I am sorry. I must go. Will you come back to see me next Sunday?" He leaned in, his eyes shining with anticipation and the passion in his plea sealed her decision.

"Yes, of course, Philippe. I'll come back next Sunday."

"Excellent." He kissed her mouth like a smitten lover, slapped the money on the table for lunch and disappeared with his friend into the crowd.

Startled, Sam remained seated at the tiny table trying to piece together the strange encounter with Philippe. By the time the waiter arrived to clear the plates and collect the money, she'd unconsciously eaten the rest of the baguette and all the petit fours. Shocked and annoyed she'd eaten so much food, she threw her bag across her shoulders and jogged out of the square. Back down the steps of Montmartre, she scrambled, then hit her stride for the few kilometres home to Hotel Hollandaise. All the while she mused over the unexpected and delightful meeting with the young, good-looking French artist.

For Philippe, the afternoon trade for sketching portraits proved unusually slow. Financially it was disappointing, but there was an upside to having so few customers. Instead of using his talent to sketch unattractive faces and flatter them on paper, he could spend more time concentrating on a truly beautiful face. That of the young Australian dancer he'd just met. Samantha possessed one of the most interesting and exotic faces he'd seen in a long time and as an artist, he longed to paint her. She encapsulated the perfect subject. At once, beautiful and mystifying. An enchanting combination of innocent, wide-eyed enthusiasm juxtaposed with a darker, unresolved yearning. Intrigued, Philippe's mind swirled with images of Samantha. Due to being called away so unexpectedly, he'd not even time to get her phone number or find out where she was living. With no other alternative, he would now have to wait a week and hope she returned. In the meantime, he could do nothing but sketch her in his mind. He suspected this imagining would become a persistent haunting by week's end.

~ ♥ ~

"Did you enjoy your day, Samantha?" Madame Lucette was lighting incense in the reception when Sam trudged through the door, sweaty and puffing.

"Yes, thank you, Madame Lucette." She shrugged off her bag and leaned against the counter to catch her breath. "I didn't go to the church, though. Too many people. But I found Place du Terte and had lunch at Le Pain de Pascal."

"Did you get a portrait done?" Madame Lucette waved the incense around in swirling circles overhead, her brightly coloured bangles jangling in time.

"No, not this time. But I might go back next Sunday again and get one."

"There are many talented artists there, Samantha. Maybe one of them will be your liberator?"

"Madame Lucette, I don't need liberating, and I don't need to fall in love. But I do need a shower. See you in the morning. *Bonne nuit.*" She blew an air kiss to her landlady and marched up the stairs for a good night's sleep.

CHAPTER FIVE

BY THE END OF the second week of rehearsals, Samantha found her body had become accustomed to the gruelling dance schedule and she'd settled into her new Parisian lifestyle. Each morning she'd wake with the sun blazing into her little *salle do soleil*, the sunshine room she'd come to love. As she stood behind her French doors dragging on her tights and leotards, the morning light filtered through the sheer curtains warming her. Then while eating her usual breakfast of a boiled egg and cup of tea, she and Madame Lucette would banter about love, liberation and the mystery of Paris. Once finished, she'd set off for the brisk walk to the Rouge, trying to warm up her muscles as winter began its embrace of the city.

Stopping at the little blue fountain of love on Saturday, Samantha threw a euro into its base.

"Wishing for love, Samantha?" His deep, lyrical voice reverberated and her skin tingled, even under her heavy coat.

How did he always creep up on her? She turned to find him standing just a couple of steps behind. With his hair tucked into his turned-up collar, shoulders hunched against the chill in the air and hands thrust deep into his pockets, Tony Di Falco reminded her of a model on a fashion magazine shoot; perennially handsome, rugged and untouchable.

"Tony, you startled me. No, I wasn't wishing for anything really. Do you live around here?"

"Not really. But sometimes I wander through this courtyard since it's the prettiest one nearest to the Rouge. See how the nymphs holding up the cup pose like dancers?" He pointed to the intricately carved sprites holding the fountain bowl aloft.

"Yes, they do. I hadn't noticed that before. But they look more like nudes since they're topless." Sam studied the nakedness of the figures.

"Yes, you are right." He paused and they continued their study of the fountain. "You know, Samantha, one day you will be a nude at the Moulin Rouge."

"I'd love to be a nude, but I don't have the body that a nude needs." Her gaze remained fixed on the statuettes, disappointment in her voice.

"I think you do. Keep dancing like you are, working hard and we will see. See you at rehearsals, Samantha."

As she turned to ask him more, Tony was already walking away through the courtyard on his silent converse sneakers. With his grey coat moving in time with his graceful dancer's stride, he cut a romantic figure in the misty autumn morning. Samantha stood there, awestruck by his assessment and with the promise of a spectacular career. Now all she had to do was make his prophecy a reality.

HE WAS PLAYING WITH fire with this one. Somehow, she'd gotten under his skin and into his crotch. He could feel his cock engorge at the thought of bending her over and fucking her stupid. It was a dangerous path he was treading, and he knew the coke was not helping. Sure, it gave him the energy he needed to keep working sixteen-to-eighteen-hour days during rehearsals, but it also increased his sex drive too much. Having a semi hard-on most of the time was difficult to camouflage and to appease.

Samantha could be a shining star at the Rouge or in any of his shows for that matter. As a team, they were a good match. She danced his choreography exactly the way he wanted. She took direction well and had the stamina to keep going. Plus, she wasn't all dreamy-eyed or crumpled under pressure. This was one dancer he needed to keep his cock away from. There was too much at stake here. Together they could further each other's careers. He clamped down on another wretched cigarette and decided to cut back on the coke and get some sleep. *Hang it, man, keep it together.*

~ ♥ ~

"SAMANTHA, YOU CAME." THE excitement in Philippe's voice was undeniable as he wrapped her hands in his, giving her kisses to each cheek.

"I said I would, Philippe. Aren't you working today?" She'd been looking for Philippe amongst the other artists in the square but couldn't find him.

"No, I changed my shift with the artist who tried to steal my place last Sunday. He wants to work Sundays, and I don't. So, it is settled. I am free all day to spend with you." He hooked his arm through Samantha's, leading her in the direction of his choosing. "Have you been to Sacré-Coeur yet?"

"No. It was too busy last Sunday so I'm waiting when there aren't so many people."

"There are always many people at the basilica. Come. I will show you around and keep you safe from the tourists." Leading her out of the Place du Terte they walked along more cobblestones up toward the famous church.

"This is the best view of all of Paris," Philippe declared with pride as they stood on the steps of one of Paris' most recognizable landmarks.

"Oh, Philippe, it's amazing. You can see forever from up here." Sam pulled out her phone and flashed a couple of images.

"Here, together." Philippe grabbed her phone, snuggled in close and snapped off a selfie of the two of them with the panoramic skyline of Paris behind them. To their left, on top of a column no bigger than one-metre square, danced and spun a street performer, executing death-defying moves and juggling acts. The hundreds of people watching him gasped in amazement each time he defied gravity and nearly lost his footing.

"God, how does he do that?" Sam admired his courage.

"*Pfft.* Claude has been doing that for years. He never falls. See how full his beret is at his feet?" Although she couldn't see clearly from where they were standing, Sam noticed just how many currency notes were being dropped in Claude's upturned beret by the impressed tourists.

"I see," she said with a knowing smile. "Claude is a showman. He makes the audience believe it's dangerous when really it isn't."

"Yes. And he makes much more money than we poor talented artists." A pout of his lips added to Philippe's 'poor-me' performance and earned a comforting pat on his cheek from Samantha. Quick as a flash, he grasped Sam's hand, turned it over and kissed her palm with gentle affection. His dreamy blue eyes peered up at her from under his shock of flaxen hair. Sam's breath hitched as if tied to a mounting post in her lungs.

"Come, *mon amie*, let's go into the church," he said. Still holding hands, they turned and ascended the basilica stairs. "It was erected over a century ago and it took over forty years to build it. More than it took to build the Parthenon in Greece. It's made from travertine stone and it always stays white . . ." and as Philippe continued in his history lesson on the Sacré-Coeur, Sam listened to her new friend with avid attention.

FOUR HOURS LATER, THEY stood in Philippe's small flat. Epitomizing the struggling artist's grotto, his one-room bedsit perched atop an old-fashioned patisserie, tucked behind the narrow Rue Saint-Rustique. An assortment of his art, framed and unframed, was tacked up covering most of the faded mint-coloured paint peeling off the weathered walls. Watercolours, pencil portraits, oils and sketches of half-finished works listed in the warm air that rose from the baker's ovens below. Through the craggy floorboards, the sweet, comforting smell of sugar, milk and flour being baked into mouth-watering delights filled Philippe's little home. For Samantha, the smell brought with it the delicious memory of childhood, of being loved.

"Philippe, these are beautiful." Sam wandered around the tiny room admiring his art. "You're really good."

"I have always loved to draw and paint since I was a little boy. To be an artist is all I've ever wanted to be."

"Well, I can see why. But surely being a portrait artist here in Montmartre is not enough?"

"The next step now is for me to have my own exhibition. But I need lots of oil paintings for that. So, I work on them now in a friend's studio. Soon I will be ready. Come, let us have some wine and baguette outside."

With a large freshly baked baguette balanced on top of a breadboard and a bottle of red wine in hand, Philippe nodded toward the French doors leading to the balcony. On opening the doors, Sam first noticed the potted yellow and purple dahlias perched on top of the wrought-iron balustrade surrounding the small balcony. Then her sightline lifted. "Oh, wow," she said scanning the view. "This is amazing."

"Yes, this is the best part of my apartment. My little balcony. It is very hard to rent a cheap room in Paris with a balcony, so even though the inside is poor and tattered, outside is glorious. It is my inspiration." The view from Philippe's narrow, semi-circular balcony cantilevered over the patisserie's awning was breathtaking. It stretched across rooftops and winding cobblestones streets reminding Sam of nineteenth-century Paris. This was the Paris she'd imagined when she accepted the dance contract. Like an artist's watercolour come to life, the view vibrated, filling her senses. With Frank Sinatra singing in her head, she finally understood why he loved Paris every moment of the year. Philippe motioned for Sam to sit. She glanced down at a weathered three-piece wrought iron garden setting that virtually took up all available space. After squeezing into a chair, she waited while Philippe carved into the baguette and scrapped on some butter. Slurping wine into the glasses, he offered one to Sam and held his up for a toast.

"To my new friend, Samantha O'Brien from Australia. An artiste, like me." They clinked glasses and drank.

A gentle rustling from one of the potted plants broke the toast and drew their attention.

"Ah, Jasper, where have you been?"

Through the flowers, the cutest apricot and white face of an exotic shorthair cat peered out. With oversized blue eyes and a mouth in the shape of an *O*, Jasper wore an expression of constant surprise. An all-white miniature body followed his curious face as he tiptoed around the railing to step elegantly onto the table. Purring, he snuggled up to his master demanding affection.

"He's a darling. I have a pet back home too. My dog, Scruffy. He's not nearly as cute as Jasper, but I do miss him." Sam reached out to the furball.

Sensing a new slave, Jasper strolled across the table to elicit more attention. Within no time, Jasper curled into Sam's lap and fell asleep.

~ ♥ ~

BY THE TIME PHILIPPE opened the second bottle of wine, they'd devoured their baguette and the sun was setting, stroking the sky in Monet-inspired colours.

"It's getting cold out here. Let's go inside, Samantha." Grabbing the wine and glasses, Philippe walked indoors while Sam cuddled Jasper to her chest and followed.

"Come on, Jasper. Time for your dinner," Philippe said.

At the sound of the magic word, Jasper sprang from Sam's arms onto the floor where he was promptly fed a bowl of dry cat kibble. While Jasper chewed through his dinner, Philippe sat on the side of his bed. Aside from a rickety table and two chairs, obscured by pencils, crayons and sketchbooks, the double bed, bedside table and a wardrobe were the only other pieces of furniture in the room.

"Sit beside me, Samantha." Assigning their wine glasses to the bedside table, Philippe shimmied back onto the bed using the wall behind him as a backrest. When she settled in beside him, he said, "I would like to paint you, Samantha. A real painting, for my exhibition. Would you sit for me?"

"I guess so." She was surprised that he wanted to include a painting of her in his exhibition.

"*Très bien.* Let's begin now." Philippe sprang off the bed and dashed to the table, where he rummaged around for the right implements. Finding a large sketchbook and several charcoals, he cleared a chair and dragged it in front of the bed. "You are my queen of the can-can. Like the famous dancer La Goulue. Here, I will arrange your pose."

Philippe fluffed the pillows for Sam to recline on, and she wiggled into place with a giggle. With great care, he clasped her arm and tucked it under her head as support. Trailing his hands over her body, he maneuvered her this way and that, edging slowly to her hips. The strength and gentleness of his touch as he rolled her forward to lay on her side ignited a subtle warmth in Sam's groin. His hand cupped her bottom, rolling her back a little to just the right angle, and she wished he'd dig deeper into her from behind. Taking her top leg, Philippe cupped her knee, bending it to drag across in the foreground. For the final effect, he reached to her other leg and pulled it straight beneath her, running his hands down her long limb to her ankle.

"There, that will be a good starting pose I think," he said. "Are you comfortable, Samantha?"

"Yes, I think so." She was anything but comfortable. Moist and ready, her sex flamed. Her nipples yearned to be teased and her arse screamed for grabbing. The seam in her jeans bit hard into the folds of her cleft. She began to unravel.

"Are you all right, Samantha?"

"Yes. Yes. I'm fine." But her dilated pupils and shallow breathing betrayed her.

She was certain Philippe suspected what she was feeling because a lazy lascivious smile graced his angelic face. Michele sensed his wild, artistic spirit swirl around her like an unpredictable tornado. Yet he remained calm and lowered his sketchbook and charcoals to the floor. Resplendent in a flowing white shirt and low-slung cargos that matched the colour of his delinquent golden hair, he fixed her in his gaze and strolled over to the bed. Gazing down at her, he moistened his lips and exhaled with a slight purr. "Perhaps I can be of assistance?"

Reaching down, he trailed his long, artistic fingers across Sam's cheek, as if assessing its structure before moving to her lips which parted to allow him access. He declined. Continuing his journey, he travelled down her delicate throat up to her shoulder and across the dip in her waist to finally rest at her hip. She held her breath and his gaze, giving him silent permission to continue. With a change of direction, he dragged his fingers across the top of her jeans, ran down the zipper line and pressed his digit deep between her legs. Desire flared inside her while Philippe's finger caught fire wedged in her jeans crotch.

Leaning down, he breathed sweet warmth into her ear. "My queen of the can-can needs some love I see." His finger began to saw in an unhurried rhythm between her legs. Back and forth, back and forth. As Sam opened her mouth to speak, his lips fell upon it and the tip of his tongue reached in to say hello. Teasing her with an open-mouthed kiss, he added another digit to the incessant to-and-fro below, digging harder through the denim into her snatch with each stroke. Sam became entranced by his arctic blue eyes as they assessed her every response while his tongue and another finger continued their torment. Leaking with wetness, her mouth and cleft yearned for closure, but he refused to allow her that pleasure. He toyed with her a while longer while the sweet smell of sugar filled her senses with the memory of love. By the time he dragged his hand between her legs in strong, hungry strokes and she was whimpering for satisfaction, he plundered her mouth, stifling her pre-orgasmic groan.

Slithering onto the bed beside her, he pushed her onto her back and slithered his hand down the front of her jeans and under her panties. On finding her wet spot, he stopped.

"Keep your legs together. Don't open them." His breath scolded her cheek while the command in his voice belied his youthful appearance.

Sam obeyed.

With his fingers inching over the top of her mons, he slipped one elegant digit into her cleft, grazing her clit. The restriction of her jeans and clamped legs made every movement difficult, so he could only just rub her bud with the tiniest of strokes until it shrieked. Suddenly, he stopped his exploration allowing his finger to massage its target a little softer.

"I love dancers. They have such discipline." He watched her bite down on her lower lip and then nipped her lip between his teeth to give it a little punishment of his own. Without warning, he slid his finger down her slippery slit, curled his wrist and dug into her as far as her jeans allowed. She gasped a breath into his mouth.

"More," she pleaded. The hammering in her head from the red wine and too little food matched the thumping desire building in her body.

"How much more?"

"Much more."

Philippe slid down the bed in delighted obedience. With each deliberate movement, he watched as Sam's chest heaved in jagged breaths. He unzipped her jeans and then rolled them and her panties down to her ankle boots, admiring the tone of her thighs and the alabaster paleness of her flesh. Left partially restrained around the ankles, Sam bent her knees and opened her legs wide, splayed on the bed. The coolness of the night air pricked her moist exposure, only heightening the agony.

"Now that cunt is what I would love to paint." Philippe bent down and lap a long, lazy lick along Sam's exposure, peeling her open even more. "God, you taste good."

Enduring her intense yearning in silence, Sam waited. But her wet, pink clit betrayed her seeming self-control by swelling plumper, pleading for attention.

"Let's see if we can't help you out a little." Crawling in beside her, Philippe brushed his hand down her stomach. With her snatch open, slick and hungry, he dipped his finger into her sweetness, removed it and slipped it into her mouth. The tang of her own desire moistened her lips. Down once more he went, dipping into her delight and returned it to his own mouth, tasting her impatience.

He locked her in his gaze. "Now?"

"Yes, please. Now."

Edging his fingers down once more, he leisurely slid one digit from clit to crack, over and over until her wetness flooded from her. Like a stealthy scout on a reconnaissance mission, one finger slipped in and out of her before being discovered. She moaned, wanting more. Finding no danger within, another finger joined its partner. With the two of them rubbing deep into her fleshy folds, and around and over her clit, she demanded more by grinding her hips against them. Finally, they rewarded her by delving deep within her, turning this way and that, preparing her for the onslaught. Three fingers now kneaded her flesh in all directions. Like a baker making dough, Philippe lavished attention on her tortured, frustrated snatch, pummelling her, opening her, rolling her. Sam lay at his mercy, the wanton thrum now coursing through her body. Unable to move, she lost herself in his incessant and excessive devotion to her sex. Philippe was an artist of the female flesh and as he brought her closer to orgasm, she gave herself over to his manipulations, her skin glowing and her brow creasing with strained anticipation.

She struggled on the brink and with her groin on fire, he jammed his three fingers deep within her, found her G-spot and thrust her to a mind-shattering climax. Her hands clutched at the quilt and her head pushed deep into the pillow as she arched her back, screaming and surging to relief. All her tensions since arriving in Paris exploded while she surrendered to the orgasm. She collapsed with an exhausted moan, her body buzzing as the aftershock waves shuddered through her muscles. When the tremors stopped and her muscles sagged, she languished on the edge of her bliss for a few moments.

With a smile of deep affection radiating from his face, Philippe gently cupped her quivering, shattered snatch, comforting it to recover. He leaned down and kissed her, soft and tender. Every part of her now too sensitive to be touched, she pushed his hand away. She needed space. Undone, Sam's emotions lay exposed and ragged. Much like how she felt lying in Philippe's bed. Embarrassed, she snapped from her afterglow and dragged her clothes back up her body, zipping her jeans fast.

"Samantha, what is wrong?"

"I'm sorry, Philippe. I have to go. It's late and I've got to get home. I've got rehearsals tomorrow." Throwing her legs past him, she jumped out of bed and grabbed her bag.

"But what happened? Didn't you like what we just did?"

"Yes. Yes, I did. That's the point. I can't allow myself to have a boyfriend or whatever. I must focus on my dancing, on my career. I'm sorry, Philippe, I have to go." She was at the door, her hand trembling on the doorknob.

Philippe's hand descended, stopping her. "But can't we see each other again?"

"No. I'm sorry, Philippe. We can't. I'm so sorry, Philippe, I have to go." She shook off his grip, opened the door and ran down the stairs.

STUNNED, PHILIPPE CLOSED THE door behind her. "What on earth just happened, Jasper?" He directed the question to his disinterested companion, who continued his *apres*-dinner grooming. "It certainly looked like she was enjoying herself. And my God, what that body of hers can do . . ." Philippe closed his eyes and recalled the vivid taste, touch and image of Samantha as she gave herself unashamedly over to him. "Maybe I came on too strong? Maybe I should have gone slower? Come on Jasper, help me out here?" His furry friend merely cast an elitist glance at his owner and resumed his toilette. Ignoring Jasper's non-responsiveness, Philippe continued his soliloquy and paced the room. "I meant it. I really wanted to paint her. Now I've ruined everything. Again. No self-control, that's my problem. I can attract women, but I can't keep them. *Idiote.*" Launching himself onto the bed, he folded his hands behind his head and stared at the dusty ceiling. "Well, we're done for this time, Jasper. We won't be seeing the beautiful Samantha O'Brien again. And what's worse, I think I was really falling for her." He reached over, switched off the light and thumped his pillow in the false belief he'd fall asleep soon.

CHAPTER SIX

BOUNDING UP THE STAIRS two at a time, Sam galloped to her room, her safe place. She needed to think, to collect herself. The sexual episode with Philippe, although physically liberating, had the potential of clouding her judgment. Once before in her life, she'd allowed her personal feelings for a man to interfere with her good sense and that had ended badly. She needed to review and regroup.

"Samantha, what is the hurry?" Madame Lucette's voice followed Sam's retreating figure up the hotel's staircase.

Sam stopped at her door, trying to mask her anxiety. She looked down at her peculiar landlady standing at the bottom of the stairs. "Oh, nothing. I'm running later than I expected. I just need to get to bed so I'll be fresh for rehearsals tomorrow."

"Why not come and keep an old woman company for a couple of minutes? I have just made tea. We can talk if you like." With her face crinkling like soft tissue, Madame Lucette gazed up at Sam with an expectant smile. She was a hard woman to whom to say no.

"Okay then. Just for a few minutes." Sam trod down the stairs at a more ladylike pace and followed Madame Lucette into her little kitchen.

"Here, drink this herbal tea. It will help you sleep." She poured a steaming brew into a fine bone china teacup for each of them. Seated next to her young tenant, Madame Lucette sipped in silence, lost in her own thoughts.

Sam examined the little room. It was as neat as a pin. Not one utensil or piece of equipment needed for food preparation or cooking could be seen. Sam reasoned they must be stored in the wooden cupboards, pantry and drawers. The façade of aging grey paint gave away nothing of the intense work this room performed in its function of feeding the hotel guests. In many ways, the room reflected its owner. Madame Lucette's elderly persona, with her grey hair and eyes, fringed shawls and flowing caftans belied the intensity and competency of the woman herself. Sam relaxed with an audible sigh. "Madame?" she said, placing her near-empty cup on her saucer.

"Yes?" She too lowered her cup.

"Can you do a card reading for me?" Sam stared into the ancient eyes of her landlady and as Madame Lucette's mouth curved upward, she wondered if her request was such a good idea.

"Of course. Let's do it now." Before Sam could change her mind, Madame Lucette rose and drifted through the door to her room, gesturing Sam to follow.

Once the candles and incense were lit and they were seated at her card-reading table, Madame Lucette handed the deck of tarot cards to Sam.

"Simply ask the cards the question you have on your mind, shuffle and then select one." Madame Lucette slid the deck across to Sam and closed her eyes to concentrate.

Sam shuffled, unsure of the words she wanted to ask. Then finding her mind straying to the amazing sexual experience she'd just had with Philippe and the unexpected feelings it had opened within her, she formulated the question in her mind. *What am I to do about Philippe?* She cut the deck, turned over a card and placed it face-up on the table.

Madame opened her eyes and peered down at the card. "The goddess of protection." Madame tapped her finger on the card and smiled. "She is strong and dependable, a safeguard. See, she holds a snake in each hand which symbolizes moving energy, the shedding of the old, making way for the new . . . of healing. On her headgear, there is a cat." She lifted the card into the light for Sam to see.

"Oh yes. I see." Sam tried not to show her alarm at recognizing the exotic shorthair cat drawn on the card. It looked like Jasper. Her heart beat faster while her fortune unfolded.

"The cat refers to the home. Cats protect the home from vermin. Both the cat and the snakes symbolize fertility, but I don't think pregnancy applies to you at the moment," Madame Lucette said, with an arched eyebrow. Sam shuddered at the thought.

"But what does it all mean?"

"The goddess of protection helps women to stand against forces that may threaten their home, their life. Her help may come in the advice and friendship from other women, or from someone who can point you in the right direction to help you discover your inner strength." Madame Lucette stroked the card with her eyes closed. "She protects those going through life-changing experiences, guiding them on the right path." Madame Lucette placed the card back on the deck and riveted Sam with a cool gaze. "Perhaps you have been liberated today, no?"

Silence hung between them, thick with secrets.

"Oh no, Madame. Nothing like that. I was just curious about getting a reading, that's all. It's a nice card, the goddess of protection. It's a little like having Mum or Aunty Michele watching over me all the way from Australia I guess." Trying to still her nervous legs from jiggling under the table, Sam flashed her showgirl smile at Madame Lucette.

"Well, Samantha. If you need any help, advice or protection, you can always ask me. I will protect you." She leaned across the table and patted Sam's clammy hand, giving it a lingering squeeze.

"Thank you, Madame Lucette, that's very kind of you." Sam withdrew her hand and made to leave.

"Remember, *chère fille*, the best advice comes from within. Do what your heart tells you to do. Protect yourself against those who would stop you from listening to your heart. If you need anything, you can always ask me." Madame Lucette released Sam with a knowing smile and returned to shuffling the cards.

Sam returned to her room with her mind in turmoil. She plonked down on the edge of the bed, her head in her hands and reminded herself why. Why she didn't want to fall in love. Why she didn't want to see Philippe. Why she didn't want to have another broken heart. She had lots of whys. Last time she felt like this she nearly ruined her life and her career. Not again. She promised herself, not again.

With the readings from the tarot cards and all the talk of liberation, something to be free of, protection, follow your heart, inner strength, healing, something coming to an end swirling in her mind, Sam undressed and slid into the quiet comfort of her bed. Confused and exhausted, she dragged the quilt under her chin, snuggling into its warmth. Surprisingly, within moments she was asleep.

CHAPTER SEVEN

THE MORNING BROUGHT NO comfort. Instead of feeling relaxed and assured as she pulled on her dance gear for the third week of rehearsals, Sam's stomach continued in its endless churning over yesterday's experience with Philippe.

Offering a silent prayer to her goddess of protection, Sam repeated her plea, "What am I going to do? What am I going to do?" Not only had she woken up still feeling confused, but she'd also woken up late.

Leaping down the stairs, she barrelled into her startled landlady. "Sorry, Madame. No breakfast this morning, I'm too late."

"But, Samantha, you need to eat."

"No time. *Au revoir.*" She rushed out the door, tossing her dance bag over her shoulder. As she hit full stride through the courtyard, Sam's anxiety rose, driving her steps faster. "Oh God. Tony is going to kill me. He's going to kill me."

RUNNING FAST AND SILENT as only ballerinas can, Sam dashed onto the stage to take her position. Red-faced and nervous, she did her best to calm her breathing. Although she looked straight ahead, ready to begin, she could feel his disappointment. She gave Tony a quick glance, screwed her face into an apology and prayed he wouldn't make an example out of her. Instead, she fell victim to his infamous death stare and the accompanying hush. Looks of disgust and barely audible tut-tuts assailed her from the cast. Holding her breath and focus, she refused to flinch. Moments lengthened but still he said nothing. Then his gaze shifted, nodding to Penny to resume.

"All right everybody. And-a-one, and-a-two, and-a-one, two, three . . ." Penny cued the routine, breaking the moment and saving Sam from further humiliation.

WHY HADN'T HE SAID something? Tony knew this was what Penny expected when he remained silent, allowing Sam's tardiness to go undisciplined. When Penny's eyebrows knitted with the 'aren't you going to say something' question, he choked. The only option was to stare Samantha down, but the little minx held firm. She had more spirit than he first thought. It confirmed his suspicions. She was only nervous when she was close to him personally, not professionally. She was a tough cookie. He nodded his head in approval. He liked this girl, but there was something else. Something that reminded him of himself, but it was still too hazy.

~ ♥ ~

"SO? WHY WERE YOU late?" Josette's eyes sparkled in anticipation. The two of them were stretched out on the floor in one of the corridors backstage sharing Josette's cheese baguette for lunch.

"Long story. I met this guy—"

"*C'est magnifique.*" Josette held her half baguette up for a toast.

"No, Josette. It's not *magnifique.* It was stupid and I've decided not to see him again." Sam chewed angrily at her half, gulping it down in under-masticated chunks.

"But, Sam, why not? Just because you had a good time and came a little late for rehearsal doesn't mean you can't see him again?"

"Yes, it does. I am here to dance, not to have sex or fall in love."

"Love? You mean you might be in love?" Josette's wide-eyed expression reminded Sam of Jasper, which in turn, led her mind back to Philippe's wondrous attack on her sex yesterday.

"No, I don't mean love. I just mean I won't be seeing him again. I don't need any further complications in my life right now."

Josette stopped chewing and cocked her head at the hint of secrets Samantha didn't want to divulge. "But what other complications do you already have in your life?"

"Nothing. Nothing. It's just an expression we use back home . . ." Sam knew she wasn't making sense, but she didn't care. She didn't need to explain herself to Josette or anyone for that matter. "Did you bring anything else for lunch? I had no breakfast this morning and I'm starving."

As Josette offered up a packet of nuts from her dance tote, Sam tore them open and palmed a handful into her mouth.

~ ♥ ~

SHE LAY ON THE cold tiles sobbing quietly; her mind a haze of loathing and anguish.

"Sam, are you in here?" Josette's high heels tip-tapped into the ladies' toilets as she rushed in, interrupting Sam's suffering.

"Yes. Yes. It's all right I'm coming." Sam scrambled to her feet, pulled tighter on her ponytail and flushed the toilet.

"Rehearsals are about to begin, and I don't think Tony will tolerate you being late twice in one day," Josette said as Sam opened the door. Sam's greyish pallor and gaunt look obviously shocked her new friend. "God, what is wrong with you? You look awful." Josette reached out, wrapping her arm around Sam's waist.

"I'll be all right. Just feeling a little sick, I guess." Sam straightened up and walked to the sink. She splashed some water on her face, looked in the mirror and hated what she saw. Rinsing her mouth out, she spat the bitter taste of vomit into the sink, wishing she could disappear into the swirling plughole with it. Her hands shook as she soaped away the remaining panda-eyes mascara then gave her ponytail another sharp tug. Josette watched in concerned silence while the first chords of the rehearsal piano filtered to them from the rehearsal studio down the hall.

"Come on, Sam. Let's go." With Josette scurrying her along, they rushed back for another afternoon of rehearsals, both of them unsure as to how Sam would hold up.

~ ♥ ~

EXCUSING HERSELF FROM THEIR weekly catch-up at Toutes les crêpes de jour, Sam laboured over packing her dance bag while the rest of the cast hurried away, chatting about their weekend.

"Sam, can I speak with you a moment?"

Sam turned to see Penny standing behind her. During rehearsals, Penny was a relentless taskmaster with the voice of a cattle drover, but up close and personal she was a sweet Aussie country girl, complete with long, curly carrot-coloured hair, freckled cheeks and soft-spoken voice. Although looking much younger than her thirty-three years, she was the ultimate professional in her job as Tony's assistant choreographer, keeping the line firmly drawn between herself and the cast.

"Of course, Penny." Since Sam hadn't said more than hello or goodbye to Penny until now, her stomach fluttered with nerves.

"Why don't we sit over here for a minute?" Penny walked to a couple of backstage chairs nearby, indicating to Sam to take a seat. Lowering herself onto the chair, Penny crossed her legs and clasped her hands together around her knees, looking every bit the elegant ballerina. "Sam, I'm not sure what happened with you today, but you know you can always come to me if you have any problems."

Sam crossed her legs underneath her chair, placed her hands in her lap and assumed the respectful position of a well-behaved schoolgirl. "Thank you, Penny. That's very kind. I'm sorry I was late this morning. I overslept. It won't happen again."

Penny looked hard at her, cocked her barely-there eyebrow and waited. Sam's practised control belied the mounting tension in her stomach. Both waited for the other to speak. Penny continued, "It was more than that, Sam. You're a really good dancer and I think you might be a nude soon and then maybe a soloist. But this afternoon you looked dreadful and your dancing wasn't up to scratch at all. Are you sure you're okay? You can take a day off if you need to go to the doctor's or anything." Penny's eyes searched Sam's face for a hint of what was ailing her young, talented dancer.

"Thanks, Penny. That won't be necessary. I just had a tummy bug. Maybe something I ate at lunchtime?" Sam made to rise, and Penny joined her.

Penny turned to face her. "Sam, we're both Aussie girls. I know it can be hard here at the Rouge when there's no one else from your own country and you're surrounded by mainly French girls and boys. I did it for years when I first came when I was twenty-three. It can be tough. I just want you to know that even though I'm the assistant choreographer, I'm an Aussie girl first. If you need anything, anytime, you just call me. Okay?" Penny took both Sam's hands in her own and gave them a sisterly squeeze.

"Thanks, Penny. I won't let you down again. I promise." Sam returned Penny's offer with a reciprocal hand squeeze and a determined smile.

"Good. Now go home and get some rest. I'll see you tomorrow, strong and terrific as normal." With a pat to Sam's shoulder, Penny left.

Sam changed into her street shoes and tucked her gear away, remembering the promise she'd made to herself before she came to Paris. She had to keep it. Today, she'd let her emotions get the better of her because of how Philippe made her feel yesterday. She needed to control herself more. She'd trained and danced all her life to get here, and she mustn't be stupid again. Nodding in affirmation to her internal pep talk, Sam hauled her bag from the floor.

"Is everything all right, Samantha?" Tony reached out to help lift her bag. When his hand glanced her forearm, familiar shivers prickled Sam's skin.

"I'm fine. Thanks, Tony. Just an upset tummy I think." Sam rubbed her stomach for effect and winced. She'd only just managed to get through the afternoon's rehearsals, and it was obvious she'd not been able to hide her struggle from either Penny or Tony.

"You should eat something substantial tonight. Get your strength back. Let me buy you dinner."

"Oh, no." Sam blinked at his unorthodox offer. "I'm not sure that's such a good idea. Anyway, I don't know if I can keep anything down." All Sam wanted was to follow Penny's advice and go home, curl up in her bed and put the whole day behind her.

"Nonsense. You need to eat and so do I. Go home, freshen up and I'll meet you at the fountain in an hour." He issued his decree with no room for negotiation.

"But Penny wants me to rest."

"Blame me if you're not well tomorrow. But I think you need to eat, then rest."

"Okay. But if I'm sick tomorrow I'll tell Penny you made me go out for dinner."

"It's a deal. I'll take all the blame. I'll see you at the fountain in an hour."

"Okay. See you then." She girded her coat tightly around her exhausted body and walked home at a slower pace than this morning's dash.

ONE OF THE ADVANTAGES of being the boss was that everyone does what you ask. Tony intended to find out whatever it was Samantha was hiding. She looked ghastly this afternoon and her dancing abysmal. Something had happened at the weekend. He was certain of it. As a choreographer and teacher, he always knew what was happening in his casts' personal lives simply by their behaviour and performance levels at rehearsals. If they were having troubles in their relationships, they'd dance with a frustrated lethargy, angry at themselves for not dancing better. If they were having great sex, they all but flew through the routines, leaping higher than normal. His intuition about such things was integral to being a good choreographer and director, and Tony had the gift. All his dancers were an easy read for him. The only way to get the truth out of Samantha was for them to be alone together, today. Tomorrow would be too late. Dinner seemed the obvious starting place. Although he didn't want to admit it, his interest was also more than professional curiosity and concern.

~ ♥ ~

SAM APPLIED A FROSTY lip gloss to her pink lip-lined mouth and no longer loathed her reflection. The hot shower had done the trick and of course, the flashback to her fantasy about Tony hadn't hurt her recovery either. With her black hair falling straight and long around her heart-shaped face and her black skivvy pulled high under her chin, she looked understated French chic.

With only two coats to choose from, Sam grabbed her 'good' coat; a Burberry double-breasted black wool trench coat, a going-away gift from Aunty Michele. She clasped all the buttons right up to the collar and cinched the waist in to keep out the advancing cold. Paris temperatures were dropping fast and as she rugged up, Sam wondered how she was going to cope with the winter freeze just around the corner. Her black jeans and black suede boots fitted like a second skin, staving off any lingering shivers. Shoving her lip gloss into her coat pocket, she turned the heat up in her little room ready for her return.

"Samantha, you look much happier than you did this morning." Madame Lucette stood at the bottom of the stairs and like the mother of the bride admired her tenant's descent.

"Yes, I feel much better. Thank you, Madame."

"Perhaps the goddess of protection has pointed you in the right direction?"

"Maybe, Madame?" Sam paused at the bottom of the stairs, thinking it might be Penny Capstan or Tony Di Falco rather than a tarot card goddess pointing her in the right direction.

"You are going out, *oui*?" The landlady leaned in, eager to hear details.

"*Oui*, Madame. I'm going out." With genuine affection, Sam kissed Madame Lucette's cheek and smiled. "Maybe you're my goddess of protection, Madame? You're strong and dependable. Maybe you're my liberator?" Without giving her time to reply Sam made for the front door.

"No, *chère fille*. It is not me. You will see. It is not me," Madame Lucette called after her.

"*Bonsoir*, Madame." Sam fluttered her fingers in the air but did not look back.

"*Bonsoir*, Samantha." The landlady wrapped her flimsy shawl tighter around her bony frame as the outside cold air swirled in the front door. With an enigmatic smile and nod of her head, she shuffled back into the dining room to attend to her other tenants.

CHAPTER EIGHT

WEDGED ON AVENUE RACHEL, the typical French brassiere with its green awning, obligatory red signage and quaint façade looked much like any other restaurant in Montmartre. Nothing about its exterior defined it as special.

"Here we are . . . Bistro de Montmartre. It has the best onion soup and lamb bourguignon in Paris." Tony opened the narrow door with a dramatic flourish, allowing Sam to enter.

Inside, its nondescript appearance continued with walls decorated in murals of nineteenth-century Paris and framed tributes to the dancers so loved by Toulouse-Lautrec. Sam imagined the grandeur and style of 1890s Paris and a small, regretful sigh escaped her. She wished she'd been born then. When ladies displayed their femininity by wearing skirts in the shape of a gently opening head of a longiflorum lily and sweetheart décolleté necklines presented their bosoms proudly, as they waltzed in on the arms of well-turned-out gentlemen clad in three-piece black-suited tailcoats with white starched shirt and necktie. The romantic notion of being one of those well-to-do ladies with a gallant lover to do her bidding skittered fancifully across Sam's skin. *But times change*, she thought. What a shame. Now, complete with red tablecloths and white napkins overflowing from the cheap wine glasses, the bistro's scattered tables waited in anticipation. Like many other eateries in the Pigalle quarter of Paris, Bistro De Montmartre tried to recapture the halcyon days of the La Belle Epoque era in the city of love. Unlike many of its competitors, the venue succeeded. This evening it teemed with local clientele enjoying the restaurant's authentic French fare.

"Ah, Monsieur Di Falco. *Bonsoir.* Your usual table, monsieur. Right this way." The friendly, efficient maître d' effused his greeting. With a hip-hoppity step, he led the way to an intimate booth tucked in a back corner of the restaurant.

He reminded Sam of the white rabbit from *Alice in Wonderland* and, in many ways, she felt a lot like Alice this evening.

"*Merci*, Pierre. Please hang these up for us, *se il vous plait.*" Tony entrusted their coats to the scurrying Pierre. After depositing menus, he darted away with his precious consignment leaving Tony and Sam to consider their order.

"I can highly recommend everything on the menu," Tony said closing his menu having already decided on his meal choice for the evening.

"As I said, not too much for me. The French onion soup sounds good. I'll have that."

"And, what about your main meal?"

"Tony, I'm not that hungry." Sam's hand lay on the menu as if taking an oath. *I promise to tell the truth and nothing but the truth. So help me God.* Sam had no idea where that pledge surfaced from, but she knew truth-telling was not going to happen here tonight. Her body begged to differ. Due to the proximity of Tony's leg under the table, her core temperature began to rise. His leg acted like a magnet, its warmth sending out little pulses of attraction, and she had to stop her wayward leg from rubbing itself against his like a queen cat on heat. She shifted her legs around under the table in the opposite direction, so they didn't embarrass herself in unimaginable ways.

The gentle touch of his hand on hers brought her attention back to the proceedings above the table. "Sam, you must eat. I will order the chicken for you. It is not too heavy and very delicious."

On so many levels Sam couldn't resist. Yes, the food sounded delicious. But it was the well-honed lines of his face, the way his hair seemed to beg her fingers drag through its curls and his generous mouth which all conspired against her. God, he was gorgeous.

An amused glint flashed in his black eyes. "It's all right, Samantha. Relax. It's just dinner."

Resolutely, she ignored the intoxicating effect his presence had on her. All this swooning was silly. With a determined wiggle, Sam straightened herself for a more dignified evening. Tony ordered their meals, the wine and eased into informal conversation.

By the end of the entrée, the mood lightened thanks not just to the delicious food and great service, but also to the pianist regaling the diners with romantic love songs. Unashamed, her legs had returned to their original position under the table, to face Tony, longing to make contact. Delicious as it was, the French onion soup had barely enough substance to counteract one glass of red wine, let alone two. Her inhibitions loosened enough for her to venture into unknown territory.

"Tony, may I ask you something?" She nibbled distractedly on her index finger as she admired the sight, smell and style of him. Scruffy around the edges with the hint of powerful predator made Tony Di Falco beyond desirable. He commanded to be pleasured and as the girl who wanted to please, to keep everyone happy, Sam longed to comply.

"Yes, Sam. What is it you want to know?"

"How old are you?" God, what a childish question. Why did she ask such a stupid question? Her index finger took the full brunt of her idiocy and self-abuse.

Tony reached over and extricated her finger from its torture. "I'll be thirty-nine on the first of November."

"Oh," she said, her finger drifting upward to her mouth.

"Why? Is my age important in some way?" Tony's lips curled in a soft smile as he saved her digit once more. This time, Sam clamped her other hand over the first in a fist lock in her lap.

"No reason, I was just interested." She doubted her attempt at nonchalance fooled him. It also did little to quell her desire to be older. Perhaps if she was closer to his age, things between them might be different. She retreated from the fantasy that threatened to expose her. "I've never been to Sicily. Where did you grow up? What was it like?"

"My goodness, you are full of questions." He leaned forwards resting his elbows on the table with his fingers steepled, tapping his lips in his usual directorial gesture.

Seemingly intrigued by Sam's curiosity and innocence, Tony allowed some of his staunch façade to be penetrated. He stretched back into the booth, holding centre stage for his recital.

"Well, I grew up in a small town called Aci Castello, about fifteen minutes outside the capital of Catania in Sicily. It's a beautiful seaside town, with the bluest water of the Mediterranean, which I swam in every opportunity I got. The town has magnificent cliffs and rocks — the perfect place for a young boy to explore, to find sea urchins and mussels. I was like a monkey, scrawny and fast, jumping from rock to rock. My favourite place of all was the remnants of a grand, old castle perched on an outcrop of a cliff high above the promenade. I used to clamber up the stairs and sit right on the parapet ledge to watch the sun go down. The sky would be filled with the brightest yellows and golds, burning hot and bright onto my face, like a stage spotlight. I'd sit for hours, dreaming of being a famous dancer while the other boys kicked a ball and harassed tourists."

Now with a legitimate reason to stare, Samantha absorbed Tony's every nuance and expression, rapt in his magnetic personality and handsomeness. The features of his face though striking in their individual structure, when combined, demonstrated masculine human architecture at its finest. Continuously moist and parted, his lips seemed to transmit unconscious messages, beckoning to be caressed. The coarse stubble peppered on cheeks and chin drove her senses positively wild as she imagined the abrasion between her thighs. A straight Roman nose added even more imperialism to his demeanour, while the lyricism and depth of his voice matched the romantic shadows dancing in his fiery eyes. He reminded her of Prince Charming from *Cinderella,* and she scolded herself for such an anti-feminist thought. Hang it, though, he could definitely play the part.

Still captivated, she said dreamily, "Your childhood sounds like a fairy tale."

"Sometimes it was." Tony's disillusioned tone forced Sam to abandon the fairy tale comparisons and concentrate. She quizzed him with a stare.

"My papa made sure my childhood was as happy as possible. He loved music, he loved to sing and dance. I remember the music playing in our little house and papa would grab my mother to twirl her around. But my mother was not a happy woman. She always seemed to be angry, with me, with papa, with everyone."

"So, you began to dance because of your father then?"

"Yes. He sent me to the best dance school in Catania — Associazione Danza Academica T.M.B. When I was young, I used to ride my bicycle along the promenade into Catania to the academy. They were happy days."

"Then where did you go after the academy?"

"I ended up at the National Academy of Dance in Rome."

"Your parents must be very proud of you?"

"My papa died nearly a decade ago. He was very proud of me, but my mother is still an unhappy woman. I don't see her much." The mood darkened, and Samantha realized she'd unintentionally touched on an emotional scar Tony preferred not to reveal.

Backtracking she said, "Oh, I'm sorry about your father."

"Yes, he was a good man. Now see. Our main meals have arrived. Let's eat and talk about you."

As they tucked into their food, Samantha chatted about her parents, her hometown of Brisbane in Australia, her pet dog Scruffy, her recent dancing contracts in London and her ambition to be a nude at the Moulin Rouge and then perhaps in Vegas.

"Well, Samantha, I think you will make it to not only a nude role but also to soloist. But you must look after yourself. You must eat and rest more. I'm not sure what happened today but it was more than an upset stomach. That I know." Tony's flinty stare nailed her.

She glanced sideways and lowered her cutlery to the plate. "It's nothing to worry about. I promise it won't happen again,

Tony. I'm sorry." Like a child waiting to be excused from the table, she remained still and silent.

He reached over and lifted her chin, turning her face toward him. "I'm not sure what your secret is, Samantha O'Brien, but whatever it is, do not let it destroy you. You have a great future ahead of you. Sometimes secrets are best shared."

"That's sort of what Penny said today."

"Well, you have a choice then. You can confide in Penny or me, but either way, you need to sort yourself out. Okay?"

She nodded and a smile creased her face. "I don't understand why they call you Ursu?" Before she could stop herself, the comment was free, and a hot flush leapt onto her cheeks. Her hand clamped over her mouth, but it was too late.

A deep, rolling laugh pealed through the restaurant. "What? You think I don't know that is what they call me. Ursu? The bear?" He was even more attractive when he laughed. His dark curls frothed at his collar and his liquid eyes shone with unrestrained happiness. Together they laughed as he imitated a gruff bear baring his teeth. No longer bound by the strict constraints of their careers, they ate and drank with the abandon of ordinary, everyday people. Being with Tony reminded her of being at home with her family; no pressures, no broken promises, no pretence. It was fun not to have to worry about anything.

~ ♥ ~

AFTER SAM THANKED HIM with a spontaneous kiss to the cheek, she did an about-face and strutted home. Tony remained at the fountain, entranced by her youthful innocence and determination. This was as far as she'd allowed him to escort her. For some reason, she didn't want his company further or maybe she didn't want him to know where she lived. But of course, he did. He knew everything about his dancers. That was his job. She amused him. Tony lit a cigarette and reviewed the night's conversation. Samantha hadn't revealed anything. Whatever was troubling her, she'd kept it well-hidden. She was as good at keeping secrets as he was. This revelation gave him cause to chuckle. Not only was she beautiful, talented and smart, she was also cagey.

He began to stroll home, his thoughts wandering in his mind. For the first time, talking about his childhood and more particularly about his mother tonight hadn't been as difficult as in the past. The residual heartbreak and pain of her domineering sarcasm and abuse had mellowed. Growing up, both he and his father had been regaled daily as to their short-comings and poor-paying creative pursuits. Her wrath had turned their little home into a battlefield. Tony had fled to the safety of the castle while his father had found comfort in a bottle at the local tavern. Over the years, Tony, like his father, found solace in substances and moved onto cigarettes, alcohol and now cocaine. He never forgave his mother for nagging his father to an early death. If only she'd showed us a little love . . . He sucked hard on his cigarette, biting down his bitterness on the filter. Yet listening to Samantha talk about her family with such love and warmth made him reconsider his mother, now old and living alone. Although he supported her financially, he rarely contacted her — or she him. They had cleaved an enormous chasm through their relationship years ago with corroding allegations and accusations. Words used as weapons leaving wounds that never healed. He'd proved her wrong by becoming a success in the entertainment industry, but it made no difference to her. All he wanted was for his mother to say she was proud of him, just once.

He threw away the butt and reached into his pocket to retrieve another nicotine crutch to squash his resentment. He stopped — both his pedestrian journey and that of his hand. It was time to take control of his life. It was time to get over his past little-boy hurts and disappointments. *Time to man-up*, he thought sternly to himself. He jammed his hand into his coat pocket, lifted his chin and strode home, his mind swirling with new plans.

CHAPTER NINE

"**T**HESE COSTUMES ARE ABSOLUTELY spectacular." Sam stood awestruck in the wardrobe department of the Moulin Rouge with Josette and the rest of the female dancers. Like a cave of treasures, the space shone and twinkled with rainbow-hued rhinestones, *Swarovski* crystals, intricate beads, glossy pearls and sequins of every size and colour sewn with meticulous care onto robes, bustiers, dresses, G-strings, bras and headgears. Examining the detail with which each extraordinary costume was delivered by the tireless team of seamstresses, Sam felt like Aladdin, overwhelmed by the encircling opulence. She shuddered to think of the number of birds stripped of their feathers to make the enormous head and back dresses that lined the walls on wig stands and hangers, awaiting the next dancer to be adorned and transformed.

"Josette Deschamps," a sharp voice called from down an aisle.

"See you later after the fitting. Have fun." Josette pranced off, her neat body and muscled legs wrapped in nude fishnet tights and leotard atop her dancing heels. She was just one of the many perfect bodies Samantha counted around her.

Stripping down to a G-sting in front of her co-workers was a normal requirement of being a dancer. It was the only job in the world where total strangers ended up naked in front of each other in a matter of weeks. No time to feel self-conscious when you have a thirty-second costume change to make backstage. Though today, Sam felt some uneasiness in a room full of experienced beauties and hers, the new body, never seen at the Rouge.

"Samantha O'Brien." Sam jumped and trotted down the aisle from which the voice echoed. In front of her stood a petite, aging seamstress, looking a lot like a St Trinian's delinquent, dressed in black everything — pinafore, patent belt, stockings and ballet flats. Elsie, a veteran Rouge seamstress and dresser, peered from under black kohl eyelids, through black-framed glasses and, as she began reciting the name of the numbers Sam performed in from her checklist, the familiar smell of cigarette smoke wafted from her black lip-lined mouth. Sam wondered if smoking was a national pastime in Paris because nearly every Parisian she'd met seemed enveloped in the cancerous vapour. Even the costumes had the sickly smell of stagnant cigarette smoke on them. She remembered what Aunty Michele used to say. "Samantha, two things motivate everyone. Pain and pleasure. Fear is the irrational avoidance of pain and addiction is the unattainable pursuit of pleasure." To Samantha, the Parisians certainly seemed to pursue pleasure on an impossibly large scale. An odd thought struck her. So did Tony. He smoked too but for some reason she hadn't even registered it until now. Ursu, motivated by the unattainable pursuit of pleasure? No, Tony's smoking was something else. Surely?

With Sam's full wardrobe of costumes and shoes displayed on a rack beside her, Elsie removed the first costume while Sam stripped down to her tights and G-string.

One after the other, Sam wiggled into her costumes and was zipped, nipped and pinned into place. When she caught sight of her reflection in a nearby mirror, she drew a sharp breath. Beguiled, she saw the image of an exquisite Moulin Rouge dancer and it was her.

"Yes, Samantha. You look wonderful." Penny appeared around the corner and confirmed Sam's reflection was indeed stunning. "You have the perfect figure for a nude. Your breasts are full, firm but not too large. A beautiful shape. Perhaps you might consider becoming a nude if you stay for the next show?"

"Thank you, Penny. Do you really think so?" In this show, Sam was a dancer which meant her breasts were covered in every number. For her breasts to be considered worthy to be exposed as a nude, was a not just a compliment, but a privilege.

"Yes, I do. And look, Elsie has to take other parts of your costume in. You have a trim figure with long lovely legs, as well as being a strong dancer. If you're willing to do the topless work, I think you'll be successful and make soloist one day."

"I agree with Penny." With his usual stealth, Tony materialized and stepped in beside his assistant, his eyes appraising Sam's body. Although he purposefully refrained from lingering too long in any place, Sam blushed at his scrutiny. "As I said from the start, Samantha, keep dancing as good as you can and becoming a nude may be closer than you think."

After Tony and Penny turned their attention to other dancers getting fitted, Samantha could barely contain her excitement. Like a student receiving a long-awaited top-grade at school, she squirmed with delight. She glanced down at Elsie, who knelt beside her, her mouth full of trapped sewing pins and drawn in a tight half-smile.

"Do you think I could be a nude, Elsie?" Sam whispered so as not to draw attention.

Elsie nodded in the affirmative and with her gnarled fingers tugging and pinning, she resumed her attack on Samantha's costume.

~ ♥ ~

"How did your fitting go?" Sam slithered into the splits beside Josette on the rehearsal floor after the fittings.

"*Bon.*" Josette's frigidity left no room for ambiguity as to her mood. With legs spread wide in a second split, her back long and straight, Josette's focus remained fixed on the far wall of the rehearsal studio as she rolled her hips forward and back.

"Josette, what's wrong?" Samantha stopped stretching and shimmied closer to her friend.

"Why didn't you tell me you went out with Tony last night?" Josette glared balefully at Samantha.

"We haven't had that much time to talk today. I was going to tell you later. I didn't think it was important. He just took me to have dinner since I wasn't feeling very well yesterday. Nothing happened. We ate and talked."

"*Pfft.* No one just talks at dinner. And now he wants to make you a nude!" Josette made no pretence of hiding how she thought Samantha gained Tony's favour.

"How do you know he wants to make me a nude?"

"I overheard Penny and Tony talking to you at the fitting today. I've danced here longer than you and I'm supposed to be the next nude, not you." Josette's claws unsheathed.

"I'm sorry, Josette. It wasn't me that brought up the subject. It was just something that Penny and Tony said to me. I don't want you to be pushed aside because of me. Really I don't. Of course, you must take the position before me." Samantha reached out to take her friend's hands. She didn't want to lose the only friend she had in Paris. "I mean it. If they offer me the job, I'll say they have to give it to you first."

With a slow thaw, Josette shelved her suspicions and relinquished her ice princess role. A cautious smile returned to her face, and she wrapped her legs around Samantha, accepting the apology with an embrace. All arms and legs the two dancers sat on the floor, giving each other a hug.

"I'm sorry, Samantha. It is all right. Whatever happens, happens. It's not your fault you are so beautiful and talented."

"Don't be silly, Josette. You are far more beautiful and talented than me." She kissed her friend on both cheeks.

Standing by the mirrors, Penny clapped her hands. "Okay, everyone, let's begin." And they leapt to their feet for another afternoon of punishing rehearsals.

~ ♥ ~

Sunday brought with it an icy snap of bitter winter temperatures, so Samantha decided to spend the day in her room, reading and relaxing. Since her wall fireplace was nothing but decorative, she pushed her little radiator to the limit, its heat battling to protect her from the outside freeze, sneaking in through the French doors. What she needed were heavier curtains to keep the warmth in and the cold out.

Dressed in sloppy sweatpants, bulky jumper, thick bed socks and a beanie sporting the Australian flag and with one of her bed blankets wrapped around her shoulders, Samantha padded down the stairs to see if Madame Lucette had any heavier curtains she could hang on her balcony doors.

Wandering up to the front reception counter, she couldn't find her landlady but instead was amazed to discover an unexpected visitor perched next to the computer. The surprised recognition on his soft white and apricot face matched hers and as he navigated toward Sam on silent feet, his purring meant only one thing.

"Jasper, is that you?" Samantha reached out to the furball, and he strained up her arm for more attention. "It is you. Jasper, what are you doing here?" She slid her hand up and down his velvety back while he maneuvered around in circles of appreciation.

"Samantha?" Like Jasper, Madame Lucette also possessed a quiet step and now stood behind Sam in the foyer.

"Madame Lucette, this is Jasper." Sam lifted the cat to her chest, offering him to her landlady.

"I know, Samantha. But how do you know Jasper?" She took the cat, who continued in his demand for more cuddles from his new handler.

"She knows him because of me, Aunty Lucette."

Sam wheeled round to see Philippe standing on the threshold as if fallen from heaven. His honey-coloured hair drifted over his forehead, and with a smile that could turn demons into angels, he gazed at her with obvious delight. "Samantha O'Brien from Australia, it is good to see you again."

Madame Lucette's head jerked left to right and Jasper pawed up at her jangling earrings. "*Mon ange*, what is this?" Madame Lucette turned her enquiry to Philippe.

"Samantha and I met a couple of weeks ago at the Place du Terte and last Sunday we went to Sacré-Coeur together, then back to my place. That's where she met Jasper."

Sam couldn't believe Philippe was here, where she lived. This time, she had nowhere to run. Even an escape up the stairs to her bedroom was blocked by his sensuous presence.

Trying to recover some of her composure, she looked at Madame Lucette. "But he called you Aunty Lucette?"

"Yes, Samantha. Philippe is my nephew. His mother, Chantelle and I are sisters. Today is Philippe's birthday and he has come here to visit me."

Of course, it's his birthday, Samantha thought to herself. *Just when I thought everything was settling down. Here he is, on his bloody birthday, looking more divine than ever.*

Philippe couldn't hide his appreciation of the situation's irony, nor did he try. He merely leaned against the column and folded his arms across chest, a mischievous grin lurking on his face.

"Happy birthday, Philippe. But I must say I'm surprised," Sam said, rattled.

"But if you two have met, how didn't you know about the connection between Philippe and me?" Madame Lucette aimed the question at her nephew.

"We didn't get around to talking about where Samantha lived in Montmartre. We talked mainly about her dancing at the Rouge, my art and other things. Oh, and of course, Jasper." At the mention of his name, Jasper strained toward his owner, who strolled over to retrieve him from his aunt. It also provided a legitimate excuse for Philippe to stand a little too close to Samantha.

Sam squirmed backwards. "Well, I must say this is strange, to find out you're related." Her hands sought out the reception counter ledge to which she clung for fear she might topple over from the hot flashes brought on by Philippe's proximity. She glanced at Madame Lucette who watched the uncomfortable tension between Sam and Philippe, and it was painfully obvious that her landlady didn't need any tarot cards to tell her what had gone on. Philippe's sexual energy and Samantha's discomfort were unmistakable.

"I can see you two didn't spend much time talking about many things, except perhaps liberation, Samantha?"

Without any chance of halting the onslaught, a flaming red blush shot up Sam's neck to settle in her cheeks. She struggled to find a response to Madame Lucette's well-aimed jibe but failed. A lame smile creased her face while Philippe chuckled quietly to himself. Jasper seemed the only one to feel any sympathy for Sam's plight, as he stretched his paw out toward her.

With unconcealed amusement and a shrug of her shawl, Madame Lucette saved Sam from further discomfort. "Why don't you join us, Samantha, for some birthday cake. The other tenants are in the dining room, and I thought we could all celebrate Philippe's twenty-fifth birthday together."

Samantha shuffled her feet. "Oh, I don't think so. I only came down to see if you have any heavier curtains that might keep the cold out in my room."

"I think I might have some, Samantha. But why don't you join us firstly for some cake and then we'll look."

On purpose, Samantha hadn't made eye contact with Philippe since he'd moved beside her. "Well, ah . . . I look terrible. I can't go to a party like this." She tried to straighten her clothes and make herself more presentable. Then realizing her woollen beanie still perched on her head, she tore it off, jammed it into her pants pocket and finger-brushed her hair. Philippe edged closer, making it even harder for her to breathe.

"Please, Samantha." His voice sounded wistful. "Come and have some of my birthday cake. My mother will be here soon. I know she would love to meet you." With Jasper secured in one arm, Philippe freed his other and it floated toward her in slow motion. She watched his hand find hers, wrap his elegant fingers — *oh those fingers* — around hers and like a pet, she followed him into the dining room. No wonder Jasper liked her. They were a match. All Philippe had to do was call them by name and beckon them with his touch. She and Jasper were slaves to the same master.

~ ♥ ~

"There they are, Philippe. Up there on the very top shelf." Madame Lucette pointed a feather duster to a bundle of dusty pink fabric wedged at the top of the storeroom closet. He dragged the step ladder closer, stepped up and pulled down the parcel. "Now go and put these up for Samantha. She is in *salle do soleil.*"

"Oh no, Madame. That's not necessary. I can do it." Although Samantha had enjoyed the last hour or so with Philippe, meeting his mother and chatting with some of the hotel's newest arrivals, she didn't want to tempt fate by having Philippe in her room, alone.

"Nonsense, Samantha," Madame Lucette said. "This is man's work and now, *mon ange* is twenty-five, he is a man. Philippe will do it." Madame Lucette's delivery of her orders meant it was futile to refuse.

"Come on, Samantha. Let me help you." Philippe hauled the curtains onto his shoulder and made for the stairs. With Jasper trailing behind his owner, Samantha grabbed the step ladder and followed suit up to her room. On purpose, she left her door open.

"I've always liked this room the best," Philippe said, unfurling and shaking the curtains.

"Really? And why is that?" Samantha and Jasper curled up on the bed together. Firstly, to give Philippe more room to get on with the job and secondly, to be as far away from him as possible in the small bed-sit.

"This is the room I used to stay in when I was young and visited Aunty Lucette on my holidays." While he spoke, his focus remained on attaching the rusty curtain hooks onto the curtains.

She watched his fingers slip the stubborn hooks into the holes of the tape and a flicker of excitement surged up Sam's legs. His dexterity is what had brought her undone. She averted her eyes and returned to the topic. "But you grew up and lived in Paris? Why did you stay here in Montmartre with your aunt on your holidays?"

"To get away from my father. My mother sent me here so he wouldn't beat me."

"What? Why did he beat you?" Samantha sat upright, legs crossed.

"My father hated that I wasn't a real man, like him. I was quiet, artistic, more like my mother and Aunty Lucette. I loved art, drawing and painting. I hated football and sports. And I certainly didn't want to be like him, lying and cheating to make lots of money. So, he beat me. From when I was a boy, he used to strap me with his belt if I didn't act the way he wanted." The more Philippe spoke about his father, the harder his fingers attacked the curtain.

"Philippe, that's awful. What did your mother do?"

"She tried to stop it, to step in, but he hit her as well."

"But why didn't she leave him. The two of you could've come here and stayed with your aunt? Madame Lucette would've taken you in, I'm sure?"

"I guess so. But my mother was scared he'd come after us and she didn't want to get Aunty Lucette tangled up in our mess as well."

"Well, I think it's unforgivable. What a terrible man." Sam said a silent prayer of gratitude for the loving and unselfish parents she'd had as a child. Her father would've no more thought of hitting her or her brother than fly to the moon. 'Poor Philippe, what an awful way to grow up.'

"So, what happened?" she asked.

"As soon as I could make enough money to support myself, I left. I was about sixteen. That is why I live in that cheap little flat above the patisserie with basically no money. But I'm happy, and I get to do what I love . . . my art." He balanced on the step ladder and hung the first curtain on the rod.

"And Chantelle, your mother? She seems lovely and she's very beautiful. Is she still with your father?"

Philippe grabbed the second curtain and began hanging it next to its partner. "Yes. She's still there. Now that I've left home, and I'm not around to remind him of his failure, my father seems much better. He never asks about me and keeps to himself mostly."

"But why doesn't Chantelle just leave him?"

"Because when I left, my father disinherited me. My mother stays because she's determined to inherit their fortune and make sure I get my share of it when she dies. My mother is an angel. She and Aunty Lucette have saved me all my life. They are wonderful women." He stepped off the ladder and surveyed his handiwork. Though creased, the curtains covered the French doors, blocking out the cold and the outside world. Samantha's room was now a self-contained, secret sanctuary.

"And if we shut the door, your room will be even more snug and warm." Philippe strode over to prove his point. Plonking down on the bed with Samantha and Jasper, he made himself at home in his old room. Up close and personal, he leaned onto his elbow and reached his hand to her face, brushing her soft cheek with an equally soft touch.

"Why did you run away last Sunday, Samantha?"

Knowing she shouldn't, she still nuzzled her cheek into his stroking hand. "Because the last time I let someone make me feel like that, it ended badly, and I got very sick. I don't want that happening again. I've worked too hard to be here at the Moulin Rouge."

"So you did like how I made you feel?" Philippe's face brightened.

"Yes," she said in a whisper.

"I can make you feel even better if you let me?" He slid in closer to her, lifting a disgruntled Jasper out of the way. With his lips not waiting for an answer, Philippe caressed Sam's neck with fluttering kisses.

"I'm not sure, Philippe. I've got rehearsals tomorrow, and I can't be late again." Though she tried to make more excuses, he rested his index finger on her mouth, stifling the rest of her reasons. Stretching up, he pressed his lips to hers. Her escaping breath belied her resolve, and she sank into his embrace. Rolling Sam under his shoulder, he gazed down at her with gentle indulgence. She thought this must be how an angel would look if she died in her sleep, and he came to take her to heaven. The peace and promise in Philippe's eyes melted her concerns.

"God, Samantha, you are so beautiful." His finger traced a delicate pattern on her cheek.

"But not as beautiful as you. You're nearly too beautiful to be a man."

"That's what my father said when he beat me."

"I'm so sorry. I didn't mean . . ." This time, he stopped her chatter with a lingering, warm kiss. One she accepted and returned with no reservations.

He continued his downward journey to her neck and Samantha rolled her head to one side and ran her fingers through his silky hair.

"Philippe?"

"Yes," he murmured through non-stop affection.

"Madame Lucette called you something this evening. *Mon ange* I think. What does it mean?"

Raising himself back onto his elbow and with his golden hair mussed, falling over his forehead, he smiled. "It means my angel."

"Oh," she said, outlining his high cheekbone with her thumb. "How appropriate."

She reached up and invaded his mouth with her tongue, her body curling into his. Without a moment wasted, they grabbed for each other's clothes, stripping them off, as if purifying themselves of the garment's sins. Now that the curtains had trapped the heat from the radiator, the room enveloped them in a heady warmth. Naked, they lay beside each other, a mutual admiration society of two.

Appreciating her body's contours with his delicate fingers, Philippe said, "Let me bathe you. Let me explore you. Let me serve you." With the agility and grace of an artist, he rose from the bed, clasped both Sam's hands in his and helped her from the bed. They embraced, and he reached behind her, slipping his fingers between her buttocks, reaching for her sweet spot.

With his hot breath in her ear, he said, "God, Samantha. I have thought of you every night this week. All I wanted was you. I've been a man possessed by you — your body, your voice, your smell, your touch, your taste." He brought his finger, wet with her juice, to his mouth, relishing it like a thirsty man finding water. "Let me show you, how much I can love you."

Again, she relinquished, and he guided her into the bathroom. Philippe's impressive erection led the way and Samantha longed to curl her tongue around his manhood, to devour and taste it. Philippe plugged the tub, turned on the water and upturned the body wash, while she waited obediently, her groin twitching, her eyes seduced by the artistry of his movement.

"Samantha O'Brien from Australia. Look at you." He held her at arm's length. Her body shuddered. Although he didn't touch her, her snatch pulsed and dripped. Engorged and ready for plunder, she rocked on her feet, longing for him to begin.

"*Mon ange*," she purred. "May I also call you that?"

"Of course. And you are my La Goulue. My queen of the can-can. Now let me see how wide you can spread your legs."

All but collapsing into his arms, Samantha steadied herself to step into the tub which by now was steaming and frothing with bubbles. Together they slid into the water, its heat welcoming their bodies. When Samantha's hand went below the surface to open and wash her snatch, Philippe stopped her.

"*Non. Non. La Goulue.* Allow me. I will clean you with my tongue."

Samantha fell back into the embrace of the tub, overwhelmed by the sheer thought of Philippe's promise. Opening her legs, he placed them on the side of the bath. With her folds open, the hot water seeped into her private place. The anticipation, the scolding heat and the soapy slick caressed her throbbing bud. Leaning forwards, Philippe cupped her breasts, circling his fingers around her tight nipples.

"My God, Samantha. You are the most perfect dancer I've ever loved." He tweaked her nipples causing a sharp, but exciting pain.

"And how many dancers have you loved, Philippe?" Her hands circled her breasts, caressing them as he watched jealously.

"More than I can remember, but none as perfect or as lovely as you." He returned to his adoration of her breasts, recruiting his lips, tongue and mouth. Samantha gasped with the pleasure and pain of it and with her legs still splayed over the side of the tub, she felt Philippe's finger reacquainting itself with her clit.

"*Mmmm*, I see she remembers me," he said with droll amusement, while her bud hardened under his touch.

"She never forgot you." Samantha heard her voice slur through the haze of sexual agony.

"That makes me very pleased, *La Goulue*." With only the softest touch, he continued to torment her clit. Perfecting his strokes, he worked on Samantha with the same diligence and attention to detail as she suspected he worked on his paintings. Lost in the anguish of it all, she only noticed the tub's emptiness when the slight chill in the air, licked at her folds, which she had held apart for her lover.

"This tub is too restrictive. I cannot love you with my tongue, my mouth or swallow your cum here. Into the bed where I can eat you all night until you are swollen and dry." Yet in contradiction to his edict, he leaned forwards and caressed her clit with the tip of his tongue. She quivered in anticipation, her traitorous body yearning for more. Philippe helped her from the tub, and she followed him into her bedroom as if in a trance. Philippe dislodged Jasper from his resting place on the bed and settled Samantha on her back, tucking one pillow under her buttocks. With their eyes locked in fascination, he knelt above her and grasped her ankles. "Now let me see you do the splits." Without the slightest effort, Samantha's legs obliged and fell open, her toes over the side of the mattress.

"Oh, *la la*." Philippe's tongue licked the perimeter of his lips while Samantha's snatch lay open and waiting for him. Every fold hungered for him, glistened for him, ached for him. As he salivated, so too did her cleft. Wet, steaming and ravenous, she needed satisfaction. Her clit swelled and when he sank to nibble at her tiny bud, her juice seeped to greet him.

"Philippe, have you got the curtains up?" Sharp knocking on the other side of the door shattered their sex play with such a shock, Samantha's legs recoiled shutting in double time, and Philippe's head only just escaped unscathed.

"Yes, Aunty Lucette. I've almost got it up." Both Philippe and Samantha looked at his rampant cock and giggled. He most definitely had got it up.

"Give me a moment and you can come in to inspect my handiwork." Philippe jumped off the bed and dragged on his clothes as did Samantha. "I will finish this another time," he whispered to Sam, kissing her on the cheek as he fought his disappointed cock into his jeans. Sam blushed but said nothing. Waiting until Sam was dressed and gave him the nod, Philippe opened the door. Madame Lucette's face wore the sweetest, most innocent smile when she glided into the room.

"Well, the curtains certainly work," she said showing little interest in the curtains. "This room is scorching." Her real interest reverted to her nephew. With unabashed confidence, Madame Lucette had foiled their liaison, and she knew it.

"Yes, the curtains are perfect. Thank you, Madame Lucette, for giving them to me. I think I can turn the radiator down now a little." Sam stepped over to the wall and turned the knob, hoping her gesture looked far more nonchalant than it felt.

"And, Philippe, I think you can turn down your charm a little too." With one eyebrow arched, Madame Lucette, wagged her finger at him. Then she turned her attention to Sam. "Samantha, my nephew inherited some traits from his father which are bound to get him into trouble. He is very attractive to the opposite sex and enjoys their company a little too often and freely in my opinion."

Philippe frowned at his aunt and pursed his lips, signifying he didn't want her to continue.

Tempering her lecture somewhat, she said, "I love *mon ange* very much. He is a good, young man but be careful, Samantha, Paris is for lovers, not always love." She allowed the comment to hang in the air for a moment while watching Samantha digest its meaning.

"*Bonsoir*, my dears." Madame Lucette kissed them both then swept from the room with her usual theatricality.

"I'm sorry about my aunt. She does tend to overdramatize things a bit." Philippe clasped Samantha's hands.

"That's okay. I know her well enough by now to understand. Regardless, it's getting late, Philippe, and I must be on time for rehearsals tomorrow. So maybe you should go."

"Yes, that's probably a good idea. But now I know where you live, you won't be able to hide from me anymore." Philippe's mouth twisted into a cheeky smile, and he squeezed her hands for added emphasis. "How about next Sunday? Can I see you then?"

"*Mmm*, let me see how this week works out," Samantha said, unsure and cautious.

"But I still have the promise I made you to keep." He leaned closer, his warm breath brushing her cheek. "To love you with my tongue until you are swollen and dry." His face remained beside hers, the tension between them arcing across their cheeks.

Samantha's groin twitched, desperate for the fulfilment of his promise. She could feel herself succumbing to his overt sexuality and persuasion. Knowing he'd ignited her passion once more, he released her hand and slipped his fingers between her legs, prodding at her crotch. "Your jeans are wet, Samantha. Oh, so wet. I need to taste her, to drink her." The tip of his tongue slipped from his mouth and stroked her cheek with a delicate lick. "Until next Sunday then," he said, barely audible. Dragging his fingers from her hot place with reluctance, he lifted them under his nose, relished her smell then slipped them into his mouth.

How she wanted to jam his angelic face between her thighs and grind her hips hard against his beauty. How she longed to have that lascivious mouth sucking and biting at her snatch until she couldn't stand it any longer. How she stopped herself from doing so, was mystifying.

In a silent farewell, Philippe pressed his lips to each of Sam's hands, then to her cheeks. He reached over, collected Jasper, and left the room as if he was no more than an apparition that never existed in the first place. Overexcited, overheated and overwhelmed, Samantha stood frozen to the spot. All her senses bristled on high alert, but the one thing she was not over was Philippe Lacroix. She was most definitely not over him.

CHAPTER TEN

EARLY THE NEXT MORNING Samantha escaped Hotel Hollandaise and what she felt certain would have been an awkward breakfast with Madame Lucette. Now sitting at a nearby café, she chomped into a chocolate croissant and *chocolat chaud*, a sinful cup of hot milk thickened with shaved and melted chocolate. With her appetite matching her mental chatter, Sam tried to think and steady her nerves before rehearsals.

Before coming to Paris, she'd expected a little stray sex would be on offer and in all honesty, she'd looked forward to a casual liaison. But falling in love with Philippe wasn't part of her plan. In fact, falling in love with any man wasn't part of her plan. What distressed her most was the total disregard with which her heart ignored her well-crafted plan. She was falling in love and try as she might ignore her feelings, she couldn't. Philippe being Madame Lucette's nephew only fuelled her angst, and she felt torn between her growing affection for both of them.

She finger-licked the last of the chocolate from the plate and slurped the dregs of melted chocolate from her cup. Shouldering her dance bag, she paid the check and stalked off to the Rouge. She hated chocolate.

SAMANTHA KNEW IT WAS too good to last. By Wednesday night, Madame Lucette had laid in wait and surprised Sam when she returned home late, having eaten dinner elsewhere after rehearsals.

"Samantha, I have not seen you for days? Is everything all right?" Madame Lucette fluttered toward her tenant, reaching to greet her. Smelling of incense and flowery perfume, she wrapped her thin arms around Samantha and kissed her on both cheeks. The genuine affection she showered on Sam alleviated some of her initial apprehensions.

"Of course, Madame. It's the last week of rehearsals. Tony is making us start early and stay late." Sam didn't like lying but she wasn't up for a long conversation or explanations. "So that's why you haven't seen me much."

"Perhaps you will keep an old woman company for a few minutes?" Madame Lucette tilted her head with a look of the cheeky girl she would have been some fifty or more years ago. "Please?" Her bony hand reached out beckoning Samantha.

Unable to refuse her landlady's insistent request, Sam acquiesced. "Okay. But just for a few minutes. I really need to shower and get to bed." Sam dropped her bag near the staircase and followed Madame Lucette into the dining room. All the other tenants were either out or in their rooms, so they had the space to themselves.

"Let's sit here," Madame Lucette suggested, pulling out a chair.

Scanning the table, Sam realized she'd been hi-jacked. Madame Lucette's tarot cards rested in a neat pile on the table, beside them a candle, waiting to be lit.

"Madame, I really don't want a card reading." Samantha remained standing, shaking her head.

"Are you sure, *chère fille*? You may not want a reading, but the cards have told me you need a reading. They will help you find the answer you seek. Please. Sit." Madame Lucette waved Samantha into a chair, lit the candle and began shuffling the cards. Without a word, she handed the pack to Sam and waited. On purpose, Sam kept her mind blank and quickly cut the pack. If she didn't think of a question, the cards wouldn't be able to tell her an answer. On turning over the card, there appeared a warrior princess with a snake curled around her body against the backdrop of a full moon and raging ocean. This time, the card was upside down.

"*Oooh*, the contrary goddess of nurturing," Madame Lucette said with restrained excitement. She studied the card and began the reading. "This is the goddess who rules the cycles of life and its creative phases. She draws the tides of the oceans, the nourishing rains and the ebb and flow of all life. She calls upon you to recognize everything has a season. In the contrary position she is telling you, you have stagnant, negative energies. You must stop damming up your energies and making yourself tired, angry and sick. You must allow your energy, your emotions to flow." Madame Lucette reached over and patted Samantha's hand. "You must let go, Samantha."

Looking at the furious storm and thrashing ocean waves on the card, Sam felt water welling in her eyes and lathering her skin. Panic grew inside her.

"Let go, Samantha," Madame Lucette said once more in a soft whisper.

With her breath shortening into jagged sobs and her shoulders beginning to heave, Sam shoved her chair back from the table. Gulping down her roiling emotions, she sprinted from the dining room, snatched up her bag and leapt up the stairs two at a time.

"Shit. Shit. Shit," she said fumbling to find her brass key. Unstoppable tears rushed down her cheeks. "Bloody cards, bloody goddesses, bloody everything . . ." The words caught in her throat, but it slammed shut, strangling her tirade. She drove the key into the lock, turned and escaped into her room. Launching onto the bed, Samantha cried with such intensity she thought her chest would cleave open. For how long she immersed herself in this catharsis, she didn't know, but she was still dressed when the sun woke her the next morning.

~ ♥ ~

"*Bonjour*, Elsie." Samantha stood beside her seamstress for final costume fittings on Saturday evening.

With her mouth full of pins again, Elsie nodded and peered up, like a little gothic pixie happy to see her giant fairy friend. "*Bonjour.*" She handed the first costume to Samantha.

Sam stepped into the magnificent, hand-sewn bustier covered in crystals and beads. Scrunching the waist in so Elsie could zip her up, Sam knew something was wrong. Her fingers didn't reach around toward the zipper as far as they should. Her waist felt thick and puffy, and the way Elsie struggled with the zipper, Sam knew it wasn't going to close. Digging her fingers harder into her rebellious flesh, Sam willed the costume to fit. It didn't.

Trying not to call attention to their dilemma, Elsie glanced around at Sam with a quizzical expression as if asking how, in seven days, could a dancer put on this much girth.

"Try it again," Sam hissed through her teeth with a fake smile. Elsie nodded and returned to the battle with the zipper. She lost. Releasing her grip, Elsie flicked the bustier from Samantha's body with a snap, hung it up and offered another costume for her to try on. Fortune smiled on the pair this time, as there was little substance to this costume, merely a G-string and bra. The fitting was successful but when Sam glanced in the mirror, there was a small roll of fat atop the G-string line that wasn't there last week.

"Oh, God." Sam's moan was just a whisper, but as if the pack knew the prey was down, a couple of the French girls stuck their heads around the corner to see what was happening. Sam's hands flew to her hips and striking a showgirl pose, she covered the offending surplus. Unsure as to what the other dancers had seen, Sam smiled and preened while the girls teetered and pointed with obvious delighted bitchiness at the rookie.

"*Pffft.*" Elsie threw a disgusted gesture at the onlookers, and they returned to their own business. Elsie turned back to Sam, but she'd already stripped off the offending G-string. Dragging her rehearsal clothes back on, Sam struggled to stem the flow of fierce tears welling up in her eyes. Biting her lip, she fled from the wardrobe department, leaving a perplexed Elsie standing with a rack of costumes and no dancer. Today was the last fitting before opening night next week. Now poor Elsie had costumes to resew with no idea of the new measurements with which to change them.

"Samantha, what's wrong?" Penny scuttled out of Sam's path to avoid a collision in the corridor, but Sam didn't see or hear her. In fact, Sam didn't register anyone or anything in her escape from the house of horrors — aka the wardrobe department.

There was only one place Sam had to be. There was only one place where she could take control of the situation. Shoving her hands hard onto the door, Sam ran in, and like a crazed criminal looked around to make sure no witnesses were present. Scrambling into the stall, she slammed and locked the door behind her, dropped to her knees and clung to the bowl with her left hand. With ferocious force, she jammed her right index and middle fingers down her throat until her body rejected the invasion. Vomiting the contents of her stomach until she retched bile, she purged herself of everything in her life she feared most — her growing love for Philippe, her inadequacies as a dancer, her fantasies about Tony, her failure, her failure, her failure. As she continued in her torment, Sam felt that if she turned herself inside-out, the world would see a better person, a better dancer, a better lover, a better daughter . . . She'd be better. Her mind swirled, a whirlpool of disgust and self-loathing, throwing her off-balance. With both hands clinging to the sacred porcelain, Sam steadied herself. There was nothing left. She had rid herself of the manic chatter in her mind. Her mouth and eyes dripped with fluids, fatigue and the euphoria of victory. She'd regained control.

"Samantha. Enough now." Penny's gentle voice filtered over the toilet cubicle, freezing Sam like a statue. "Why don't you come out and freshen up? There's no one else here but me, and I won't tell anyone."

Sam grimaced, swearing under her breath. When her brain rebooted a few seconds later, she pieced together the past minutes. She remembered nearly barrelling Penny over when she ran out of the wardrobe department and then, due to the echo in the stall, she'd not heard Penny follow her into the toilets. *Shit.* Penny had been on the other side of the door, listening to Sam purge.

"Samantha. Please come out."

Sam leveraged herself off the floor and flushed the toilet. God, she hated this. She wiped her mouth as best she could, and the stench of her own puke offended her on so many levels. With Penny waiting outside, Sam had no other option. She unlocked the door and stood shamefaced.

With her arms spread wide, Penny said, "Samantha honey. What are you doing to yourself?"

Sam stepped into Penny's arms with hiccupping sobs. "I'm sorry. I'm sorry. I'm too fat. My costumes don't fit. I've been eating and eating all this week. Chocolate and cake and bread and chocolate and—"

"It's all right. It's all right." Penny patted Sam's damp back. "Come on. We'll get it all worked out. I promise." She held Sam at arm's length, encouraging her with a kind smile. "Throw some water on your face, and we can talk." Penny ushered Sam to the basin and continued reassuring her while Sam obeyed. When she lifted her head, Sam cringed at her reflection. Like a death mask, her haggard face stared back, taunting her and telling her she'd never be good enough. Sam wanted to put her fist through the mirror, but as her eyes travelled over her shoulder, she saw Penny's compassionate smile. Unable to keep this secret any longer, Sam surrendered, and the fight left her body.

Penny reached over. "Come on. I'm taking you home with me."

~ ♥ ~

PROPPED UP ON THE sofa, Sam tried not to feel like an intrusion. Penny's long-time partner, Jacques had been intuitive enough to vacate their flat to get some milk, leaving Penny to brew a pot of strong, black, sweet tea, the solution to all ills and upsets.

"Now drink this." Penny handed Samantha a mug of the steaming brew. The invigorating taste and comforting temperature of the tea worked its magic immediately. With a deep sigh, Sam settled in on the lumpy, yet comfortable velveteen couch. Penny and Jacques lived in a small, three-room apartment within a fifteen-minute walk of the Rouge. It was old, needed a face-lift but Penny had made it feel like home with a blend of Australian and French nuances. A friendly, warm little place which Sam felt comfortable in, it embraced her like a mother's unconditional love.

Penny allowed her guest a few more sips of tea in silence and then said, "Now, Samantha. I think it's time you told me the truth. How long have you been purging like that?"

Sam stared into her cup, not wanting to meet Penny's gaze. "I haven't done it very often." She glanced over. Penny reminded Sam of Aunty Michele. She had the look of someone who'd wait all night for the truth, so there was no point in not telling it right now.

"It started well before I auditioned for the Rouge. I was dancing in London. I met this English guy, and we fell in love. He made grand promises to me about the life we'd have together. He loved me, he said. Anyway, I forgot to take the pill a few times and before I knew it, I was pregnant. I wasn't going to have the baby. I had no intention of giving up my career to have children like Mum did . . ." Sam paused, but Penny didn't comment.

"So, I told Richard, that was his name, about the baby and that I wasn't going to have it and he just flipped out. Called me every name under the sun and left. Just walked out, never called, never supported me, nothing. All those promises meant nothing to him. I went through the termination all alone. I couldn't tell anyone."

"You never told your parents or family back in Australia?"

"God, no! And have them think what an idiot I was for forgetting to take the pill? Or that I should marry Richard and have the baby? No way. It was my mistake, and I had to fix it, by myself."

"So why the purging?"

"After the termination, I couldn't get it out of my mind. Had I done the right thing? What about the tiny foetus? Was it already a human being? Over and over it all went in my mind. The doubt never stopped. And then I began to eat. I couldn't stop eating. I kept shoving all my guilt down with food. I just kept gaining more and more weight. Suppressing emotion is what they call it, that's what Edith, my counsellor said."

"And did Edith help you?"

"Not really. Because all she talked about was getting in touch with my emotions and letting go." As Sam spoke, she realized this was the same message of the last tarot card she'd pulled with Madame Lucette, the contrary goddess of nurturing, telling her to let go.

"By this time, my producer was threatening with me with breach of contract because I'd put on too much weight. I was going to lose my job. Then what would I do? I needed to lose weight fast. Another dancer in the company told me she often purged and over-exercised at the same time and it worked. I thought, why not?"

"And?"

"That's what I did, and it worked. I kept my job, lost the extra weight I'd gained, got over Richard and now I'm here in my dream job at the Moulin Rouge." Although the events were true, the emotions attached to them didn't make Sam proud of her actions. Desperation and doubt crept under the surface of her rationalization. This was the first time she'd ever spoken about these episodes aloud, and she wasn't impressed with what she heard. She turned her attention back to her mug of tea. Unburdening herself to Penny made her feel lighter, but she was uncertain as to where all this truth-telling might lead. The wait for Penny's response seemed interminable. Sam's restless legs began to tap out a random beat on the threadbare carpet. Penny moved from the single armchair she was sitting in and slipped in beside Sam on the sofa. When she put her mug down on the coffee table, Sam did likewise.

"Well, Sam. I'm sure you know that if you keep this behaviour up, you'll make yourself so sick and weak you won't be able to dance?"

Sam nodded in silence. Her hand drifted to her mouth, where she attacked her finger, tearing at the cuticle skin.

"I'm not going to ask you what brought on this excessive eating over the past week but from where I sit, I think you're being too hard on yourself. I understand you want to be perfect, a perfect dancer with the perfect body so you can then go on to be the perfect nude, soloist and principal. But your perfectionism is strangling the life out of you and your dancing. You're making it so hard to live up to the ideals you set for yourself, you're bound to fail. I tend to agree with Edith. You need to let yourself go a little. Enjoy life. Just because you had one bad love affair doesn't mean all men are bastards." Penny rescued Sam's finger from the abuse, squeezed her hand and smiled, which Sam reciprocated albeit without much conviction.

"Well, there is someone who I have strong feelings for, but what if it doesn't work out? What happens then?" Sam thought of the angel-faced Philippe and his love-making talents. Her fingers fidgeted with the zipper on her tracksuit top, running it up and down with a whirring sound to match her X-rated thoughts of Philippe.

"If it doesn't work out, there'll be another one. It doesn't mean you have to overeat and purge. You can always do what most girls do at the end of a love affair — scream and cry — then kick him out. Sam, honey, you need to be gentle on yourself. You can't jeopardize your career just because you're frightened of the future of a love affair."

Sam considered Penny's logic and her mind wandered away from Philippe to the other important man in her life. "You're not going to tell Tony, are you?" Sam feared she may have already threatened her Rouge career just by this conversation.

"No. I'm not going to tell anyone, but I want you to promise me you won't do this purging again." Penny's tone sounded hard and resolute, the same tone she used in rehearsals when giving directions.

"Okay. I promise," Sam said, determined to keep her pledge. "But what about my costumes? They don't fit. I look terrible. I've got these rolls of fat . . ." Sam pinched at her hips.

"Stop worrying. I'm sure if you return to your usual eating and stop gorging yourself with sugary foods, it'll only take a few days for your body to find its shape again. Tomorrow drink lots of clear fluids, stay away from the alcohol and come Monday, after a full day of dress rehearsals, we'll see if any costumes need changing. I have a feeling that with all this emotional tension and if you return to your normal diet, your body will respond quickly."

"Okay," Sam said, feeling more confident.

"Good. Now if you want my advice, I think you should consider letting yourself go a little with this young man you mentioned. Allow a little love into your life. I've always found that love is the best remedy for overeating and hot sex is the best way to over-exercise." The golden flint in Penny's pale green eyes sparkled with experience and wickedness. As if on cue, Jacques strolled into the apartment. Unaware of the increasing heat level of the girls' conversation, he smiled and turned to the fridge with his carton of milk.

"See what I mean?" Penny shot goo-goo eyes at her partner, who looked like a young Olivier Martinez.

Samantha leaned closer. "Yes. I see what you mean."

CHAPTER ELEVEN

"OH, PHILIPPE. IT'S EXTRAORDINARY." Sam craned her neck skyward. "It's even bigger than I imagined."

Beside her, Philippe stood bursting with Parisian pride and read from the tourist guide. "One of the seven wonders of the modern world, the Eiffel Tower is the most recognized and most popular architectural achievement in the Western world."

Impressed by the massive steel structure dominating the land and air space around them, Sam clung to Philippe's arm as they wandered under the tower, its core stretching above them like a giant rainforest canopy of latticed metal. Its four enormous wide-spread legs mounted on concrete columns housed souvenir stores and ticketing shops, feeding the hordes of people lining up to eat and ascend the monument to the rarer air at three hundred metres.

Philippe stopped directly under its centre and joined Sam's upward gaze. "When I was very young, Aunty Lucette used to bring me here. She told me the Eiffel Tower was made long ago by a gentle giant who became very sad when the woman he loved left him. In his torment and anguish, the giant thundered through Paris, demolishing all the buildings. As he despaired for his lost love, he twisted the metal girders from the ruins, sculpting the wreckage into a form that matched his broken heart. That is how the Eiffel Tower was created. The colossal legs of the tower, represent the steady strength on which his love was built while the tip of the tower symbolizes the deadly point of love's arrow, which pierced his heart and left him destroyed."

"Oh, Philippe, what a tragic story. I've never heard that before. It's so beautiful and so sad." Sam squeezed his arm with affection and imagined a passionate ballet depicting the story. She could see the dancers, costumes and sets swirling in her imagination with a forlorn giant puppet sitting in the middle of the stage, wringing the prop girders and crying.

"I'm sure Aunty Lucette made it up just for me, but I've always remembered it. The lonely, abandoned man who yearns for his lost love to return . . . His pitiful misery speaks to my artist's heart. I much prefer this romantic notion of the Eiffel Tower to it being built by Gustav Eiffel for the World Exposition of 1889."

Laughing and chatting, they strolled over to the Champ de Mars, the sprawling grass field near the tower. Being a chilly Sunday, they had no difficulty finding a spot on the grass directly in line with the apex of the tower. Philippe shrugged off his backpack and not unlike Mary Poppins with her carpetbag, extracted an inordinate amount of supplies from his knapsack. Within no time, they were seated on a thick red, white and blue French flag picnic rug, with little tubs of salads, a crusty baguette, camembert cheese, Evian water, red wine, glasses and plates laid before them.

"Some wine, Samantha?" He offered a bottle of cheap, yet palatable red wine to her.

"No thanks, Philippe. Not today. Water will be fine," Sam said honouring her promise to Penny and herself.

"Some baguette? Cheese? Salad?" He flourished his hands over the assortment of mouth-watering food, reminding Sam of a peacock displaying its luminescent feathers in the hope of enticing the peahen.

She giggled. "Philippe, this is so wonderful. But today I think I'll just have a little cheese and salad. No bread thanks."

Once they were settled in, ready for lunch, Philippe lifted his glass. "*Salut.*"

"*Salut.*" Sam clinked her glass with his.

During the afternoon, they laughed and shared stories from their lives, warming each other's hearts, despite the chill. Sam listened to Philippe's discourse on his painting and dreams of becoming a famous French artist, the new Monet of the twenty-first century. He aspired to big dreams much like Sam and his energy for life was infectious. So much so, Sam accepted his offer to return to his flat for a coffee to ward off the increasing cold.

"Jasper, it's good to see you again," she said, as the exotic shorthair cat purred around her ankles as soon as she entered Philippe's flat.

"Come on, Jasper. Dinner." The familiar rattle of the kibble bag and Philippe placing his bowl on the floor drew Jasper's immediate attention. "I'll make the coffee while Jasper eats. When he's finished can you let him out onto the balcony? He likes to prowl a bit before bedtime."

With wistful memories of Scruffy back home, Sam watched Jasper devour his food, go straight to the balcony doors and with tail in the air, dart outside in search of adventure.

"Here you go. Coffee." Philippe handed her the Eiffel Tower souvenir coffee mug he'd bought earlier that day. "Your first coffee from your mug."

With lips warm and bitter from the plunger coffee, they remained indoors rather than venturing onto the balcony with Jasper. Looking out through the closed French doors they watched the lights of Paris come to life against the velvety blue of early evening. The sweet smell from the downstairs patisserie and the faint mist of baking sugar as it wafted up through the floorboards, settled in Sam's mug, improving the taste of the coffee.

"I think I'm getting used to the coffee in Paris. It's still bitter, but the colder the weather gets, the more I appreciate it." Sam sipped the last from her mug.

"Would you like some more?"

"No thanks. One's enough for me." She handed her mug to Philippe, who took both back to a little sink suspended in a corner on the wall. He walked back to Sam and clasped her hands.

His nose brushed hers in a playful fashion. "Samantha, I still feel the same."

Sam looked up at him from under lids heavy with sexual desire. "In what way?"

"I want to eat you all night until you are swollen and dry."

She melted as her insides liquefied. "Then do it."

Philippe encircled her face in one hand while the other found the small of her back. Holding her in his grip, his eyes like chips of ice, he parted his lips ready to kiss her. Fascinated, Sam watched the saliva dance on his lips and tongue, preparing him to receive the juices she longed to give him until she was spent. With utmost gentleness, his tongue slinked into her mouth, and she stumbled. He embraced her with more force and his tongue lashed hers, saving her from the threatening collapse. Deep, hot and slow he plundered her mouth until she moaned. Her head lolled back as she gasped.

"*La Goulue*, my queen of the can-can. Have you never been loved before?" Philippe murmured his question into Sam's exposed neck.

"If this is love, then no, I haven't been loved before." She tilted her head up and through blurry eyes, offered him her mouth to make love to. A knowing smile drifted across Philippe's face as the tip of his tongue floated onto her lips, licking them, teasing them, but not venturing into the orifice she presented.

"Oh, Samantha. You are ready for love, and I will love you beyond your wildest dreams." With deceiving strength, he lifted her into his arms and carried her to the bed. Instead of laying her down, he set her on her feet where she remained like a dutiful child. He pulled her sweater up over her head but didn't remove her bra. He then bent down, unfastened and removed her boots and socks. Finally, he unzipped her jeans and scrunched them down to her ankles.

"Sit," he said in a subtle, yet commanding whisper, and Sam lowered onto the bed. "Lift your legs." She did. He removed her jeans and laid her back, still in her panties and bra. He grabbed a blanket and with delicate care, laid it over her. Sam lay outwardly still with every fibre of her body screaming for action. Her drenched panties needed to be tugged from her hungry cleft and replaced with Philippe's glorious tongue, but where was he? Sam lifted her head to see

Philippe industriously working at the sink. Shrouded in silence, she wondered what on earth he was doing. Like a physician, he returned with a bowl of steaming water and a face cloth. She didn't understand what he was doing but she didn't care. All she knew was Philippe was her angel, *mon ange*, at last she was going to know what love was really like.

He leaned in, his hot breath against her ear. "Your cunt needs washing before I tongue fuck you, my love. And I am very good at washing beautiful cunts." Although she hated the four-letter word, Philippe's use of it didn't diminish his attractiveness. In fact, the word's incongruence with his angelic features and French accent sharpened her desire. At any other time, she'd be insulted by the word, but with Philippe it was different. Everything was different.

He threw back the blanket and the air rushed over the lower part of her body. Wide-eyed, Sam shivered from the shock, the cold and the anticipation. Without waiting for assent, his fingers fluttered across her hips. Pushing them into her panties, he peeled them off in one graceful move as Sam lifted her hips to help. Bringing them to his nose, he breathed her scent deep into his face. "You smell so wicked, Samantha. Maybe I will just eat your wickedness and not wash you?"

She watched him wrap his tongue around her wet panties, sucking her moisture from the crotch. She didn't know how much more of this torment she could stand. Philippe had no shame, and she wanted to join him in his wanton debauchery.

"No, wash me. Make me clean, *mon ange*," she said, her voice breathy and hoarse.

With nothing but a shrewd smile, Philippe bent to the bowl and rinsed the cloth. After wringing most of the moisture out, he unfurled it, dragging its damp folds up Sam's leg until it came to rest on her waxed mons. Inserting his fingers into the cloth, he pushed it between her legs and rubbed, slow and even. She moaned. Every orifice in her body dripped.

"Open your legs," he instructed. She shimmied her legs wider.

His eyes never left her crotch as he removed the cloth to rinse it again. Sam shuddered when once more the heat assaulted her folds and exposed clit. His touch, the excruciating dichotomy of gentle but insistent teased at her. Her snatch engorged and her clit hardened beckoning him, begging him to begin. Thrice he rinsed and washed her snatch. His labour-intensive methodology drove her mad, fuelling the carnal fascination glinting in his eyes. Finally, he dropped the cloth in the bowl and stood beside the bed. He rolled his designer beige cashmere jumper over his head, discarding it as if worthless. It was a birthday gift from his mother, and Sam thought how shocked Chantal would be if she saw how her son treated it. Probably more shocked to see how her son was treating her. Philippe's trim, athletic body flinched as he rubbed his hands over his torso, drawing Sam's attention to his tight nipples which he tweaked for her pleasure. The soulful way in which he moved mesmerized her, making her forget the cold air creeping into her exposure. Still in his jeans, he leveraged himself onto the bed, planking above her. He leaned down and kissed her with such affection and warmth, Sam felt giddy.

"*Mon ange*, you are such a contradiction," she said after their mouths drew apart for respite.

"Why is that?" His eyelids fluttered on her cheek in innocent butterfly kisses.

"Because you're graceful and beautiful like an angel, yet in bed, you're dirty and depraved." She wrapped her arms around his back, trying to pull him down on top of her. She wanted to feel his skin on hers, let it burn his brand, his smell into her flesh. He resisted with surprising power. Throwing his head back Philippe laughed, then nailed her with a fiery glare. "Because, Samantha O'Brien from Australia, in every angel there lives a nasty, little devil who loves to shock and fuck."

Sam giggled and he slid down her body, trailing his hot tongue over her mid-section. At her navel, he circled its pucker with feathery strokes and wasted little time slithering down to her mound. He dug his chin into her and looked up over the alabaster-smooth landscape of her body, catching her attention.

"I will now eat you until you are dry and swollen. I am a man of my word, Samantha. I always keep my promises." The wicked smile creasing his face all but curved up to his ears.

"I do hope so as I like men who keep their promises." Sam opened her legs wider to give him access but he moved them closed again. Grasping her ankles together and pulling her legs straight in the air, Philippe rolled her backwards until her feet touched the bed head. In this position, Sam could feel her snatch trapped, tight and impenetrable, between her locked legs.

"Perfect," he said.

Sam felt his hot breath flutter across her screaming cleft. Her ankles remained clasped in one of Philippe's hands while his tongue caressed and teased her closed oyster, searching for the pearl while it remained reluctantly imprisoned.

"Oh, God." Sam's legs fought their restraint, but he held firm, his tongue licking and twisting, digging for the jewel within.

"Please, please." She squirmed looking for freedom and satisfaction. He obliged only by offering long wet laps deep into her screaming folds as they plumped up like ripe fruit. Gently rocking her back and forth, he toyed with her flesh, licking in ever longer arcs forwards and back, while she moaned for release. Sweet juice seeped from her straining slit, begging his muscular tongue to peel her open and suck her ripeness. His oral teasing seemed endless until she finally succumbed and gave in to his erotic machinations. The moment Sam released her leg muscles, he allowed her freedom. Legs wide open, her snatch gaped up to devour him. He wrapped his mouth around its pink fleshiness and drove his tongue deep within her, seeking her sweetest seed. With his teeth nibbling at her clit, Sam pulled her labia apart and he sucked, licked and lapped her until she lay battered and bruised. Red and swollen her slit ached, but it was hungry for more. Sam lifted her head and grinned at the honey-coloured crown her mons now wore as Philippe continued in his feasting. He alternated between tickling and sucking her clit with violent passion and tender regard. The more he slurped her juices, the wetter she became.

"More, more," she said writhing around on the bed.

Philippe drove two fingers into her and hammered a hard beat on her G-spot while sucking with all his might on her clit. Sam exploded. She ejaculated, spraying her essence into Philippe's face while inhaling the sweet smell of the downstairs patisserie. Little particles of baking sugar settled in her nose, enjoying their new home for an instant. Perhaps this was how a gobstopper felt after being sucked to oblivion in a child's mouth? Because of the unrelenting attack on its hardened exterior, the candy's systematically reduced to layers of blissful sweetness. That was exactly how Samantha felt — blissfully sweet. Lying in her afterglow, Sam didn't notice Philippe's absence until she felt his naked body remount her. His hand was guiding the head of his cock into her slippery slit. Although she was well satiated, Sam splayed herself, allowing him full access. Probing her by degrees, Philippe entered her, filling her crevice with his long, sleek cock. He buried his head into her neck and encircled her shoulders in his arms. Secured, she lay trapped in his embrace.

"*La Goulue* . . . this is love," he whispered into her ear. With deep unhurried strokes, he began to claim her as his own. Like its owner, his cock was athletic and lean, its length more than average. Sam could do nothing but enjoy her entrapment under his weight and passionate restraint. Each time, he drove a little deeper, quicker and harder, curving the head of his cock up to antagonize her G-spot. Every breath she took was sweet, every sensation, one of bliss. Even Philippe smelled of an exotic aftershave with subtle sweet overtones. Sam's mind wandered to images of the sugar-plum fairy dancing in the *Nutcracker* ballet, all controlled and delicate. A comparable performance to how her snatch contracted around its latest, and most welcome, partner. Shattering the sweet images from Sam's mind, Philippe drove the tempo harder and faster. Gripped in rising ecstasy, she equalled his rhythm, her body responding to Philippe's pace. Faster and fiercer he rode her until he released his grip, drove his hands deep into the mattress beside her shoulders and arched back. With his golden hair thrown from his face and eyes shut tight, he yowled in delight as he came deep within her. Small tremors shuddered through his body like the fluttering of hummingbird wings until at last he withdrew and rolled off her.

Scrunched under his arm, Sam snuggled in peace. Watching his chest heave, she traced his smooth body with her fingers. Smiling indulgently, he leaned down and kissed her forehead. "Now how about I walk you back to the hotel? You don't want to be late again tomorrow for rehearsals." Philippe tweaked her nose in a playful mood. Although not anxious to leave his embrace just yet, Sam considered his offer. She'd much prefer some post-coital cuddling and love-talk, but she didn't want to appear needy.

"Okay. I guess so, *mon ange.*" She reached up and kissed his cheek, her lips lingering on his silken skin. He rolled over on top of her and kissed her, slow and tender. Charmed, Sam didn't want to break the attraction, but time proved her enemy and Philippe's confederate.

"Then let us away, my love." He sprang out of bed and dressed in double time, giving Sam little chance to appreciate his magnificent young body. Once clothed, he dashed to the balcony doors where an impatient Jasper stood, waving his tail in displeasure.

"Sorry, Jasper, come in." Philippe opened and closed the doors in one deft movement. Jasper made a beeline to the bed where he scratched a tidy spot in the middle of the warm mattress, ready to sleep. Now dressed and ready to leave, Sam palmed his head with affection. "Bye, Japer, see you soon."

"Come, Samantha. We'll have to walk quickly to keep the cold out." He stretched out his hand into which she thrust hers with a squeeze. They strode out the door, and with a final glance back, Sam cast an envious look at Jasper, wishing it was her, curled up on Philippe's bed for the night. Maybe next time . . .

~ ♥ ~

Reefing his scarf tighter around his neck, Philippe huddled into his wool overcoat as he strode back to his flat at a less hurried pace. The pinching crispness in the air tweaked his nose but improved his thinking processes. For the first time, Philippe found himself considering the current woman in his life in more than a casual way. Although he was looking after Sam's interest in getting her home early, if he was honest with himself, he'd rushed her from his flat. Her lustful willingness in their sex play and the growing affection she unearthed in his heart, bewildered him. He felt he was losing part of his identity. An identity he'd lived with happily up until now.

Surrounded by doting women all his life, Philippe had discovered their gender's softness, gentility and irresistibility early. He could recall as a young boy, he sought out the touch and smell of full breasts and fleshy hips. His young hands slid accidentally across women's bodies, and since he appeared so young and innocent, the women ignored the touching, unaware of the sexual effect it had on him. As a maturing boy, he'd heard arguments between his mother and father through his bedroom wall, where Chantal accused his father of some uncontrollable addiction. Accusations of mistresses and sordid sex parties filled his head with licentious thoughts of the thrill of such things, and he'd tug his cock mercilessly in his young palm. Artistic by nature, he'd been born with a finely-tuned sensuality and heightened sex drive, which propelled him toward the fairer sex with what some would call an insatiable appetite. Aside from his art, sex was his favourite past time. And although he hated his father for the beatings he'd inflicted upon him, he was his son, and he'd inherited his father's darker desires.

Yet in Samantha, he wondered if he'd found a kindred spirit both artistically and sexually. She seemed to understand his passionate obsessions — for art and sex. In fact, her needs all but matched his. Added to this compatibility was a new emotion. Perhaps he was falling in love? Perhaps as his mother and aunt had long wished for, he was growing up? Whatever it was, Philippe's deepening attraction to Samantha had become his new habit, one he didn't want to give up.

CHAPTER TWELVE

BY THE TIME THE cast arrived for the technical and dress rehearsals on Monday, the entire backstage area, stage and dressing rooms were abuzz with anxious activity. Racks of couture costumes, sparkling sets, scrims, screens stretching tens of metres overhead and innumerable props filled every conceivable space. Dressers, wardrobe masters, backstage crew, stage managers, Penny and the dance captain all scurried around calling and shouting orders to the vast numbers of cast and crew on the cavernous stage. The entire area resembled controlled chaos, and Sam couldn't have been happier. She flattened herself against a corridor wall as a rack of costumes whizzed past her, expertly maneuvered by Elsie. Although not lit, a cigarette dangled from the dresser's lips, giving her comfort on this stressful day.

"*Bonjour*, Elsie," Sam called out and waved her hand high above the passing costume rack. Elsie propped. Her diminutive head, looking like it had just been dipped in a black ink pot, appeared through the hanging costumes. She kept perfect time with their violent swaying in an effort not to get hit and of course, she succeeded.

"With me. Now." Without pleasantries or cordiality, Elsie spat the order. Her bespectacled face retreated, and Sam trundled behind the rack as it whirled off once more.

Within the hour, every dancer had been allocated their spot at a bench in a dressing room. Here they unpacked their makeup and good-luck paraphernalia. For Samantha, she'd brought with her treasured pictures of her parents, her brother Jason and Scruffy as well as a picture of her mother and Aunty Michele taken when they were Moulin Rouge dancers, years before. Sam slipped the photos into the perimeter of her mirror where she could see them when applying her makeup before every show. Making sure no one was watching, she placed a small silver medallion with the Gemini zodiac symbol engraved on it, in her porcelain trinket box under her chignon pins and other hair accessories. A gift from her father on her seventeenth birthday, he'd given it to her before she left to go overseas and continue her dance studies. It was her good luck charm and she'd never danced without kissing it on opening night. The dancers settled in and when they flicked on their mirror Hollywood lights, the dressing room temperature began to steadily rise, and the air conditioners rattled in a lame effort to keep the room cool.

"*Bonjour,* Sam. Look we are sitting beside each other." A perfect picture in her designer rehearsal clothes and her face in basic stage makeup, Josette bent down and wrapped her arms around Sam's neck.

Jumping to her feet, Sam squeezed Josette in a much fiercer hug. "Oh, Josette, I'm so pleased you're sitting beside me. Really I am." The two girls teetered and chatted as Josette unpacked her bag and set up her dressing space. In no time, the dancers in their dressing room, which was only one of many, had their makeup laid out on clean towels, good luck trinkets in place and their costumes organized in performance order hanging in massive open closet compartments across the narrow aisles behind them. Dressers fussed about, consulting their checklists and assuring themselves and their designated dancers as to the whereabouts of every item of clothing, shoes, headgears and accessories. Now in rehearsal gear of flesh leotards, fishnets and high heels, the girls found any small space they could to limber up. Legs up walls, tugged overhead, split to the side and wrenched behind in grotesque shapes, every dancer primed herself for the big day.

"I love tech' runs and dress rehearsals," Sam said, sporting a big, fat smile.

"Me too, it is my favourite time. But is that all you love, Samantha?" Josette probed for more, obviously intrigued by Sam's continued privacy about her love life.

From a standing split, Sam released her giraffe-long leg and it momentarily hovered in mid-air beside her ear, before gliding down to earth. With both feet now on the ground, she leaned over to Josette. "Well, there is this guy I met . . ."

"Ah, ha. I knew it. You have found yourself a boyfriend and some good sex, *oui*?"

"Well the sex is more than good and whether he is to be my boyfriend, it's a bit too early to tell, but I am enjoying myself." Sam's face burst open in a vibrant smile, like a schoolgirl in the throes of first love.

Josette clapped her hands in childish glee. "*Bon. Bon.* This is good news. Who is he? Tell me more?"

"I might tell you more later, but for the moment, he's my little secret until I see where it leads. Okay?"

Josette shrugged and pouted, disappointed not to know all the story, but she still planted a kiss on each of Sam's cheek. "I am happy for you. When you are ready, I will meet him then."

Loud smacks of clapping hands broke the chatter. "Okay, everyone. Tony and the crew are ready for the tech' run. Downstairs with you." Performing her normal mother hen duties, Penny shooed the dancers from the dressing room. When Sam passed, Penny reached out and clasped her hand, pulling her aside. "You look much better, Sam." Genuine affection creased Penny's cheerful face.

"Thanks, Penny. I am. I took your advice and let a little love into my life."

"Well, it certainly seems to be working. Now go, dance your heart out and have a great day." Penny gave Sam's butt a sharp slap, and they both galloped down the stairs to the stage.

"*BONJOUR, BEDDI*," TONY WELCOMED the hundred-odd faces of cast and crew in front of him as they gathered like aimless cattle on the stage. "As you know, tech' runs are normally stop–start until we finalize the lighting plan and stage management. Dancers, take it easy. It's more a mark through for you. If you have to change your spots, Penny will let you know. Please remember your new spots because we won't be going through tech' again. Thank you, everyone. Now let's begin."

Sam noticed Tony seemed more relaxed today. No longer wearing his dance pants and rehearsal gear, he was dressed in rough blue jeans and white shirt with the cuffs rolled up. His ponytail barely stayed constrained by the elastic and his signature white converse sneakers shone with every step he took. As the choreographer and stage director, the truly arduous work for him was over and now he could concentrate on bringing the final components of his vision to life. He oozed ease and success while everyone did his bidding.

Scuttling off in all directions, everyone took their places. Once Tony, the lighting director and stage manager concluded the last of their discussion, Penny managed the rehearsal on stage. Tony moved to the back of the auditorium and with headsets in place and lighting plan in hand, he readied himself to liaise with the lighting director in the booth. Three long hours ticked past until the finale's last pose was lit to Tony's approval.

Everyone broke for an hour's lunch before an afternoon of dress rehearsals. While the rest of the dancers threw on clothes and coats to venture outside for coffee, cigarettes and perhaps some food, Sam returned to the dressing room alone. Here she found Elsie sitting on a low stool like a gnome in a garden, furiously finishing off some detail on a costume. Over her thick-rimmed glasses, Elsie peered up at Sam. Although the morning's unlit cigarette no longer dangled from Elsie's mouth, the sickly smell of it wafted around the dresser. Elsie's eyes darted to Sam's midriff, and she sniffed.

"Elsie, I think my bustier might fit today. Can we try it on before everyone comes back please?" Terrified of her dresser's disdain, Sam hoped Elsie would have pity and fit the costume on her now in private. The last thing she needed was more humiliation in front of the glamorous French girls. With a raised black-pencilled eyebrow, Elsie obliged and placed her sewing kit on the floor. Standing up, she grabbed the dazzling black and silver sequined bustier and flicked it open for Sam to slink into. Like a frightened worm, Sam wiggled out of her leotard, spread her arms wide and allowed Elsie to jerk the bustier around her body. Sam dug her fingers in tight at the waist, praying the zipper would now meet at her back. She felt Elsie jiggle the zip lock into place just above her butt and begin to pull. Costume zippers were legendary. For dancers, they acted as an insurance policy — heavy-duty engineering feats made to withstand enormous pressure. The trick was to get them zipped up and locked. Carefully, Elsie maneuvered the zip up Sam's lower back toward her waist and paused. Sam contracted her tummy, sucking all flesh in as much as possible while giving her waist an extra hard dig with her fingers. With only a little effort, Elsie man-handled the zipper until the resistance eased and *voila*, it continued its journey up to Sam's shoulder blades. Although still too snug, the bustier fitted and would hold. Both Sam and Elsie breathed a sigh of relief, and Sam knew that within a week of strict eating, the costume would again be less restrictive.

Once out of the bustier, Sam faced Elsie. "Thank you, Elsie." Elsie shrugged with usual French insouciance.

"No, I mean it. Thank you for not telling anyone. I promise not to put you through that again." Elsie's cheeks received an appreciative peck each from Sam. A brisk nod of her head and a glimmer of a smile demonstrated Elsie's understanding. Like an impatient elf, she shooed Sam out of the dressing room and resumed her last-minute sewing duties.

BACK AFTER LUNCH, THE magical transformation began. Like ducks in a row, the dancers sat in front of their Hollywood-light mirrors, their chatter as loud as the din of a farmyard. The first part of the enchantment was the disappearance of their hair. Pulled tight to their scalps, their hair was sprayed sleek and curled into low buns, which they speared mercilessly with chignon pins.

'You have plenty of pins, *oui*?" Josette spied Sam's stash of pins in her porcelain trinket box.

"Yes. I've got lots." Sam shoved another couple into her flattened black bun.

"*Bon.* I would hide them if I were you. There are some girls who don't have enough, and they will steal them if they see them." Josette nodded to Sam and then leaned forwards and glared at Bridgette, the dancer on Sam's other side. Sam raised her eyebrows to Josette with a quizzical stare, and Josette returned a silent shake of her head with a sharp look at the pins. Taking the hint, Sam put her surplus pins out of sight, while Bridgette sneered back across at Josette.

After the battle with the hair, the girls applied layers of makeup. Sweeping strokes of pancake base became the canvas for multiple tones of striking eye shadows and glowing blushers. Then with the precision of surgeons, they glued on luscious stage eyelashes and finished off their artwork with lashings of eyeliner and mascara. The final touch was the Moulin Rouge red lipstick outlining the perfection of each girl's mouth in a perfect bow. Only thirty minutes before, they were hard-working dancers. Now they were moving masterpieces of extraordinary beauty. In their opening costumes, they cantered from the dressing room down the old steep timber staircase. Fish-netted legs stepped out in uneven timing, and Sam thought they resembled an awkward giant centipede tumbling down to backstage.

"Here are your headdresses," Elsie said to her small handful of charges. "You put them on here with me and when you are ready you look in this mirror here," she pointed beside her on the wall, "and you call 'check.' I then will check you and then you can go onstage. *Oui?*"

"*Oui,*' Sam said the loudest, excited to be harnessed into her headdress. She jiggled it in place ensuring it was balanced, turned to the mirror, scrutinized her body and proudly said, "Check." Running over to stage left, she waited for the other girls in her group to join her. With luxurious orange, yellow and lime green feathers cascading down her back to her ankles and a flurry of feathers on top of the headdress which stretched nearly one metre above, Sam finally felt like a Dorris Dancer at the Moulin Rouge. Not only did she look magnificent, she felt it. Her career dream had come true and what's more, she'd found Philippe, someone to love and make her feel loved in return. Professionally and personally her life was as bright as her spectacular opening costume. An old tune Aunty Michele used to sing sprang to her lips, "Walking on Sunshine, whoa-oh . . ." and she certainly felt good.

Dress rehearsals started on time. To have the full orchestral soundtracks, lights and crew working with the dancers brought the production to its magical climax. No longer a show, it became an extravaganza worthy of the Moulin Rouge brand.

The first section of the *Partie Paradise* went without a hitch. Tony clapped and called his approval as they reset the stage for the next segment after the guest act. Normally the dancers would have a twenty-minute break while the act performed during a live show, but as today was a dress rehearsal, the acts weren't required, making the costume change faster than normal. Buzzing around, Elsie assisted her dancers in the wings, prodding, zipping and sewing anything loose, making sure none of them would be cited for a costume malfunction. When Sam turned to the mirror for her check, she felt someone tear a chignon pin from her bun.

"Ouch," she said, her hand slapping her head as she spun around.

Holding the orphaned pin, she'd just forcibly detached from Sam's bun in her elegant fingers, loomed Bridgette.

"Give that back." Sam stuck her hand out for her pin.

Instead of complying, Bridgette offered a cattish smile and stuck the pin into her own bun. She then spun on her three-inch heeled pump and flounced off. Shocked, Sam swung around to see if anyone had witnessed the attack but of course, Bridgette was too skilled at bitchiness to ever get caught.

Enraged, Sam stormed after her and grabbed Bridgette's arm, spinning her around. "Why did you do that for?"

Bridgette merely shrugged and pouted as if pretending nothing had happened. Cool, calm and collected, Bridgette epitomized the arrogance her mother had warned Sam many French dancers possessed. Knowing this wasn't going to end well in her favour, Sam released Bridgette's arm, shot her a contemptuous look and stalked back to her position in the wings.

Josette joined her seething friend. "She is a bitch that one." They both eye-balled Bridgette. "Because you hid your pins so she couldn't steal them, she pulled one from your hair." Bridgette glanced in their direction with a sarcastic smile and Josette flicked her the finger. "Bitch," she hissed, making sure Bridgette read the message, loud and clear.

"I've never had to work with girls like this before," Sam said, upset her favourite day had taken an unexpected and vicious turn.

"*Pfft*, do not let her worry you. It is really me she hates. She will leave you alone now I think." Josette rubbed Sam's shoulder helping her forget about the petty altercation.

By early evening, the day was finished. Costumes were either stored ready for tomorrow or being hurriedly mended by tired dressers, desperate to have a cigarette. The dancers rubbed off their stage makeup with such force their faces contorted in odd looks but eventually shone with clean, rosy skin. Freed at last, their hair was released from its entrapment and given a good upside-down shake to ease the scalp pain. The magic was over, and they once more returned to hard-working, underpaid dancers.

"Well done, everyone." Tony strolled into the dressing room with Penny beside him. "I'm very pleased with how you all worked today. You did a good job." Everyone clapped, not so much for themselves but to Tony's genius in bringing together such an illustrious production. "Tomorrow is opening night. I want you to be here early, to check your costumes with your dressers and make sure you warm up well. I don't want to hear of any injuries. Okay?"

"Yes, Tony," they chorused like good school children.

"Now, home to bed for all of you. Get plenty of rest. You can party tomorrow night after the show." With a satisfied smile and a quick nod, he departed the dressing room after Penny scribbled down his final notes on her clipboard.

"That's exactly what I'm going to do. Home to bed. I'm knackered." Sam was already on her feet, dance bag in tow.

Josette joined her, and they flicked off the lights around their mirrors. "Alone?"

"Definitely alone." With aching muscles and happy hearts, the two girls linked arms and wandered out of the dressing room.

CHAPTER THIRTEEN

SINCE TONIGHT WAS OPENING night, today was unlike any other day. Sam woke with a tummy full of butterflies, each bouncing off the walls of her insides trying to escape. It was a sensation that never quietened until she stepped out onto the stage at night. Little appetite also accompanied the day of opening night, but Sam forced herself to eat a solid lunch knowing it would be the first and last meal of the day she could keep down. Like a thoroughbred racehorse, her muscles twitched throughout the day, eager to explode and release their energy. Pacing, stretching and occasional finger gnawing filled in the hours of waiting. Relieved when mid-afternoon arrived, Sam hitched her dance bag to her shoulder and controlling her over-excitement, strolled at a leisurely pace to the Moulin Rouge.

With plenty of time to spare, Sam applied a fine line of glue to her upper eyelid and with tweezers in hand, fidgeted her false eyelashes in place and pressed. While she concentrated on the delicate manoeuvring of the lashes to her other eyelid, the dressing room echoed with giggling voices and chit-chat, as the dancers burned off excess tension before the performance. Within a few minutes, Sam's face was stage perfect, except for lipstick. She never applied it until just before warm-up. Tidying her space, she was confident and ready for opening night. Beside her, Josette applied her pancake in big wilful strokes, like a circus clown applying white face paint. Following her normal opening night routine, Sam slipped her hand into her porcelain trinket box, but it was empty. She picked it up and peered in. It wasn't her chignon pins missing. It was the zodiac medallion her father had given her.

"Josette. It's gone. My good luck charm." Sam stared at her friend, dread rising inside her

"*Non*, it must be there." Josette stopped in mid-stroke and turned to her friend, concerned.

"It's not. Someone's taken it." Sam's teeth clenched tight, barely containing her emotion.

"Look again." Josette peered over to see if the medallion lay hiding. Sam thrust her trinket box under Josette's nose to prove its emptiness.

"*Mai oui*, it is empty. This is not good." Suspicious, Josette leaned forwards to sneak a peek at Bridgette. She appeared unaware of Sam's dilemma or their conversation. "You must report this to Pierre, the stage manager. Go now."

Without hesitation, Sam got to her feet and glared down at Bridgette. Bending over, Sam whispered in her ear, "I'm going to tell Pierre about my stolen medallion. I'm going to say I think you did it. So, I suggest it be here when I get back with him or else." With her heart beating like a trapped bird in her chest, Sam turned and strode from the dressing room. Outside she steadied herself against the wall. Sam hated confrontation and she couldn't believe she'd just instigated one with Bridgette, the dancer in the cast no one ever crossed. Sprinting down the stairs, Sam continued her brisk pace over to the stage manager's corner. With each step, her anger and upset grew. When she threw back the heavy black wing curtains to cross the stage, she all but hit Tony in the face.

"Oh, Tony, I'm so sorry." She stretched out her hands toward him, deflecting the swirling curtain.

He dropped his hand from protecting his face. "Sam, what's the matter?"

"The good luck medallion my father gave me as a present has been stolen, and I think Bridgette did it." The emotion began to bubble over, and Sam realized she was more upset about the whole episode than she thought.

"Are you sure?"

"Of course I'm sure." Her sharp tone snapped at him, surprising both of them. She forced herself to calm down. "I always kissed my medallion for good luck on opening night. And now it's gone. You know how it is with superstitious pre-performance rituals?" With a lame grin, she sniffed back the threatening tears pricking her eyes. She couldn't possibly let herself cry, not in front of Tony and not in full stage makeup. God, she was such a putz.

She lowered her eyes and fidgeted with her fingers, trying to control her anxiety. It was then she noticed Tony wasn't wearing his converse sneakers. In their place, black patent leather shoes gleamed like those worn by Gene Kelly in the movie musicals. Also absent were his dance pants or jeans, replaced by sleek black, well-cut trousers. Edging her gaze up his body, she felt her skin tingle but did her best to ignore it. Tony's muscular frame, stood but a breath away, dressed in a midnight black designer dinner suit and white silk mandarin-collared shirt with diamanté neck stud. *Delicious* was the word that sprang to Sam's mind and her mouth salivated, craving to taste. Freshly washed and still slightly damp, his hair fell over his collar while unruly black curls flopped on his forehead. Doused in an expensive aftershave, his fragrance surrounded them in a vaporous cloud of exotic scent and his face, now free of stubble, appeared even more chiselled. Her mood changed from one of childish anxiety to a more adult version of sexual tension.

His dark eyes drilled hers. "I'm sure it will turn up, but still you must tell Pierre for his report."

"Yes, Tony." She could barely speak. Here they were secreted away in the wings of the Moulin Rouge on opening night, their nervous energy skyrocketing. Around them but unseen, they heard crew and dancers busy with pre-show preparations, yet here they stood seemingly invisible. As if magnetized to each other, the only movement was their chests rising and falling in the same tempo, in unison, together.

Trapping her in his gaze, he spoke in a whisper, his husky voice reminding her of the lilt of a waltz. "Since your medallion is gone . . ."

"Yes, Tony?"

"And I know how important superstitions can be, especially on opening night . . ."

"Yes, Tony?"

"You might like me to replace your medallion and kiss me for good luck instead?"

There was no breath left in her to answer. All energy sucked from her, leaving Sam hovering on the spot, drained and motionless. Taking her silence as affirmative submission, Tony cupped her cheeks and an indulgent smile graced his handsome, fragrant face. "Samantha, there is so much I can teach you if you will let me." His scent caressed her as he drew closer. With the lightest touch, he pressed his soft full lips to hers and their breath met. There was no frenzied intensity, no snaking of tongues, just a perfectly polite open-mouth kiss, tender, moist and moreish. Still clasping her face, he detached his mouth from the charming ritual. Sam's eyes fluttered open to find Tony's hot gaze fixed upon her.

"Good luck, Samantha. Be a star tonight," he said with a smile so seductive it was criminal.

"Thank you, Tony," she mumbled through tingling lips.

He released his hold on her and with his usual grace, turned and stalked away, once more the stage director and master of all he surveyed.

TONY HAD NO IDEA what possessed him to do such a thing. *For God's sake*, he was the stage director and he'd just given a chorus girl a kiss, a real kiss, in the wings on opening night. Something he'd never done in his directorial career of over fifteen years. He must be mad, and he wasn't even coked. He'd stopped doing lines a couple of days ago. Maybe that was the reason. When he stopped taking coke, his brain stopped working too. The compulsion to quieten Samantha's anxiety overtook his better judgment, as did a deep desire to take her in his arms. No time for self-chastisement now. His show was about to be laid bare to an audience of over a thousand highly critical theatregoers, critics, producers and investors. He brushed the imaginary lint from his jacket shoulders and prayed no prying eyes had seen their spontaneous liaison. Thank God Samantha wasn't wearing her stage lipstick, he thought as he dabbed her pancake from his lips. The last thing he needed was to expose his stupidity to the producers. Or to expose his heart — women you love, oftentimes break it.

It took a few moments for Sam to recover her senses. Tony Di Falco, the stage director and choreographer of the Moulin Rouge had just kissed her in the wings on the opening night of the *Partie Paradise* production. His scent still infused the air, his taste still lingered on her lips and his energy still seemed to prowl over every inch of her body looking for a way in. Why did he kiss her? *Why does he have such an effect on me?* Shell-shocked, she filed away the experience in her mind for later analysis. Now wasn't the time or place to fathom what just happened between them.

Marching over to the stage manager's corner she found Pierre and gave her account of the missing medallion. Troubled by an accusation of theft, Pierre accompanied Sam to the dressing room. Together they walked in, Pierre with a deliberate casual gait, and Sam with a determined stride. When she reached out to show Pierre her empty trinket box, she gasped. Sam lifted her eyes to see Bridgette with a sarcastic smirk on her face as Pierre said, "Is that the medallion you said was stolen, Sam?" He reached in and lifted it from the box.

Sam wrapped it in her fingers. "Yes, Pierre. It seems to have been returned. Thank you, Bridgette." Sam made no pretence as to who she thought was to blame.

Bridgette stuck her nose so far in the air, the other dancers who were watching, giggled. Pierre scrutinized Bridgette and rumbled something in French to her, then turned his polite attention back to Sam. "Maybe it would be a good idea to take anything of sentiment or value home, Sam. The dressing room is not the place for valuables." With a final accusatory stare and terse whisper at Bridgette, he left the dressing room.

Sam took her seat and met Bridgette's cold stare in the mirror. Uncomfortable at having to spend the next twelve months of the season sitting next to her under these hostile conditions, Sam nodded and mouthed a thank you to her. On the surface, Bridgette ignored Sam's olive branch, but couldn't hide the slight smile curving up the corners of her lips. This time, it looked genuine, so perhaps a truce had been made.

A stern voice called over the intercom, both in French and in English. "Thirty minutes beginners." This signalled they had only thirty minutes until the curtain went up. Time for last preparations. Before hiding it away, Sam kissed her medallion and patted more pancake over her lips. With the memory of Tony's good luck kiss stirring within her, she prepared to apply her lipstick. Suspending her hand holding the lipstick over her mouth, she gave her reflection a thoughtful smile. Dreams do come true, she mused. Disbelief stole a peek into Sam's thoughts, but she shook it away. Not tonight. Tonight she'd made it. Nothing could take this moment away from her. Wearing her showgirl smile, she pulled her lips taut and painted them in a splash of red. Now all that remained was to warm-up and dance her heart out.

THE ROAR OF APPLAUSE thundered through the auditorium as if breaking the sound barrier. Sam had never heard such enthusiasm from an audience as she posed on stage for the bows. After the nudes, soloists and principals took their bows, the specialty artists flounced down stage for theirs. Following them, Tony strode onto the stage, where he was heralded the newest sensation in Paris. With an armful of at least four dozen red roses, he nodded, smiled and bowed graciously while the audience cheered, clapped and stamped their feet in appreciation of his brilliance. Every performer on stage wore smiles so big their faces looked ready to split. Even the crew and dressers standing in the wings clapped furiously. God, Sam loved this. Nothing compared to a great production well-conceived, well-executed and the subsequent adoration of the audience. Her mind flashed to the French addiction to cigarettes, and she realized she was addicted to the magic of theatre.

Within the hour, the audience vacated the auditorium and the stage's transformation was complete. All the sets and proscenium curtain had been flown into the flies — the large air space above the stage — and tables strewn with supper, cake and champagne were set awaiting opening night celebrations. Speeches of appreciation for Tony were made by the Moulin Rouge management. Tony then thanked his team of designers, costumiers, builders, cast and crew. The bubbles flowed, disco music filled the auditorium, and everyone cut loose. Opening night parties signalled a beginning and an end. The end to all the hard work of rehearsals and uncertainty as to whether the production would be well received, and a beginning of a gruelling twelve, one hundred and five minute shows a week schedule, for the next year. Like a volcano on the verge of eruption, opening night parties promised the venting of some serious energy, both positive and negative.

Tony sidled up next to her as she stood sipping champagne by herself. "Samantha, you were spectacular."

"Thank you, Tony, but your show was spectacular. It's easy to dance your best when you have great choreography and a great director." She held her champagne up to his in a salute.

"So why aren't you off celebrating with everyone else?"

"I can't speak French. But anyway, I'm very happy standing here looking out into the auditorium. I've dreamed of being here since I was a little girl, and I still can't believe I danced opening night in your show. I guess I'm just a little awestruck still." Her eyes sparkled with delight as her gaze returned from the back row of the venue to settle onto the striking architecture of his face.

"Perhaps the good luck kiss worked for both of us?" He sipped more champagne and cast her an amused glance.

Mirroring his action, Sam tasted from her glass. "Perhaps?"

"Samantha, would you like to continue celebrating with me at my apartment tonight?" The delivery of his unexpected offer flowed like melted chocolate, sweet and tempting. The warmth of it drizzled over her body. Sam had little trouble imagining what a night it would be if she accepted. However, she resisted and reciprocated with only a beguiling smile.

"Tony, I don't think that's such a good idea." Although her body believed otherwise. "Tonight, I promised to meet up with some friends who came to see me perform." She glanced down at her watch. "And they'll be waiting for me now, in fact."

"Very well, Samantha. Another time then."

"Congratulations again, Tony. I love working in *Partie Paradise*." She reached over and kissed his cheek, which surprisingly still smelt as powerfully seductive as hours before.

"And to you too, Samantha. Enjoy the rest of your night." Stepping into her space, he brushed his body on hers, the force of his intention unmistakable. Turning as smooth as an Olympic skater on ice, he hailed the show's specialty artist who swam with her pet python and wandered over to join her.

MORE APPLAUSE GREETED SAM the moment she swanned into the foyer at Hotel Hollandaise.

"*Bravo, Bravo.*" Madame handed Sam a bright, straggly bunch picked from her garden while Philippe offered a professional bouquet of pink roses tied with an oversized pink ribbon.

"Samantha, you were wonderful. You were the best on stage." Dressed in a flowing vintage black sequined cocktail dress with matching shawl Madame Lucette reached up to embrace Sam kissing her on each cheek.

"Madame Lucette, you look marvellous. Like a devotee of the Rouge from last century."

"Please, my dear. I'm not that old." They laughed as Madame executed a pirouette and curtsy, proving her agility and youthfulness.

"Aunty Lucette is right, Sam. I think you were the best too and you stood out from the other chorus dancers." Philippe leaned in and kissed Sam's cheek.

"You two are biased, that's all I can say." Sam juggled the flowers while Philippe collected her dance bag. Madame

Lucette ushered them into the dining room where a bottle of champagne sat chilling in a crystal ice bucket. Here Philippe did the honours of opening the bubbly and filling their three glasses while Madame arranged the flowers into vases.

"A toast to the beautiful Samantha O'Brien from Australia. The newest star of the Moulin Rouge." Philippe held his glass high in the air. The sapphire glints in his eyes sparkled all but outmatching the effervescence of the champagne bubbles.

"Yes. To Samantha. Long may she live here and love Paris." Madame Lucette lifted her glass to join her nephew's.

"Thank you both. To my dream come true — dancing at the Moulin Rouge." They all took a hefty sip of champagne.

"And to love," Madame Lucette said, a broad grin creasing her face.

"And to love," Philippe added, with a wink to Sam.

"And to love," Sam said, with only the slightest hesitation.

~ ♥ ~

Surprising herself, Sam declined Philippe's offer to stay and party with her privately in her room. Even his wicked promises couldn't sway her. Wild sex wasn't what she wanted tonight. She needed time alone to digest the fabulous new experiences and sensations in her life. Wrapped in a blanket with a cup of steaming coffee clasped in her hands, she leaned on the balcony railing of her bed-sit and waved to a reluctant Philippe as he departed, blowing kisses up to her. Feeling like a love-struck Juliet, she returned his affection and wondered if perhaps a good romp in bed mightn't have been a better option.

After he bid a final farewell, her attention turned to the moonlight dancing on the linden trees. Tonight was a full moon. Exactly one month ago, on a full moon, she'd arrived in Paris. Reflecting how much her life had changed in such a short time, Sam granted herself a satisfied smile. Though the cold night air nipped at her hands and wriggled in under the blanket, Sam remained leaning on her balcony, admiring the moon, her thoughts keeping her warm.

She'd made her dream come true. Here she was dancing in a Tony Di Falco production at the Moulin Rouge. She was injury-free and committed to becoming a nude in the show as soon as possible. She lived in a comfortable little hotel with a sweet, although slightly eccentric landlady, whom she liked. She'd found a good friend in Josette and enjoyed working with her, even if some of the other girls were bitchy. Also, she'd taken Penny's advice and let a little love into her life with Philippe. In all, everything seemed to be going along smoothly. The only hiccup was Tony. Between them, an undeniable attraction pulsed. Sam was uncertain whether he just wanted to notch her up as one of sexual conquests or not. He was her boss, and Sam couldn't venture down any path with Tony, regardless of how tempting his offer was and no matter how much she wanted. If only he wasn't so damned gorgeous, talented and persistent, he'd be much easier to ignore. Sam sighed and looked at the moon. Full moons were for lovers and here she was alone having sent her lover away. Perhaps it was time for her to let more than a little love into her life? Maybe it was time to take a leap into the sea of love. Go with the flow like the tarot cards suggested and ride the relationship with Philippe to its unknown destination. She was here in Paris for at least another year or longer if she signed a contract extension or became a nude.

Maybe she wouldn't have to choose like her mother had done? Perhaps Sam could have both — her beloved career and a loving, committed relationship. She also figured, allowing herself to fall in love with Philippe would lessen her attraction to Tony. After all, love is the key to life. Being in love with Philippe might fasten the lock on her fantasies about Tony. It was worth a try.

CHAPTER FOURTEEN

As Sam pulled back her heavy curtains to let the sunlight brighten her room, her phone buzzed with a call from her mother in Australia. After ten non-stop minutes of excited interrogation about the previous night's performance SallyAnn said, "Oh, darling, I'm so pleased everything went well for the opening. I'm sorry we couldn't be there, but Aunty Michele and I will come over soon."

"It's okay, Mum, really it is. There's plenty of time for you to come over. I'll be here for another eleven months at least." In some ways, Sam was pleased they weren't there last night as it would have only added to her nerves. Later in the year, once she settled in, was better timing for them to see the show.

"Is everything else okay?"

"Yes, Mum. Everything's fine. I'm really enjoying it here and now the show's up and running, I'm going to get out and see more of Paris, I think."

"Good idea. Pity it's going to be so cold soon. But Paris is still beautiful in winter. I'll call you in a few days. Love you."

"Love you too, Mum. Give everyone a kiss from me and hug Scruffy as well. Talk soon."

After Sam ended the call, she strolled over to her little fireplace mantle and sniffed the flowers given to her last night by Philippe and Madame Lucette. She lifted one of the pink roses from its vase and holding it to her chest, leaned on the wall surveying her tiny room. With the radiator toiling away, the sunlight streaming in through the French doors and her bed a ramshackle pile of mismatched quilts, pillows and blankets, Sam revelled in the peace welling up within her. This was her home now. No longer a dream, her new life had begun.

~ ♥ ~

Bouncing down the stairs to breakfast, Sam called a cheery "hello" to the other tenants before they set off on their way to work or Montmartre excursions. She slipped into a table nearest the radiator, content with her view of the courtyard garden. Now devoid of all flowers, the garden readied itself for winter. Although the clouds had begun to cluster overhead and play tag with the sun, Sam's mood still shone.

"*Bonjour*, Samantha." Madame Lucette approached Sam's table. "You are very happy this morning. This is good to see." Nodding her head in agreement with her own observation, the landlady shot Sam a motherly smile.

"Yes, Madame. I am very happy this morning. I'm going to celebrate and have two boiled eggs but no toast and a big pot of English breakfast tea please."

Madame Lucette whooshed into the kitchen and returned soon after with Sam's order. While Sam ate, they chatted about last night's show and shared the tea. When the conversation turned to more mundane things like the weather, Madame Lucette dug around in her apron pocket.

"Time for a *Gitane*, Madame?" Sam had taken to teasing her landlady about her nicotine addiction on a regular basis.

"*Non, chère fille,*" she said. "Time for the cards." Madame Lucette placed her tarot cards on the table, her scrawny hand resting sagely on top of the deck.

Sam laughed. "Madame Lucette. You and your cards. Really? Where did you learn to read the tarot cards in the first place?"

"Ah, all my family comes from the Romani gypsies. Chantelle's, and my father was brother to the famous flamenco dancer, Carmen Amaya. She was magnificent — full of fire and mystery. Our Aunt Carmen also had the gift of sight. When I was a young woman, I went to Spain, and I found I had the gift too." Madame's eyes sparkled with fervour and pride. "And since then, I read the cards, and they are rarely wrong. Samantha, I am sure they have been right for you to now. *Oui?*" She eyed Sam as if she knew what had transpired in her tenant's life over the past weeks.

"I'm not going to say, but I will let you do a reading for me." Sam reached out and claimed the deck from Madame Lucette. No longer fearful of the message of the cards, Sam shuffled them, mulling over the question she wanted to ask. *Show me what my future holds. Show me what my future holds. Show me what my future holds.*

Sam cut the deck and upturned a card, placing it on the table. On it, a beautiful young woman, dressed in a white sari levitated on top of a pond full of white lotus flowers. Behind her, a swan nestled and across her body was poised a lute she was playing. "Oh, Madame Lucette, what a lovely card."

"Yes, Samantha, this is the goddess of knowledge, beauty and grace. She is the inspiration behind the arts, reminding us the most sublime music, dance and art are drawn from the well-spring of human experience. She is worshipped through evening prayers, and sweet words of wisdom pour from her like a flowing river." Madame Lucette's apple-shaped cheeks lifted so high with obvious glee, the skin around her soft grey eyes crinkled tightly. She reached out her hand and tapped Samantha's. "*Mon cher*, this is a wonderful omen." Sam slid the card closer to her. Picking it up she studied the image and although she'd not believed in the fortune the cards foretold before, she liked this one.

"Madame, would you photocopy this card for me?"

"Of course, *chère fille*, I'll do it now." She left Sam alone with her thoughts and returned only a few minutes after with a neatly cut copy of the tarot card. "There you are, Samantha. Whenever you look at his card, you will think of the crazy, old landlady you stayed with in Paris."

Sam slipped the card into her wallet, stood up and kissed her landlady's soft, powdered cheeks. "Merci, Madame, I don't think you're crazy at all. I think you're very sweet and kind. Now, I'm off to see Philippe for a few hours. I'll see you later." Sam shrugged her coat on and wrapped her scarf high around her neck. As she walked through the foyer, she noticed the clouds turning ominous. Grabbing the last umbrella from the hotel's stand, Sam marched out into the promise of a miserable, wet day.

~ ♥ ~

"SAMANTHA, COME JOIN ME where it is warm." Philippe held open the door to his flat and pulled Sam in from the cold. When he placed her wet umbrella in the sink, Sam noticed he was clothed only in a loose-fitting, slate grey wool sweater and colour-coordinated cotton stretch trunks. She also noticed his underwear did little to conceal his promising bulge and everything to enhance his flinching tight arse as he led her to the bed. She figured he must have been having a nice morning with Mrs Palmer — his own hand — before she arrived. The slang term made her grin with the memory of Aunty Michele's sort-of-brother, Uncle Mark, who used the term a lot.

He slid into bed, squeezing himself up next to the wall and patted the space beside him. "Hop in. It's nice and warm under the covers."

Disappointed he hadn't kissed or hugged her hello, Sam slipped off her coat and scarf with little enthusiasm.

"What's wrong?" Philippe asked, dropping the bed covers to stop the warmth from escaping.

"Is this all we're ever going to do, Philippe? Have sex?"

"No, Samantha. I don't have sex with you. I make love with you, and I want to make love with you today, to show you how wonderfully you performed last night in the show." With his hair flopping over his forehead, his white angelic smile and the contrast of his golden glow against the masculine grey of his clothes, he looked irresistible.

Making him wait, Sam wandered around the flat, lingering now and then to admire his art. "Where's Jasper?"

"He's asleep in his bed over near the radiator." Philippe pointed to the corner under the sink where Jasper, curled in a padded basket, opened his bleary eyes at the mention of his name. Bending down, Sam gave her furry friend a pat. Satisfied, he then settled himself back into a ball to fall asleep once more.

"Samantha. Get into bed." It seemed Philippe had wasted enough of his time and the command in his voice sparked an immediate response between Sam's legs. She moved over beside the bed and began to undress. With a minxy smile, she removed her boots, socks, jeans and jumper.

"Wait," he said. Ready to unbutton her white silk blouse, Sam's fingers paused.

"Leave your blouse on. Take your panties off." Intrigued by his game, Sam obeyed. "Now dance for me."

"Like this?" Sam glanced down at her half-nakedness. Her flimsy blouse barely covered her nude private parts. Although on stage, it appeared to audiences as if dancers had little on, in fact, a dancer was fully clothed in G-strings, tights and costumes. What's more, being on the stage under bright lights, performing in the magical fantasy of the theatre, a dancer was removed from the audience. Even doing topless work, a nude or soloist never felt exposed. Here in his cramped flat with the morning light flooding in, Philippe's up-close-and-personal request proved challenging for her.

"Please dance for me. Something slow and graceful, like a ballerina." His eyes travelled from her trim ankles up her long, lean legs to rest on her crotch, her waxed mons just hidden underneath the gossamer film of the silk. Though her insecurity considered Philippe's salacious request unseemly, Sam's body responded with an immediate clitoral thrum.

"But what about music? I need music," she said, stalling for time.

Philippe reached over to his phone on the nightstand and flicked through his playlists. For Sam, it was a split-second decision. Was she going to say no to the very person, only the night before, she committed herself to fall in love with? Or was she going to step out of her comfort zone and let herself go a little? Live a little? After all, isn't that what you're supposed to do when you're young? She remembered when she was just a girl and Aunty Michele twirled her around in the kitchen singing along to Cyndi Lauper's "Girls Just Want to Have Fun." Even then she told Sam that's what she needed more of . . . fun. Well here was her moment.

"What about this?" Philippe hit play and beamed at her. "Please . . .?"

Although Sam remained unsure, it was the enchanting and familiar sounds of the clarinets, bassoons, oboe and harps that sealed her decision. The music of Tchaikovsky breathed life into her soul, his melody seducing her body to freedom. Then as the harpist built the tension up and down on her heavenly instrument of the gods, Sam drifted into an indescribable rapture only dancers understand, and she sacrificed herself to the music. The hiatus lingered and her eyelids fluttered closed. With her breath held, she waited, waited and then catching the rhythm, Sam stepped off on her right foot as the French horns heralded the haunting melody of "Waltz of the Flowers." Gripping the old floorboards with her dancer's feet and cat-like balance, Sam padded out the three-four time in front of Philippe's bed. Philippe tucked a pillow hastily behind his back against the wall and got comfortable. Scrunching the covers under his chin, he looked the perfect audience — enraptured, engrossed and enamoured. It was all Sam needed.

As the string section claimed the melody with triumph, Sam took flight. Her steps lengthened, her body pirouetted, and her arms flew into the air, abandoning any lingering concerns about her semi-nudity and the assaulting chill between her legs. She was free. She was alive. The rich smell of baking bread wafted up from the ovens downstairs heightening another sense in her performance. With arched feet and explosive muscles, she transformed into the ballerina she had trained to be. Floating like a cloud, she soared around the small flat, dancing intricate steps in time with the music. Folding forwards and backwards around Philippe's table, she hovered in mid-air before curving her supple spine until her head almost touched her buttocks. Sam was lost to the magic of Tchaikovsky and Philippe seemed lost to the magic of her. Then on the second chorus, she lifted first one leg and then another, extending each overhead in elegant développés with feet pointed to the heavens. Philippe sat mesmerized as she exposed not only her body but her soul, just for him. On and on her solo continued interwoven with the oboes and flutes. Pat de chats, arabesques, glissades, step after step, Sam executed with complete control and yet with complete abandon. Twirling to and from the bed, reaching to Philippe then pulling away, she resembled a nymph in the forest, untamed and delicate. Her black hair whirled around her face while her blouse seemed to transform to sprite's wings. With crescendo building, she gathered speed without faltering in the tiny space. With nowhere to go, she leapt high on the spot scissoring from one side to the other, until, having used every inch of the space, she spun, arms outstretched for a grand landing on the bed.

Philippe sprang to his feet applauding loudly. "*Magnifique. Magnifique.*" He dropped to his knees beside her and peppered kisses all over her face.

Big heaving breaths escaped Sam's chest as a satisfied smile spread across her face. She licked her lips, eager for a drink. Registering the need, Philippe bounced from the bed and returned with a glass of water. 'Samantha O'Brien. You are indeed a star." He handed her the glass and she sipped slowly. Her lids fluttered at him and her awareness of her nakedness returned, as did the ache between her legs.

When she regained control of her breathing she said, "So, Philippe, perhaps it's time to show me how much you enjoyed my performance both last night and now." Sam was surprised at how brazen her remark sounded, but she didn't care.

His lips were upon her throat before she took her next breath. "Of course, *La Goulue.* I have a little surprise for you, though. Why don't you undress, and I will return." Philippe left the bed like a thief in the night. Now hungry for the promised love-making session, Sam unbuttoned her blouse and slipped out of her bra in double time. Just as she was about to jump under the covers, Philippe leapt on the bed and stood over her straddling her naked body.

"Lie down," he said. She did but her body was beginning to chill. She needed warmth for her muscles. Just as she began to shiver, Philippe raised his hand high in front of him and from it drifted a flurry of white powder. It sprinkled all over her like tiny snowflakes.

"Philippe, what are you doing?" She coughed a little as some caught in her throat.

"You are my star. You are more beautiful than Tchaikovsky's sugar plum fairy, so I am covering you in sugar dust." In his voice humour and passion partnered while in his hand he held a flour sifter. With each punch of the handle, he released another dusting of baking sugar over Sam's body until she resembled a human pastry dusted in sugar. Once satisfied with the result, Philippe jumped from the bed, throwing the sifter to the floor.

"Now I will eat you." He stood straight and tall, legs splayed, hands on hips, his shorts trying to contain his manhood.

"Philippe. You look like Peter Pan." Sam giggled with girlish innocence, causing the powder to tremble on her body like water on a beating drum.

"Is that so?" Philippe did his best impersonation of J. M. Barrie's boy hero as he tore off his sweater. Spinning it three times above his head, he flung it to the far corner of the room where it obviously surprised Jasper who meowed in disgust.

Dropping the act, Philippe skulked over to her. The mood changed to one of intense sexual tension as he growled his pledge. "Now I will eat you."

Sam's nipples hardened at the promise, catching Philippe's attention. He leaned down and licked the sugar in lazy strokes from the plump fullness of her breast to circle the areola and tease her nipple. Repeating this pattern, he laved her breast on all sides until it was clean yet sweetly sticky. Then with deliberate circles, he ran his tongue over the tip of her nipple before devouring it, sucking it and engulfing as much of her breast as he could in his mouth. Sam moaned. "God, Philippe. Thank goodness I've only got two breasts."

"Maybe so. But I will make you wish you had more." He trailed his tongue over her other breast and fulfilled his promise.

"Now let me see what I can do with the rest of this sweetness?" Philippe's voice didn't belong to such a refined, young man but to someone darker and more twisted. Sam opened one eye to check it was still Philippe preparing to feast on her body and that he hadn't metamorphosed into some wicked hobgoblin. Assured her angel partnered in this lustful coupling, she relaxed and waited. He opened her legs and knelt between them, scraping the powder from her torso toward her mound, most of which sprinkled down into her cleft and onto the sheets. Sugar dust filled the room in a delicate cloud of sweet scent and her wetness felt like a syrupy delight. Without a word, she stretched back, and Philippe lowered his face. Dipping his tongue on her clit, he irritated it enough to cause Sam to groan in pleasure.

"*Mmm*, Sam. You taste so sweet." He wiggled his tongue into the folds of her cleft, licking her plump flesh. As she pushed her snatch into his face, he equalled her desire. Lapping harder he drove his tongue into her, seeking out any last hint of sweetness, both hers and the sugar. He relished her like a sunbird sucks nectar from a flower. Over and over he tongued her cleft and clit, this way and that, pausing only to lick more sugar off her body to deposit into her private place. Her blossoming snatch opened for fulfilment, but he ignored its plea. Instead, he straddled Sam's chest, his balls and cock drifting in the remaining sugar dust at the hollow of her throat.

"Suck me." The icy command in his blue eyes left no room for refusal as he repositioned his manhood higher up over her face. Sam licked the sugar from her lips, opened her mouth and his powder-coated cock was there, eager for attention. With her tongue loitering on its smooth orb, rolling around its cap and tickling its opening, Sam took firm control of the sex play. Careful to find the right angle, she accommodated more of his length as the taste of sugar and pre-ejaculate mingled in her mouth. Philippe's neatly shaved shaft base and balls, played on her chin, heightening her own arousal. With a steady rhythm, she made love to his cock, kissing, sucking and swallowing as much as she could. When she felt him strain wanting to plunge her hard, she tried to oblige his wish but gagged. Anxious for release, Philippe pulled himself free and thrust his impatience deep between her legs. The force drove the breath from her. As he hammered them both to a climax, Sam matched his fervour, wrapping her legs around him, spurring him on.

With their bodies and hair tacky from perspiration and baking sugar, they laid together as if glued with carnal viscosity. Enjoying their afterglow, Sam cuddled onto Philippe's chest, delicately picking sugar powder from his fine chest hairs. He cradled her in his arms, stroking her raven hair, likewise matted with their love-dust. Laughter and animated voices from the bakery below drifted up through the floorboards and for the first time, Sam realized how entertaining their lovemaking must be to the bakers downstairs. Philippe seemed totally oblivious to the downstairs impersonations of their recent rutting.

"Now that it's coming into winter, I'll be in my friend's studio preparing for my exhibition," Philippe said, speaking to the ceiling. "I'd like you to come and model for me, Samantha." He looked downward at her upturned face.

"Of course, Philippe. When will we start?" She hooked her leg over his and squeezed.

"We'll start over the next month. I have some preliminary sketches to do first. Then you can come and sit for me." He kissed her forehead, his lips gentle, sticky and warm.

"Will I see you this Sunday, *mon ange*?"

"No not this Sunday. I'm sorry. I must prepare in the studio," he said in apology.

"Oh." She winced at the disappointment in her voice. She sounded like a spoilt child whose toy was about to be confiscated. Now that she'd given herself fully to Philippe, she wanted to spend more time together as a couple.

"Don't be angry with me. Like you, I am an artist and I must prepare. Like you, I must rehearse. You understand, *oui*?"

What could she do? Metaphorically stamping her foot in demand of his time was immature, particularly since he made such a valid point. Philippe possessed the same drive for success in the expression of his art as she did. Similarly, he needed time to create and practice, alone. She snuggled into him and in a soft, breathy voice said, "Of course I do, *mon ange*. I will see you the following Sunday. But in the meantime," — Sam ground her snatch into his thigh — "since we won't be seeing each other this Sunday—"

Needing no further encouragement, Philippe's mouth possessed her, bruising her lips. Eager to perform in another encore, his cock swelled pushing against the weight of her leg slung over his groin. Sam reached down and stroked its silky shaft as her hips continued grinding against his body. Lifting herself up onto her knees, she straddled Philippe, his cock in her hand, its slippery head rubbing on her open snatch. The more she rubbed, the more juices seeped from her, christening his cock with her divine liquid. She tormented him, rubbing him unhurriedly but forcefully on her folds, around and around, but not allowing him entry. Then she slithered his head in and out until she could stand it no longer. With the slowest tempo, she guided him into her. With his ramrod cock at attention inside her, she clasped her pelvic floor muscles around it and squeezed.

"Fuck, what are you doing?"

"Dancers have strong muscles in lots of places, Philippe. Let's see if I can milk you upright?" Philippe laid back enthralled by the sensation of his cock being massaged by Sam's internal muscles. Like being well-sucked, his cock throbbed from the continual pulsing she applied up and down its length. Lost to the sensation, his body wanted to penetrate her deeper, to take control. Teasing him further but not wanting to break her ride, Sam finally allowed Philippe to join her quickening rhythm. Hands chased over each other's body, touching and tweaking hidden places while mouths nipped and licked at anything on offer. Then on crescendo together, his hands clamped hard on her hips and she dug her nails into his shoulders. Pummelling her down on his angry cock, he bucked beneath her and she milked him into mind-shattering orgasm and to the cheers of the bakers below.

CHAPTER FIFTEEN

WHILE **S**AM LIMBERED UP in the wings before the first show on Saturday night, she sensed his presence. Instead of turning around, she continued stretching her leg on the banister, her face to foot. "*Bonsoir*, Tony."

He bent around her elevated leg, turning his face to meet hers while her pointed toes added a third party to the conversation. With similar cheeky grins and twinkling eyes, Sam and Tony both appreciated the situation's silliness. When limbering up, a dancer never stops to chat. You just keep stretching. Still twisted to meet her face he said, "*Bonsoir*, Samantha. Can I have a word with you please?" The authority in his voice broke the prankish interaction, making Sam recoil her leg off the railing quick smart.

"Of course, Tony. What have I done?"

"Relax, Samantha. You haven't done anything wrong. Your dancing has been superb. I'm very pleased." Once more his engaging smile beamed, and she swooned just a little. "Samantha, remember when we went to dinner and you asked when my birthday was?" She nodded, casting her mind back. As she remembered her initial discomfort that night, which turned into a naughty desire to rub against his leg under the table, her finger drifted upward to her mouth to be nibbled. Tony stretched out his hand and clasped it around Sam's, stopping the habit, but not her anxiety.

"Yes," she said, unsure of where the conversation was heading.

"Well, my birthday is tomorrow. Sunday the first of November."

"That's right. It is too," she said, glad he'd reminded her. "Happy birthday for tomorrow, Tony.

"That's not why I mentioned it. Samantha, I'd like you to join me tomorrow evening to celebrate my birthday. I'm just going to invite Penny and Jacques, I think. I love to cook so it'll be my favourite Sicilian dishes on the menu. Will you join me?"

Shocked that Tony would even consider asking her, Sam wanted to jump up and down like a lottery winner, but her professionalism restrained the glee. "But what will people think, Tony? I'm not sure if that's a good idea." Sam visualized the bitchy, horrid remarks and stares from the other dancers if they knew she'd been invited to Tony's apartment. Still having another eleven months left on her contract and enduring that hideous persecution would be too much to bear.

"Samantha." Tony took both her hands in his firm grip. She glanced around to see if anyone else was watching and realized he'd picked his moment perfectly again. The man was a brilliant director with impeccable timing and delivery. "I doubt very much that anyone will find out. Penny and Jacques won't say anything, and neither will anyone else if I choose to invite them. It'll be fine. Please join me." His sincerity was hard to refuse.

"But you know I don't eat much."

"Samantha . . ." An edge of impatience crept into his voice.

"Okay. I'll come and celebrate your birthday."

"Good. I'll give you all the details tonight before you leave." A panic spread across her face. "It's all right. I'll make sure no one sees." With a squeeze to her hands, he turned and disappeared into the inky blackness of backstage.

Dusk settled with biting winds and grey skies, as Sam alighted from her taxi at the Black Cat Hotel on the Boulevard de Clichy. Although she could have walked the thirty or so minutes to Tony's apartment building, she instead decided to splurge on a cab. She hurried under the historic building's red awning where she collected herself and finger-combed her hair. Madame Lucette would have something superstitious to say about a building called the black cat. Sam couldn't remember whether it was good or bad luck if a black cat crossed your path. Tonight she hoped it was good luck because she certainly didn't need anything bad to happen with Tony.

Like so many doorways in the old red-light district of Paris, the private entrance to the seven floors of apartments was barely visible, concealed from curious eyes. She pushed into the little foyer, leaving the world of Montmartre and its fierce weather behind her. She buzzed 701 and a click of a latch signalled she'd been permitted entry into the inner sanctum of the hotel. Painted in art deco black and red designs, the elevator foyer looked like a theatre set from a 1920s cabaret. The only thing missing was Liza Minelli singing the title song with a chorus of decadent, debauched dancers cascading down the stairs. Even the smell of decades-old cigarette smoke lingered through the layers of fresh paint. Ah, the French's addiction to nicotine.

Into the elevator cage, she stepped and slid the rattling door across behind her. She understood how a canary must feel when caged and taken down the mines as an early warning of gas leakages for the miners. Trapped in the ancient elevator, she prayed her early detection system with Tony wouldn't let her down. As the cage trundled its way to the top floor, the narrow stairs spiralled around the elevator well, showing her the route she'd have to take if she needed to make a hasty escape from tonight's party. Once on the seventh floor, she dragged back the heavy cage door and turned right down the narrow, dimly lit hallway. The quaint wall-sconces emanated a soft amber glow, and she half expected to see Hercule Poirot standing at the end of the hall with his homburg hat royally dipped. Before knocking at apartment 701, she readied herself. She'd made a promise not to encourage any of Tony's advances and to most definitely not be left alone with him. Although she'd made a commitment to Philippe, she still found it difficult to not be affected by Tony's dynamic personality and authority. As an added safeguard against doing something she might regret, she planned to leave the celebration with Penny and Jacques.

When she raised her hand to knock, the black glossy door opened. It was only then she noticed the peephole and realized Tony must have seen her standing there. To think she hadn't even walked into his apartment and was already suffering untold embarrassment. *Mon dieu!*

With his well-built body back-lit by the smouldering lamp glow coming from within his apartment, Tony's silhouette towered in the doorway, dark, mysterious and imposing.

"Samantha. Come in. Let me take your coat." He stepped back, allowing her entry. She dropped her tote bag, and he helped shrug off her coat. The rich scent of musk wafted from him as his breath skimmed across her hair. Was that an imperceptible pause over her hair so he could inhale? Sam didn't have time to think further on the thought due to the all too familiar tingling when his hands brushed past. She chided herself for being so easily distracted. She turned to face him, and they each gave a small gasp. Both had chosen black turtleneck wool sweaters and black jeans, creating a mirror image of the other. Aside from the obvious difference in gender, Tony wore his usual white converse sneakers and Sam wore a pair of jet drop earrings. Apart from these slight differences, they were dressed like twins. The irony of the situation was not lost on either of them.

With unconcealed amusement in his voice, Tony said, "Samantha, you look ravishing. How did you know tonight's dress code was black?"

"Just lucky, I guess." She fluttered her eyes, performed a curtsy and extended her hand to her escort.

"Allow me." Tony bent to kiss her hand, but instead he upturned it, kissing her palm with more affection than needed for their satirical role-play.

Reclaiming her hand, Sam met Tony's inscrutable expression with a meek, silent smile.

"Come inside, Samantha. You're the first to arrive."

Of course I am, she thought, uneasy that the night hadn't even started, and they were alone.

Tony's apartment epitomized designer chic. With vivid white walls providing the backdrop for elegant and obviously expensive furniture, the apartment suited its sophisticated tenant. Atop a faux black and white cowhide rug and taking pride of place in the living area, rested an enormous red leather lounge winged by two smaller tub chairs. Nearby hovered a modern black glass and aluminium eight-person dining suite. Low slimline, hi-gloss black cabinets cloaking a hidden sound system meant the room was uncluttered and felt much larger than it was. Everywhere were strewn tea-light candles as if a fairy had flown in depositing them wherever her gossamer wings touched. On the walls hung oversized art pieces in a black, red, grey and white palette to complement the art deco theme of the apartment. It was all so strategically placed, much like Tony was in his designer jeans.

"Tony, this is lovely." Sam tried hard not to appear awestruck.

"Thank you, Samantha. It's where I always stay when I live in Paris. I like this apartment best of all the rooms here. Now would you like some wine?"

"Yes, please. Just a white wine would be wonderful. Thank you." Sam's gaze remained on the tasteful nuances in the apartment as the dulcet tones of Tony Bennett crooned from the speakers. This was the life she dreamed of — doing what she loved, making money out of performing and living the good life. Maybe when she reached thirty-nine like Tony, she too could have all this. Realizing she was here to celebrate his birthday she dashed back to her bag and fumbled out the present, then went in search of her host. Walking toward a wall painted in a sprawling modernist abstract, Sam discovered Tony behind it in a hidden galley kitchen. On the hotplate, pots and pans bubbled away giving off the most appetizing aroma.

"That smells amazing," she said. Across the countertop lay herbs, vegetables, meat and bread all tossed with abandon as if artistically laid for a photoshoot. "Sorry, Tony. Happy birthday. Here." From behind her back, she gave him a small gaily wrapped gift and card which he exchanged for a glass of wine.

"Samantha, you shouldn't have bought me anything," he said, but his delighted smile proved otherwise.

"It's just a silly little thing, but when I saw it, I thought of you."

He tore open the bright paper and his hand curled around something soft and furry. Lifting it from its hiding, Tony chuckled. In his hand lolled a children's small stuffed toy — a black bear wearing a red bow tie and a pair of white shoes.

"I know I'm cheeky but it's you — Ursu, the bear."

Tony threw his head back and laughed a warm, rich, happy chortle. With the bear in one hand and his glass of red in the other, he said, "Thank you, Samantha. I'll treasure it always and when I look at it, I'll think of you." He clinked his glass to hers, and they both sipped.

"Don't forget the card." She pointed to the yellow envelope on the counter.

He removed the card embossed with a bunch of balloons on its cover and read aloud, "To, Tony, the best director in the world. I hope you have a fabulous thirty-ninth birthday and I hope I can work with you again in the future. Love Sam." As he folded the card and placed it back in the envelope, Sam lowered her eyes. His reading of the card made it sound more than the admiration of a dancer to her director. She shouldn't have included the 'Love Sam' bit. Just Sam would've been enough. Too late now. She felt his touch under her chin, and as he raised her face, their eyes locked.

"Thank you, Samantha, for the gift and the card. I have no doubt we will work together again. And thank you for accepting my offer to celebrate my birthday with me." The insistence of his hand under her chin never faltered. Even with the kitchen blazing in fluorescent light and the hiss of cooking turmoil in the background, Sam remained transfixed. Leaning into her, he pressed a soft kiss to her lips. He was doing it to her again, making her surrender. Eyelids heavy with submission, Sam granted this one indiscretion, reasoning it was a birthday kiss. Though for her it resonated with much more than a simple light-hearted celebratory kiss and from the amorous look in Tony's eyes as he pulled away, she supposed the same was true for him. Perhaps she'd never know. Between them, the moment lingered, a stillness with no end until a knock at the door broke the spell.

Snapping back to normality Tony said, "Let's see who that is?" Grabbing her hand, he led her toward the door. Stumbling a little, Sam allowed herself to follow, enjoying the spontaneity and naturalness of the gesture. At home, she felt at home.

"Penny, Jacques, come in, come in." Tony kissed the couple while Sam joined in the welcomes. Within minutes, they gathered in the kitchen with glasses of wine to toast Tony's birthday. Enthused to watch him cook, they settled in, but as usual, Tony held court and directed the event.

"Samantha, you can stir the basil into that tomato salsa simmering over there, while I fry the eggplant. Penny, you grate the ricotta and salata cheese, there on that board. And Jacques, you can be in charge of the pasta." With each command, his finger pointed in a different direction.

"Yes, boss," Penny said with a sarcastic smirk as she took to her task. Tony's minions obeyed, setting about their assigned jobs while he kept a sharp eye on their progress.

Now that Penny and Jacques had arrived Sam's nervousness dissipated. Chatter and laughter filled the apartment's tiny kitchen as they all enjoyed their free time. Playing the impeccable host, Tony changed the music, topped the glasses and offered a delectable Reggiano cheese drizzled with an orange blossom honey to nibble while they cooked.

After quaffing the second glass of wine, their level of cheekiness had escalated to overt dissension and the three guests had turned into mutineers. Rabble rousing, they taunted him, until with plates in hand, he turned on them in mock anger. "Sit. Sit all of you." Tony ordered his guests to their dining chairs for the entrée — *pasta alla norma*. Originating from Tony's hometown of Catania, this was one of his specialties and was the dish they'd all helped prepare.

While they tucked into the authentic Sicilian pasta, Sam ate a couple of mouthfuls then pushed her food around the plate like a kid in a sandpit with a toy grader.

"Don't you like it, Samantha?" Tony asked, disappointment evident on his face.

"Oh no, Tony. It's delicious. I just don't want to eat too much. You understand." She looked at Penny for help, but she pursed her lips with a small shake of her head.

"Samantha, it's my birthday. Eat." Tony's voice rose with command as he tapped his fork twice on her plate and waited. Forced to eat her full serving, Sam complied knowing that her waistline would pay for it tomorrow. *I'll eat less tomorrow to make up for tonight*, she promised.

By the time the *cotolette*, similar to schnitzel was cooked and served with an enormous bowl of Italian salad, Tony opened another bottle of Santagostino red. On topping up the glasses, he raised his and said, "Thank you, Penny, Jacques, and, Samantha, for celebrating my thirty-ninth birthday with me today. It means a lot to an old gruff Ursu like me." A broad grin split his face and they laughed at his self-deprecating humour.

"Happy birthday, boss." Penny leaned over and gave him a kiss on the cheek.

"*Bon anniversaire.*" Jacques tapped his glass to Tony's and gave him a manly slap on the shoulder.

"Happy birthday, Tony." Sam clinked her glass likewise. Tony leaned over proffering his cheek and refused to leave without Sam giving it a kiss.

"Now everyone, eat, enjoy," he commanded. The continuous sound of cutlery on crockery and a decrease in conversation demonstrated they did.

WHEN SAM OPENED THE door to the bathroom to leave, Jacques barrelled into her pushing her back inside. "Sorry, Jacques, I didn't see you," Sam said but realized he was closing the door behind them. "What are you doing?" Sam pushed against him, trying to pass.

"Samantha, you are very pretty, and you and I could . . ." His hand was making its way between her legs.

"Stop that. Stop that right now," she barked her objection forcefully but kept it low enough not to alert Tony or more importantly, Penny. She grabbed his hand and reefed it out from where it didn't belong. "What are you doing," she hissed into his ear. "You get out of here right this minute and go back to Penny. If you don't, I will scream." Sam shook with fear and fury. How dare he do this? How dare he put me at risk, both personally and professionally? How dare he — everything.

Jacques took a step backwards and leered. He brought his fingers to his nose, breathed in her sex, then licked them. Sam shuddered. She felt like throwing up.

"Oh my God. Get out!" she spat the words with as much venom as she could. Never had this happened to her. Although unnerved by his disgusting lechery, Sam held her ground, but if he didn't leave now, her knees were going to give way and so would her bravado.

Without a word, Jacques turned and left. Sam clutched the vanity bench and tried her best to control the panic lodged in the pit of her stomach. She took a deep breath, pulled her shoulders back and lifted her face to catch his reflection in the mirror.

"Is everything all right, Samantha?" Like a sentinel, Tony loomed behind her, concern and suspicion on his face.

"Yes, yes, Tony. Everything's fine." She preened and fussed about in her bag, trying to divert his attention from her flushed, panicked face.

"You know, Samantha. French men can be very persuasive. Some say, overconfident. Others say a few French men have such egos they think they can take what isn't theirs."

Tony occupied the space between them not just with his striking presence but with his astounding insight. Hot tears stung her eyes, but Sam remained silent. "Remember, Samantha. Some secrets are best shared. You gather yourself together, and I'll get dessert ready." When Tony left her alone, she reached over and locked the bathroom door. The familiar feeling of twisted eels fighting in her stomach transferred to frenzied thoughts. Her gaze fixated on the dreaded toilet bowl. The sheer force of will with which she fought against her overwhelming desire to control the situation by purging caused perspiration to bead all over her body. She could smell the fear emanating from her body. Her temperature escalated, and she knew if she just threw up, it'd be over. She would be better. The bowl beckoned, its coolness, its privacy, its promise of a better future. But not here. Not in Tony's apartment. White-knuckled she clung to the bench. If she could keep her fingers away from her mouth for just a little longer, the moment would pass. Shutting her eyes tight, she prayed it would end soon. She gulped down a lungful of air, then another. Slowly, her temperature reduced and as she opened her eyes, the seduction of the toilet bowl became nothing more than a nasty nightmare. With one more, deep sigh, she released her fear and with it, her need to purge.

Tony was furious. He knew all about Jacques and his wandering eyes, wandering hands and his wandering cock. Penny had confided in Tony some time ago. He'd told her to leave him, but she didn't. Said she was in love with him. The usual shit women say. Jacques needed a good beating in Tony's opinion and now the French prick was hitting on Samantha. Not in my fucking apartment.

"Jacques, you want to help me in here a minute?" Tony called from the kitchen. "Penny, you and Samantha sit on the couch. I'll serve dessert there. Grab some of the dessert wine and pour it for us. Thanks, Pen'."

By the time Tony finished issuing his remote orders, Jacques leaned on the bench beside him, a smug look on his face. Resisting the urge to smack him in the mouth, Tony reached down and grabbed his guest's cock. Hard. Jacques tried to squirm away from the searing pain, but Tony held firm.

"You listen to me you motherfucking French fuck. You think you're so fuckin' smart, don't you? Well, let me tell you . . ." Tony twisted the knob of Jacques cock tighter. "If Penny wasn't my assistant and friend, you'd never step foot in my apartment. But she is, so you're here by default. Penny knows all about your screwing around. *Stronzo*. And I don't know what game you're playing with Samantha, but I can promise you, it stops now!" Tony squeezed again for emphasis. Jacques began to falter and turn green with searing agony. "So, you go back in there. Make some excuse why you can't stay for dessert and get the fuck out of my apartment. Otherwise, I'll expose your sick, twisted perversions to Penny right here, right now." With a final twist, Tony released Jacques's cock just before his guest passed out.

Incredulous and with both hands gripping his excruciating crotch, Jacques stared at Tony, speechless. Not because of his egotistical nature, but because the relentless pain burning in his crotch prevented his mouth from moving. The silent grimace plastered on Jacques' face made Tony smile. Pleased with himself, he nodded and turned back to sprinkling chocolate dust on the top of the tiramisu.

MUCH TO PENNY'S SURPRISE, she and Jacques made a hurried exit before dessert. Instead of pretending to be disappointed in their early departure, Sam wished Tony had thrown Jacques' sorry arse out of the apartment, but she suspected he'd already orchestrated their unexpected exit. After Jacques' abhorrent behaviour, Sam didn't feel nearly as anxious about being left alone with Tony. Quite the opposite, in fact. He'd been nothing but a gentleman, quite the hero. Now curled up on Tony's couch sipping her dessert wine, she felt safe and secure. His apartment was warm, spacious and glamorous, and although she loved her little room at Hotel Hollandaise, this made for a welcome and fashionable change.

He placed a plate of creamy dessert in front of her. "I make a really great tiramisu, Samantha. And regardless of your obsession with your weight, you will taste it." Again, he left no room for debate.

"What do you expect? I'm a dancer with hopes of being a nude and then a soloist. I can't afford even the tiniest bit of fat anywhere on my body." She cast her mind back to the recent chocolate week and its immediate impact on her body. From now on, she pledged to be far more careful, every day.

"I applaud your dedication but at the same time, dancing is about joy. So is life. And you need to enjoy yourself a little more, Samantha. Eating is the Sicilian way of enjoying life." With that, he dug his fork into the exceptionally enticing dessert and spooned a big mouthful of creaminess into his mouth. Sam enjoyed watching him relish his own culinary creations. There was a natural fierceness and playfulness about Tony she admired. He seemed to have everything worked out. As he swirled the dessert in his mouth, he pointed his spoon to her plate, nodding for her to begin. Not willing to argue, Sam picked up her plate and dipped the spoon in. "What did you say to Jacques?"

"I told him to fuck off out of my apartment and to keep his fucking hands off you."

Sam blinked. Tony nodded at her again to eat her dessert.

"But how did you know?"

"Jacques is one of those arrogant pricks who screws around behind his lady's back. Penny knows of course but she won't leave. I've seen his play before on other dancers and it boils my blood. So, I told him to fuck off out of my apartment. What he does elsewhere is their business, but not in my home." He shovelled in another heaped spoonful, and since he delighted in his own cooking so much, Sam finally decided to eat.

With a ladylike spoonful, she popped the tiramisu into her mouth and nearly orgasmed. She rolled her eyes as the sweetness and bite of coffee and marsala assaulted her tongue simultaneously. "Oh, God," she murmured through creamy lips. "This is delicious."

A childlike grin spread across Tony's face obviously pleased with her critique. Returning to the topic, Sam said, "So what now? What am I supposed to say to Penny?'

"Nothing. You say nothing. Nothing has happened. She is still your boss as am I and the beat goes on. It's none of your business. Jacques is a prick. Penny knows that. She doesn't need you to tell her again. Stay out of it and stay away from any place where Jacques could get you alone. Although with what I did to him tonight, I think he'd run a mile in the other direction if he ever saw you again." Tony chortled softly to himself as he swept his spoon around his near-empty plate.

"What? What did you do?" So engrossed in the conversation, Sam had quite forgotten about not eating too much and had caught up with Tony. Her plate was now nearly as clean as his.

"Never you mind. Trust me. It's sorted." He stood up and extended his hand for her plate, then took both back to the kitchen and returned. "Here's the last of the dessert wine." On pouring the sweet, syrupy liquid into their glasses, he settled back into one of the tub chairs, gazing at her. "*Salute*, Samantha." He raised his glass to her, his eyes twinkling with a hot sparkle.

"*Salute*, Tony." She mirrored his toast and tried to stop her eyes from reciprocating the same level of heat.

"So, where to from here, Samantha?" He reached over to his packet of cigarettes, selected one and twirled it in his fingers like a cheerleader's baton.

With his flawless, black-clothed body reclining in the red tub chair, his right ankle propped on his left knee exposing his tight crotch and his thick hair longing to be ruffled, he looked delicious. Sam wished she had some of the creamy tiramisu left to rub all over his body and lick it off. *Stop!*

When a predatory smirk crept across his face, she froze. Her fleeting fantasy had betrayed her, and it was obvious Tony intuited her naughty thoughts. Embarrassed seemed to describe her constant state of being whenever she stayed too long in his presence. Reverting back to the conversation, with as much nonchalance as she could muster, she said "I don't understand,

Tony? What do you mean, where to from here?" This was not the conversation she wanted. Home was where to from here, and as fast as possible.

"I meant would you join me on the balcony while I have a cigarette?" His smile broadened in a checkmate grin as he stood up, offering her his hand.

Bastard, she thought. *He's toying with me.*

"Oh, yes. Of course. The balcony." She accepted his assistance to stand. Level with his face, she couldn't help but feel the electricity surge between them, and she swallowed down the desire bubbling up in her body. She licked her lips and noticed his attention on her mouth, his breath hot against her face.

"You do feel what I feel, don't you, Samantha?" With her hand still clasped in his, he twirled his thumb on the back of her hand with a delicate but deliberate touch.

Now she was trapped. Truth or dare. "I don't know what to say, Tony."

"One day, you will." He leaned in and lightly brushed a kiss to her cheek. "One day, we both will."

Back in the kitchen after getting Samantha safely into a cab, Tony went to work cleaning up his birthday masterpiece. The night worked out better than expected. His food was terrific with each of his mother's recipes working to perfection. Maybe he'd call her and open a conversation based on her great recipes? Maybe? Then there was the showdown with Jacques, which he'd been anticipating for months. He hated the prick and now he wouldn't have to tolerate him again. After tonight, Jacques would always make the excuse not to see Tony. This left Jacques being the bad guy and Tony being the good guy in Penny's eyes, which was important because Penny was one of the best women Tony knew. Sorting Jacques out was definitely one of the highlights of the night. But the big, starring moment was Samantha. Although there was the carnal part of him that longed to fuck her brains out . . . God how he wanted to smear tiramisu all over that luscious body of hers, bury his face between her legs and suck the fuck out of her . . . there was another part of him, a deeper part of him he'd not known before, that wanted more. Normally, whenever he'd had a dancer back in his apartment at night alone, he would have produced some cocaine and encouraged her to partake. Then, ripped off their tits, they would have banged their way till sunrise. He'd taught so many dancers how to fuck and be fucked, he'd lost count. But tonight, the thought never occurred to him with Samantha. Well maybe just that once with the dessert, but not long enough for it to take hold. Tonight, something shifted. And he knew she felt it too. She was just young, not sure of what was going on and she was smart enough not to jeopardize her career with a director who could turn out to be just some lecherous bastard. Smart girl. He liked her even more for that. Samantha O'Brien was no cheap starlet, fucking and sucking her way to the top.

As the old parable said, the tortoise wins the race, so slowly, slowly, he thought. If he wanted a real relationship with Samantha, he'd need to pace himself. After all, he was nearly fifteen years older than her. She needed time to adapt to the idea, or so he thought. But, in truth, he had no idea what women thought. He knew what turned them on. That, he was good at. But fulfilling the emotional needs of the female of the species was new territory for him. He further contemplated his shortcomings in this department while he continued in his domestic duties, long taught to by his surly mother. She may have whipped him into keeping a clean and tidy house, but she'd not shown him how to love a woman. With pots and pans splashing in the sink, he set about his tasks determined to find a solution to his dilemma of successfully wooing the young Samantha O'Brien. Like Gene Kelly in love, he began to dance to a melody swirling in his memory. "I've Got You Under My Skin" was an award-winning tune by the inimitable American composer, Cole Porter which described precisely where Samantha had taken up residence.

Humming and singing, Tony cleaned up with the carefree spirit of a 1940s movie musical hero.

By the time he went to bed on his thirty-ninth birthday and jerked-off, his kitchen shone as brightly as his hope for the future.

CHAPTER SIXTEEN

The bone-chilling cold of November turned into a mind-numbing freeze in December. Paris became a low-lying canvas of the beauty and dreariness of winter. Stripped bare, the linden trees reached their elongated branches into gloomy skies like the appendages of a grotesque character from a horror film. Juxtaposed to the trees' vicious outlines, lay fine blankets of crystal snow sprinkled onto the streets and parks as if protecting them from the trees' wrath. Yet this delightful snow scene lasted only fleetingly. Within no time, the snowy wonderland turned to treacherous pavements and footfalls when the city's dirt and sleet mingled in a slippery sludge. Perpetually dark, rainy and snowy days, with shorter daylight hours meant the city of love retreated from its open spaces where lovers reclined in each other's laps under the glow of the sun, to the indoors, where fires burnt, and they romped naked in front of their licking flames. Although Philippe's flat lacked the thrill of a roaring open fireplace, the warmth from the baker's ovens below compensated, ensuring she and Philippe lacked none of the fiery passion of winter lovers. Obsessed with each other, they spent Sam's Sundays off in Philippe's bed having wild, abandoned sex.

Now propped naked on a chaise lounge, with a filmy crimson shawl draped seductively over her body, Sam held the pose for Philippe as he sketched. This was her fourth visit to the studio owned by Philippe's artist friend, Jean-Paul. She'd met him only briefly on her first visit. He and Philippe had gone to school together but unlike Philippe, Jean-Paul remained on good terms with his father. He approved of Jean-Paul's artistic endeavours and as such paid the rent on this modest studio. Tucked in an aging part of the arrondissement, the run-down studio looked battered and tired. Its timber walls managed to remain standing only because the layers of wall paint slapped on them over the years acted like a cement adhesive. Large sections of paint had peeled away exposing the history of changing colours used by the different tradesmen. The ceiling disappeared upward giving the studio a cold, cavernous quality, as the warm air escaped up toward the rafters. Philippe propped a small electric heater near Sam, so she remained relatively warm throughout the sitting. Without its comforting heat, she would have only been able to sit for short periods of time before shivering and having to cover up. Small and compact, the studio burst at its seams with canvases, at all stages of completion, stacked against its walls. The air smelt of acrylics, oils, charcoals, the ever-stewing pot of coffee and of course, cigarette smoke. Thankfully, not only was Philippe good-looking, talented and a generous lover, he wasn't a smoker which pleased Sam immensely. It was another of the many boxes Philippe ticked in her life. But because Jean-Paul was a chain-smoker, no doubt like the hundreds of artists before him who used the studio, the acrid odour of cigarettes hung in the air. Now having lived nearly three months in Paris surrounded by cigarette smoke, Sam realized she'd become a passive smoker. Its pungent smell no longer repulsed her as much as before, but as the small electric heater pushed up the temperature, her throat closed over every now and then, begging to differ. On an elevated dais in the middle of the studio perched the chaise lounge on which she now posed.

"By God, Samantha, you look beautiful. Now drop your chin just a little and look to your left over your shoulder at forty-five degrees." Philippe with charcoal in hand stood at an enormous easel on which balanced a virgin canvas. Scrutinizing her with deep intensity, he watched the light on her cheek drift until he called, "There. Stop there. Perfect. Now don't move."

Sam enjoyed doing these sittings for him. Each time, Jean-Paul would open the studio for them and then bid farewell, leaving Sam and Philippe alone for her nude sittings. Today Philippe was sketching her in a more revealing position than usual. His forthcoming exhibition was entitled A Celebration of Woman, and he'd decided to paint a series of six portraits on the female body in all its glory. Three of the series were already completed, a little girl sitting on her mother's lap, an adolescent girl playing in the park and a naked pregnant woman caressing her unborn child. These canvases were hidden away in the studio ready for the exhibition. The other three of the series were due for completion before his showing at the Art Paris Art Fair on April 2.

His mother Chantal and Madame Lucette were sitting for the mature and older age woman portraits, while Sam was sitting for the sexual woman portrait, hence the reason for her nakedness and posture. Over the previous weeks, he'd sketched her in a variety of poses but today's was the most revealing. Reclining in a slovenly fashion into the back corner of the lounge, her left arm lay slung out and over the side of the armrest. Her left leg was splayed forwards, her knee bent. Her right leg bent slightly, also splayed open and her right arm was positioned loosely over her head. Both her inner thighs were exposed meaning the lips of her vagina opened as if beckoning for satisfaction. Fortunately, the shawl draped between her legs for dignity. Philippe had her face turned away from the audience in a manner of disinterest, leaving the entire titillating focus of the painting on her hidden gaping maw.

SIMPLY BREATHTAKING. THESE WERE the words repeating themselves in Philippe's mind as he admired Sam. She was the perfect subject — obedient, patient, physically tough for the long hours of posing and a body and face of exquisite proportions and symmetry. Unaware of her uniqueness, she was able to convey her captivating presence when completely still. Philippe had been planning and sketching for this sitting for weeks. The excitement to finally be confident enough to paint Sam bubbled up inside him, as did his intense sexual desire. The soft light filtering into the studio today possessed just the right amount of brightness. It caressed Sam's creamy skin as if in awe of her beatific youth, casting a heavenly glow. A red velvet shawl lay abandoned covering her modesty, while every other inch of her body exposed its perfection to the viewer. After rearranging his brushes, paints, easel and canvas one more time, he stood back for a final inspection of his subject. With a deep sigh and some trepidation, he decided to explore how far Sam's artistic appreciation stretched.

PHILIPPE SCUTTLED OVER TO make another postural adjustment. Leaning over, he said, "Samantha, you have a glorious cunt and now the whole world will see it." He dragged the shawl from between her legs, tickling her folds with its fringing. She longed for his mouth to soak up her juices like the shawl had just done, lick her, drink her, fuck her. Only just restraining herself from shoving his face between her legs, she waited for him to redress the shawl on her body. Instead, he discarded it, leaving her totally naked, exposed and dripping with yearning. He reached down and with one easy swipe of his finger opened her slit a little more. "Now this is the painting."

Sam upturned her face with a snap. "Oh no, Philippe. You can't paint me like this. I don't mind sitting in this position for you, but only you. You must cover me with the shawl. Make the painting tasteful, not pornographic. Oh God, what would my parents say?"

Philippe pouted and waited a beat. Then knelt beside her. "But, Samantha, I need to paint you like this. You are the star of my exhibition — the sexual woman." His throaty voice ignited the burn in her groin, but she remained firm.

"No, Philippe. If you paint my body wide-open, then you must not paint my face. Or if you want my body and face, then you can't paint me open like this. You must put the shawl between my legs. It's one or the other." She was decided and no matter what he said, they were her conditions.

He nuzzled into her breast, his tongue licking its nipple. "But, Samantha, your delicious cunt is screaming for stardom. Please?" It wasn't stardom her snatch was screaming for.

"No, Philippe," she said, her voice in command, but her body at his bidding. He slid his expert fingers into her cleft and her head collapsed back onto the lounge. Like jelly she gave up the will to argue while he swirled around and around in her folds, making her ooze. Her breathing quickened and as her eyes closed, she gave herself over to the orgasm soon to come. Next, his tongue was upon her, then inside her, probing her, fucking her. His lips clamped onto her labia kissing and sucking. Increasing the torture, he gently slipped his fingers inside, swivelling them around to irritate her G-Spot as he tormented her clit, needling it with his tongue tip.

"Oh God, Philippe, that's so good," she moaned, as he lapped and slurped her juices.

"Do you want more?" came his muffled reply.

"Yes please." She drifted into a sexual delirium as her left breast yielded to squeezing and nipple tweaking. And then her right breast found equal pleasure. Buckling under so much stimulation, Sam's body shuddered toward orgasm. Then it hit her, the smell of a just-finished cigarette. And there were three hands on her, not two. She snapped her eyelids open to find Jean-Paul looming above. It was his hands fondling her breasts with Philippe's face and fingers between her legs.

"Fuck!" she screamed leaping up off the chaise lounge. Trying to cover herself, she snatched her clothes off the stool and ran into the bathroom. With a thunderous sound, she slammed the door and the studio shook as if ready to fall. "What the fuck?!" Even through the bathroom door, her voice filled the studio, its pitch and power soaring ever upward. Jumping up and down on the spot, pounding her fists on the wall, she screamed over and again. "Fuck. Fuck. Fuck."

After moments of repeated expletives, Sam collected herself. Outside she could hear heated arguing between Philippe and Jean-Paul but, as she didn't understand French, she had no idea what their disagreement was all about. Controlling her breathing, she tried to stop the shock trembling through her body. She dragged her hand across her mouth and swallowed hard. Lathered in perspiration, her body buzzed with adrenaline and fury. She glanced at the toilet bowl but today she wasn't feeling insecure or frightened. Purging was not an option today. She was beyond livid. She was on the warpath. Dressing in super quick time, she laced up her boots, nearly hang-noosed herself with her scarf, jammed her hands into her coat pockets and took a deep breath. She glared balefully at the mirror. "Fuck them. Fuck them all." Thrusting her chin up, she paced into the studio where Philippe scurried to her side, like a conciliatory mouse.

"Samantha. I'm so sorry. I didn't know Jean-Paul was here. I didn't know. And I certainly didn't know he was touching you. He is no longer my friend. See I have stacked all my paintings to take home. I cannot work in his studio anymore. He is dead to me." With a look of anguish, Philippe gestured to some pieces covered by a painting tarp. As far as she was concerned the bundle could have been anything and the excommunication of his friend did little to assuage her anger. With the same determination she used when dancing, Sam ignored him. He wasn't in her sightline. Therefore, he didn't exist. She blocked every one of her senses to his presence. At the studio door, she stopped and spun on him.

"Do you honestly expect me to believe that you had no idea Jean-Paul was in here watching us, waiting to join in. You've got to be fucking kidding me! I may be young but I'm not stupid." With a final contemptuous glare, she stalked out onto the street. Philippe scampered beside her, making strange mollifying noises. Due to the day's end upon them, the temperature was dropping fast. Dressed only in his trousers, shirt and boots, Philippe's lips began to quiver and turn blue in the five-degree winter cold. "Please, Samantha. Believe me. Please." His begging only made it worse.

She snapped to a stop and turned on him. "Get inside, Philippe. You're freezing. Don't contact me again." She knew the pace with which she set off couldn't be matched by Philippe in his current attire. She heard him sprint back to the studio and its door shut behind her, but she didn't look back.

Marching back through the dank streets, angry tears burned her eyes. Sam's heart hammered an unhappy beat in her chest and her gloved fists swung in the momentum of her stride. Hiccupping sobs tried to break free of her throat, but she gulped them back. She squeezed her eyelids tightly, wondering if tears freeze in these temperatures. With a stream of salty water trickling down her cheeks, she discovered they didn't.

WITH HIS BACK PRESSED against the door, Philippe stared manically into the studio. He shivered in convulsions, both from his falling body temperature and the horrendous fight with Samantha. His panicked breathing burned his lungs, while his mind spun in confusion.

Crazy with dread, Philippe yelled in full voice, "What the fuck is wrong with you, Jean-Paul?" He breathed deep and hard. "Look what you've done?" Launching himself from the door, Philippe stormed into the studio. "Where are you?" Like a cat tracking a defiant mouse, Philippe combed the studio, but couldn't see his rodent friend anywhere.

A lecherous snigger from behind an easel tucked in a far corner, caught Philippe's attention. "Get out here right this minute."

Jean-Paul sauntered out with a lifeless cigarette clamped in his pursed lips.

Philippe growled and marched over to stand eye to eye with him. "You stupid, dumb fuck. What possessed you to get in on the action?"

Jean-Paul shrugged. The cigarette slid from one side of his leering mouth to the other. He remained silent while his feet fidgeted.

"This was not a three-way deal. I told you that. Go get your jollies off somewhere else." Jean-Paul pouted. "Go on. Fuck off. God knows how I'm going to get Samantha back now."

"But, Philippe, there's plenty of other women out there we can fuck together." Jean-Paul sounded as stupid as he looked.

With scathing contempt, Philippe snorted and jammed his arms into his coat. "That's the point, Jean-Paul. Samantha is not a share fuck."

~ ♥ ~

LIKE A DEMON ON the winter wind, Samantha blasted full speed through the front doors of Hotel Hollandaise. Unconcerned if her recklessness caused injury to some unsuspecting person, she barged in and through the foyer. Leaping three steps at a time, she hurdled to her room shutting the door behind her, before anyone knew what caused the commotion. With a fierce twist of the key, she was safe in her room. Safe and heartbroken. Standing still, or more rightly, still standing, she felt her heart crack. Like shattered glass, all the love she'd allowed herself to feel in this relationship with Philippe tinkled down into the bowels of her soul. Having heard so many people express their own despair with just one word, she now understood what gutted meant. Someone had just reached inside of her, grabbed everything she held sacred and tore it from her. He'd lied. He'd set her up. He'd played her for a fool. She slumped on the bed, head in hands. She was too tired to cry, too tired to be angry, too tired even to throw up. She was too tired to be anything but what she was born to be — Samantha O'Brien, Moulin Rouge dancer, soon to be nude, soon to be soloist. Philippe, along with the rest of the male of the species could all go fuck themselves. They required too much energy, too much pandering, and too much effort. Dancing twelve shows a week was easier than this shit. She was done.

~ ♥ ~

"SAMANTHA, ARE YOU ALL right?" Madame Lucette tapped lightly at Sam's door at nine A.M. the next morning. "Are you coming down for breakfast?"

Monday mornings had become somewhat of a ritual for Sam and her landlady. Normally, they met in the dining room usually around eight-thirty to share a pot of tea, a light breakfast and chat about life and love. More so love, since Philippe had become a regular fixture in Sam's life.

"Not this morning, Madame Lucette. I'm not feeling very well. I think I'll just sleep a little longer." From under the quilt, Sam called her apology. All of it true. She wasn't feeling well, and she longed to sleep, hopeful she'd wake up from the nightmare of yesterday.

"Samantha *chère fille*, Philippe has called a dozen times. He told me what happened. Please open the door. I have a tray with some tea and toast for you. You cannot stay in your bed all day. Better to talk." Madame Lucette's melodic voice and offer of sympathy soothed Sam's upset. Her mother used to do the same thing when Sam locked herself away after being belittled by some of her ballet peers.

Sam considered and called back, "All right, Madame. But I don't want to talk about Philippe." She waited for the mandatory promise.

"Very well, *chère fille*."

Throwing off the covers, Sam pushed herself up out of the mattress's embrace and pulled her gown around her, cinching the waist cord. She dragged her fingers through her bed-hair and opened the door.

"*Bonjour*, Samantha." Madame Lucette glided into the room with a breakfast tray and deftly deposited it on the bed. "Would you like me to pour us tea while you use the bathroom?"

"Thank you, Madame. That would be wonderful." Samantha left to freshen up and returned to find her curtains drawn with the first sunlight for over a week peeping into her room. Madame Lucette offered Sam a piping cup of English Breakfast and patted the bed, beckoning for her to sit beside her.

"*Chère fille*, I am so sorry about what happened to you yesterday. Terrible, terrible." Madame Lucette shook her head with deep regret, her brow furrowed in long creases. "I am so ashamed to be French after what took place."

Sam reached over to squeeze Madame's hand. "Thank you, Madame. But it's not your fault."

"And I am sure it is not Philippe's fault either." Madame Lucette's teary grey eyes beseeched Sam to listen. "*Mon ange* would not do that, I am sure," she said. "He promised me he didn't know Jean-Paul was there."

Out of respect for the old lady, Sam kept a lid on her bubbling indignation. "Madame, I know you love Philippe very much." She wanted to add, so did I, but refrained. "However, I think he's lying. After all, how could he not know Jean-Paul was there, touching me?" A part of Sam wanted to tear Philippe to pieces while another part of her wanted to re-establish the status quo and be convinced of Philippe's innocence so she could return to being happily in love.

Madame Lucette put down her cup of tea and took Sam's hands in hers. "Samantha, I know my nephew is not an angel when it comes to the opposite sex, but I know he feels very strongly for you. I am sure he would not jeopardize what you have by doing something so crude as what happened yesterday."

"I wish I could believe that, madame, but I don't." Sam paused. "As I said when I first arrived here, I came to Paris to dance, not fall in love. I should have stuck to my original plan. You can tell Philippe not to call anymore." Madame Lucette looked so frail and disheartened, Sam wanted to change her mind, but she couldn't make up with Philippe just to please her landlady.

"Very well, Samantha. But Philippe is a stubborn young man. He says he loves you, so I do not think he will give up that easily. But I will tell him as you wish." Madame Lucette rose and clasping Sam's face between her shaky hands, she kissed her on the forehead with affection. The sweet scent of incense wrestled with the stale smell of cigarettes, much like the emotional skirmish happening inside Sam. Still holding her face and looking deep into her young charge's eyes, Madame Lucette said, "Sometimes hurt is needed to make us grow, and time is needed to help us know." With a soft smile, she turned, leaving Sam to her meagre breakfast and unsettling thoughts.

CHAPTER SEVENTEEN

WITH JUST OVER TWO weeks until Christmas, Sam was in full swing with the festive season. Over the past few hours, she and Josette had burned through more money than any sane person would, buying expensive gifts and delectable goodies. With overfull shopping bags stacked beside them and their hands wrapped around mugs of steaming hot chocolate, they perched like two merry Christmas gnomes next to the café window watching the snow fall.

"I just love the Opera district," Sam said for the umpteenth time that day. Josette beamed. Today she'd taken Sam to the ninth arrondissement. A district drenched in artistic history and bursting with grand shopping boulevards and flagship department stores. It proved the ideal location for a marathon shopping spree.

"*Oui*, Sam. It is one of my favourite places." Josette was also delighted by their successful day of shopping and sightseeing. Looking fashionably chic with her blonde hair hanging like golden curtains around her face and a bright red woollen beanie pulled down over her ears, Josette surveyed the crowds milling around outside. Her *Chanel* red lips colour-matched her beanie and red roll-neck sweater, as did her fingernails. She was the picture-perfect advertisement for Christmas in Paris.

"Thank you, Josette. I've had the best day." Sam peered out the window with the unrestrained joy of Susan Walker, the little girl who believed in Santa Claus in *Miracle on 34th Street.*

Josette giggled, and Sam glanced back at her. "What? What is it?"

"It is good to see you happy. No more boyfriend troubles then?" Josette cocked her head to the side with a wry smile, waiting for information. Sam had purposely not said anything to Josette about Philippe, or that she no longer had a lover in her life. She figured the less said, the better. Many years ago, she'd overheard a private conversation between her mother and Aunty Michele. Most of it was whispered but one sentence remained firmly etched in her memory, loose lips sink ships. Sam's experience over the years as a dancer proved this to be true. Many times, she'd seen the damage caused by people sticking their noses into others' business, dancers telling too much about their personal lives and careers devastated by gossip. She preferred her privacy even if it meant at times, she seemed aloof to others.

"No boyfriend troubles," Sam said in her best merry Christmas voice. "Everything is fine and now that mum and Aunty Michele are coming over for Christmas, I couldn't be happier."

"When do they arrive?"

"On the twenty-third, for a week." Sam could barely contain her excitement. "And Madame has two rooms available at the hotel so they can stay there with me. I can't wait." The waiter deposited two plates, each containing a slice of sumptuous strawberry shortcake. The high-sided, high-caloric pastry wobbled from the weight of the plump heavy fruit on top while the syrupy glace winked under the café's bright lights.

"Josette, I can't eat this." Sam was astounded that this was what her friend had ordered.

"Of course you can. It is nearly Christmas, and this is our celebration together. One piece of strawberry shortcake will not kill you. And besides, we have lots more walking and shopping to do this afternoon."

Sam gave her friend an appreciative smile. "Thank you, Josette, for being my friend. You've helped me settle into Paris and the Rouge. I don't know what I would've done without you." She reached over and squeezed Josette's elegant hand.

"*Bon, bon.* Now eat," Josette said, obviously embarrassed by Sam's sudden display of affection.

Admiring their wicked indulgence, the girls paused, forks in hand. Then with a last glance at each other, they popped a forkful of lusciousness into their mouths, murmuring in delight. Sam winked at Josette. "Orgasmic, simply orgasmic."

~ ♥ ~

TEETERING ON TOP OF the wooden stool, Sam stretched up to the lattice panelling in the internal foyer doorway. With a streamer of glistening green tinsel in her hand, she threaded it through as far as her arms could reach. Then she shimmied down from the stool, repositioned it a little further along and repeated the process once again. She loved decorating for Christmas. Back home, anything that glittered, dangled or tinkled made it up on the walls, dressers and tables — in fact, she filled every surface or empty space with some sort of sparkling garland or bauble. The more, the merrier. Just as she was about to step down, she heard the outside door open behind her, letting in a gust of freezing air. She turned toward the cold. "Can you close the door please, I'm trying to . . ." She lost her footing and began to topple. Falling backwards she let out a yelp and shut her eyes, but she was spared the anguish of hitting the floor by a pair of strong, familiar arms which brought with them a different sort of anguish.

"It's all right, Samantha. I've got you." Philippe's arctic blue eyes and angelic countenance gazed down at her, pricking her heart with fond memories. Shocked but unhurt, Sam allowed herself a moment to recover, quietly grateful she hadn't injured herself. Realizing the awkwardness of the situation, she freed herself from Philippe's embrace and straightened, brushing off her clothes. What she was brushing off herself she had no idea, but it gave her something to do while she averted her eyes and collected her thoughts.

"Hello, Philippe. Thank you for breaking my fall." She gave him a sharp nod and curt smile then returned to her box of decorations. *What is he doing here?*

"I've missed you, Samantha. Did you get the flowers I sent? The messages I left?" In his voice, the plea for an answer sounded tremulous.

With her back still to him and pretending to rummage for a trinket in the box, she said in a flat, even voice, "Yes the flowers were lovely, Philippe." It was true — they were. Every second day for the past fortnight, he'd sent beautiful pink roses, like the ones he'd given her opening night. She had no idea where he got them in this frightful weather or how he paid for them, but their constant delivery made it more difficult to forget him. Their beautiful blooms filled her room, sending her to sleep in a fragrant sea of loving scent and waking her each morning with a perfumed "hello." She had no doubt Philippe had sent them hoping to charm her back. In many ways, his strategy had worked because the roses acted as a constant reminder of Philippe and his sweet nature, or what she thought was his sweet nature before the threesome incident at the studio. Each time, the bouquets had arrived with the same note:

I'm sorry. Please call me.

"I got your messages, but I really don't think there is anything for us to discuss." Was she being too hard, too cruel? She'd not given him any chance to explain or redeem himself at all? She began to feel sorry for him and what's more, she missed him. Surely if he'd been complicit in that awful, humiliating scene with Jean-Paul, he wouldn't be wasting his money on flowers all this time? She felt his tentative touch on her shoulder, and she shuddered. Her traitorous body took the affirmative side in the debate, urging her to forgive. She relented a little and turned to face him but kept her eyes downcast.

"Samantha, I don't know what else to do or say to tell you how sorry I am. Please, I had nothing to do with what happened. I miss you. It's nearly Christmas, a time for forgiveness and love. Won't you show some to a poor, struggling artist like me?" By now he'd lowered his face and was staring up under hers, his winter-chilled cheeks and childish pout the perfect addition to his appeal. The begging mischief in his eyes became too much for Sam to bear. Try as she might, she couldn't stop the smile from creasing her face. Philippe whooped with glee. He sprang up, wrapped his arms around her waist and twirled her around in circles.

"Put me down, Philippe. Put me down," she said in a stern tone. "Just because I smiled doesn't mean we're back together again." She pushed down hard on his forearms, dislodging herself from his grip.

Dropping to one knee, like a man about to propose, he grabbed her hands. "Please, Samantha. Take me back. Let's celebrate Christmas together. It will be such fun. Please."

God, why did he have to act so sincere and be so beautiful? With his fine, chiselled features all he needed was a set of wings and she could have stuck him on the top of Christmas tree as the angel. His dazzling spirit and beguiling smile only added to her dilemma.

"All right. All right," she said with clipped irritation in her voice. "But I'm warning you, Philippe Lacroix, if you as much step out of line, even a little, I'll throttle you." She wagged her finger at him while he cowered under her grim frown and strict conditions.

He bowed to her authority. "Your wish is my command, *La Goulue*. Now let me help you decorate so you don't hurt yourself." He sprang to his feet and grabbed the stool. Holding it steady with one hand he extended the other to help Sam climb up safely. Stepping on top of the stool, Sam returned to her tinsel threading feeling safer now Philippe was there. God, she hoped she wasn't turning into one of those needy girls who must have a boyfriend in order to feel safe and whole in their lives. While she mused further on this depressing topic, she felt his head nuzzle into her legs. She peered down, and he raised his face upward. "I have missed you, Samantha. Really I have. You complete me."

When she returned his lover's pledge with an air kiss and a grateful smile, a lurching in her stomach reminded her not to lose control.

~ ♥ ~

THEY GATHERED LIKE EAGER schoolgirls in the dining room, chirping and talking over one another, all smiles and gleeful faces.

"Oh, darling you look wonderful. I can't believe we're actually here." SallyAnn, Sam's mother, reached out and caressed her daughter's heart-shaped face. Sam hadn't inherited her mother's strong jawline, blonde hair and blue eyes. Instead, her wild exotic appearance, raven-black hair and flashing green eyes were a blessing given by her father's Irish ancestry. But of all the characteristics she had inherited from her parents, it was her mother's statuesque frame and grace, which set Sam apart, both on and off the stage. Never one to think of herself as extraordinary, Sam nevertheless knew her genetics played a role in her success as a dancer and for that, she was grateful.

On the other side of the table, Aunty Michele held Sam's hand in both of hers. "My Tiny Dancer. Look at you now. Dancing at the Moulin Rouge. I knew one day you'd make it here. I am so proud of you." Michele kissed the top of Sam's hand with deep affection.

"I'm so happy you're both here to spend Christmas with me and to see the show. And, Aunty Michele, I can't believe you came all this way, just to see me." She stretched over, wrapping her arms around Michele's neck in a tight hug.

"Of course, I would. I couldn't let your mother have all the fun." Michele cast a cheeky sideways glance to her friend of over thirty years. "And besides, who's going to look after you two in Paris in the holiday season. That's when the maddest love affairs of all happen." The three of them laughed, not just at Michele's naughty inferences but at the absurdity of SallyAnn or Michele having affairs. Both were married to adoring husbands and neither woman seemed keen to run off with a lover.

"Those days are over for me, Michele," SallyAnn said. "No more mad French love affairs for this old girl." A faint reminiscence twinkled in her eye.

"What do you mean? What happened?" Sam leaned forwards intrigued by what her mother had said.

"Nothing, darling. It was a long time ago when I danced at the Rouge. Before I met your father . . ." SallyAnn's voice trailed off to join her memory as it disappeared down a long-forgotten lane.

Sensing SallyAnn needed to follow her memories, Michele explained, "I think it was one of your mother's greatest love affairs, aside from your dad of course. He was the quintessential French lover, young, well-bred and born to be successful. Your mum was a young, fresh-faced Aussie dancer on a short-term contract at the Rouge. They had a mad, impetuous affair for six months. He wined and dined her, and they made love in his apartment on the right bank of the Seine in the ninth arrondissement."

"I was in the ninth only a couple of weeks ago with Josette. It's a beautiful district," Sam said.

Michele continued, "Well, he stole your mother's heart. When she finally returned to Australia, she was quite devastated, having left her love behind."

Never one to reveal much of her past, SallyAnn normally stopped Michele whenever she told stories of her younger days to Samantha. But today, being in Paris with the memories fluttering around her like falling snow, SallyAnn seemed oblivious to Michele's storytelling. Sam sat enchanted by the story of her mother's passionate past. To think her mother felt the same feelings with a young French lover all those years ago as Sam did now with Philippe seemed out of character. Her reliable, duty-bound mother who gave up her career to marry her father had been once a wild, love-sick dancer in Paris. Who would have thought? This revelation shifted Sam's perspective, allowing a new appreciation and affection for her mother to settle into her heart. Without a word, she reached out and clasped her mother's hand in female understanding. SallyAnn smiled at her daughter and slowly returned from her mental meanderings.

"*Mmm*, what is it, darling?" SallyAnn asked, quite out of sync with the conversation.

"Nothing, Mum. Nothing. I love you."

"I love you too, darling."

"Excellent. We all love each other," Michele said, and their laughter broke the pensive mood.

After fifteen minutes or so of casual chit-chat, Madame Lucette appeared with a tray laden with Laduree macaroons, her best china tea service and an enormous pot of tea.

"Merci, Madame Lucette." SallyAnn helped the landlady place the service in front of them.

"You are most welcome. I am very happy to have Samantha's mother and aunty stay at Hotel Hollandaise for this week. I hope your rooms are satisfactory?" At her gracious best, Madame Lucette poured the tea while the women complimented her on her lovely hotel. Normally, the bitter weather kept most of the tourists or short-term residents away, so accommodating SallyAnn and Michele in the hotel, proved an unexpected and beneficial surprise.

"Here, Mum. Have you tried these before? The famous Laduree macaroon?" Sam lifted a plate of gaily coloured macaroons to her mother. The distinctive pink, green, yellow and crimson-hued meringue wafer scattered between their darker versions created a kaleidoscope of delicious colour.

"Oh, yes. My favourites." SallyAnn's elegant fingers selected the famous peppermint green macaroon and she bit into it, closing her eyes in pleasure. "Remember these, Michele? God, I love Paris."

Michele's mouth was likewise orgasming over a strawberry-flavoured sugary disc. "So many good memories and fabulous food." She licked the sugar from her fingers.

"I'm pleased you like them. I bought a big box for you both to enjoy over the next few days," Sam said, thrilled to see her mother and Michele enjoying her gift.

"Trust me. They're not going to last that long." SallyAnn she reached for another.

~ ♥ ~

Following a protracted and delicious afternoon tea, Sam said, "You know, Mum, Madame Lucette does tarot card readings. Why don't you let her do a reading for you?"

"No, no, Samantha. We're not here to impose on Madame Lucette . . ." But before SallyAnn could continue in her excuse, Madame Lucette produced the pack from her trusty apron pocket and deposited them in the centre of the table.

"Nonsense. It would be an honour. Now all you have to do is shuffle the cards and ask them a question. Then when you feel ready, you cut the deck and show me the card. I will then do your reading."

SallyAnn glanced sideways at Michele, who smirked. Although Michele believed fully in spirituality and that everything happened for a reason, good or bad, SallyAnn was yet to be convinced.

"Go on then." Michele nudged her friend in the arm. "Let's see what the cards have to say." She couldn't wipe the smile from her face as SallyAnn began to shuffle the cards with obvious reluctance.

The four of them fell silent as SallyAnn pretended to focus on the task. Wasting no time, she cut the deck and exposed a card to Madame Lucette. All eyes bore down on the image of a fierce-looking woman, dressed in red flowing robes, clutching a long wooden staff with skeletons scattered at her feet. Fascinated, SallyAnn, Michele and Samantha looked at Madame Lucette and waited for the reading.

Madame Lucette lifted her eyes and regarded SallyAnn. "This is the goddess of battle, of struggle, of love scorned." She paused for effect. "She is also known as the banshee and her wild cries herald death."

Samantha giggled. "That sounds about right, Mum. Sometimes you sounded like a banshee when you'd yell at Jason and me."

Michele sniggered.

"Yes, yes but what does it all mean for me?" SallyAnn grew impatient with the game.

"Perhaps you seek revenge for a love-scorned? Perhaps it is time to clear the air even if it is in anger? But trouble most definitely lies ahead, but you will prevail. As the goddess of battle says, 'what doesn't kill me, makes me stronger.'"

"Well, there you are, SallyAnn, off to battle you go." Michele's mischievous spirit danced. "I'll come with you if you like and together we can slay whatever it is that's pissing you off."

"At this point in time, that would be you." SallyAnn fixed Michele in her sights and a sly smile stole across her face. "You're incorrigible."

SallyAnn turned to Madame Lucette. "Thank you, Madame, for my reading. I will bear this in mind for the future."

"*Non, non*, it is not the future. It will happen while you are here in Paris." Madame's solemn expression stopped the shenanigans.

After Michele eyeballed the landlady, she turned to SallyAnn. "She's right, honey. Something will happen while you're here."

"What? What's going to happen?" Rattled that something bad might befall her mother, Sam wished she hadn't insisted on a reading.

"There, there, *chère fille*. It is all right. It is not bad. Your mother will sort something out, she will win. Nothing bad will happen to her." Madame Lucette patted Sam's hand, reassuring her.

"Okay then," Sam said, somewhat pacified.

SallyAnn rose pushing back her chair, leaving no doubt the reading was over. "Now, I think it's time we showered and got ready to go to the theatre."

Michele also stood. "Yes. It's a big night tonight, watching our Samantha dance in the Moulin Rouge."

"We'll see you later, Madame Lucette," Sam added, keen to get ready. As the three women left the dining room, Madame Lucette collected her faithful deck of cards and returned them to her apron pocket exchanging them for her trusty companions, her *Gitanes*, and shuffled off to smoke in private.

~ ♥ ~

AFTER A LUKEWARM SHOWER and change of clothes, SallyAnn and Michele waited in Sam's room while she finished dressing for the show. SallyAnn checked out her daughter's meagre amenities while Michele scrutinized the large number of pink roses scattered throughout the room. "Okay, Tiny Dancer. Who is he?" Michele called out to Sam who was in the bathroom talking with SallyAnn.

"I'm not sure I should tell you anything." Sam walked into her bedsit with a watchful expression.

"Out with it. Who is he and what did he do that was so wrong that he had to send this many roses?" Michele flourished her arm in a wide arc demonstrating her point, determined to receive an acceptable answer.

"Never you mind what he did. It's all over with now. His name is Philippe and you'll meet him on Christmas Day here for lunch. He's Madame Lucette's nephew if you must know."

SallyAnn and Michele raised their sculptured eyebrows on cue at the revelation of Sam admitting to a boyfriend and one related to the landlady.

"French then, is he?" Michele asked stating the obvious while SallyAnn remained tight-lipped allowing her friend to conduct the interrogation.

"Ha, ha. Yes, he is French. He's also an artist and a very nice young man." With her chin held high, Sam threw the last of her gear into her dance tote and shrugged on her coat.

"Well, I for one am glad you finally have a lover. It's about time. I hope he's good in the cot."

Sam sensed the blush racing over her cheeks.

"But don't tell me you do it in this lumpy old bed?" Michele pushed up and down on the mattress multiple times, watching it sag beneath her bouncing hand.

"Aunty Michele, you are shameless." Sam giggled, delighted to be bantering with her again. Turning to her mother, she added, "I don't know how you put up with her, Mum?"

"Trust me, Tiny Dancer, your mother is far worse than me.' Michele and SallyAnn exchanged cheeky glances with their mouths closed tight in secret smiles.

"Okay, you two. Let's go to the show." Sam hooked her arms through the other women's and they all but skipped out of the room together like Dorothy, Tinman and Scarecrow.

~ ♥ ~

Waiting in the backstage foyer after the show, SallyAnn and Michele felt depressed and elated. Depressed because even after thirty years they still missed performing and dancing as much as ever, and elated because Samantha had been breathtaking to watch. Both lost in their thoughts, they gazed at the familiar surroundings they remembered so well. Even the dank smell of makeup and sweaty costumes brought back cherished memories. Breaking through their haze of recollection, Sam raced up to them still in her stage makeup, with her enormous showgirl smile splashed across her face.

"Darling, you were wonderful. Truly you were." SallyAnn tried but failed to control the tears misting her eyes as she hugged her only daughter.

"Thanks, Mum." Sam kissed her mother, giving her a reciprocal hug.

"Absolutely, Samantha. You were spectacular. You have a big career ahead of you." Michele also tried to control her emotion as she kissed her unofficial niece.

"Come on. Come backstage while I take off my makeup. The stage director, Tony Di Falco is here for the next week or so and I want you to meet him." Sam led the way, though SallyAnn and Michele needed no help. They recalled every corridor, staircase and door from having been Dorris dancers themselves years ago. They weaved their way backstage while Sam explained that Tony had left early in November to fly to Las Vegas, where his pitch to produce and direct a major production had been accepted. "He's back for a week or so just to check up on things here and then off to Vegas for his next big production." Sam sighed and her shoulders slumped.

"What is it, darling?" SallyAnn stopped and looked at her daughter.

"I don't know. I really loved working with Tony and I'm sad to see him go. I'm happy here really I am but—"

"Samantha, I've been looking everywhere for you." Out of the darkness, Tony appeared like a magician. Having gotten used to his stealth, Sam didn't flinch, but both SallyAnn and Michele started with surprise. Dressed in his signature blue jeans, white converse sneakers, white silk shirt opened enough to expose his sculptured chest, he oozed sex appeal and authority. A sparkle danced in his liquid eyes on seeing Sam before he turned their gleam upon her guests.

"Tony this is my mother, SallyAnn, and Michele. They were both dancers here at the Rouge years ago."

"Go steady, Sam. It wasn't that long ago." Michele fluttered her eyelashes and extended her hand to Tony who promptly accepted and kissed it.

SallyAnn nudged Michele in the ribs. "Yes, it was. A long, long time ago."

Tony chortled softly, obviously enjoying the sarcastic dance of the two ex-showgirls.

"Ladies, please allow me to escort you all backstage." Tony brandished his arm in a chivalrous manner. With askance glances and amidst titters of laughter, the three Dorris dancers, past and present, stepped off together, allowing the stage director to be their tour guide.

WHILE SAM DASHED TO her dressing room, Tony escorted SallyAnn and Michele on a quick revisit to their old stomping ground. Wandering across the stage, he explained the changes to the theatre over the past few years and how technology had transformed the venue. Looking up into the flies and around the curtained stage, SallyAnn and Michele fell silent.

"I miss this all so much," Michele said, a lump in her throat. She stared at the back of the proscenium curtain; a deep longing evident in her gaze.

SallyAnn stepped in beside her, to hold her hand. "Me too." Together they stood staring into the cavernous folds of the curtain. A whirring sound broke their reverie and the heavy, red velvet curtain began to ascend. Michele looked stage left to the stage manager's corner to see Tony there, smiling. She returned his considerate gesture with a silent "Thank you" to which he nodded with obvious understanding.

Frozen, SallyAnn and Michele waited, longing for the stage lights to blind them, and their heat to assault their faces. Although the theatre was dark and the stage lights were off with only the workers giving enough fluorescent light for the wait staff to clear up in the auditorium, it was enough. Releasing hands, their bodies transformed, and they became showgirls once more. Standing erect and elegant, feet placed and angled, arms drifting upward, and chins raised, they entered a time warp. For a moment, they were nudes again, stunning and sophisticated. They strutted downstage recalling the weight of the headdresses and the care and strength it took to keep them balanced. To the silent beat in their minds, they wafted across the stage, lost to the rhythm.

Unbeknownst to them, Sam sidled up next to Tony to watch.

"Samantha, you come from a very good line of dancers, you know that don't you?" His eyes remained riveted on the two ex-showgirls while they worked the stage with grace.

"I know but I've never seen them do this. Oh my, God, they must've been amazing."

"They still are," Tony said. Having replaced his onstage career with his longer-life directorial profession, he knew exactly what SallyAnn and Michele were feeling. "Samantha, the pain a dancer feels in their heart when they give up the stage, never goes away. It may retreat under cover, but it never dies. It is a longing of indescribable proportions. I feel this pain as much as your mother and Michele do, so I understand. One day, unfortunately so will you." Still enthralled by the impromptu performance on stage, Tony sought out Sam's hand and gave it a squeeze. Standing in the stage manager's corner together, holding hands as her mother and Aunty Michele relived their halcyon dancing days, Michele clung to this moment in time. She sneaked a glance up at Tony's face and his relaxed expression of admiration for the ex-showgirls made Sam's heart flutter. She would miss him terribly.

A loud clatter of plates from the auditorium broke the moment deflating SallyAnn's and Michele's posture like burst balloons. They spiralled back into the present moment to loud clapping by Tony and Sam.

"*Bravo. Bravo,*" he called, striding onto the stage. "I only wish I could've had the chance to be your director. Magnificent, ladies."

"Thank you, Tony, that's very kind of you." SallyAnn straightened her jacket, self-conscious that Sam's director was complimenting her.

"Mum, Aunty Michele, you were wonderful." Sam hugged them both with pride.

"Thank you, Tiny Dancer. What can I say? Your mum and I are just showies at heart." Michele forced a wide smile on her face to replace the threatening melancholy.

"Tiny Dancer? What is this name?" Tony asked. Embarrassed, Sam ran off to get her bag while Michele explained her pet name for Samantha. On her return, the three of them were deep in conversation about Sam's prospects.

"I do think Samantha will be a nude and perhaps a soloist when a position becomes available here," Tony said with confidence. SallyAnn and Michele nodded, pleased with his prediction while Sam hovered on the outer, eavesdropping on her future.

"And do you think that's likely during this twelve-month contract, Tony?" SallyAnn asked. Sam suspected her mother was mentally planning flight schedules based on how long Sam might work in Paris.

"Depends. Unless we lose a nude perhaps not, but there is plenty of time for Samantha and her career." Tony glanced at Sam with a promising, affectionate smile. Reverting to the older women, he said, "Now if you'll excuse me, ladies." Tony bid them goodnight and retreated backstage.

~ ❤ ~

Tony wandered off, ruminating on the meeting. He liked Samantha's mother and her friend Michele, intelligent, straight-to-the-point type of women with only the best intentions for Samantha and her career. They must've been a wicked pair in their day too, he thought, a sly smile on his face. He plonked himself down in his director's chair tucked inconspicuously in a small, unused space backstage. A fluorescent lamp light hung over his shoulder which he switched on to read the notes he'd written from tonight's show. But he couldn't concentrate. Today he'd rung his mother to tell her the great news about his show being accepted in Las Vegas. Mistakenly he thought she'd be delighted to see her only son make it in the live entertainment capital of the world, but she still "hummed and harred" about him getting a real career, rather than wasting his time on dancing. What a bitch! After all this time, she still got under his skin and that made him even angrier. *Damn her.* No wonder he never wanted to get too close to women. All of them ended up making him angry. Then there was Samantha, the surprising exception to the rule. But still, he wasn't getting close to her either. Tony Di Falco, the great stage director, an absolute failure in love. He saw the slogan emblazoned on an imaginary theatre sign in his mind's eye. In another couple of weeks, he'd be gone, Samantha would still be here and what would he have done about it? Sweet FA. This was most out of character for him. At the highlight of his career, he should be celebrating his success, kicking his heels up, partying and enjoying this once-in-a-lifetime opportunity. Instead, he was sitting alone backstage unable to concentrate, cursing his wretched mother and wondering what he was doing with his life. What a fucking loser. Now was not the time to be mooning over a young, inexperienced dancer such as Samantha. Now was party-time.

Tony stood and threw his book on his chair with a growl. He speared his fingers through his thick hair, giving his neck and scalp an aggressive massage. All his good intentions amounted to nothing whenever the memory of his mother's disapproval slashed through his mind like Freddy Kruger. Try as he might, his resolve weakened, and he became enslaved once more to old habits. Habits which blocked out the unjustified inadequacy he felt. Leaning over he switched off the light, sending him into total blackness. Pushing his fingers into his jeans coin pocket, he fished out a small packet. No one could see and that was the point. He rubbed the cocaine in the packet between his fingers, shrugged and went in search of someone to party with.

~ ♥ ~

WHEN THEY TURNED TO leave the theatre, Michele tapped her finger on her lips. "I think Tony Di Falco has more than a professional interest in you, Sam. I've a feeling he's quite smitten."

"Don't be silly, Aunty Michele." She purposely kept her gaze from meeting Michele's.

"I'm seldom wrong about these things." Michele waited a beat. "And if I'm not mistaken, you said before you were sad to see him go. I wonder if there isn't a little mutual adoration happening here. You know, Sam, you could do far worse than Tony Di Falco." Unlike her normal delivery, Michele voiced her opinion in a thoughtful, measured manner.

"He's my director and fifteen years older than me. I couldn't possibly . . ." *Damn*, Sam thought. Her eagerness and speed to refute the attraction had exposed a deeper truth.

Her mother stopped, turned and placed her hands on Sam's shoulders. "Samantha, whatever you do, just make sure you consider every possibility. Talk it over with us or someone you trust. Then make a decision. Okay?" SallyAnn waited for Sam to digest her advice. "You know what your father would say . . . fools rush in." SallyAnn cocked her head to one side and eyed Sam.

"I understand. Okay, Mum." But talking things over and not rushing in was exactly what Sam had been doing, but sometimes things were more complicated than her mother realized.

"Good. Now no more talk of my baby's sex life." SallyAnn cast Michele a sharp glance. "Let's find somewhere to have a hot chocolate." A consensus reached, they dragged their coat collars up under their chins and set off in search of a nightcap.

CHAPTER EIGHTEEN

TRADITIONALLY, EUROPEAN CHRISTMAS WAS celebrated on Christmas Eve with tables groaning under the weight of scrumptious food and drink. But since Sam was rostered to work both shows on the nights of Christmas Eve and Christmas Day, she couldn't enjoy a traditional European Christmas. So, she organized for an Australian Christmas Day lunch to be served at Hotel Hollandaise. This meant she could celebrate with her mother and Aunty Michele and still get to work in plenty of time. Madame Lucette supported Sam's plan and prepared the roasted meats and vegetables per Samantha's instructions. Sam even found the time and ingredients to whip together a delicious trifle and make some rum balls, which Madame Lucette thought were little orbs from chocolate heaven.

By noon on Christmas Day, the hotel's dining room glittered in true festive style, Christmas carols rang out from Sam's phone and chilled champagne waited to be popped and poured. A few tables were rafted together and dressed in festive red, white and green, awaiting the six guests.

Madame Lucette glided from the kitchen carrying a platter of hors d'oeuvre and offered them to SallyAnn, who accepted a tasty morsel. "I hear your nephew and my daughter are seeing each other?"

"Yes. Young love is sweet, don't you think?" Madame Lucette hovered on the spot, with an expectant expression.

"Maybe so, but sometimes it can also break a young girl's heart." SallyAnn cocked her eyebrow at the old lady, probing for more.

"Yes, it can do that too. But I hope not in this case." Madame Lucette's expression mimicked SallyAnn's, with the addition of a reassuring smile.

"Then we are on the same wavelength, you and I, Madame Lucette," SallyAnn said, satisfied. "To know you have not only your nephew's but also my daughter's best interest at heart is appreciated."

"But of course, Madame O'Brien. We must all look after our young lovers and love will look after them." Madame Lucette turned and drifted over to Samantha and Michele, who chatted next to the small Christmas tree in the corner.

The foyer door slammed, signalling the arrival of the other two guests.

"They're here." Excited, Sam ran out to greet them and returned with Philippe and his mother.

"Mum, Aunty Michele, this is Philippe and his mother, Chantelle." Sam stepped back awaiting the prerequisite hellos and kisses. In that split second, SallyAnn clutched Michele's arm, squeezing so tightly, her friend grimaced. Michele looked at SallyAnn, whose colour had drained from her face. "Honey, what's wrong?"

"Nothing, nothing's wrong. I'll tell you later." She hissed the words through her teeth like a ventriloquist.

"*Bonjour*, SallyAnn, Michele, I am so pleased to meet you." Chantelle swanned over to them both, kissing their cheeks.

"*Bonjour*, Madame O'Brien, Madame Stavros. It's a pleasure to meet you." Although exuding his usual, angelic charm, Philippe seemed very cautious and approached the ladies with due respect.

"Philippe, so nice to meet you." SallyAnn sounded somewhat stilted, as she offered him a shaky hand. As they chatted, Sam pulled at Michele and whispered, "What's wrong with mum? She's acting very weird?"

"No idea, Samantha. Maybe she's just nervous meeting your first real boyfriend. But look, she's settling down now. Everything's fine."

SallyAnn gestured to them to join the party and while the women chatted, Philippe retreated to bartending duties, opening and serving the champagne. A faint scratching noise drew their attention.

"Jasper," Sam said. "Look, Mum. It's Philippe's cat Jasper, there in his bag." The exotic short-hair cat wiggled out of the knapsack on the floor and with a final stretch freed himself to wander over to the group. He seduced Sam's leg with a slow, sensuous rub and was rewarded with a cuddle. "Jasper, this is my mum and Aunty Michele." Everyone made the necessary fuss and cooing noises over Jasper before Sam released him to prowl around the dining room where he found the best spot nearest the radiator, curled up and fell asleep.

The next couple of hours passed amidst good conversation, delicious food and lots of laughter. It was late afternoon when Philippe, Chantelle and Jasper made ready to depart. Philippe caught Sam's attention and motioned for her to join him in the foyer in private.

"Yes, Philippe, what is it?"

"I have a gift for you, Samantha."

"Oh, Philippe, we promised not to exchange gifts, remember?" Since they'd only recently made-up and Sam was still a little hesitant as to their future together, she'd not wanted any gift-giving between them. Now here he was with a gift, and she felt awful.

"I know we said that, but I had to show you how I feel. Here." From behind his back, he presented a jewellery case.

Even worse she thought. *He's bought an expensive gift.*

She prized open the lid and gasped. "Oh, Philippe, you shouldn't have." Inside rested a delicate Moulin Rouge pètillante necklace, dressed with pink and red *Swarovski* crystals — its design inspired by the roaring twenties. She knew the details about the piece because she'd been ogling at in the Moulin Rouge store window for some weeks. "Philippe, this is too much. Really it is."

"*Non, non*, Samantha. Nothing is too much for *La Goulue*, my queen of the can-can." Lifting the necklace carefully from its case, Philippe unfastened the clip while Sam held her hair up off her neck. He stepped behind her, fastened the pendant in place then returned to view its brilliance. Against Sam's creamy Irish skin and flanked by the open collar of her red blouse, the jewels sparkled. "Like the lights on the stage, they illuminate your beauty. The crystals dance nearly as good as you, Samantha."

Sam was breathless, her hand fingering the exquisite necklace. Philippe leaned over and kissed her like the first time he kissed her, at Le Pain de Pascal in the Place du Terte. A smitten lover's kiss, but this time, it lingered between them, filled with smouldering passion and expectation. She gave herself over to him, wanting him in her bed as much as he obviously wanted her. But today wasn't the day.

She came up for air. "Thank you, Philippe. This is lovely." She touched her hand to the pendant once more. "But I have mum and Aunty Michele here until the thirtieth, so we won't be able to spend any time alone until they leave."

Though he nodded in acceptance, he grabbed her hand and forced it against his pants' crotch where his raging cock showed its dissension. She smiled wickedly, pleased she had such an immediate and intense effect on him.

"Until then, *mon amour*, I will have to look after myself." Philippe raised his hand and displayed his palm to Sam, a resigned smile on his face. She giggled. It was good to have him back — him and his carefree spirit and naughtiness. Just then, the ladies ambled into the foyer saying their farewells. Philippe bid his final goodbye to everyone and helped his mother shrug on her coat. With Jasper stuffed snugly in Philippe's backpack, mother and son departed for the short walk to Chantelle's car.

Inside the dining room, the four of them tended to the last of the clean-up. Having spied the sparkling necklace, the three women fussed around Sam, admiring her new gift.

"Well that is beautiful," Michele said with obvious approval. "At least he has taste. That's a start." She kissed Sam on the cheek.

"I did say my nephew was a stubborn young man. I knew he would do everything he could to win you back." Seeing the other two women didn't seem to know the full circumstances of the young lovers spat, Madame Lucette said no more and hurried off to the kitchen.

Sam turned to her mother. "Do you like it, Mum?" Sam's voice lilted with the brightness a young woman should have when given a lovely present from an adoring young man.

"Yes, darling, it is very beautiful," SallyAnn said except her voice expressed no joy. Instead, a miserable resignation cloaked her words.

"What on earth is the matter?" Michele asked, surprised by her friend's response.

"I'll tell you. But not here. Not now. Let's finish helping Madame Lucette and when we're in private, I'll explain." SallyAnn gave them both a pleading look and set about carrying dishes to the kitchen. Not happy with having to wait to find out what was going on, Michele and Sam joined in, bustling double-time to clear away the Christmas luncheon.

Within the hour, the three of them gathered in SallyAnn's room, which was slightly larger than the others, with a small two-seater sofa jammed against a wall. SallyAnn perched on the bed while Michele and Sam sat upright on the couch, sipping their teas, ready for the explanation.

"Okay, spill it," Michele said.

"It's Philippe." SallyAnn peered into her teacup.

"What? What's wrong with Philippe?" Sam readied for a fight with her mother if she disapproved of him.

"Nothing's wrong with him. His mother Chantelle is a lovely lady and his father's name is Anton." SallyAnn raised her eyes to look directly at Michele, who stopped mid-sip and lowered her cup.

"Not Anton Lacroix?" Michele said in a whisper.

"The same." SallyAnn nodded with a grim pursing of her lips.

"Well, I'll be . . ." Michele couldn't find the words.

"Will someone tell me what is going on?" Sam demanded to know the secret.

"Anton Lacroix was my young French lover I told you about when I was a dancer at the Moulin Rouge. Phillippe is his son."

"Don't be silly," Sam said. "I'm sure there are plenty of Anton Lacroix in Paris. How do you know it's the same man?"

Sam thought the idea preposterous and wasn't in the least convinced.

"Because I asked Chantelle a lot of leading questions about her husband and her answers proved it was him. My Anton, from all those years ago. I knew it the moment I saw Philippe. He's so much like his father . . . boyish good looks with an irresistible charm." SallyAnn's eyes glazed over for a moment.

"So that's why you nearly tore a hole in my arm when they walked in." Michele gave the spot on her forearm a brisk rub.

"Sorry about that, but I just couldn't believe what I was seeing. I thought I was going to faint."

Sam remained silent, trying to stop the confused spinning of her thoughts. *With all the people in the world, how could I possibly have fallen in love with the son of my mother's ex-lover?* The odds seemed astronomical.

"Samantha, I'm telling you because I think you should know. Anton Lacroix was a very charming young man, so handsome and a generous lover." SallyAnn paused. "As a parent, I know the 'apple doesn't fall far from the tree' so I must tell you a little more about my affair with Anton." The air crackled with tension, as if the room was an animate object, holding its breath. Sam figured Aunty Michele knew the rest of the story by the expression on her face, but she was uncertain whether she wanted to hear it all.

"Mum, maybe you shouldn't. You know Philippe's father beat him when he was growing up because he was nothing like him. Philippe wanted to be an artist while his father wanted him to go into business like him. Anton was a terribly wicked man. I don't think Philippe could be anything like his father. He has a softer, gentler spirit."

SallyAnn remained motionless on the bed. "It doesn't really surprise me Anton got physical with his son. He never abused me but . . ." She struggled to find the words. "But he did like things rough." She paused for effect. "Sometimes he also wanted to explore other avenues, wanting to introduce other partners into our bed." Sam pursed her lips tight so her shock wouldn't find voice. "In the end, it was, shall we say, his perversions that finally broke us up. I left broken-hearted but not damaged. I came home with my self-esteem, my integrity and my ability to love again."

Before Michele reached to clasp Sam's hand, Sam sprang to her feet. Hot and furious, she glowered at her mother. "I am sick and tired of you and your sayings, the apple doesn't fall far from the tree, fools rush in, loose lips sink ships." She turned her scorn on Michele before spinning back to berate her mother. "I'm sick of all of it. I'm twenty-four years old and I can make up my own mind who I sleep with and who I'm going to love. I don't need your advice. Now if you'll excuse me, I've got to get ready for the show, which I'm dancing in and you're not." She spat the last insult with such venom, SallyAnn recoiled on the bed. Sam wished she hadn't said it, but her outrage carried her out of the door, back to her room.

SALLYANN TRIED TO HOLD back the tears but failed and Michele rushed to her side.

"What have I done?" SallyAnn spluttered. "It's Christmas Day and I've alienated my daughter. How could I be so stupid?"

"Well, your tarot card reading did talk about the goddess of battle, seeking revenge for a love scorned and clearing the air in anger. Well, that's sort of what just happened?

"I didn't get angry. Samantha did." SallyAnn's indignation halted the tears.

"I know that, but just the same you did get the whole Anton episode off your chest. You cleared the air. And remember what Madame Lucette said in the reading, 'what doesn't kill us, makes us stronger?' I think this tiff will make you and Sam stronger individually and together. It's just you told her things she wasn't prepared for, but that doesn't mean she thinks you're wrong. Maybe you hit a nerve?"

SallyAnn considered her friend's opinion. "You really think so?"

"She'll calm down, honey. I know she will. I guess it's as much as a shock to her as it was to you, about Philippe being Anton's son. Let's give her a little time to cool down and I'll go and see her. Okay?" Michele cuddled her friend's shoulders, trying to lighten her spirits.

SallyAnn nodded, hoping Aunty Michele could pave the way to a truce.

~ ♥ ~

THE KNOCKING AT THE door disturbed Sam as she finished packing her bag. "Who is it?" came the curt question.

"Tiny Dancer, open the door please."

Sam *harrumphed* and opened the door. "Yes?" She dragged out the question with a little too much indignation.

"Listen, your mother is gutted. She didn't mean to upset you. She's just trying to protect you—"

"I don't need protection, Aunty Michele." As the words flew from her mouth, Sam remembered the tarot card she'd pulled from a reading with Madame Lucette weeks ago — the goddess of protection. Faintly in the back of her mind, she recalled something about women to stand against forces that may threaten their home, someone who can point you in the right direction, finding her inner strength. Although her memory was blurry on the detail, Sam realized her mother's love, although overprotective at times, made her feel safe and secure.

"Samantha, are you listening to me?" Michele interrupted Sam's musings.

"Yes. Yes, Aunty Michele. Sorry. It's all right." Sam refocused on Michele and the subject at hand. "I was just upset. I guess I overreacted. I'm sorry. I know mum was only trying to help but she does tend to worry too much.

"I think that's part of a mother's job description." Michele gave Sam a tight, swift squeeze. "Now go in and see her. She's so upset."

Sam trundled off to her mother's room and within no time they were in each other's arms, full of apologies and promises.

~ ♥ ~

THE NEXT FIVE DAYS rushed past. During the short, bleak daylight hours Sam, SallyAnn and Michele crammed in as much sightseeing, shopping and spending time together as they could. Visiting museums and galleries, lunching in quaint little cafés and, even in the biting cold, they filled their time ambling through the historic beauty of Paris. The three of them blended into the city of love, arm in arm while snow fluttered onto their hoods and faces. Now with the air cleared between mother and daughter, their relationship blossomed into a more adult version. The three of them resembled the camaraderie of good girlfriends rather than the differing company between two generations.

In the evenings, Sam danced in the shows and returned home to her effusive mother and aunt. One night, Tony invited SallyAnn and Michele as his special guests for the late-night performance. They dined with him at his reserved table, appreciative of the privilege he afforded them with his kind gesture. From this vantage point, they had one more opportunity of watching Samantha before leaving Paris. As much as for SallyAnn and Michele, this night proved to be the best for Samantha because she knew her mum, aunt and director all watched her perform. During the applause, she imagined the looks of pride on their faces and it made her heart sing.

Far too fast, the thirtieth of December arrived, and it was time for goodbyes. No longer filled with the excitement with which they greeted each other a week ago, the three of them stood in the foyer looking miserable.

"I miss you already." SallyAnn hugged Sam one last time.

"Me too, Mum."

"You take care, Tiny Dancer. Remember if you need anything just call." Michele wrapped her arms around Sam, hugging her tightly. Having not had any children, Michele loved Sam as if she was her own. "Right, let's go before we all break into a waterfall of tears." Michele and SallyAnn heaved their suitcases behind them and left Hotel Hollandaise to catch a cab to the airport.

Sam watched them vanish into the mist and wondered when she'd see them again. If everything remained unchanged, she had another ten months to run on her dancer's contract at the Rouge. That meant she wouldn't be leaving Paris until next September and they probably wouldn't be returning before then. It felt a long time to be alone without family. Although she'd made the decision to accept the Moulin Rouge contract knowing all the pros and cons, having had her mother and Michele there for this past week and now watching them leave triggered a lonely ache, one which Sam hadn't experienced as acutely before. Though the tangible rewards on offer to stay, lifted her spirits, becoming a nude was a positive possibility, but when? And if that opportunity eventuated, how much longer would she stay in Paris? Like Penny did with Jacques, perhaps she'd settle down and build a life in Paris with Philippe. Sam paused to consider this more closely. The life Penny had built with Jacques wasn't what it seemed. Maybe Penny stayed because she loved her job but at the same time, was caught in an unhappy relationship?

The more Sam followed her options, the more her fingers toyed with the pendant at her throat — her Christmas gift from Philippe. All she was doing was increasing her anxiety levels by worrying about what might happen. Like a mouse in a maze, her thoughts scurried in one direction and then another, contemplating situations that hadn't even happened and may never happen. This worrying had to stop. She knew if she didn't get a grip on her mental state, she'd wind up hugging the porcelain again, trying to take control of her life. She so wished she had Scruffy with her or even Jasper, a little furry friend who wanted nothing more but to sit beside her and love her.

Sam wandered over to the small sofa in the foyer and sat down and imagined Scruffy and Jasper sitting on either side of her, purring and rubbing against her, showing how nothing matters nearly as much as she thought it did. A quiet peace descended upon her, slowing her thoughts and shooing away her anxiety. Here she was in Paris, living her dream, she had a terrific director who was convinced she was going to go far, she lived in a safe, quaint hotel within walking distance of work with a caring, compassionate landlady and she had a boyfriend, who although having suffered a damaged childhood, was doing his best to love her. All in all, Sam thought her life was pretty damn good. She smiled down to the imagined pets either side of her with a silent thank you. *Decision made. I'm going to take each day as it comes, stop worrying as much and enjoy myself more.* With a nod of her head, Sam left the foyer and ambled casually up the stairs to her room. For once, it felt good not to run.

CHAPTER NINETEEN

New Year's Eve in the city of love . . .

ALTHOUGH SAM HAD BEEN on stage for two performances tonight, she imagined what commotion had taken place outside the famous Moulin Rouge. The non-stop twinkling of the season's festive lights festooned in the trees, passing motorists and riders tooting their funny-sounding horns, laughing crowds with conical hats, streamers and whistles milling on the streets, lovers embracing and kissing on the stroke of twelve, not caring if they blocked pavements or traffic. Sam was certain it had been an extraordinary party atmosphere for one of the world's party capitals. Now after curtain down on the second show, the energy in the dressing room was just as exuberant, with champagne bottles popping and dancers slurping giggle juice in between removing their makeup and getting ready to join the celebration.

"Samantha, you are coming downstairs for the New Year's Eve party with the audience, *oui*?" With speedy efficiency, Josette had already removed her stage makeup and was applying her 'town' face.

Keeping up with her French counterpart, Sam added the final touches to her face as well. "Of course, Josette. And tonight, you'll get to meet my boyfriend." Josette struck her hand down on her dressing table and with eyes wide open, stared at Sam. "He came to watch the show tonight so we could celebrate New Year's Eve together now."

Still surprised, Josette said, "*Non?* A boyfriend? I finally get to meet your boyfriend?" She gave a short, sharp laugh.

Sam smiled a sassy grin and screwed up her nose at Josette in the mirror. "Yes, my boyfriend," she said with finality. "So, get a move on girl."

By the time they reached the auditorium, the venue buzzed. Audience and performers mingled, thrilled to celebrate new beginnings. Tall as she was, Sam still strained on tiptoe searching the sea of faces for Philippe. Then she spotted him, forging his way through the crowd to join her. His blond hair shone like a beacon, and she didn't take her eyes off him.

With a final push, he freed himself into her space. "Happy New Year, my queen of the can-can." Grabbing her waist, he dragged her to him, kissing her long and passionately.

Although she enjoyed the kiss, Sam sensed that such a public display of intense affection was inappropriate, considering this was her workplace. Hoping no one had taken too much notice of them she extricated herself from his grip. "Happy New Year to you, Philippe. I'd like you to meet my friend Josette."

Josette had joined a group just to Sam's left and was chatting away with a champagne glass balanced in her hand. When Sam tapped her on the shoulder, Josette spun around and the French fizz swirled over the side of the glass. "*Ooops*, sorry," Josette said.

Sam repeated the introduction. "Josette, this is my boyfriend—"

"Philippe," Josette screamed and as she threw her hands into the air, the last drops of the champagne rained down on them.

"Josette," Philippe yelled, obviously as delighted and surprised to see her. The two of them embraced giving each other multiple cheek kisses while Sam propped to one side like the third wheel.

"I cannot believe it," Josette said. "Philippe is your boyfriend?" She tweaked his chin and he gave her waist a tighter squeeze.

Sam stood blinking like the proverbial possum in the headlights through this effervescent reunion.

Philippe grabbed Sam and gathered her into his side. Lowering his voice, he explained, "Josette and I first met years ago when she came to stay at Hotel Hollandaise, when she began dancing at the Moulin Rouge."

Josette cut in, "Remember I told you, Samantha, when I took you to the hotel and you met Madame Lucette. Well, it was while I stayed there. I met Philippe." She snuggled into him once more. "How did you two meet?"

Philippe filled in the gaps of the story while Sam watched on, an ironic smile flickering on her face. She wondered if Josette and Philippe had been lovers as well. Not the most appropriate question to ask, but judging by their body language she wouldn't be surprised. All that whooping and jumping up and down seemed *OTT* for a pair of friends who hadn't seen each other for a while. But if they'd been lovers, would they be this pleased to see each other again? God, the French were so hard to fathom.

A waiter whooshed by and Sam snatched a glass of champagne and swilled it down too fast while Philippe and Josette played catch-up. When they slipped into their mother tongue, Sam slipped further into her thoughts. She looked around for another waiter and exchanged her empty glass for a full 'soldier.' Another drink she sculled recklessly.

"Happy New Year, Samantha O'Brien." The greeting purred next to her ear, warm and breathy. For a change, she delighted in her body's response to Tony's enigmatic presence. As if sensing her rapture, Tony kept his face close to her ear allowing his breath to caress her neck and his scent to envelop her. With a sensuous roll of her hips, she turned to face him. Unsure of whether it was the champagne too quickly drunk or the effect Tony had on her, Sam swayed uncertainly on her feet.

He reached out to steady her. "Are you all right, Samantha?"

Regaining her equilibrium, she said with a sultry smile, "Yes, thank you, Tony. Happy New Year to you, too." A flirtatious smile slinked across her face and she didn't care.

Tony conducted a quick reconnaissance of the surrounding crowd then returned his attention to her. "Are you here alone?" He leaned in to be heard above the din, but he was closer than required.

"No, my boyfriend, Philippe is here." Sam turned to discover Philippe and Josette had joined another couple of dancers a few steps away in the crowd. "Oh, he's over there with Josette, talking." She noticed her speech slurred and thought her mind and body seemed to be going their separate ways, much like Philippe had just done, leaving her alone.

"Samantha, since Philippe seems to be busy catching up with his French friends, why don't we go and sit down, over there?" Tony pointed toward the chairs in front of the stage.

"Okay," she said and turned to tell her boyfriend. At that moment, Philippe waved back to Sam, who sign-messaged where she was going. Philippe nodded unconcerned and returned to his animated conversation with the dancers. In an instance, Tony held her hand leading her through the crowd. She'd never seen him so focused, so intense, except at rehearsals. People congratulated him and tried to stop him on the way, but he nodded politely not slowing his pace. When they reached the chairs, he continued up the side steps onto the stage. "Where are we going?"

His pace quickened and his grasp tightened on Sam's hand causing her a prickle of anxiety. Within moments, they were secreted away in the heavy, black velvet wing curtains with Tony's dark eyes scanning her face. He held her to him in a tight embrace, his excited cock hard against her body. She moistened at its insistence.

"Do you think this is wise?" Sam asked.

"I noticed you haven't asked me to stop, so yes, I do think this is wise." At the omission of a refusal from Sam, Tony's cock swelled, and his eyes danced with delicious wickedness.

"I'm not sure what you expect?" she said, beginning to feel highly aroused but also uncomfortable at the professionally dangerous the situation.

"I expect nothing. But I needed to get close to you, to feel you against my body." His arm cinched her tighter causing her to release a sharp exhale. With his muscular thigh jammed between hers, she wanted nothing more than to ride it deep into her crotch, which she caught herself beginning to do. Tony smiled checkmate and ground his cock harder into her.

"Come with me." He released his grip, grabbed her hand and threw back the curtains. They marched off backstage to his director's corner. Not a soul was around as everyone was in the auditorium partying. He guided her into his chair then knelt beside her.

"Tony, we can't possibly do anything here."

He chuckled and fished out a small packet of cocaine from his jeans. Turning to her, he cocked an eyebrow. "Have you had cocaine, Samantha?"

"No," she said, but she'd heard about how it keeps you awake for hours and full of energy. Like the Energizer bunny, you never wear out when you're coked. Also, the sex was supposed to be amazing.

"Then you must try it." Tony had already sprinkled two small lines of the white powder on his side table and was rolling up a twenty euro note. With a quick snort, he sucked back one line and rubbed his nose. Lifting his head, he offered the note to Sam, who sat motionless.

What the fuck are you doing man? The moment he looked up at Samantha, he realized he'd made a monumental mistake. *That's what happens when you're too coked to think and your cock takes over.* The Samantha Effect, as he'd come to refer to Samantha O'Brien, was systematically undoing his sanity. Not only had she gotten under his skin, but he also couldn't rid himself of the growing sexual fascination. No matter that over the past week or so, he'd found other willing lovers to party with, he remained unsatisfied. His carnal thoughts kept returning to the talented, statuesque dancer and his body ached for her. Going to sleep at night fantasizing about what he could teach her and what they could do to each other had transformed from a nightly sleeping relaxant to a nightmare, one he endured savagely with his cock in his hand. Although physically spent at the end of every fantasy, he remained anxious and unfulfilled. This was what really unsettled him. He couldn't rid himself of the nagging feelings of attachment. And because she'd rushed home over the last few nights to be with her mother and aunt, he'd discovered he missed her. He missed her sunny smile, their bright banter, and her hopeful innocence which inspired him. At no time in his life had he missed anyone, except his father. Now this wretched combination of lust and affection strung him out so badly he'd lost his common sense. With too much coke and craving in his body, he'd just exposed his shortcomings to the one person he wanted to impress. *Recover and plead insanity*, he thought.

IN WHAT FELT LIKE an interminable silence while Sam sat and considered her options, Tony seemed to drift away to a place on his own. Glad of his wanderings, Sam collected her thoughts, ready to respond.

Just as she was about to speak, Tony snapped back to the present moment. "Oh, Samantha, forgive me, please. I don't know what came over me. I should never have offered you cocaine, and I certainly shouldn't have taken you away from your boyfriend. I'm so, so sorry. I need to clean this up." Agitated, he bent over the line of coke, snorted it, gave his nose a rough rub and returned the note and packet to his jeans pocket.

Springing to his feet with cat-like stealth, he proffered his hand and she accepted, rising beside him. When she locked eyes with him, she sensed the heightened energy as the drug sped through his body. Although the return to his gallant, controlled self was admirable, she wondered what fucking Tony Di Falco on coke would be like. No doubt, it'd be unforgettable. The longing to fulfil her initial fantasy starring Tony returned — the one where his demanding hands soaped her body, his fingers slipped in and out of her cleft and his breathy demands scorched her ear. Her knees weakened.

"Are you all right, Samantha?" He held her up, a look of concern on his face.

"Yes, I'm fine, Tony." When she clasped his forearms, his taut muscles flinched under her grip, and she wanted to drop to her knees and suck his cock.

"As I said, I'm sorry. I hope you'll forgive me?"

Looking at him, Sam realized his plea wasn't just personal. It was professional. "Don't worry, Tony. Everything's okay. I understand. We all do stupid things now and again to help us through. I know I have, dozens of times." She thought back to the times when fear overtook her, convincing her to purge herself in the false hope that all would be better afterwards. She cocked her head and smiled. "My Aunty Michele used to say addiction is the unattainable pursuit of pleasure. You like to pursue pleasure through cocaine. None of my business." She shrugged. "I won't be telling anyone. Your secret is safe with me."

A small sigh escaped his lips, and he relaxed. As he caressed her cheek, Sam closed her eyes for a moment, wanting to snuggle his palm, but didn't. "I always knew you were special, Samantha O'Brien. May I kiss you Happy New Year?" he said.

Sam opened her eyelids in a lazy manner. "I'm not sure if that's such a good idea—" And then he did. Ignoring her common sense, his mouth silenced her speech with a deep kiss filled with heat and longing. The attraction was too great for Sam, and she pushed herself into him, returning his passion. In the darkness, for a few fleeting moments, they sealed his secret with a clandestine kiss. Seemingly, one from which neither of them wanted liberation.

~ ♥ ~

"WHAT A NIGHT." PHILIPPE'S bubbly voice matched the champagne he'd drunk. Rugged up in their hooded coats, gloves and scarves, they strolled hand-in-hand to Hotel Hollandaise in the wee hours of the morning.

"Yes, it was," Sam agreed as she recalled her first New Year in Paris. It was a clear cold night and they joined the throng of people wandering home after celebrating. Even in the bitter cold, couples still canoodled, and families played in the freshly fallen snow. After Tony had made his exit, she and Philippe had finally found each other and enjoyed the rest of the night together, undisturbed by others. Strolling home, the quiet burbling of the *petite fontaine bleue* caught their attention. When they stopped to admire how the lights in the fountain danced upon the water, Philippe pulled off one of his gloves and fished out two one-euro coins from his pocket.

"Here, Samantha, let's make a new year wish." He handed a coin to her. "I'll go first," "I wish that Samantha stays with me for a long, long time in Paris." Philippe threw the little coin into the fountain and it clattered down to drown silently in the water. "Now your turn." He fixed her in a steady gaze.

Making wishes remained a private matter for Sam. Being asked to divulge any wish made her feel uncomfortable, especially since she suspected what he wanted to hear. "Oh, Philippe, I'm not sure. You know my greatest wish is to become a nude and then a soloist."

Philippe looked crestfallen. "But careers are short-lived whereas love lasts forever. Don't you want to stay with me, here in Paris for a long time?"

"Of course, I do, Philippe. But—"

"But what? What is it? It's not that thing with Jean-Paul at the studio?"

She could hear the irritation rise in his voice. "No. No, Philippe. It's just . . . Oh, I don't know. I'm just being stupid." She kissed his nose and turned to the fountain. "I wish to stay in Paris for a long, long time with *mon ange.*" The coin struck the top of the water, rippling it outward in small circles.

"*Bon.*" Philippe wrapped her in his arms. "Then let us away to do what all lovers do on New Year's Eve." He squeezed her hand and set off at a brisk speed back to the hotel.

~ ♥ ~

"My God, Samantha, I can't get enough of you." With his face nuzzled into her neck, his voice sounded muffled and breathy. Plunging his cock deep inside her with a steady, unhurried rhythm, he clung on as if for life. With his arms wrapped around her shoulders and his weight upon her, she couldn't move. Not that she wanted because she was well and truly satiated. Drained, she lay legs splayed underneath her lover while he wrung out every last ounce from them both. They'd spent over an hour or more feasting on each other in a series of ever-changing positions. Atop his face, she'd orgasmed multiple times, drenching him with her essence. Next, like a rodeo rider, she'd bucked as he tongue-fucked her and chewed her clit until it burnt. If he slowed the pace, she arched her back, thrusting herself harder on his tongue while grabbing his lonely cock, using it as a whip to spur him on. Then he tossed her face into his crotch and thrust his cock deep into her mouth. With her thighs wrapped around his ears, he continued to eat her pummelled snatch, her perfect orb buttocks tempting him like a brazen hussy. If she tried to wiggle away for respite, his tongue speared into her anus, making her gasp and lift her screaming snatch back into his mouth for retribution. With faces devouring each other's sex, they groaned and came, giving each other more and more. His long persistent fingers had teased, rubbed and tweaked her flesh all over and without mercy. Her breasts, nipples, clit, cleft, G-spot and even her arse had been conquered by Philippe's artful fingers. He'd wasted nothing of her. He'd consumed all of her. Now exhausted, raw and euphoric, she lay beneath him, while he dragged his cock in and out of her with a relentless hunger. Like a glutton, he couldn't be sated.

"Enough, Philippe," Sam said as the first light of dawn peeped in through the curtains. "I need to sleep. You mightn't have to work today but I've got two shows tonight." She pushed at him, rolling him off.

He slumped next to her and cradled her into his shoulder. "I think I love you, Samantha," he said, in a tender whisper.

"What did you say? Sam tilted her face upward at his untimely admission.

"Yes, I think I love you," Philippe repeated his confession more audibly before drifting off to sleep. No sooner had he met the Sandman, Sam joined him.

CHAPTER TWENTY

EVERYONE IN THE DRESSING room gathered around Madeleine as she gripped her ankle, crying hysterically.

"Madeleine, calm down." Penny tried to soothe the dancer while placing an ice pack to the injured joint.

"*Non, non*," Madeleine yelped, refusing to allow Penny anywhere in the vicinity. As the calamity worsened, Josette leaned over to Sam and said in a matter-of-fact tone, "She is done. She will not dance again for a long time. I saw her twist it. It is bad." The crowd dispersed when a medic rushed into the room and took control. Followed by another equally efficient and handsome young man, the two of them heaved Madeleine up, and supporting her weight, manhandled her off to the hospital.

"Okay, everyone. The commotion is over. Back to your places." Penny clapped her hands and shooed the gossiping dancers away.

At their mirrors, Sam spoke aloud to no one in particular, "It's only the third of January and we already have someone out."

Out of the corner of her eye, she saw Bridgette glance at her and then cast a further look sideways to Josette. Her expression indecipherable, Bridgette nevertheless seemed to be conveying something to Sam but before she could ask, Josette said, "So I wonder who the permanent nude role will be offered to now?"

"I don't know. It's up to Tony since he doesn't leave for another few days. I bet Penny's pleased he'll be making the final decision." With a cotton wipe drenched in makeup remover in her hand, Sam swabbed off her eye makeup in one long stroke. She changed the topic. "I guess you and Philippe go back a-ways then?"

"Oh yes. We are like brother and sister, Philippe and me. He saved me from many a bad love affair when I lived at Hotel Hollandaise."

"Oh." Sam hoped she sounded nonchalant.

"*Oui*. I am very happy you are with Philippe. He is very handsome, *non*?" Josette crinkled her perfect nose like a minxy rabbit and waited for Sam to agree.

"Yes, Philippe is very handsome." She felt her cheeks blush.

"And a good lover too, I think?" Josette raised her right eyebrow in a high, enquiring arch.

"All I will say is that he suits me." Sam wiped at her cheeks, removing long streaks of makeup, self-conscious at her friend's candid question.

Josette cast a cheeky look at Sam in the mirror. "Every woman needs a good lover. One who will give her lots of eating and fucking." She drove her hand between her legs, rubbing it up and down in an exaggerated manner.

"Josette, stop that." Sam tried to keep a stern expression but failed.

"Ah, ha. I see he is a good lover by your face. This is good, Samantha. I'm pleased for you." Josette returned to her own post-show ablutions.

After a few moments, Sam ventured onto shaky ground. "So, you and Philippe never . . .?"

Josette's laughter filled their side of the dressing room. "*Non, non*. Never. We were too busy with other lovers."

"I see." Sam thought Josette's response was much like Philippe's when she asked him the same questions a few days ago. Somewhat vague and unsatisfying. It appeared they hadn't been lovers. Not because the desire wasn't there, but because they were with other people at the time. No matter, though. It was all in the past and of no consequence to her renewed relationship with Philippe. *And anyway, Philippe told me he loves me. It doesn't matter what's happened before, he's with me.* And she put the matter and her accompanying anxiety to rest.

~ ♥ ~

Subdued, Sam walked into the boardroom. It wasn't a room a dancer wished to visit because it usually meant a warning or dismissal. Though Sam had no idea why she'd been summoned, she feared it wouldn't be good news. With a variety of enormous Moulin Rouge posters adorning the walls and a couple of green leather Chesterfield couches forming an L-shaped conversation nook in one of the corners, the room possessed an atmosphere of austerity and history, which only added to her discomfort. An imposing teak table surrounded by at least a dozen equally grand high-backed chairs occupied the space, leaving just enough of a gap for one person at a time to pass behind them. Seated at the far end of the table Tony glowed in his directorial magnificence and to his right sat Penny, forever his trusted assistant. Sam paused at the doorway and tried to quell her apprehension before meeting the two people who held her future in their hands.

Tony rose. All official and remote, he nodded to Sam. "Samantha, please come in." She walked toward him, noting his hair was pulled back in a loose ponytail, his normal style for work, and he wore an open-neck, lilac striped business shirt. She'd never seen him in a business shirt and as usual, he looked drop-dead-gorgeous. Moving closer, she could see he still wore his blue jeans and white converse sneakers which helped her relax a little.

Penny stood up next to him. "Thank you for coming in, Samantha, at such short notice."

Sam had been called in at two P.M. on her rostered day off. Not a good sign. With dread in her heart, she'd dressed *tout de suite* and hightailed it into work. Now her nerves rattled around in her stomach like unsecured crockery on a fishing trawler. What's more, the image of stale fish made her nauseous.

With a gracious smile, Tony motioned for her to sit on the opposite side of the table to Penny, making a triangular formation with him at the head of the table.

It was Penny who opened the conversation. "Sam, you know Madeleine injured her ankle." Sam nodded and tried her utmost to stop wringing her hands in her lap. Penny continued, "It seems she's fractured her ankle, so she'll be off for some time."

"Oh, that's awful." Sam sympathized with Madeleine's plight of not being able to dance and the uncertainty of return.

"Her swing can't continue to do Madeleine's nude role because she'll be leaving the Rouge shortly to take up a contract elsewhere. Besides, we'll need a permanent dancer to take on the nude role — and the sooner the better, for the show."

Sam's heart skipped a beat and her hands froze.

Tony spoke, his voice resonant and calm. "So, Samantha, we've decided to offer you the nude role for the rest of your contract." Both Tony and Penny broke their authoritative air and grinned.

A reciprocal smile rushed to Sam's face as did her hands. With a whirlpool of happiness spinning in her stomach, Sam said, "Oh thank you. Thank you both. I always hoped to be a nude here, but this is so soon. I can't believe it. Really I can't."

Tony reached over and took her hand, giving it a congratulatory pat. "As I've said many times, Samantha, you were born to be a nude and then a soloist, and Penny agrees with me. You are the dancer for the role. We're very proud of you." Just as Tony and Penny congratulated her further, Sam stopped. The colour and smile drained from her face.

"What is it?" Penny narrowed her eyes at Sam's change of mood.

"I don't think I can take the role."

"What? Why not?" No longer tranquil, Tony's tone became gruff and terse. Ursu, the bear, had awakened from his long hibernation and was not pleased.

"Because I promised Josette that if a nude role ever came up, she should have it. After all, she's been here much longer than me and she is just as good a dancer." Sam's shoulders slumped as she remembered the promise she'd made only a couple of months before.

"But, Samantha, we're not offering the role to Josette. We're offering it to you," Penny explained, seeing Tony's lips purse and his arms fold irritably across his chest.

"But why aren't you offering it to Josette?" Sam knew it was none of her business how they promoted the dancers, but the impertinent question escaped before she could stop it.

Tony rolled his chair backwards with a hard shove and stood. With both women still seated, he rose to a towering height, his fierce stare firmly fixed on Sam. From above, he placed his hands wide on the table and leaned down toward her face. There was no doubt as to his mood and there was certainly no romance or affection in it.

"Samantha," he growled, long and deep. It reminded her of the first time at rehearsals when she displeased him. Her hands once more found each other and began their endless fidgeting torture in her lap.

"Yes, Tony," she said, meek as a mouse.

"The decision to promote from within and offer you the role of nude is not one we take lightly. How we came to this decision is not your concern." He waited a beat. "Penny and I have thought long and hard about this and we believe you are the best dancer for the job. This is a great opportunity you're being given." His dark eyes drilled her, waiting for her to accept.

Penny tried tempering his annoyance by breaking their stalemate and getting Sam's attention. "Josette was considered for the role along with a couple of other dancers, but when we took all things into consideration, we decided you were the best dancer technically, physically and professionally."

Sam remained silent. Tony pushed back from the table with a grunt and began to pace. Sam knew this wasn't a good sign and that a whole lot of bad was about to befall her if she didn't say something — something that would bide her time and placate Tony, but she just wasn't fast enough.

From the other side of the room, he bellowed, "You want to think about an opportunity of a lifetime because you made a silly dancer's promise?" He pounded his fist on the table. With a vicious shake of his head, he turned and stalked to the boardroom's door. The temperature in the room dropped as if the demons of hell had been unleashed upon the planet. He propped at the doorway and over his shoulder glowered another incredulous stare, shook his head and made a perfectly timed, theatrical exit.

~ ♥ ~

WHAT THE FUCK IS wrong with this girl? Tony thought, stalking down the corridor. A couple of dancers on their way to the administration office were about to say good afternoon to him, but on seeing his alter ego, Ursu in full expression, they shimmied up against the wall allowing him to pass. *For God's sake, the girl has real star quality.* She told me she wanted to one day be a nude and then a soloist and now she's turning it down? He prowled off his initial anger through the theatre, growling at anyone who merely glanced in his direction. He needed to get out of here. After grabbing his coat from his office, he slammed out the backstage doors onto the street where the January freeze, not only assaulted his physical senses, it dug into his emotions with a savage bite. He came to a dead stop.

"Fuck," he said out loud.

Pulling his coat collar up and wrapping his scarf around his neck like a noose, he turned away from the Rouge. Head down, brows furrowed, and his hands jammed deep into his pockets, Tony took off. It wasn't so much she was turning the job down; she was turning him down. As a type-A personality, Tony was a man used to getting his own way, both professionally and personally. And here was this talented, beautiful dancer turning him down. Maybe he'd been right in the first place? Maybe Samantha wasn't the exception to the rule? Don't get too close to them because sooner or later, all women make you angry. This should have been a no-brainer. He should've walked away the hero after making her dreams come true, and she should have been eternally grateful. Anyway, he was leaving soon, and all this would be behind him. With a deep growl, Tony hunched over against the sharp wind and lurched off to his apartment. Though he continued his internal tirade, a stray thought found just enough space to bring a reluctant smile to his face. *But the girl's got integrity. I've got to respect that . . .*

~ ♥ ~

ON THE SLAMMING OF the boardroom door, the unsympathetic energy in the room dissolved. Feeling like an utter idiot, Sam propped her elbows on the table, head in hands and exhaled. The proceeding silence was broken only by her heavy sighs and moans.

"Sam," Penny said. "Just take the job."

Sam lifted her eyes, moist with threatening tears. "Penny, please listen. Josette has been a wonderful friend to me here. Without her, I think I would've gone mad. She so wants to be a nude. I can't believe you'd offer it to me rather than her."

"Over the time she's been here, Josette's name has come up in a number of instances of unprofessional behaviour. Nothing we could find evidence on, but like we say back in Australia, where there's smoke, there's fire. She's been the common denominator in a few things. So, whether you take the job or not, we won't be offering it to Josette. You have had an exemplary record, except for that one occasion when you were late. But that's all sorted now. Correct?" Penny tilted her head, waiting to be told Sam had no longer been purging.

"Absolutely, Penny. All sorted." Sam nodded her head vigorously.

"Good. So, you're the dancer for the job."

"But I told you about the broken promises Richard made to me in London and what a horrible effect that had on me. I don't want to be like him. I don't want to be a promise-breaker. I don't want to break my promise to Josette," Sam pleaded with Penny to understand. "I want this job more than anything else in the world. I just don't know what's going to happen if I take it. I'm sure Josette will never speak to me again. How can I possibly stay here if that happens?" Sam's teeth tore at her finger with such vengeful efficiency, her cuticle began bleeding.

"Sam. Stop." Penny slapped her hand on the table. "You're working yourself up over this. Just go home, relax and think about it. Today is Monday. We'll need a decision no later than Friday. That gives you two days over the weekend to learn the part, sign a new contract and begin as a nude the following Monday. I'm giving you four days to make a decision that normally takes any other sane dancer four seconds to make. If you need to talk to anyone, I'm here for you but you know what I think you should do."

Sam nodded in reluctant acceptance.

"Now go. And if I were you, I'd stay out of Tony's way until this is sorted. Understand?" Penny's suggestion sounded more like a command.

"Yes. I understand. I'm sorry, Penny. I'll work this out, somehow."

Signalling the meeting was over, Penny rose. "Now go. Get some rest but sort yourself out. This is your future here, Samantha. The future you wanted." Penny turned her attention to the manila folder on the table and shuffled the papers back into place. Sam realized her new contract was probably in there. A nude contract she should now be signing. Instead of celebrating her promotion, Sam walked away like a scolded puppy, tail between her legs.

At the door, she turned the doorknob and glanced back at Penny who nailed her in a stare. "Life doesn't always work out the way you want it to, Samantha. Sometimes great opportunities come at the same time as great challenges. True success is how you handle both the opportunities and the challenges. Never make decisions based on your fear of the challenges. Make them based on the potential of the opportunity. I'm sure you'll make the right decision. Good luck." With a sweet smile and dismissive nod of her head, Penny resumed her paper shuffling.

Sam departed thinking she'd left her sparkling future behind in the hands of a 'salt-of-the-earth' woman. One who seemed to speak from experience and who'd helped her through her darkest hour of self-abuse. She wandered home trying her utmost not to return to her old habit of self-recrimination and doubt. Instead, she steeled herself for the inevitable repercussions of the opportunity.

~ ♥ ~

"WHAT DO YOU THINK, Madame Lucette?" Sam had spent the last fifteen minutes explaining her dilemma to her landlady over a pot of English breakfast tea. Outside, the moon hid behind looming clouds while the wind scampered through the trees making them creak like decrepit wooden boards. The bleak, imposing night shrouded the hotel in a damp, swirling mist, and threatened to deteriorate, mirroring Sam's worsening despair. She and Madame Lucette were dressed in their pyjamas and dressing gowns, huddled in the dining room. During Sam's dissertation, Madame Lucette had remained silent and pensive, listening to the pros and cons on whether Sam should accept the role of a nude and break her promise to Josette or keep her promise to Josette and turn down the role. Now as Sam waited for an answer, Madame reached over and poured them each another cup of tea. When she released the teapot to resume its position in the middle of the table, Madame tugged her lavender, chenille dressing gown across her chest. "*Chère fille*, many years ago I faced a similar situation with a friend and an opportunity. Like you, I was torn. I went to my grandmamma. She was a wise, sensible woman, and I hoped she would tell me what to do. Grandmamma told me this . . . a promise is a commitment by someone to do or not to do something. Promises hold enormous power, for when we keep the promise, we show how much we value ourselves or the other person. When we break the promise, it shows a lack of value for ourselves and the other person." Madame Lucette paused allowing Sam time to digest her words. "Promises are made to be kept otherwise we should not make them, but we should only make promises on which we feel confident to deliver."

"Madame, I'm not sure any of this helps me at all." Although Sam heard what her landlady had said, it sounded convoluted and didn't offer any clarity whatsoever.

Madame Lucette's face brightened with a cunning smile. "Then let us see if the cards cannot shed some light on the situation for you."

"Very well." Sam acquiesced. "Let's see what the cards have to say." By the time she finished the sentence, the dependable pack of tarot cards rested on the table, calling Sam to shuffle. The now familiar image of the full moon peeping out from behind storm clouds on the back of the cards had a soothing effect on Sam. She remembered how at the beginning, the thought of a card reading worried her, whereas now she gave herself over to the cards' fortune-telling with quiet trust. Shuffling them in her hands, she took her time asking for their guidance in the tricky situation in which she found herself. Splitting the pack, she upturned the card and studied the gleeful yet ancient goddess looking directly at her. Dressed in a flowing lavender robe, an exact colour match to Madame Lucette's gown, the goddess stood in front of a Greek temple with a spinning wheel to her right and a spindle in her left hand.

Madame Lucette nodded, threaded her fingers together and gazed at Sam. "This is the goddess of fate, Samantha. She weaves the tapestry of life and destiny. She is also known as a fairy godmother. Whenever a child is born the fairy godmother pronounces the child's fate and it cannot be changed."

Sam listened intently to Madame Lucette, a deep sense of knowing rising within her.

Madame Lucette continued with more authority in her voice, "Samantha, we are all born with a life purpose and a destiny to fulfil. When we travel the path we are meant to, it becomes easier. If we veer from the path, it becomes more difficult. The goddess of fate is asking you to think carefully about what your life purpose is and how best you can fulfil it."

By now tears welled in Sam's eyes because she knew what she must do. "I understand, Madame. As hard as it will be, I must follow my life path. I must take the job."

Madame Lucette reached over to take her hand. "Yes, you must take the job, Samantha. The promise you made to Josette was not yours to make. You have done all you can. You told Tony and Penny how much Josette wants the role. You even told them she should have it. But it is not a decision you can make. You have kept your promise as much as you can within your control." Resting on Sam's hand, Madame Lucette's skin felt like soft tissue paper against Sam's taut flesh. She looked down at the old lady's hand and then into her grey eyes and realized Madame Lucette was soft all over — a soft, gentle, wee sparrow of a woman with the strength, wisdom and heart of a goddess.

Sam leaned down and kissed the back of Madame's hand, with the reverence and loyalty of a liege to her sovereign. "Thank you, Madame Lucette. Thank you for everything. You have shown me the utmost kindness since I've been here. I'll never be able to thank you enough."

"Don't be silly, *chère fille*, this is my destiny, my purpose. Now go and fulfil yours."

~ ♥ ~

SHE LEAPT UP THE stairs two at a time like an impala on the Kenyan plains. Once at the door, she knocked a demanding *rat-a-tat-tat* knowing Philippe was probably still asleep. She heard his muffled swearing through the aging timber door and imagined him dragging out of bed, tired and cranky at whatever nuisance was waking him so early on a Tuesday morning.

Bleary-eyed, he cracked open the door a little and scowled. Then his face brightened. "Sam, what are doing here? It's so early and it's freezing outside. Come in."

"I have news." Sam stepped thankfully into the warmth of his little grotto, shrugged off her coat and strode over to stand in front of the radiator. Philippe bent over and adjusted the tap trying to get more heat from the wheezing heater.

"Thanks, Philippe." She encircled his torso and snuggled closer not just for his body warmth but also for the affection. With deep sleep still cloaking his limbs in heat, he felt like a comforting doona enfolding her shoulders.

"Now what's going on? What's this news that has you in a flap to be up here so early? Sit down and tell me while I make us a coffee unless you're here for some early morning delight?" He glanced down with a wry smile at the tent his morning glory was erecting in his satin sleeping shorts.

Sam curled a sassy grin on her lips. "Maybe later" and gave his cock a tender stroke.

"Okay, later. Coffee it is for now." He ambled to the sink to begin the process.

After the incident at the studio with Jean-Paul, Philippe had said he'd not spoken to his friend since and that he'd found another studio to work in. Because of that, Philippe's flat now had only the bare artist's necessities and some newly finished canvasses draped in painting covers. They leaned as hidden secrets against one wall, destined to be publicly revealed at his exhibition in a couple of months' time. She never asked about her portrait, and Philippe never requested her to sit for him again. The whole matter had been forgotten by mutual agreement.

With most of his painting gear gone, the two chairs at his rickety table were vacant and there was enough space on the table to place a couple of coffee cups and a bowl of sugar. Sam chose the chair closest to the radiator and sat down, pushing Philippe's pencils and crayons into a small pile to one side.

A soft yet persistent head nudged at her ankle. "Jasper, good morning to you too." Sam lifted the cat and cradled him in her arms. "Come on, I'll give you something to eat." By the time she'd poured a bowl of kibble and Jasper was munching away contentedly, Philippe sat at the table with two steaming mugs of rich percolated coffee.

"Tell me, my queen of the can-can, what is so important you run here on such a freezing winter's morning?" His arctic blue eyes danced above the mug as he sipped his brew. She noticed he'd not got dressed. Bare-chested he slouched in his chair waiting, and Sam suspected he was waiting for more than her story.

"I've been offered the job of a nude in the show," she blurted out. "I have to make a decision as soon as possible whether I'm going to take it or not. If I do, I go into rehearsals straight away and start in the role next Monday." She was breathless not with the cold, but with excitement.

"*Magnifique*, this is what you've always wanted. Why haven't you already said 'yes'?" Philippe put down his mug and leaned forwards onto the table, crossing his arms.

"Because I made a promise to Josette that if we were offered the job, I wouldn't take it because she should have it." As the words tumbled from her mouth, Sam realized how silly the whole promise was.

"But was she offered the role as well as you?"

"No. They only offered it to me, and they said if I don't take it, they won't be offering it to Josette anyway."

"Again I ask, why haven't you just said 'yes'?" He reclaimed his mug, leaned back and waited.

"Because I know Josette will be devastated that she's not getting the role and then what happens. I've got to sit beside her in the dressing room for another ten months. If she blames me, it'll be unbearable. I want this job, and they want me, but this silly thing with Josette has me worried sick." The more Sam talked about the possible repercussions of Josette's disappointment, the more she doubted taking the job. Sam hated confrontation and especially with another dancer who'd been so good to her. Her fingers drifted up to her mouth to take the brunt of her insecurity.

Philippe shuffled his chair around next to her and took her hands in his. "Sam, I want you to take this job. It means you will be here in Paris with me, for not only the rest of this year but maybe for another contract. Perhaps, you'll stay even longer?" His eyes searched her face as if waiting for an answer. For the first time in her life, Sam contemplated not only having the career she loved, but also the love of a good man.

"Oh, Philippe, do you mean that?"

"Yes, I do. Let me prove it to you." He rose from the table and rummaged through his bedside table drawer. Finding what he wanted, he returned and placed a key on the table in front of her. "This is a spare key to my flat. Although it's not much, I want you to know you have free access to my home, my life and to me whenever you choose."

Sam studied the tarnished key for a moment. This wasn't what she expected when she bounded up the stairs this morning. All she'd wanted was his support, but this overt display of his commitment changed everything. She sprang from her chair and threw her arms around his neck, smothering his cheeks in kisses. "Thank you, Philippe. Thank you." Her heart danced a fluttery beat in her chest to match the tempo of her feet pattering on the floor.

Laughing, Philippe pulled her arms from his neck. "If I'd known such a simple little thing like a key would make you so happy, I would've given it to you when we first met. Please. Sit." He guided Sam back into her chair, but her feet kept up their merry dance under the table for a few more moments.

"It's not the key. It's what it means," she said, holding onto his hands. "It means you really do want us to be together, to be a couple."

"Of course, I do, Sam. More than anyone else, I want to be with you. I love you." He lifted her hands to his soft lips and kissed them with such tenderness, Sam was swept away by the romance of it all.

"Oh, Philippe."

"Now, about your new role as a nude . . ." He returned to the reason for Sam's visit. "Josette will just have to get over it. Would you like me to talk to her for you? Maybe I can ease her disappointment and point out it's not your fault?"

At this added ray of hope, Sam straightened, and her sunny expression brightened even more. "Oh, Philippe, would you? Do you think you can help Josette see I didn't do anything wrong if I take the job?"

"Of course, *La Goulue*, anything for you." Philippe encircled her in his arms, nuzzling into her neck with soft murmurs. Then with subtle extortion, he asked, "And will you do anything for me?"

"Of course, *mon ange*, anything," she purred and slipping her hand into his shorts, she took care of his morning glory.

Meowing for breakfast, Jasper prowled on the table as Philippe kissed Sam farewell. True to her word, she'd taken care of his morning glory with an outstanding head job. Now, he had to fulfil his promise of speaking with Josette. Knowing Josette better than most, he didn't relish the task before him. Stubborn and unpredictable, Josette could be a handful of trouble. Convincing her Samantha was in no way complicit in her not being offered the job, was going to prove difficult. Josette was just too volatile, too hot-blooded. It was one of the reasons he kept his distance on first meeting her years ago. But as he contemplated their meeting, another part of him awoke at the prospect of dealing with an impassioned woman. Smacking the head of his cock, he pushed out of his chair to feed Jasper.

~ ❤ ~

The word had already circulated that Samantha had been called to the boardroom yesterday for a meeting with Tony and Penny. Like any theatre, the gossip mill was in full swing with everyone speculating on what had happened. No one wanted to wait for an official announcement, so rumours became certain facts although nobody could corroborate anything. Sam had asked Josette to meet her in the dressing room an hour before the rest of the dancers usually arrived so they could have some privacy. Not wanting to be late, Sam dashed up the backstage stairs to the dressing room and skidded into the chair beside Josette who merely zeroed in on her with an icy stare. With nothing more than a slight snarl, Josette crossed her arms, sitting rigid and still.

Sam puffed out a breath. "Josette, I have to tell you something."

"I already know," she spat.

"Know what?" Josette was obviously furious, yet Sam hadn't even started a conversation.

"You've been given Madeleine's role, haven't you?" Josette snapped around in her chair, her arms beside her, hands clenched.

"Josette, let me explain—"

"Explain what? You promised me you wouldn't take the role of a nude before me. You promised me." Josette was in full French shriek, standing over Sam, her face reddening.

Determined to defend her case, Sam jumped up. "No, Josette, that's not true. Now sit down please and I'll explain." She touched her friend's shoulders gently, hoping she' d relax and listen. With an exaggerated *harrumph*, Josette plonked down in the chair with arms crossed once more. Refusing to look at her, Josette gave her mirror a frosty stare. One which reminded Sam of the wicked queen in *Snow White* and here she was, the innocent princess about to get her heart ripped out.

Sam swallowed and focused.

"Josette, Tony and Penny did offer me Madeleine's role yesterday, but I told them I couldn't take it because of the promise I made to you."

A more rapid change of mood Sam had never experienced. Josette flew from her chair with peals of laughter, hugging and kissing Sam's cheeks.

"Josette, stop. Sit. Please. I need to finish." Sam wriggled out of the embrace, her stern instruction halting her friend's lavish demonstration. Josette's eyes narrowed and returned to their hard stare as she cautiously lowered her bottom onto the chair.

"As I was saying, I told Tony and Penny that you've been here longer than me and that you deserved the role more than I did."

"*Bon.*"

"However, they made it clear to me that even if I don't take the role, which I haven't done, they wouldn't be giving it to you." Sam winced, preparing herself for another outburst. Instead, Josette's head swivelled toward Sam, like a snake eyeing a cowering rodent for dinner.

"They said what?" she hissed.

"I'm sorry, Josette, but if I don't take the job, they still won't offer it to you. I've been sick over this because I don't want to lose our friendship. But I can't give away this opportunity. I did try. Really, I did. But they want me to have the role and I want to take it. Please understand. It's out of my control." Sam wanted to get down on her knees and beg forgiveness from Josette. But she hadn't done anything wrong. A long pause ensued, and Sam wondered if she should present her case once more.

Then, Josette reached over and held Sam's hands. "It is all right, Samantha. I understand. You cannot help it if they want you rather than me for the nude role. I'll just have to try harder for next time." Josette sighed and her expression was one of wretched resignation. With pursed lips, she dragged her fingers through her blonde hair, fluffing it around her neck. "I'm happy for you, *mon amie*. Really I am." She leaned over and gave Sam a kiss on each cheek.

"Thank you, Josette. Thank you. I'm so pleased you understand. If there's anything else I can do, please let me know. Really . . ." Sam held fast to Josette with an appreciative hug.

"Thank you, Samantha. Everything will work out. I'm sure it will." Josette's tone was flat and measured. In so many ways, Sam knew she'd made the right decision and now she needed to tell Penny. But as Josette's embrace lingered longer than expected, tightening ever so slightly, Sam had a distinct feeling that everything hadn't been worked out.

CHAPTER TWENTY-ONE

"**Let's try that one** more time please," Penny called. Since they were the only two people in the empty studio, her crisp command bounced off the walls, adding to the intense experience of rehearsing one-on-one. Both Sam and Penny wore the same determined expressions while working together in this private capacity. With hands on hips in front of the rehearsal studio mirrors, Penny gave Sam a couple of extra notes before Sam repeated the routine again. Sam knew that once she accepted the role of nude, it'd mean long daytime rehearsals for both of them. And they loved every bit of it. At the end of the number, Sam held her pose chin lifted with imaginary stage lights on her face, her heart beating wildly.

"Excellent. You nailed it that time." Approval filled Penny's voice.

The sound of slow clapping reverberated in the rehearsal space. Sam glanced up to see Tony gracing the doorway, applauding her performance. "Well done, Samantha. I knew you were the dancer for the job." His praise sounded as much self-congratulatory as it was meant as encouragement for her. "Why not take a lunch break, Penny? Start again in thirty minutes."

"Thanks, Tony. I'll be back then." She threw her towel and bag over her shoulder and strolled out of the room, closing the door behind her.

Following Penny's advice, Sam had stayed out of Tony's way. Even though she'd accepted the role, Sam had steered clear of him, hoping Ursu had been tamed. In many ways, Tony was her nemesis. Every time Sam got comfortable in her life and her own skin, he'd appear as if challenging her, demanding more of her. His confident swagger teased at her insecurities, his power weakened her resolve, while his command of life made her ache for him to take command of her. Perhaps they were both driven by some purpose to be more and that was why she couldn't quite extricate herself from him, from wanting his approval? And perhaps that was why his presence ignited such a yearning in her?

"Samantha, I'm very pleased you decided to take the role. You look magnificent doing my choreography. It suits you." Tony edged beside her in front of the mirrors, their energy magnified by their reflections. Dressed in his standard rehearsal gear with his large male package cupped in his black dance pants, he pulsed sexuality. His upper body wore only a white singlet, exposing his well-cut muscular arms and chest whose veins sketched a road map of his masculine beauty.

Trying not to follow the route they plotted, Sam said, "Thank you for offering me the role. I'm sorry, Tony, I didn't accept it straight away. I love performing the nude role and I love dancing your choreography. It feels so natural to me." As did being next to him. The familiar tingling raced over her skin, and she wondered if he could see it ripple up her arms. Perspiration dripped from her body saving her from certain exposure. She was always grateful to speak with Tony when she could blame her hot-and-bothered look on having just danced.

"I've been working on a routine for my Vegas show. It's a *pas de deux* for lovers. Would you partner me so I can see how it looks on the woman?"

It was as if the floor fell away. To be asked by one of the world's leading choreographers to partner with him while he tried out his choreography was a dream Sam hadn't dared to dream. "Of course, Tony, where would you like me?"

I KNOW EXACTLY WHERE I'd like you. In my bed with my face buried between your legs. He realized he'd begun to lick his lips. Fortunately, Sam didn't see his expression because she turned away for a sip of water. Pulling himself from the fantasy, he shifted his growing cock giving it a hard squeeze to behave. When Penny had told him the good news about Sam accepting the nude role, he'd felt vindicated. Sam's acceptance meant he'd made the right choice. He wasn't an idiot, after all, contrary to what the voice in his head, which sounded remarkably like his mother's, said. Sam was a beautiful dancer, and he was pleased he could further her career with this opportunity. She was also a beautiful woman, not just physically but as a human being, and as much as he tried to rationalize the situation, his attraction and attachment to her strengthened.

"Actually, the man begins centre stage and you make a stage right entrance," Tony said, walking her to the spot. Side by side they stood, poised and ready to begin a choreographic coupling of love expressed through dance. When he took her hand, guiding it upward to her opening pose, the air in the rehearsal room sparked. Sam had partnered with many male dancers in her career, but nothing like this had happened. Sure, there was usually a zing between partners, but this was beyond mere dance chemistry.

"Now you'll come in like this . . ." He marked out the steps, and Sam followed memorizing each with accuracy and skill, mirroring his flow and expression. "Then once you get to me, you développé your left leg into my hand . . . here." He held his hand out and Sam obeyed. "Then you go into a full backbend . . ."

Sam arched backwards as Tony traced his fingers up her body, counting out the beats. During the next fifteen minutes, he taught her the basics of the routine, enough for him to get a feel for how it would look when performed as a *pas de deux*.

"Okay, let's try it, shall we?" Anticipation lit up Tony's face. He was in his element, bringing his creative vision to life. "I've got the music on my phone, so we'll plug it in and see how we go."

Sam nodded. "Okay. I'll do my best." Her determination to get the steps and style right, and not to disappoint him squelched the heady, sexual energy from before.

"It's an old 1972 classic sung by Roberta Flack. It's a number I've wanted to choreograph for years. 'The First Time Ever I Saw Your Face.' Do you know it?"

"I think so." Tentatively, Sam began to hum the melody.

"That's it. Good. Okay, here we go." Tony hit play and rushed to his position centre stage.

The opening piano chords filled the studio and Sam's spirit awakened. Transported by the music and the lyrics, she stepped into the space that only dancers inhabit. Lost to the emotion, she danced as if weightless, travelling toward Tony, hypnotized by the seductive depths of his dark eyes. Gliding up next to him, her hand caressed his face with a feathery touch and she too thought the sun rose in his eyes. She swooped her long body across his, and catching her in his arms, he supported her backbend, long and slow. Straightening her until erect, Tony's hand slithered down her spine, and they drifted into the next languorous phase, giving themselves over to the dark and endless skies.

With hands held, they circled each other producing enough air current to flutter the wisps of their hair. Like children playing, their smiles revealed the happiness they experienced in the music and the movement, and when he snatched her to him, her breath hitched. Face-to-face, they were a mere finger width apart. In the hiatus, their breathing synchronized, and he found her mouth with his generous, full lips. Even though it was only a stage kiss, it resonated through every fibre of Sam's being.

Ever in control, Tony dipped her with reverence into a deep, lingering lunge while Roberta sang about the earth moving in her hands. And Sam wanted to never leave his hands; his powerful, manly hands. Spinning into a cascade of pirouettes, she understood the trembling heart of a captive bird, until finally, with her body pressed to his, she abandoned herself to the dance allowing him the command she so longed for.

She stepped into an arabesque and with his hands secured at her waist, she encircled him with her raised leg like the wing of a swan, caressing and protecting him. She swivelled her face to his and they held their breath, making the moment last. Shoulder-to-shoulder, they watched each other in the mirror, stepping and gliding, reaching and stretching. Awash with bliss, their reddened faces shone with sweat and satisfaction.

Every movement became not just an extension of their bodies, but of their spirits.

Spontaneously, he changed the choreography and nodded for her to step back and launch into an overhead lift. Without hesitation she obeyed, putting all her trust into him. As she threw herself further into the joy, he lifted her with such confidence, power and grace, Sam felt like she was flying. High above on his outstretched arms, she floated and soared, while he paraded proud and tall beneath her. Gradually, he lowered her, his muscles flexing under the excruciatingly slow descent, placing her to the floor as if she was a delicate flower he didn't want to bruise. Overlocking his arms and taking her hands, he tumbled her, slowly unravelling her body like a ball of yarn to the floor. Motionless, Sam lay on her back for him to straddle and descend on her in a controlled plank. Totally still, he hovered above her while Roberta trailed off . . . your face, your face, your face.

Sam lay unflinching beneath him, their perspiration and breath mingling. His delicious dark curls stuck to his face like lashings of melted chocolate, and Sam so wanted to reach up to taste them. With eyes locked and air surging in and out of their heaving chests, neither wanted to break the spell they'd woven.

"Oh no." Sam's face contorted into a grimace, prompting Tony to dismount.

"What is it, Samantha?" He sat upright beside her. A look of concern now replaced the desire previously displayed on his face.

"Oh God," she moaned. "I've hurt my ankle." By now Sam cradled her right foot, rubbing it, hoping to reduce the pain and restore full mobility.

"Here let me see." Crawling around, Tony grasped her ankle and carefully moved the joint, testing it. "What happened?"

"I think it was when I took off for the lift. I felt it twinge but then it seemed okay." Sam leaned back on her hands, wincing at Tony's manipulation.

"It's only sprained. But to be on the safe side, I'm taking you home and I'll get my osteopath in to look at it. No more rehearsals or show for you tonight. We need you back in full working order to take the nude role on Monday."

Sam was about to protest, but he cut her off. "Samantha, I am the director, and you will do what you're told." He stood and helped her to her feet while Sam tried to ignore the flash of fire in her ankle. If she wasn't in pain, the fire would have been burning somewhere else in her body at Tony's non-negotiable command. No time for any wanton thoughts now. She needed to have her ankle examined. RICE was a dancer's strategy — rest, ice, compression and elevation — and that was exactly what she was going to do.

"Don't put any weight on it. Here let me help you." Tony circled his arm around her waist and shouldering her weight, half carried her to the mirrors. As Sam teetered upright, Tony helped her towel off and dress. Interspersed with a couple of sharp gasps from Sam when her ankle twisted, they both dressed in silence. With Tony once more suspending her weight, they hobbled to the studio door.

"Oh my God, what's happened?" Penny rushed in and dropped her gear, looking in horror from Tony to Sam.

"Samantha's twisted her ankle. I'm taking her to my apartment, and I'll get Pierre to look at it. I think she'll be all right in a day or so. You'll have to do the re-blocking for the show and sort things out here Pen'. I'll call you once we have a prognosis."

Penny nodded and stepped back giving them room to leave. "Okay, don't worry about anything here. You rest up, Sam, and do what Tony tells you."

Tony and Sam were out the door by the time Penny wished them luck. They lumbered along the corridor in silence. Then Tony looked at her. "It'll be all right, Samantha. I promise." She couldn't speak because a terrifying lump of fear blocked her throat and churned in her stomach. She was left with only one alternative . . . To keep a brave face even though tears rolled down her cheeks.

CHAPTER TWENTY-TWO

"*MERCI*, PIERRE. THANK YOU for coming so quickly. *Bonjour.*" Tony closed his apartment door and returned to his new patient. No longer lathered in perspiration, but still wearing his dance clothes, Tony strode back into the living room with a satisfied grin on his face. With her leg hoisted on a pillow, her ankle strapped tighter than a straitjacket and an ice pack perched precariously on top, Sam was completely immobile propped up on Tony's couch. Unlike Tony, she looked miserable.

"Well, good news, Samantha." He clapped his hands, rubbing them together, his eyes twinkling. "Pierre expects that if you rest fully for twenty-four hours, there is every possibility you'll be back in rehearsals, mark-through only of course, but ready to dance the nude role for Monday night's performance." He towered over her, delight spreading across his face.

"Really?" Sam struggled upright, her hope returning.

"Yes. He says it's just badly bruised, but you mustn't put any weight on it for at least twenty-four hours. Keep it up and keep it iced. So, you will stay here with me." He raised his eyebrow at her, ready for a rebuttal. Foiled, she lowered her chin and nodded in agreement. "That way I know you're behaving yourself." Tony wagged a finger at her, then bent down and fluffed her pillows. "Now, I'm going to shower and change and then it's your turn."

"What?" She blinked, wondering if she detected an ulterior motive in his offer.

"Samantha, you can't remain in damp dance clothes for the next day. I'll give you something to wear. Don't worry. We'll sort it out." Before she had time to discuss the logistics of what he'd said, Tony vanished into his bedroom, leaving his door ajar.

No sooner had she rested her head back onto the pillows, she heard the shower raining down in his bathroom. At the sound of falling water, her tensions soothed, and her mind began to wander. But before it made its getaway into another Tony Di Falco fantasy feature, she brought it back to reality with thoughts of Madame Lucette and Philippe. She must let Madame know where she was. She'd be worried sick if Sam didn't come home tonight. Madame could then advise Philippe, who wasn't expecting to see Sam anyway, because he knew she was rehearsing all day and performing all night this week. Still, he should know what happened in case he found out and started to worry. With her action plan decided, she relaxed once more, drifting into a light sleep.

She smelt Tony before she saw him. His aftershave with its musky, heady overtones, crept into Sam's senses, stirring a feminine yearning. Barely opening one eye, she watched him tiptoeing around the apartment trying not to disturb her. There was something about Tony, maybe his maturity, that Sam found intoxicating. His dark, smouldering looks, almost predatory power, creative brilliance and intense personality intrigued and seduced her on so many levels. And then there was Philippe — the ivory to Tony's ebony. Philippe's angelic, golden good looks, unbridled passion, joy for life and graceful artistry enchanted her, making her approach to life more adventurous. Never had she been attracted to two such different men. Yet destiny and professionalism decreed Tony remain off-limits. While Philippe's recent declaration of love offered Sam a security she'd not realized she sought. Fate ordained Sam would remain here in Paris with Philippe, fulfilling her life-long dream of being a nude at the Moulin Rouge. But fate had also given her the next twenty-four hours to enjoy the fantasy of being with Tony before he began his new life in Las Vegas. Taking all things into consideration, Sam felt quite blessed to have sprained her ankle.

Dressed in tight grey jeans, a loose-knit charcoal-coloured jumper scrunched up to his elbows and the obligatory white converse sneakers, Tony looked good enough to eat. His newly washed hair tumbled untethered over his face and neck, accenting his sexy Sicilian heritage and wild spirit. With his rock-hard arse stuck up in the air as he reached over to sort a pile of magazines, Sam shuddered and a quiet, appreciative murmur escaped her lips.

Tony glanced over his shoulder and a wicked smile tickled his mouth. "Good, you're awake. Now let's see if we can't get you cleaned up as well. Come on, let me help you." Bending down, he scooped his arm under Sam and lifted her to hop on her left foot. "Now off we go," he said, and they hobbled off to the bathroom together. "I've left this tracksuit here for you. It'll be too big but at least it's warm and won't be too much trouble for you to get into to. Okay?" Tony patted the garment and the clean towel he'd placed on the vanity bench.

"Thank you, Tony. This will be fine. I can take it from here." She shuffled over to the stool next to the vanity and shimmied down. With the heady smell of Tony's aftershave filling the air, Sam wasn't sure whether it was that or the twinge in her ankle, making her feel a little faint.

"If you need anything, just call." He gave her a stern look. "Samantha, I'm a dancer too you know. I've seen and helped many naked female dancers in my career. So, seeing or helping you undress is not going to make any difference to me."

"Well, it makes a difference to me. Thank you, but I don't need your help." With a dismissive wave of her hand, Sam shooed him away. Tony bowed like a feigning courtier, and with his eyes flashing up at her through his thick black eyelashes, closed the door behind him.

After Tony left the bathroom, he reeled in his lustful thoughts of Sam's nakedness just a room away and set about making dinner for them. That she'd sprained her ankle and was now holed up in his apartment amused him greatly. *Man, it's now or never. You've got to make a decision.* He set about grating a solid wedge of parmesan and mulled over what it was he wanted from Samantha O'Brien. Taking her into his bed would now be much easier since he was leaving the production and going to America. No more professional ethics standing in the way, and based on Sam's responses to date, he was certain she felt the same sexual heat. *Tonight's the night for that move*, he thought. Lascivious images flashed through his mind and as he chased after these wayward thoughts, his finger replaced the cheese on the grater. Damn. Instinctively his finger went to his mouth, reminding him of how Sam's fingers found little solace in her mouth, only punishment. She needed to relax more. He could help her with that. He could teach her many ways to relax.

Shaking the pain from his hand, he moved onto preparing the salad and got the vegetables out of the fridge. Cutting them into pieces, he paid more attention both to the activity and to his thoughts. He questioned whether a brief one-night stand would be enough. Was that all he wanted? But what else was on offer? He'd purposely kept his distance. They both had. Sam was ensconced in what appeared to be a growing relationship with that young French fellow. What was his name? Philippe, that's right. And now that she'd accepted the nude role, the opportunity for anything becoming more serious between him and Samantha was a moot point. *That boat has sailed, man.*

Realizing the shower had stopped some time ago, he walked over to the bathroom door and knocked. "Is everything all right, Samantha?"

"Yes. I'm fine. Thank you, Tony. Won't be a minute." Her voice sounded more relaxed. The brightness was back. He was pleased he'd made her stay. She needed looking after, and he was just the man to do it. Then it struck him. Out of nowhere, when he least expected it, the city of love had bewitched him. *Damn.*

He'd fallen in love. *Damn.*

He'd fallen in love with Samantha O'Brien and had missed his chance.

~ ♥ ~

SAM COULDN'T WORK OUT what had happened. Before she'd had a shower, Tony was his usual, naughty playful self, but when she came out of the shower, the gruff, grizzly Ursu had made a reappearance. Not that Tony has been rude or unkind. He'd just been reclusive, aloof and non-communicative. During dinner, he seemed distracted and hardly ate anything. Even when she asked him if everything was all right, he nodded but remained pensive. Then when he'd helped her to bed and settled her in, he seemed to all but bolt from the room as if she was infected with some serious form of contagion.

Here she was thinking they'd have a wonderful last night together. Laughing, talking and discussing her new role and his new show in Las Vegas. Although she'd been determined to keep it platonic, she missed their covert flirting. She missed the askance looks he gave her which made her feel not just desirable, but valuable.

In fact, the more she thought about it, the more disappointed she became. He never even commented on their dancing together today. It was such a special moment as far as Sam was concerned. Magic happened between them. Or so she thought. She must have been mistaken. Doubt throbbed in her mind and her ankle joined in. Tony's change of mood toward her stung more than she wanted to acknowledge. Her whole body ached and no matter how much she squirmed around in bed, she couldn't seem to get comfortable. Disappearing into sleep, her hand drifted to her chest. Heartache.

CHAPTER TWENTY-THREE

"*CHÈRE FILLE*, I HAVE been worried about you." Madame Lucette fluttered at the front door of the Hotel Hollandaise as Tony helped Sam into the foyer.

"I'm fine. Truly I am. Madame Lucette, this is my director and choreographer, Tony Di Falco. Tony, this is Madame Lucette."

Madame Lucette scrutinized Tony from head to toe. The warm, scented air of the foyer seemed to chill slightly as Madame's eyebrows arched high up on her forehead while her grey eyes narrowed. After what seemed like minutes, she returned her steely gaze to peer into his fathomless eyes. She snorted. "I see." A deliberate nod suggested she was satisfied. "Yes. I see." Her tone thawed. "A pleasure to meet you, Monsieur Tony Di Falco." Rattling bracelets provided the soundtrack when she extended her scrawny hand to Tony.

Not missing a beat, he said, "And a pleasure to meet you, Madame." He took her hand and kissed it with respect, leaning over in an exaggerated bow.

Sam watched this odd, almost theatrical introduction. It reminded her of some royal ritual. Madame Lucette, with her majestic posturing, was Queen Elizabeth I while Tony was the heroic Sir Walter Raleigh, forever grateful for his Queen's support in his expedition to El Dorado. *By love and valour,* Sam thought, having no idea from where these imaginings had sprung. Shaking the illusion from her mind, she returned to the present moment with a worrisome ankle. She needed to lie down with an ice pack.

"Madame Lucette, if you'd get an ice pack, I'll help Sam to her room. Which one is it?" Tony said, awaiting direction.

With a grand sweep of her arm, Madame Lucette pointed up the stairs, then without a word, turned to attend to Tony's request.

"This is going to be fun," Sam said in a cheerless voice.

"Nonsense. I'll get you up the stairs, no trouble at all." Tony bent down and collected Sam in his arms and began the climb. She clung to his neck, breathing him in. She loved the smell of him. He'd woken much happier this morning although her disappointment still lingered. Fussing over her, he'd made a breakfast of pancakes, strawberries and clotted cream with the best coffee she'd had since living in Paris. As the day progressed, her wish from the night before came true. They'd laughed, talked, played music and divulged years' worth of memories and events to each other. Now, snuggled into his strong neck, she missed him more than she was prepared to admit. The door to Sam's bedsit was open, so Tony eased her through the tight doorway. Madame Lucette had cleaned the room in preparation for Sam's return and placed a vase of flowers on the mantle.

Positioning Sam gently onto the bed, Tony propped the pillows behind her and another couple under her ankle. "How's that?"

"Thank you, Tony. Much better." She looked up at him with no words to say.

"Here you are. An ice pack." Gliding through the door, Madame Lucette appeared with a plastic bag of crushed ice and a damp cloth. She wrapped the cloth around Sam's bandaged ankle and steadied the bag on top. "There. I'll be back in thirty minutes with a fresh one." Before anyone could thank her, she waltzed from the room, closing the door noiselessly behind her.

"She's a strange old bird," Tony said with a smile.

"I thought so too when I first met her, but she really is a dear. Quite eccentric, but I've never seen her wrong on anything."

"Well, I guess I'll leave you in her capable hands then." Tony's smile weakened but his eyes blazed. The silence stretched. "Samantha, you are happy here in Paris, aren't you?

"Oh yes. Very happy. I have my dream job and on Monday, if my ankle is strong enough, I'll dance the nude role at the Moulin Rouge."

"Good. I'm pleased to hear it. And you'll be magnificent. I have no doubt." He reached down and patted her hand, then entwined his fingers with hers. "Samantha, although I said I'm not leaving until Tuesday, something's come up, and I have to leave earlier."

"But you said you'd watch me dance the nude role. You were looking forward to it." Her voice cracked with emotion.

"I know but I have to go. I'm sorry I won't be here, but I know you'll be breathtaking." The admiration in his eyes made it even harder for her not to feel disappointed.

Sam slumped. "When do you leave then?"

"Monday."

Neither spoke. The tension thickened until the air pricked her skin. On the edge of tears, she couldn't speak for fear of making a fool of herself. She didn't know whether her intense upset came from his leaving early or from his leaving, full stop.

"This is a sweet room, Samantha. It suits you." Tony walked to the French doors and pulled back the curtain to admire the view of the courtyard. Sam turned her head and stared at him. *What is wrong with me?* she thought.

"Such a pretty view. It must look beautiful in spring when the linden trees are all shades of green and the moon is full . . ." The trailing of his words hit Sam like a body blow. There he stood, his outstretched arms reaching to either side of the French door frame. The perfect triangle of his body topped with a shock of unruly black curls and toed with his white-sneakered feet, stirred the roiling emotion in Sam's stomach. Tears rolled down her cheeks, and she swallowed hard trying to stop the audible escape of the sobs filtering upward to her throat. He was leaving . . .

The door opened and Madame Lucette swept into the room. On seeing Sam, she hovered over her, protecting her. "There, there, Samantha. Your ankle must be hurting. Let me help you." Madame Lucette peered down into the emerald swimming pools which were Sam's eyes, registering their distress. While she maneuvered a fresh bag of ice into place with a sympathetic smile, Sam looked at her with gratitude.

She blinked hard, hoping the tears would stop. Sneaking a peek over her shoulder, Madame noticed Tony still with his back to them, lost in thought.

"Tonight is a new moon." Madame Lucette drifted over to him, shrugging her shawl around her shoulders. Standing side by side, they studied the dark night sky. Devoid of the moon and with the stars hidden by wispy clouds, the sky seemed painted in syrupy, black ink. "A new moon symbolizes new beginnings. It is a time when you look at old goals and set new ones. The new moon brings with it the opportunity to start anew, to refresh your dreams, your desires, and your future goals."

Tony stared down at the small-framed elderly lady beside him while Madame Lucette's gaze remained fixed ahead. Sam watched this unmoving tableau from her bed, unsure of its meaning. At least, she'd stopped crying. Tony nodded to Madame Lucette and she stepped back, allowing him to squeeze past her.

"Samantha, you rest up now. I'll come and see you in rehearsals." He bent down, kissed her cheek and pushed back a stray tendril from her face. "Everything will be all right. I promise." Before she could say goodbye, he was gone.

"Now you rest, *chère fille*, I will be back soon with some more ice." Like Tony, Madame Lucette made a hasty exit, leaving Sam alone in her room with nothing more than sadness for company.

Determination drove Tony from Samantha's room. That and something the crazy old landlady had said, but he couldn't quite get a handle on it. By the time, he reached the foyer, he heard her call out to him in a loud whisper, "Monsieur Di Falco. Monsieur Di Falco."

He pivoted around and spotted her gliding across the floor to where he stood. *She's an odd one*, he thought and shook his head. "Yes, Madame Lucette, what I can do for you?"

She clucked her teeth and mirrored his head shaking. "There is nothing you can do for me, but I wanted to thank you for giving Samantha the wonderful opportunity of the nude role at the Moulin Rouge. She is so excited about it."

"She deserves it. She's the best dancer for the role."

"And I understand you are leaving and going to Las Vegas soon?" She cocked her head like a hen, brisk and inquisitive.

"Ah, yes. I'll be leaving Monday at this stage."

"At what time?" Her head cocked to the other side.

Tony thought she'd looked very comical and her inquisition strange, but he certainly wasn't going to offend Madame Lucette by not answering her questions. "I leave on the Delta Airlines eight A.M. flight Monday morning."

"*Merci.* It's been a pleasure to meet you, Tony. I wish you every success with your new beginnings in Las Vegas." She proffered her hand once more, obviously finishing the conversation.

Accepting her hand obediently, Tony shook it politely. "And you too, Madame Lucette."

With a sweet smile and folding her arms under her shawl, she waited for him to depart. Bewildered, Tony walked to the front door and stepped out into the night of the first new moon of the year. It was then he knew what he must do.

CHAPTER TWENTY-FOUR

PIERRE HAD BEEN CORRECT in saying the recovery of her ankle would be successful if she kept off it fully for at least a day. The past day and a half of bed rest had worked. Further complying with Tony's added instructions, Sam had only marked through today's rehearsals with Penny and found her confidence returning.

"Excellent, Sam. You know all the routines now. Well done." Sitting beside Sam as she foisted another bag of ice on her ankle after rehearsals, Penny patted her young charge's shoulder with professional affection.

Sam gave a deep sigh of relief. "Yes. I feel confident with the new routines and my ankle feels remarkably good. Even after being up on it today, I can feel its strength and flexibility returning."

"Just to make sure you're ready for Monday, we're giving you tonight and tomorrow night off to fully recuperate."

To be given two nights off, particularly a Saturday night was a rare privilege. "Oh, thank you, Penny." Sam stretched over and gave her a spontaneous hug. "I'll take it easy. I promise."

"Good. Then I'll see you here Monday afternoon ready for your first performance as a nude at the Moulin Rouge." Penny beamed a radiant smile of pride at Sam, then collected her things and left the studio. Sam was in no hurry to leave. She needed to keep her ankle elevated and iced for at least ten minutes before making her way home. Sitting alone in the quiet studio proved the perfect relaxation. Sam began to hum "The First Time Ever I Saw Your Face," remembering the routine Tony had taught her yesterday. Although she'd injured her ankle, the sweet memory of their dancing together was worth it. Swaying where she sat, Sam hummed the music, moving her arms to the flow of choreography. She became so lost in the memory that she didn't hear the door open, nor the soft padding of his sneakers.

"Hello, Samantha," he whispered beside her cheek. She jumped and blinked up into Tony's face. "Sorry to startle you, but Penny tells me the rehearsals went well and that your ankle is much better. I'm pleased to hear it." He pulled out the vacant chair, turned it to face him and threw his leg over it to sit, open-legged, staring at her. Sam tried not to appreciate his poise and position but failed. Disobediently, her eyes travelled down to his crotch only to make a hasty and obvious return. Her inability to hide her delight seemed to please him, because his smile broadened into a cheeky grin. Were you mentally marking through the routine I taught you yesterday?"

"Yes. I loved it." Drifting back to the moment, she relaxed and began to sway again to the silent melody in her head.

"You danced it very well, Samantha. Very well indeed."

"Really?"

"Absolutely. I'm sorry I haven't mentioned it until now, but you were the perfect partner. We are well-suited in height and style for my choreography." His dark, pooling eyes never wavered from her face and the rising heat racing over her body made Sam blush. To think that Tony Di Falco was giving her such a wonderful appraisal and compliment compensated for her ankle injury. She'd remember this conversation forever.

"Would you like me to help you home? I'm going that way and can carry your bag for you. It'll save you overworking your ankle." Not waiting for a reply, Tony was on his feet with her bag over his shoulder. "And you think I'm too old for you. Ha!" he snorted. "Look at you, hobbling to stand up."

Sam stopped mid-hobble, surprised at his odd comment about their age difference. Why would he say that? What did he mean? Unsure of what to say, Sam gave a gracious smile. "Thank you, Tony. That's very nice of you to offer."

"Let's go then," and with his hand gently resting on the small of her back, he guided her from the rehearsal studio.

The slow stroll home proved uneventful. Little conversation passed between them and a comfortable silence warmed their way. Stopping at *petite fontaine bleue*, Tony turned to her. "Remember when we stood here some months ago, and I asked you what you wished for?"

How could she forget? "Yes, I wished I could be a nude at the Moulin Rouge."

"And that's exactly what's happening? That must make you very happy, Samantha?"

God, why did he keep asking if she was happy? "Yes. It does. It's what I've wanted for so long." Again, he searched her face, with an unspoken question teetering on his lips. *Just ask whatever it is?* she screamed in her mind.

"I'm pleased," was all he said.

ON PURPOSE, HE DIDN'T go into Hotel Hollandaise. He said his farewell at the door, telling Samantha he'd see her tomorrow to check on her recovery. It took enormous willpower on his part, not to scoop her up in his arms and ask her to go with him to Las Vegas, but he withstood the temptation. He couldn't ask her to give up her dream. Of all people, he knew the power and promise of a dream come true. Not only that, he'd given her the perfect opportunity today when he broached the matter of their age difference. She could have negated the fifteen years between them with one of her sassy comebacks, but she hadn't. Instead, she'd chosen just to ignore his remark. It seemed that it did matter, at least to her.

WITH AN ICE PACK lodged on her ankle, she lay on top of her bed resting. A knock at her door brought a flutter of excitement with it. The door cracked open just enough for a bunch of red roses to appear at the end of a hand.

"These are for the most beautiful girl in the world," Philippe's cheery voice called from the other side of the door. Before she knew it, he was sprawled on her bed like a cheeky pet, lavishing her with kisses.

"Philippe, Philippe, stop." Although the affection was appreciated, his jumping around sent slivers of pain up her leg.

"Sorry, Samantha. Sorry. These are to help you feel better again." At arm's length, he held out the bouquet.

Taking his gift, she buried her nose into the flowers' silky petals, delighting in the sweet scent. "They're beautiful. Thank you." She motioned for him to place them on the mantle. She'd get a vase later.

"How's your ankle?" Philippe brushed his hand lightly over her lower leg.

"Much better, thank you. I got through rehearsals today, and I think I'll be ready for Monday."

Philippe crawled back on the bed and snuggled beside her. "I am so pleased. I've been worried about you. But you are strong. You are my queen of the can-can. You will dance wonderfully on Monday night." She nestled into his shoulder while he stroked her cheek and dotted her forehead with kisses. She'd missed his affection and bright spirit. His hand drifted down to her breast, circling its firmness and rubbing his thumb over the nipple.

"Philippe, that's just not going to happen. Not with my ankle." Regardless of how her body immediately responded to the contrary, Sam wasn't having sex. She couldn't afford to jeopardize her ankle's recovery.

"That's a pity. For I have something I know you'll like." He dragged Sam's hand over his crotch where his lean, hard cock lay trapped beneath the denim.

She gave his yearning an affectionate squeeze. "Sorry, Philippe. Not tonight. Let's wait until Monday night. You come to the show and then afterwards, we'll celebrate. All of us." She tweaked his cock once more for emphasis.

He pouted. "Very well. I'll have to wait until then."

"By the way, did you speak to Josette?" Since Sam had been so busy in recovery, she'd not known if Philippe had followed up on his promise to sort things out with Josette.

"No. Not yet." He shrugged. "I've left messages, but she hasn't returned them."

"Oh well. Please keep trying. I haven't seen her either, but I was hoping all could be sorted before Monday's performance. I really don't want any bad blood between us, but I have a feeling it's not going to work out that way."

"Love will win out in the end," Philippe said, thumbing her chin. "Even if Josette isn't happy about you getting the job to begin with, I'm sure she'll come around. Leave it to me. I'll find a way . . ." He cradled her into his shoulder and planted a soft kiss on the top of her head.

Within fifteen minutes, Sam drifted to sleep, and Philippe made a quiet departure.

Sunday morning arrived like a miracle. Sam's ankle felt strong and healthy as she put her weight on it to walk to the bathroom. Because she'd fallen asleep so early last night, it was only five A.M. and the sun hadn't yet risen. But a different sunny idea sprang to her mind. Sam hurried to shower and dress, put the key to her surprise in her bag, then tiptoed down the stairs out into the courtyard. Thrilled her ankle felt so fit, she strode off to fulfil her mission. Because she worked at the other end of the spectrum, Sam seldom saw the dawn unless she was still awake from the night before. This morning, though, she appreciated what other people said about this time of the day. There was a serenity, a peaceful expectation of a good day dawning. Her pace slowed to a stroll and she considered the life before her. A schoolgirl's crush was what she had on Tony Di Falco — that's what she put it down to. Once he left tomorrow, she'd feel better. It was like whenever she left her mum and dad, the ache would go away, eventually. Besides, Philippe was such fun, so alive, always looking for new adventures and experiences. Being with him invigorated her. Yes, she'd be happy here in Paris.

WITH AS MUCH STEALTH as she could muster, she picked her way up the dilapidated stairs. Fossicking in her bag, she produced the key and slid it into the door lock. She wanted to surprise Philippe with some early morning lovemaking. He'd been so patient last night, and this morning was going to be his reward. She listened hard at the door and heard muffled sounds in his flat. Then something clattered to the floor. *He must be awake*, she thought. No need for secrecy now. She turned the key and threw open the door.

Philippe was naked on his knees on the bed, his hands digging into a woman's waist with his cock shafted up to the hilt in her. Sam couldn't tell whether his cock was in her arse or her vagina from where she stood *but fuck! What did it matter?* His golden hair was lank and straggly, meaning they'd been fucking themselves stupid for hours. Wedged under the woman was another man, his erect ugly cock visible as his mouth slurped at the woman's snatch. He was sucking her juices and face-fucking her, while Philippe slammed into her from behind. Although repulsed, Sam's eyes travelled to the woman who was still moaning and grinding her hips on Philippe's cock. On all fours, her head hung between her arms, her breasts full from gravity and excitement. She was blonde and had a perfectly proportioned body, long, lean, muscular . . .

As the sunrise inched over Philippe's balcony, so too, did Sam's new dawn. "What the fuck?" The words barely escaped Sam's throat in a rasp. The three-way orgy screeched to a halt.

Artfully, the blonde lifted her head, the frigid ice of her blue eyes glancing on their unexpected guest. "Samantha, won't you join us?" Like the venomous creature she was, Josette hissed her invitation with Philippe's cock still wedged deep within her. Sam's jaw locked like a vice. She could feel her lips tightening and loosening, flexing ready for the words about to spew forth, but she had no idea what they would be. Her body was on full alert, her amygdala igniting its ancient fight or flight response.

Through gritted teeth, a powerful voice emanated which didn't sound like Sam's, but one which she willingly owned.

"Philippe. Is this what you meant by sorting everything out with Josette?" A beat. Then dripping with sarcasm, she continued, "'Leave it to me,' he said. 'Love will win out in the end,' he said. 'I'm sure she'll come around', he said. Well. She. Certainly. Came!" Sam yelled so loudly that the bakers downstairs shouted back.

Anger rocketed up her body, and as the guy underneath Josette cautiously shimmied out, her amazed fury transferred to him. "Jean-Paul, is that you? But of course it is. You sick bastard." Sam swung to glare at Philippe and back to Jean-Paul. "You two are a fucking freak show."

With a sheepish look, Jean-Paul ventured a lop-sided grin, grabbed his pants and scurried into them like a weasel. Seizing the rest of his clothes he made a dash to the door, slamming his shoulder into the frame trying to stay clear of Sam.

"Serves you right," Sam sneered at him, wishing she could break his jaw. Nevertheless, she felt avenged when she heard him stumbling and crashing down the stairs. "I hope you fucking break a leg, as we say in the theatre," she yelled after him, a bitter taste of bile lining her mouth. She swallowed hard. The only purging happening today was Sam hurling her anger externally, not internally.

Not concerned with anything other than herself, Josette wiggled her arse back onto Philippe's groin, to keep his cock hard inside her. There was no mistaking her message. She was the only one having any fun — her expression, a hideous mask of hateful revenge and self-satisfaction.

Tugging himself free, Philippe wrenched his cock out with an audible pop and pushed her away. "Samantha, let me explain," Philippe whimpered, his dick as weak and limp as he sounded. "Josette came here and threw herself at me—"

"Oh, *puh-lease* . . . You are kidding me, aren't you?" Sam spat with an incredulous hoot. "Yes, yes I can see now. You weren't just fucking Josette. You were fighting off her advances, weren't you?" With her fists clenched and legs locked, Sam remained rigid where she stood, although a part of her wanted to turn and run — run and never stop.

Philippe sprang off the bed, babbling lame excuses and struggled into his pants. If he so much as stepped toward her, Sam knew she wouldn't be answerable for her actions. She understood how crimes of passion could so easily be perpetrated by normally sane people.

Josette spun around on the bed, exposing herself and dipped her finger into her slimy slit. She dragged the cum up over her belly and sucked it into her mouth. "*Mmm*, your boyfriend tastes good, and I taste even better. Here try." She pulled her slippery folds apart, inviting Sam to taste her demonic juice. Sam turned her head away in disgust. Josette laughed — a high-pitched cackle.

"Shut up, you stupid cunt," Philippe commanded through clenched teeth. When Josette hissed back at him, Sam's anger finally broke its leash, rising in full voice.

"You stupid, French cow. You think fucking Philippe is going to make me upset? You must be mad! I don't give a rat's arse what he does with his flaccid French cock."

Philippe lowered his eyes in a sulk.

Not to be outdone, Josette propped upright, crossed her legs elegantly and stuck her chin high. "You took my job, so I take your boyfriend."

Sam shook her head in amused pity. "Have him. He's not worth anything."

Philippe slumped even more.

"And as for being a nude, if you took your fingers out of your pussy long enough, you'd realize you're not good enough to be nude."

"That is not true! That job was mine. Madeleine hurt herself because I—" Josette clamped her lips shut, but it was too late.

"You what?" screamed Sam. "What did you do?"

Josette kicked her leg lazily to and fro, obviously satisfied with whatever despicable accident she'd set up for Madeleine. Sam cast her mind back to the event. Bridgette's strange look in the dressing room on the day of Madeleine's accident now made sense. She must have somehow known Josette was complicit. Poor Madeleine had been the victim in Josette's plan to become a nude.

Incensed by this revelation, Sam zeroed in on Josette with laser accuracy. "You lousy bitch! You're just a two-bit dancer with no talent. A cheap slut, trying to suck and fuck her way to the top, and you don't care who you hurt to get there. No wonder Tony wouldn't give you the job. He must've suspected something all along and that you were at the root of it. You'll be fired now!"

Howling a string of French obscenities, Josette lunged at Sam, tripped and landed heavily on her knees with a crunch. She yowled like a spoiled child who Sam ignored. With the hounds-of-hell released, Sam eyeballed Philippe. "And you! You and your talk of love. My mother was right. The apple doesn't fall far from the tree. You're no better than your father. Screwing around, lying and cheating. You said you didn't want to be like him. Well, guess what? You are!" Sam's fury metaphorically burnt up the walls of the apartment. Shooting a contemptuous glare from one to the other, Sam blazed. "You two are just perfect for each other. Sly, selfish, narcissistic liars. You can both go fuck yourselves stupid and leave me out of your fucking French games. I'm over all this shit."

Sam pivoted violently on her right ankle and yelped, but she didn't waver. On her way to the door, her wrath dissolved on seeing poor, little Jasper cowering in the corner. She collected him in her arms and spun around facing Philippe. "You don't deserve this sweet little creature and Jasper doesn't deserve to live in a disgusting place such as this. I'm taking him back to the hotel to give to Madame Lucette. He'll be safe there."

She snatched the key from the door and glowered at Philippe. "And keep the key to your flat, to your life, to everything. There's nothing here of value anyway that needs to be kept under lock and key!" She hurled it at his feet. Then spying the canvasses leaning against the wall, she marched over and tore back the cover sheets. The most exquisite portrait of her leapt from one of the large oil paintings. Philippe had captured the depth of her soul and the love she'd felt for him in every unique brushstroke. With tears stinging her eyes, Sam's gaze flashed and finding what she was looking for, she lunged. With the scissors in her hand, she attacked the canvass like Norman Bates in Psycho, hacking it to pieces. Horrified, neither Philippe nor Josette moved.

As Philippe opened his mouth to speak, Sam hurled more vengeance at him. In a deep growl, her threat reverberated through the small flat like an impending earthquake. "Do not speak. Do not come near me. Do not follow me and do not make a promise you cannot keep ever again." The scissors clattered from her hand. With Jasper nuzzled into her neck, Sam snapped a more careful about-face and marched out of the flat, away from the promising future she'd woken up with this morning.

CHAPTER TWENTY-FIVE

BY THE TIME SAM reached the hotel, the searing pain in her ankle signalled she'd reinjured it badly. Opening the hotel door, Sam peeped in praying Madame Lucette was not yet up and about. In answer, Sam found the foyer still unlit with no smell of burning incense. Treading as lightly as she could on her throbbing ankle, she struggled up the stairs while holding Jasper to her chest. She pushed her key into the lock, opened the door and slipped inside. Plonking down on the bed, Jasper escaped her arms and propped himself next to her, as if in sympathy. His big, round eyes regarded her in the most loving fashion.

"Oh, Jasper. Why can't all men be as loving as you?" A jab of pain shot up her leg. "God, what have I done? My ankle is killing me." She collapsed back on the bed with a heavy grunt. Sensing her distress, Jasper nuzzled his head into Sam's ribs, trying to comfort her. Absentmindedly Sam reached over to stroke him, prompting Jasper's purr to grow louder. Back rushed vivid memories of the times she and Philippe had shared in his flat with Jasper as the playful third wheel. They'd been such happy times. Times she'd come to depend on and cherish. Now they were gone. They'd been a lie. Philippe was a lie and she'd been played for a fool.

Spying the roses on the mantle, Sam hopped off the bed using her one good leg. She grabbed the bouquet and beat their red heads until the petals lay scattered on the floor. Like little puddles of blood, they reminded her of the emotional blood-letting Philippe had put her through. Up to this point, her anger on discovering the truth about him had squelched the tears, but now they flowed unabated. The emotion stirred deep within her gut — its energy gushing up firstly in small sobs, followed by bigger gulps until she slid down the wall, weeping. With her head in her hands, she rocked back and forth, bruised and beaten.

Why did she take Philippe back after that incident in Jean-Paul's studio? Stupid, stupid girl. After what she'd been through with Richard, she should have known better. *All men are bastards.* Her thoughts spun out of control and she chastised herself for her naivety. Grappling to her feet, she hopped over to the box of tissues on her nightstand and reefed out a fistful to wipe her face. Eyeing Jasper, who'd settled between the pillows, she said, "I should have stuck to my original plan. I didn't come to Paris for love, I came to dance. And now look at me." She waved her hands at Jasper. "Not only did I not get love. I got my heart broken — again! And now I can't dance," she wailed miserably. She was past caring who heard. Her career, her wonderful career was now gone.

Like a trapped tornado, Sam's confusion spun violently, knocking her off balance. She fell and screamed as her ankle twisted beneath her weight. She needed ice or at least cold water. Crawling, she pulled herself along the floor to her bathroom. She could let cold water run on her ankle until she felt better to get some ice. Between each drag of her body, Sam gulped back more sobs. She was a blubbering, defeated mess. Oh God, how she hated herself at this moment. Every muscle ached. Every breath gagged. Everything was gone.

I can help you take control. The voice in her head seemed to come from over there. Sam crawled faster and heaving herself up, she clung to her old friend, the porcelain. *That's a girl. This way you'll be free of all the pain.* Back in control. Sam slowed her breathing and pushed to her knees. Replaying the old habit, her fingers drifted toward her mouth,

"Liberation, Samantha." A lilting voice drifted from behind Sam. "It is just as the crone goddess forecast. There is something you are now free of . . ." Soft footfalls padded up next to Sam and a bony hand stroked her damp hair. "*Chère fille*, my dear girl. Come away. You longer need to do that. It is over. You have exorcised your demons."

With more tears streaming down her face, Sam looked up into the sympathetic, wise, old face of Madame Lucette. With surprising strength, she reached down and tugged Sam to her feet. "Come, I have an ice pack. You must lie down." Exhausted, Sam hobbled to the bed and allowed Madame Lucette to tend her pain, physical and otherwise. Once the pack was secured on Sam's ankle, Madame Lucette perched beside her on the bed. Sam snuffled through more handfuls of tissues and when she released a long sigh, Madame Lucette nodded in approval.

Madame Lucette stroked Sam's hand. "If you recall, Samantha, when you arrived, I said Paris is for lovers, not always love." Barely able to see out of the slits of her puffy eyes, Sam nodded and dragged another tissue across her reddened nose. "And you and my nephew have been passionate lovers, enjoying the fire of young bodies." A knowing smile creased Madame's face. Embarrassed, Sam downcast her eyes, fidgeting the tissues into a papery coil. "But sometimes the flames become so hot, the lovers get burnt and suffer painfully. However, fire brings with it liberation and freedom. The parched heart it leaves behind is fertile ground for new beginnings."

As usual, Madame Lucette's riddles left Sam's mind straining to find the message. "Samantha, you have a strong heart." To this, Sam nodded. She most definitely had a strong heart. "And inspiration comes from the well-spring of human experience." Sam recalled this had been another message of one of Madame Lucette's tarot cards. "You know your destiny is to dance."

"Yes," Sam said in a soft voice, hoarse from the shouting and crying she'd done.

"So, there is nothing for you to worry yourself over. Your ankle will soon repair itself. You will be a nude at the Moulin Rouge and whatever has happened between you and my nephew will pass. You never have to see him again if you do not want." Not waiting for a reply, Madame stood up and kissed Sam's cheeks. The familiar whiff of her cigarettes wafted under Sam's nose. But instead of wincing at the overpowering smell, Sam found it strangely comforting as fond memories flitted through her mind.

Madame Lucette's obvious concern and wise advice triggered the image of the goddess of protection card in her memory. Sam smiled weakly, realizing Madame had been protecting her from the beginning. "Thank you, Madame Lucette, for looking after me. Thank you for everything."

Madame Lucette patted Sam's hand once more. "Now you rest and dream of liberation."

EXHAUSTION FORCED SAM TO sleep but raised voices woke her. Before, when Madame Lucette left, she'd not closed her door completely. Because of this, the argument raging downstairs funnelled up the staircase and into her room. The noise also woke Jasper, who huddled closer to Sam, eyes wide with fright. Sam couldn't make out what the argument was about, but she recognized the voices — they belonged to Madame Lucette and Philippe. Between them, they hurled words in French like a bombing raid, neither giving the other a chance to speak. Sam shimmied off her bed and shuffled to her ajar door. Peeking out, she could see them standing nose to chest, in the foyer. Even from this distance, Sam saw Madame Lucette shaking with rage. Her landlady's distress alarmed Sam so much, she couldn't allow the scene to continue.

She stepped out onto the landing and called down, "Philippe! Leave your aunty alone. She's an old woman and you must show more respect." On seeing Sam, Philippe began to bound up the stairs. "Stop," Sam commanded. "Don't come up here, Philippe. You're no longer welcome." This had the desired effect for he halted on the sixth step, stranded half-way between Sam and Madame Lucette.

Madame Lucette spoke directly to Philippe, in a conciliatory manner. "Philippe, *mon ange*. I love you. Was it not I who cared for you when your father beat you?" Philippe nodded reluctantly. "Was it not I you came to with your problems." Again, Philippe nodded. "Was it not I who smoothed the way for you and Samantha to be together again?" Another nod. Then with a power in her voice unexpected in a woman of such small stature, she roared, "And this is how you repay me? By lying to me? By breaking my trust? By making promises to me you had no intention of keeping?" Sam could've sworn the lights flickered on and off and the hotel actually shuddered at Madame's accusation. Perhaps she truly was a goddess after all?

Under Madame Lucette's wrath, Philippe crumbled. Sam reasoned it was because of the beatings his father inflicted upon him as a child. Madame Lucette had been his protector throughout these abusive, childhood years and now, as she berated him, Philippe simply wilted. Like a precious flower left in the scorching heat, he couldn't withstand his aunt's ire. Dropping to the stairs, he landed with a thud while Madame continued in her tirade.

"You have forsaken me, *mon ange*. You have forsaken Samantha, but worst of all, you have forsaken yourself." From where Sam stood, she couldn't see Philippe's face, but she could tell by the slumping of his head and shoulders, Madame Lucette's words struck like deadly weapons, straight at his heart. Sam felt sorry for him, but he'd brought this on himself. The damage ran deep in Philippe, but he was a man now. It was time for him to grow up, to stop playing out the sins of the father.

Like the crone goddess on the tarot card, Madame extended her skeletal arm toward the door in one rigid movement, pointing to the tip of her arthritic finger. "Philippe, you must leave. Do not come back until you are a real man, a man who appreciates love."

"But, Aunty Lucette, please?" He jumped up and dashed down the stairs, pleading. Taking her hand, he lavished it with kisses, apologizing over and over.

"*Non*, Philippe." She remained firm, with chin lifted. Philippe encircled her neck in his arms and sobbed on her shoulder. As his body trembled with despair, her mood softened. She pushed him away and cupped his face in sympathetic hands. "Perhaps we will talk soon, but not today, not tomorrow or this week. Perhaps not next week either. But soon." Madame Lucette pressed a soft kiss to each of her nephew's cheeks and sent him on his way.

At the front door, Philippe turned. Even from where she stood, Sam could see a deep sadness settle upon him. He straightened and said, "I now understand the story of the Eiffel Tower — of the giant who in torment and anguish on losing the woman he loved, demolished Paris. My heart now feels like the twisted wreckage, pierced by the deadly point of love's arrow, for now, my love is destroyed. Forgive me, Samantha. Forgive me."

Samantha remained silent and hoped Philippe couldn't see the water brimming in her eyes. Still, after everything, he appeared angelic. The golden glow of his charm that attracted her to him in the first place still emanated from him. Like a heavenly halo, it silhouetted his body, hovering in the doorway. He remained a beautiful, talented, young painter, perhaps irrevocably damaged, but struggling to find himself and in the process, fulfil his destiny of being one of this century's world-famous artists. In her heart, Sam wished him luck. He had a long road ahead of him.

"Goodbye, Philippe," she said without emotion and returned to her room.

~ ♥ ~

By mid-afternoon, Sam surprised herself by feeling quite positive about her future. She'd called Penny and told her of the confrontation with Josette, although not all the graphic details. Penny promised to investigate Madeleine's accident further. If she discovered evidence of Josette's complicity in the event, Josette would be terminated, effective immediately. Knowing Penny was on the case, lifted Sam's confidence to stay on as a nude at the Moulin Rouge.

"It sounds like you took my advice then, Sam?" Penny said just before hanging up.

"What advice is that, Penny?"

"Well, I think you made lots of good decisions today, as hard as they were. None of them were based on your fear of the challenge but on the potential of the opportunity. What do you think?"

Sam considered Penny's words. "Yes. I guess you're right. I never thought much about it. I just acted on instinct I guess."

"Instinct will never lead you astray. Keep me posted on how your ankle recovers. In the meantime, I can re-block the nude line for a couple of days until you return. Rest up, kiddo." With a cheery farewell, Penny was gone, and Sam found herself smiling, feeling pleased with herself.

Standing in front of her mirror, brushing her hair, Sam heard her door open. "Madame Lucette, I'm in here," she called brightly. She bent forwards to tousle her hair, giving it a good finger ruffle. When she threw her head back, her straight lengths of thick black hair splayed over his face. But he didn't flinch. He never did. Nothing ever seemed to faze Tony Di Falco.

Startled, she said to his reflection in the mirror, "Tony what are you doing here?"

He wrapped his arms around her waist. "Madame Lucette called me."

Sam's skin ignited as she fought the desire to lean back into his protective chest. "But, why? Why would she call you?"

"Because she knows I love you."

Sam's major senses shut down, leaving only her heart thudding faster and louder in her chest. Open-mouthed, she stared at him in the mirror.

"Did you hear me, Samantha O'Brien? I love you." His smile flashed like summer lightning, illuminating his face while its electricity surged through her body buckling her knees. "Here let me." Tony swooped her up, carried her to the bed and lay her down like precious cargo.

Sitting beside her on the bed, he gazed down into her radiant yet startled face. With his arms splayed wide on either side of her body, she was his willing captive. He moistened his lips. "I've been thinking about a lot of things, Samantha, but the main one has been you." Another captivating smile. "I haven't been able to stop thinking about you. Nor have I been able to stop thinking about the words you said about addiction being the unattainable pursuit of pleasure. You're right you know."

"But they're not my words. They came from Aunty Michele," Sam corrected.

"No matter where they came from, the message hit me. Cocaine was only me trying to pursue pleasure because I hadn't found you." Tony's intense oration made Sam giggle.

"What? What's so funny?" he said, with only a hint of indignation.

"You are. You sound so romantic, like one of those heroes in the movies. You're supposed to be Ursu, the gruff, hard-to-please bear. Tony Di Falco — world-famous stage director." Sam declared in a circus ringleader's voice.

"Are you going to let me finish or not?" Ursu made an appearance just for her benefit, or so she thought.

"Yes, Tony," she said, suitably chastised.

He continued in a less theatrical voice. "Good. So, I've decided that me to give up cocaine, I need to have the real thing. Real pleasure in my life and it appears to be you." He rose abruptly and began to pace the room. "I didn't expect this in the least. However, it is what it is. Samantha O'Brien, I've unexpectedly fallen in love with you and I'm hoping we may be able to see where this might lead." He glanced furtively at her to gauge her response and continued regardless, "Madame Lucette has informed me you are no longer with young Philippe. Good. She also inferred you feel similarly toward me and that by telling you how I feel, I wouldn't make a fool of myself."

"No, Tony. You're not making a fool of yourself. Madame Lucette is right." Sam lifted her arms out to him into which he yielded, embracing her.

With a sigh, he pulled away, his brow furrowed. "Samantha, come with me to Las Vegas. Let's start a new life together there."

A swirl of conflicting emotions and feelings spiralled in Sam's body. Disappointment at not getting the chance to perform as a nude at the Moulin Rouge, utter shock Tony was pledging his love for her, excitement at the prospect of going to Vegas and sadness to be leaving Hotel Hollandaise and Madame Lucette.

Sweetening the offer, Tony continued, "There's a spot for you in my show. You'll have to start as a dancer, but I've no doubt, you'll be performing the nude role within a matter of months. Please come with me, Sam. I think we need to give this a try."

Aunty Michele's familiar voice filtered into Sam's mind. "Samantha, two things motivate everyone. Pain and pleasure. Fear is the irrational avoidance of pain and addiction is the unattainable pursuit of pleasure. But freedom is beyond both."

"Okay. I'll come to Vegas with you, but on one condition. We start from scratch. I'll get my own apartment. I'll be just another dancer in the show with no special treatment from you. If I do something wrong, you'll treat me the same as everyone else. If you want to see if a relationship is possible between us, you'll have to court me and prove to me you're ready and that you won't break any promises." Her hand flew to her mouth, covering her giggle. "I know it all sounds very old-fashioned. But I've discovered I'm worthy of a good man and I'm not settling for anything less."

Tony scooped her to his chest, and thumbing her chin, lifted her sunny face to his. "You have yourself a deal, Samantha O'Brien." Pressing his soft lips upon hers, he sealed it with a kiss.

CHAPTER TWENTY-SIX

BEFORE THE SUN ROSE again the next day, Sam stood dressed and ready to leave. This time, with her luggage packed and Madame Lucette beside her in the foyer. Both their eyes brimmed with tears.

"*Chère fille*, I will miss you." Madame sniffled, dabbing a lace handkerchief to her damp eyes.

"Me too, Madame. So much." Sam reached down and hugged her eccentric, wonderful landlady.

Composing herself, Madame Lucette focused her steely gaze on Sam. "You have made the right decision, Samantha. You are fulfilling your destiny. I sense it will be in Las Vegas you will find true love with Monsieur Di Falco." Madame Lucette cast an approving smile toward Tony, who stood nearby. He responded with a silent nod.

"Oh, Madame Lucette, what am I going to do without you and your tarot cards?" Sam sniffled into her tissues,

"Here. Take them. They are yours." Madame thrust her favourite pack of cards into Sam's hands with single-minded conviction.

"Madame, I can't take these." Sam's voice broke at Madame's selfless farewell gift.

"*Pfft*," she snorted. "I have many more packs of cards. These are yours now. Use them well. Use them often. They will never lie. *Au revoir*, Samantha. Until you return to Paris." Stretching up, Madame kissed each of Sam's cheeks abruptly, turned and scurried away, leaving gentle sobs in her wake.

"Come on, Samantha. We have to go." Tony collected her bags and helped her out the door.

As she limped away from Hotel Hollandaise, Sam couldn't resist one final farewell. Turning back toward her home away from home for the past few months, she said, "Paris is love and I love Paris." With trembling lips, she blew a kiss to the quaint little hotel and its eccentric landlady who taught her the real meaning of love.

~ ♥ ~

With an uneventful take-off behind them and settled into the flight, Sam rummaged through her bag while Tony read quietly beside her. Finding her wallet, her fingers dug out the hidden treasure. Unfolding the paper, she stared affectionately at the photocopy of the card — the goddess of knowledge, beauty and grace.

Madame Lucette's voice lilted in Sam's mind. "*Mon cher,* this is a wonderful omen. Whenever you look at his card, you will think of the crazy, old landlady you stayed with in Paris." Indeed, she would. Indeed, she would.

Placing the paper back into her wallet, Sam continued digging around in her bag.

Curious as to all the activity, Tony leaned over. "What are you doing, my Tiny Dancer?"

Sam paused, considering whether to permit his use of her family nickname and decided she would. She reached over and twirled one of his luscious locks in her fingers. "I think I like it when you call me that." A smile lit her face, as bright as the future before and beside her.

"Good. I'm pleased." Tony reciprocated her smile and squeezed her arm affectionately.

Then with a triumphant gesture, Sam presented the pack of tarot cards Madame Lucette had given her and handed them to Tony. "Now all you have to do is shuffle the cards and ask them a question. The cards never lie . . ."

THE END

STAND-ALONE CONTEMPORARY ROMANCE FEATURING STRONG HEROINES AND PAGE-TURNING PLOTS

TEMPT ME

One woman . . . Two men . . . Threesomes change everything

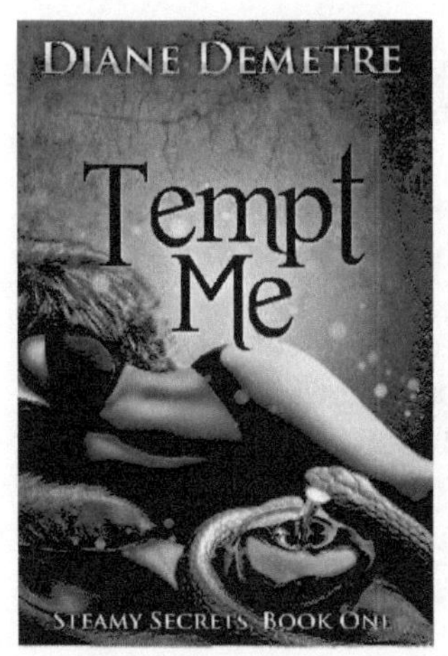

When Michele Johnston, a forty-two-year-old ex-dancer from the Moulin Rouge gets divorced, she leaps into her new world of singledom with unbridled passion.

Aided and abetted by three vivacious girlfriends, Michele embarks on her steamy, erotic adventures, but gets more than she expects when mysterious yacht captain Mark Miller unleashes her wanton desires.

Further complicating matters, debonair Greek businessman Nick Stavros arrives on the scene and falls madly in love with her, promising the happy-ever-after ending. But will she give up her newfound freedom? Will she choose one man over the other? Or can she continue loving them both?

Tempt Me is the first stand-alone Contemporary Erotic Romance in Diane Demetre's genre-busting series, Steamy Secrets. If you love strong heroes, hot sex, and feisty heroines, don't miss this page-turning love story with a twist.

EXCERPT

Squeezing her way through the nightclub crowd, Michele made for the bar where she stepped nimbly into a space just vacated by a large Negro man.

"I must try one of those as well," she mused to herself, watching his tight buttocks retreat.

Leaning across the bar to be heard, Michele ordered her poison. The service was fast, the vodka and tonic cold and the music hot. With all the accoutrements to suit the scene, she settled in to scope the room, enjoying the buzz of sexual energy.

It took only thirty minutes before an extra drink arrived in front of her. The bartender pointed to the big guy at the other end of the bar who tipped his glass and smiled. She accepted his offering with a reciprocal gesture. Her drink patron stood nearly a full head height above everyone else and was built like an Arnie Schwarzenegger double with a twist of Crocodile Dundee about him. Accentuated by his casual clothes, his face and manner had Aussie written all over them. After an initial assessment, Michele gave him only fleeting attention as she'd already chosen her mark for the night; the young bartender with the trim body, aquiline face, and gelled hair.

The night progressed, and another couple of drinks arrived compliments of the titan, who remained fixed as if supporting the other end of the bar. She acknowledged each drink with a gracious smile, which he returned with the unwavering stare of a wildcat, mouth curled waiting for its prey to make a move.

While the bartender showed initial interest in her flirtations, he disappeared at the end of his shift leaving her advances unrequited.

Nothing new there, she thought, *God, what's wrong with me?* Feeling the familiar sense of rejection left over from years living with her husband, she sculled her drink and turned to leave.

But there he stood, her drinks benefactor, wearing an inscrutable expression as he blocked her exit. From a distance he'd looked a solid guy, however up close he must've been virtually a hundred kilos of pure muscle.

With a smile twitching his lips, he initiated the conversation. "You're the horniest thing I've seen in years. Why are you chasing pencil dicks?"

His brash opening remarks pinned her to the spot and, as a half-smile flitted across her face, she took a closer look at this man with the roguish sense of humour. He wouldn't be classed as typically handsome, but his sheer presence and blunt approach caused her skin to tingle. Impeding any escape, he flashed a wide, white smile, and waited for a response. His eyes, a vivid marine blue, twinkled with life experience and his collar-length soft brown hair framed his sun-tanned face. He encroached into her personal space, towering over her with the promise of a real man, and he smelt good. The scent of masculine musk mingled with the bittersweet overtones of a world-class aftershave triggered a positive response in her brain.

"Thanks for the drinks. That was very generous of you. And your name is . . .?"

"You can call me Mark. And you are?" His voice was like the breath of a friendly dragon, warm and playful.

"Michele." Her initial obligation to be polite since he'd spent money buying her drinks had softened to casual interest. "Tell me a little about yourself, Mark."

"Not much to tell really. I'd rather talk about you."

"Either you're very chivalrous or very secretive. I suspect it might be the latter. You don't give too much away, do you?"

"Not only good looking but clever as well. What is it I can do to make you choose me instead of that gay bartender?"

Shit, she thought. After all she'd been through, she'd chosen a carbon copy of her ex-husband. Why hadn't she'd seen it? But it wasn't too late to save the night. "Well, I guess you can buy me another drink, Mark."

~ ♥ ~

TAKE ME

How far would you run to find love?

Aiden Bishop is a successful young lawyer hiding out in sunny Spain to escape unsavoury clients in Australia. At twenty-seven, Ace as he's known to his mates, happens upon a local flamenco club in Seville where he's befriended by Rafael Flores and beguiled by Carla Armando — a famous flamenco couple well-known for their fiery performances both on and off the stage.

With ancestral links to the famous gypsy flamenco dancer Carmen Amaya, Rafael and Carla have mysterious Romani culture coursing through their veins. Sensing Aiden's love of adventure, they invite him on a road trip from the Costa Del Sol to Granada in search of Carla's true Romani gifts. However, as the trip stretches deeper into less travelled emotional geography, long-kept secrets are exposed.

Brimming with gypsy traditions, the passion of the dance, mysterious rune readings and intrigue, Aiden realizes that he may be able to evade his clients, but he can't escape his destiny no matter how far he runs.

Take Me is the third stand-alone Contemporary Erotic Romance in Diane Demetre's genre-busting series, Steamy Secrets. If you love strong heroes, hot sex and feisty heroines, don't miss this page-turning love story with a twist.

EXCERPT

"Well, tango is like having sex. Except instead of being horizontal, you're vertical. Here. I'll show you." Carla slithered her right leg in between Aiden's, the top of her thigh easing towards his crotch. "Now when we dance tango, we have to remain locked in this position, so we move as one."

"Carla, if I remain locked in this position, I won't be doing any dancing."

She giggled. "Why not?"

"First of all, I can't move, and second, I'd rather be doing the horizontal tango." A half-smile lurked on his face and his eyes twinkled with mischief.

"I see," Carla said in a soft, sultry voice. Tiny tingles raced from her toes, surging to her face in a hot flush. He'd not released his grip on her, nor the intense stare in which he'd trapped her. "Well, Aiden. That is tango. Tango is love. Tango is passion. You must love your partner. You must want to be passionate with your partner." The more she spoke, the slower her speech became. Gazing into his eyes, she recognized he had the requisite love and passion to dance tango. She moistened her lips, noticing how the slight movement with her tongue seemed to mesmerize him. "Let's proceed, shall we?" She tried to direct his attention back to tango.

Not breaking his stance or stare, Aiden said, "I'm ready."

"I'm going to step back on my right foot, and you step forwards on your left. Ready and step . . ." As Carla stepped back, Aiden obeyed with his left. Unsure of the power needed, he pushed too hard, and they stumbled. Quick as lightning, he crushed her in his arms lifting her up before they fell. He found his footing for them both though her feet dangled off the floor. His chest heaved, and she could feel his heart beating as fast as hers. With her arms wrapped around his neck, her face hovered at kissing distance and the yearning she'd disregarded since meeting him, resurfaced with a vengeance.

"Are you all right?" he asked, his masculine breath resting on her lips, making them ache.

"Yes. Thank you," she said, whispering her unspoken permission to be kissed.

"I told you I had two left feet." Aiden still held her firmly in his embrace, seemingly unaware of her weight and unwilling to let go.

Naked under her caftan, Carla felt her nipples harden against his bare chest. Glancing downwards, Aiden moaned. Suspending her in one arm, he slid his other hand to cup her buttocks, dragging her closer onto his body. His hot breath scorched her neck, and she pushed against his cheek like an affectionate cat. With his face tucked into her neck, his breathing deepened like he was trying to suck the life from her. Big heaving breaths tied them together as they caught each other's tempo. Expertly, his supporting hand under her buttocks flexed and contracted, squeezing her arse and made Carla squirm with desire. Unable to stand the insistence of his hand any longer, she crawled onto him, wrapping her legs around his trunk. The thin silk of her caftan did little to conceal the wetness between her legs when her cleft opened onto his bare stomach. "Oh God, Carla," he groaned.

Wrapped like two desperate souls, they clung tight to each other — she like a frightened child reluctant to let go and he the championing hero to her rescue. "Carla."

AUTHOR BIOGRAPHY

Diane began her career as a schoolteacher before moving into the entertainment industry as a choreographer, director, event manager, dancer and actress, working in television and live theatre, and managing multi-million-dollar productions.

Following her onstage career, she spent many years as a stress & life skills therapist, keynote speaker and presenter, appearing on national radio and television under the pseudonym of the Goddess of Love.

For her outstanding contribution to the arts, Diane was awarded the 2019 SBAA International Women's Day Leader Award for Leadership in the Entertainment, Creative Arts and Media Industry.

She is an award-winning author of contemporary, genre-busting romance, suspense and mystery novels. Her intuitive insights into human behaviour are woven into her casts of characters, heightening the intrigue in her storytelling. Set in exotic locations, her stories are packed with emotional punch and feature empowered heroines who live life to the fullest, much like the author herself.

Connect with Diane

https://dianedemetre.com/

AWARD WINNING AUTHOR

> 66 . . . Dare to dream bigger than ever before, dare to forge our own path no matter how hard the challenges. But most of all, dare to be you and let the chips fall where they may. We are all warrior women with gossamer wings . . . It's time to roar! 99
>
> — Diane Demetre

Winner of 2019 SBAA International Women's Day Leader Award for Leadership in Entertainment, Creative Arts and/or Media Industry.

Diane was nominated as a finalist in the ARRA Awards 2018 for Favourite Romantic Suspense, for her novel *Retribution.*

In 2017 Diane won the Romance Writers of Australia Emerald Pro Award for Best Unpublished Romance Manuscript.

ALSO, BY DIANE DEMETRE

ISLAND OF SECRETS

Two love stories separated in time. Two women following their dreams. In a paradise littered with painful secrets, will love turn the tide?

1973. Cecilia "CiCi" Freemont has a restless soul and the voice of an angel. Leaving her privileged upbringing behind, she chases her dreams to the sandy beaches of an unspoiled Hawaiian paradise, Harbor Island. But life takes an unexpected turn when she falls for the island's young heir-apparent and her newfound adventure becomes too much to bear . . .

2017. Investigative journalist Tina Templeton has dedicated herself to the pursuit of truth. But when she inherits Harbor Island, her career plans take a confusing twist. Managing the sprawling island estate is tough business even with the help of aging cabaret singer, CiCi Freemont. Especially when a massive ecological disaster threatens to destroy her beautiful beaches — and the responding coast guard captain steals her heart.

As the investigation into the disaster reveals a 40-year-old mystery that could change their lives forever, will Tina find love among the secrets, or will CiCi's painful past dash her dreams on the rocks?

Island of Secrets is an epic love story. If you like generations-spanning drama, characters with hidden pasts, heart-warming romance and intrigue, then you'll love Diane Demetre's powerful novel in paradise.

~ ♥ ~

RETRIBUTION

Winner of Romance Writers of Australia Emerald Pro Award 2017.

**She's a ballerina with a dark secret.
He's a retired sniper with a tortured past.
Will they find love or fall prey to a stalker's deadly game?**

Professional ballerina Jessie Hilton wraps her battle scars in satin pointe shoes, but there's a deeper hurt that haunts her sleep. When a handsome man steps in to save her from a mugging, something about her hero makes her heavy heart leap. Though her career can't afford distractions, he may be her sole source of safety when she gains the unwanted attention of a relentless stalker.

Ex-sniper Brad Jordan survived his tour of duty, but a tragic accident cost him the lives of those closest to him. With his faithful border collie Whiskey by his side, Brad gets a second chance when he protects the beautiful Jessie from danger. When the ballerina's stalker grows more brazen, Brad's tactical training may be their only weapon against tragedy.

Will Jessie and Brad survive a deadly game or will the assailant destroy their chance at love?

Retribution is a stand-alone romantic suspense novel. If you like tough-as-toe-shoes heroines, second-chance romance, and page-turning plots, then you'll love Diane Demetre's heart-stopping saga.

PRAISE FOR DIANE'S WORK

An exciting and erotic read A refreshing genre-busting story of a divorced, older (I hasten to add by society's standards not mine) heroine who is determined to embrace her singledom while simultaneously casting aside her self- and societally-imposed sexual repression through casual erotic encounters. Diane Demetre offers a story that challenges our pre-conceived notions of what "women of a certain age" should or should not be doing and she does this in an empowering manner. The heroine embraces and cherishes her female friendships and though this aided in the flow of the plot, it also highlights the importance for women of having encouraging and supportive female companionship. Most importantly, we see the heroine herself allow the experiences of her new-found freedom to shape her own future thus enabling her to escape the repressive nature of her pre-divorce life. All in all, an erotic and exciting read sure to captivate and thrill readers of any age.

— AusRom Today

I found this to be an amazing read and I adore the author's writing style. I was captivated by the setting, the characters, the Romani culture and the story line twists and turns. A fast flowing novel with just the right amount of eroticism thrown in. I fell in love with one of the lead characters (Aiden Bishop) very quickly and the relationship between Rafael & Carla had me wondering what would eventuate next. Well done Diane Demetre.

— 5 STARS, Robyn Powers

> This is the third book I've read by Diane Demetre and I was absolutely delighted! What a great read. It has everything: a great story line mixed with sensual exploration; mystery; spirituality and wonderfully complex main characters. Couldn't put it down. Loved Aiden – just gorgeous and every woman's dream. Looking forward to the next book.
>
> — 5 STARS, Deborah Bispham

> Demetre paints vividly the atmosphere of Paris and the Moulin Rouge with such detail that it adds yet another layer of intimacy to the story. A wonderful read that we highly recommend.
>
> — AusRom Today

> I bought this book and wow what a read! To every young woman it's a must! Life lessons learnt in an amazing story told! Though I had other things to do, I had to finish this amazing story! Bring on book 3!
>
> — 5 STARS

> A well-written erotic romance with its share of twists and suspense. Love the characters and the way the author describes Paris and behind the scenes of the Moulin Rouge.
>
> — 5 STARS, Peter Brady

> Michele, a former pro dancer, has finally extricated herself from a very unsatisfying marriage, & is ready for a chance to kick up her heels, sexually & emotionally. Intent on a one night stand, she finds, instead, Mark, a most inventive & attentive lover, something she has never experienced before. As she falls in love with him, against her better judgement, she finds that he has way too many secrets that threaten to derail their fledgling relationship. By the time Nick inserts himself into her life, insisting he is just her type, despite her thoughts to the contrary, Mark has disappeared & bad people are after both him & Michele. Under Nick's protection, Michele finally figures out what she wants from life, in a very good

heroine's journey. There's an abundance of very hot sex, & the love of a good man.

> — 4.5 STARS, Alberta, ManicReaders

Fast Pace!! Erotic!! Read it in 2 days!!!! What a book Woo Hoo!!!!! Congratulations Diane Demetre, I thoroughly enjoyed your book . . .

> — 5 STARS, Amazon

DIANE DEMETRE